COMRADE STALIN
CHANGED HIS HAIRCUT

COMRADE STALIN
CHANGED HIS HAIRCUT

Roman Rutman

Copyright © 2004 by Roman Rutman.

Cover design by Bruce Maddocks

Front cover image, *Tachanka* © by Sergei and Svetlana Tarasenko, by permission

Back cover image, *Piano Arithmometer* of Thomas de Colmar, 1855, photo courtesy of Robert K. Otnes

Frontispiece image: from *Liber Vagatorum*, Nuremberg, Germany, 1529

Library of Congress Number		2004093924
ISBN :	Hardcover	1-4134-5888-2
	Softcover	1-4134-5887-4

All rights reserved. No part of this book may be reproduced or transmitted in any form or by any means, electronic or mechanical, including photocopying, recording, or by any information storage and retrieval system, without permission in writing from the copyright owner.

This is a work of fiction. Names, characters, places and incidents either are the product of the author's imagination or are used fictitiously, and any resemblance to any actual persons, living or dead, events, or locales is entirely coincidental.

This book was printed in the United States of America.

To order additional copies of this book, contact:
Xlibris Corporation
1-888-795-4274
www.Xlibris.com
Orders@Xlibris.com

25475

To the memory of my grandparents,
Hirsh and Rachel,
murdered in Kalai, the Crimea

Acknowledgements

I owe a great deal of thanks to Cathy Madsen, Eleanor Roth, and Diane H. Hartnett, who read the manuscript. Improvements are theirs, remaining flaws mine. I am ever so grateful to Bruce Maddocks, the fellow admirer of *King, Queen, Knave,* whose imagination, generosity, and boundless patience with me have made the cover look the way it is. My warmest thanks go to Mila Orlova for her unwavering support.

The scenes of the Yalta Conference were influenced by the accounts of Hugh Lunghi, Justice James F. Byrnes, and Miss Sarah Churchill. I advanced by a couple of months King Ibn Saud's remarks made at his meeting with FDR in Egypt in February 1945, as reported by Colonel William A. Eddy. The primary source of information on the Soviet mobile gas chamber was the article by E. Zhirnov in *Komsomolskaya Pravda.* On Beggar's Welsh I owe much to *Wörterbuch des Rotwelschen* by Siegmund A. Wolf. Alfred Tennyson, Sir Walter Scott, William Wordsworth, and Vladimir Mayakovsky inspired the unattributed poetic quotations and misquotations.

R.R.
Dartmouth, Massachusetts
April 2004

PROLOGUE

I n the early hours of February 13, 1945, the marines on night-guard duty at the United States Embassy in Moscow heard bursts of automatic gunfire. The clatter came from behind the Kremlin walls across Manege Square. Then searchlight beams performed their brief, nervous dance over Red Square and died down. The night was chilly, the air crisp. The compound lay dark against the gloom, rigid in the cold.

The marines reported to the Political Affairs Officer and went to bed. The Embassy staff went to town to touch base with their contacts. On their return to the gracious yellow-ochre mansion, they broke the news. Rumor had it that German gliders had landed in the Kremlin to kidnap the Soviet dictator Stalin. Sweeping arrests had begun in academic circles.

German gliders? Now that the frontline had rolled back from the outskirts of Moscow to the borders of Nazi Germany?

The Political Affairs Officer, a slight redhead in granny glasses and ill-fitted tweeds, dropped a scholarly journal on his lap, keeping his thumb in for a bookmark. He was sitting in for those luckier ones who'd gone to the Allies' Conference at Yalta, down in the Soviet Crimea, and he conducted the interrogation with thinly veiled ennui.

Were their contacts positioned well enough to know?

Yes, they surely were.

What if they merely transposed the Mussolini rescue onto Russian soil?

The staffers exchanged glances. Everybody in the Embassy knew the Mussolini episode. German SS-commandos had fallen out of a clear sky upon a mountain castle in the Apennines and

·9·

snatched the deposed Italian fascist dictator from under his jailers' very noses.

Neatly done, the Political Affairs Officer continued. A brilliant operation of the sort that grows into folklore. The story has reached Moscow, hasn't it?

But the gunplay, protested the staffers. The rattle in the Kremlin—how about that?

Well, the Political Affairs Officer said; a play indeed. Doesn't the Kremlin house a garrison? Right over there, in the Arsenal? Young men are prone to joy shooting in all epochs, under all governments. For all we know, they celebrated the Republic of Uruguay's declaration of war on Germany. As for the arrests, that's hardly good copy in Moscow.

All the same, the Political Affairs Officer summoned the marines back and pressed for more detail. One of them, who'd seen action on the Normandy beaches, identified some of the night sounds as the report of Schmeisser MP-44 assault rifle, German paratroopers' firearm of choice, whereas the other guard, a brawny armaments buff with a collection back home in Esmond, North Dakota, was positive that the rattle had come from the German machine gun Maxim MG 08, the workhorse of the First World War.

World War I?

Yes, sir. Obsolete as of now, but deadly all the same. And handy—the mount folds into a sled so that you drag it through the mud and slush of trench warfare.

For Christ sake, we're not in trenches.

No, sir, we aren't. May I remark, though, that the sled hauls still better in the snow.

Ugh. And how much did the contraption weigh?

One hundred and forty pounds.

Hardly the first choice for a glider operation.

No, sir, it isn't. But there was a lighter version, too. Nicknamed the Devil's Paint Brush.

Funny name.

Funny peculiar or funny ha ha, sir?

Why?

It made for more casualties than any single weapon before and after. *Sir.*

The marines went back to sleep, the staffers back to town. From his second-floor office, the Political Affairs Officer peered out at the red-brick crenellated walls shielding the seat of the Soviet Power, the jumble of palaces, office buildings, churches, squares, and gardens, the medieval fortified town measuring twenty football fields: the Kremlin. A red flag hung listlessly above the green cupola of the Senate, as the Muscovites, by force of habit, called the yellow-and-white neoclassical palace. Above, the pale disc of the winter sun dimmed by thin clouds began sliding down from where it had climbed, which wasn't very high in the first place. Must've given up on spying into the dark secrets of the United States and Great Britain's uneasy ally.

The Political Affairs Officer shrugged and went back to his reading.

Something was amiss in the January issue of the *Proceedings of the Soviet Academy of Sciences* that he'd held open. The article by Arnold Hramoy, Division of Linguistics, contained nothing new—and here was the sticker. Why would a top linguist of the land, the father of the controversial theory of the genesis of the Indo-European languages, who had of late published solely on exotic subjects, such as the kinship of Tocharian and Illyrian, and for whom the German language and German linguists had been little more than the object of an old, bitter feud—why would he have bothered with a compilatory report on a contemporary German dialect, *Rotwelsch*, an arcane jargon of thieves and vagabonds?

This was what the Political Affairs Officer found in the article.

Rotwelsch, or Beggar's Welsh, came from the Middle Ages, when it was spoken among uncounted hordes of lice-infested vagrants dressed in tatters, begging a crust and a mug of wine in the German countryside. They paraded their wounds and ulcers, sold false relics or quack medicine, or collapsed in sham fits, foaming at the mouth. Or they passed themselves off as pilgrims, friars, or university students. During the Great Peasants' Revolt of the sixteenth century, those "rebels against the suffocating society" often served as scouts or spies or message runners for the peasant armies.

The glossary of Beggar's Welsh, Hramoy wrote, abounded with Hebrew and Aramaic borrowings, Hebrew being the language of the Old Testament and Aramaic spoken in Judea / Palestine in the epoch of the great revolts against the Roman Empire. By 1528, Beggar's Welsh must have become fairly common in Germany if Martin Luther found it expedient to launch an invective against it. He did so in his *Introduction* to the popular anonymous pamphlet, *On the Knaveries of the False Beggars.* Luther wanted to suppress another threat to the purity of standard German, which he was forging out of prevailing dialects.

He only succeeded so far, Hramoy wrote. Alongside the normative High German, the other language grew and developed in a sphere beyond Luther's control. It had preserved the richness and beauty of the medieval vocabulary and metaphor. *Meschuge, Chutzpe, Schicker*—the modern German language had borrowed all those little gems from Beggar's Welsh. They alone, together with the immortal pages of *Das Kapital* and similar Marxist classics, saved the contemporary reader of German from jaw-twisting yawns.

Hramoy had included a woodcut done in the naïve technique of the period. A countryside road; the spires of towers on the horizon; a man beneath a soft flat hat, stumping on a wooden leg. The blind cripple was heading towards the town in the company of a little boy, his guide. The artist had rendered the puzzled frown on the face of a female passerby as she took a close look at the wretch's bandaged foot, as if the good woman was trying to say: come night, won't the false cripple throw off his crutches, bathe his eyes, and turn into a highwayman?

End of article. The subsequent article called on the Academy's scholars, scientists and staff to rise to the occasion of the upcoming fiftieth anniversary of the first printed work by Comrade Lenin, titled *What the "Friends of the People" Are and How They Fight Us,* and to mark it with no less than eighty-six major discoveries, breakthroughs, innovations, and inventions, eleven of them seminal.

The Political Affairs Officer was a linguist himself. The State Department had yanked him from his desk at Princeton for his fluency in Russian and German. His narrower field was Low German dialects, and he was no stranger to Beggar's Welsh.

He asked the switchboard to put him through. Hramoy's secretary answered in a strained voice ranging on hysterics. Corresponding Member of the Academy of Sciences, Professor Hramoy, departed yesterday for an inspection tour in the provinces . . . No, she didn't know . . . Why don't you call back in a month..

The Political Affairs Officer hung up.

Had Hramoy been arrested?

Meanwhile a staffer came in. His informer had seen for himself a cordoned-off square in front of the Senate and plasterers patching the pockmarked façade.

The Political Affairs Officer's stomach churned. Stalin's Kremlin apartment and his main office were generally believed to be located in the Senate, and he was well known for his late-night work.

Did the contact say what had happened to Stalin? the Political Affairs Officer inquired.

The staffer had, of course, put the question to his source, but his man had only smiled mysteriously, his gaze brushing over the barren poplars lining the boulevard they strolled. And would the Political Affairs Officer please write off two bottles of Jack Daniel's bourbon and three pairs of nylon stockings as operational.

The following morning, a messenger brought a letter from the Peoples Commissariat for Foreign Affairs. Minister Molotov requested the pleasure of the company of the ambassador and ranking staff at St. George's Hall in the Grand Kremlin Palace for the banquet celebrating the successful completion of the Allied Heads' conference at Yalta. Marshal Stalin would make a brief appearance.

And so he did, imposing in his resplendent gold-braided uniform in spite of his short stature and pockmarked face. Aloof from the servile retinue and deferential foreigners, he stood under the lofty vaulted ceilings sparkling with crystal chandeliers and decorated with white-and-gold stars, crosses, and St. George striking down the dragon. The imperial grandeur of the Hall didn't dwarf him. It served to enhance his magnificence.

So much for the speculations. The Embassy duly reported to Washington, where President Roosevelt had just returned from his trip to Yalta and a Suez Canal stopover to meet with Arab rulers. No request for a follow-up had come back from the State Department.

The rumors, however, splashed up once more several days later. Allegedly, an entire company of the Kremlin Garrison was arrested on the day of the shooting. Some in the know maintained the soldiers had been dispatched to Siberian labor camps; others said, summarily executed. As traitors? the Muscovites asked one another, scandalized by treason in the Kremlin praetorian cohort. Not necessarily, answered the more sophisticated. Things happen to people who see too much. But the gossip came to a quick end, dispelled by Soviet battlefield victories. Almost nightly anti-aircraft batteries in Lenin Hills rumbled with salutes to Red Army's progress, and tracer rounds cut through the night air.

In the British Embassy, though, some knew a thing or two . . .

Forty-odd years later, a hurricane raged through the Soviet military establishment. Heads rolled; careers terminated. On that day in May, 1987, a teenage German amateur pilot had hobbled through four hundred miles of the Soviet airspace for five hours undeterred and landed his Cessna 172 on Red Square, smack in the Kremlin's shadow.

I stood with the throngs of Muscovites cordoned off near the redbrick History Museum, catching glimpses of the little scarlet hopper down the cobbled slope. The crowd's speculations about the pilot's identity ranged widely, from a jerk to an anti-imperialist refugee to a scout of an imminent NATO invasion. Could one fetch a ride with him back to Helsinki? Or still better, to Hamburg? Hamburg, gasped the crowd, and doubled their pressure on the police line.

On my right, a stooped man with a three-day grey stubble grumbled, "They did it again, those Germans. We licked 'em in the War, and guess who's keeping who on the dole? Like Stalingrad never happened. Like we never hoisted the red flag above the wrecked Reichstag."

The green military trucks came over and dragged the Cessna away. The crowd began thinning out.

"And all 'em rockets and radars," the stubbly man went on. "Blew it big time again, like in '45. When the fritzes did a three-pointer on Ivan Street."

The long open stretch bearing that name lay within the Kremlin walls.

"You surely don't mean it," I said.

He started. His sunken eyes turned at me. "You English? American? Got a couple of them Marlboros for a former Kremlin guard?"

I gave him a pack. It proved to be a sound investment. For the next two days, over many a beer, there was no stopping Afanasy Glebov's tongue.

Much as his stories were implausible, they launched me into the Soviet secret archives, which gingerly crack-opened their doors to dollars and marks before slamming shut again. I had come to Russia to look for my family roots; I found much more.

I offered my findings to the New York Museum of Jewish Heritage, but the negotiations broke down over their refusal to allocate a special display.

PART ONE

CHAPTER ONE

Max Ebert stepped out of the food store into a cold, drizzly Kazakhstan morning. He stood roughly at the middle point of the Soviet Union. To the Baltic and to the Pacific the distances were the same; the arctic tundra and the Afghan mountains were equally remote. Ebert had checked it out on the station's map when he first registered with the local KGB. You couldn't be exiled to a place more central. Not that being closer to a border would have amounted to anything. The borders of the Soviet Motherland were securely sealed against those ingrates seeking to flee it.

Ebert held a fish in his hand, rolled in a newspaper. That and some bread, that would keep him through the day. The large silver herring was his remuneration for the repair of the store manager's cuckoo clock. He'd made the clock chime *Ach Du lieber Augustin* all right, but the figurines wouldn't dance. The mechanism was busted. A fascist bayonet, the woman'd told him. Her brother acquired the clock in close combat on the enemy turf.

Ebert carried his tall frame down the middle of the road. Mud squelched from under his feet and stuck heavily to his high boots. He paused, lodged the roll under his arm, took hold of the tarpaulin top of the right boot, and pulled it up. More filling, he thought. I need more filling for this one. Perhaps it was one size larger than the left boot, but Ebert felt lucky to have gotten the pair as it was. The herring, now again in his hand, oozed out brine.

Down the single street of the settlement, treeless and fenceless, squatted barracks. The road was deserted except for a stray dog and an oncoming Army jeep topped with olive-green tarp. It passed Ebert, spattering slush on his shabby wadded trousers.

Ebert let the vehicle go and stepped into the tracks left by the deep-treaded tires. The shaggy grey dog tagged along at a safe distance. Where the brine hadn't yet blotted the paper to dark saturation, Ebert read, "On this January 19, Red Army kept rolling into East Prussia, the enemy's lair—"

The dog had stolen up and jumped for a kill. Ebert jerked his roll up. Teeth clutched. The mongrel jumped off, licking brine off its nose.

The jeep must have made a U-turn. It overtook Ebert and stopped.

Too late, Ebert thought. Anything he did would look like running away.

As he drew nearer he saw no statutory driver. The officer under a blue-banded peaked cap was alone in the Willys.

"Over here!"

Ebert slogged up deliberately, playing for time. On the officer's greatcoat, the blue shoulder boards of State Security carried a larger star. A KGB major. Eyes dark and unblinking. In his early thirties? Ebert would have about fifteen years on him.

"Get in."

"I'm almost there, Comrade Major." Ebert pointed to the barracks ahead.

"Don't play dumber than you are." The officer motioned to his right.

Ebert set out to walk behind the vehicle.

"Wrong way! Come around the front."

While Ebert performed the maneuver, the major, his large hands set on the wheel, kept his gaze on him.

"Drop the filth you're carrying."

Ebert hesitated but obeyed. The dog snatched the herring midair and ran away, leaving behind shreds of paper. Ebert ducked his head and stepped into the car.

The major drove without saying a word. The vehicle cleared the last barrack. The tires tore through the mud and skidded. The wiper rushed before Ebert's eyes: leftward—*that's the end*; rightward—*not yet* . . . At two stunted poplars the major made a right onto a barely visible track between the trees. The jeep struggled a hundred yards and stopped.

The major reached to the back seat and came up with a grey cardboard folder. He half-turned to face Ebert, keeping the file close to his chest.

"Max Ebert, administratively exiled to this blessed Central Asian asshole of the universe. Regime violations are gently discouraged by incarceration in corrective-labor camps for up to ten years."

Ebert resolved to remain silent.

"You were a humble watchmaker in Alupka, near Yalta on the Crimean South Coast. Then on August 18, 1941, the KGB rounded up local ethnic Germans on the grounds of Prince Vorontsov's former seaside palace. The war raging for two months, all ethnic Germans in this country were deported to hospitable Siberia. The whole catch, except for you and your family. You dodged the dragnet. You holed up in the Crimea until April 1944, throughout the German occupation."

"It's all in my file. I've reported it."

"What did you do under the Germans?"

"Repaired watches."

The major read from the file. " 'Provided logistics for German units' rendezvous and partisans' executions.' Which means—"

"I repaired watches."

"The German soldiers' watches," the major persisted. "The Wehrmacht watches."

"Theirs too."

"But you didn't go with them when they pulled back. Why?"

"The Crimea is my country."

"Not Germany?"

"Why? I was born in the Crimea. My parents never left the Crimea. Same for my grandparents. Only my great-grandparents started in Germany."

The major repressed a yawn. "You were left behind to spy and sabotage. I wonder why the watchful SMERSH didn't shoot you on the spot."

The SMERSH. The military counterintelligence. They all but did so.

In the corner of his eye Ebert saw a column of men in dirty-grey padded cotton jackets, five-wide, pulling onto the main road to halt there. German shepherd dogs growled at their sides. Behind marched uniformed men with rifles. The wind brought in the punctuations of the ritual notice: "A step . . . right . . . left . . . shoot without warning . . ." The marching resumed.

"They even didn't throw you to labor camps. Why?"

Ebert shrugged. "How'd I know?"

"They told you why."

"The commandant said my file'd been misplaced."

"A clerical error, eh?"

Ebert said nothing. Did he see the major before?

"To be straightened out soon."

Ebert squinted across, trying to read the purple type. He'd never seen his file that close.

"So they shipped you here. You and your family. How about them?"

"My daughter died in the railroad car." Ebert made an effort to keep his voice even.

"On your way here?"

"On our way here."

"And that little wife of yours?"

"She—she died here."

The major's finger ran along a line. "What, your journey lasted five weeks?"

"You arithmetic is excellent, Major."

They glared at each other without blinking. Ebert felt his jaws tighten. His fists clenched. If that was the end, so be it.

The major slammed the file shut. His eyes locked with Ebert's, he tied the dangling ends of black ribbons together.

"Hand me your ID."

Ebert reached out with a piece of yellow paper, folded in four.

The major tucked it away in and buttoned up his breast pocket. He cranked up the engine. "You're leaving with me."

"How about my belongings over there?"

"You'll do without."

The engine was running, but the major didn't slip into gear.

"So you blundered by being born in Russia with German blood coursing through your veins. Never mind Thomas Mann, Friedrich Engels, or Karl Maria von Weber. It's a crime, walking around with the enemy's blood, even if the enemy burns the books by the aforesaid Mann, despises the forenamed Engels, and prefers Wagner to Weber."

A strange major. A most strange KGBist. And who were the men he'd listed alongside Engels?

"Therefore, you aren't to be trusted with a certificate of Soviet citizenship, the internal passport, the inalienable property of the good, loyal Soviet man, the first and foremost source of his pride, assigning him his station in life. The magnanimous Soviet Government gave you a chance to partially atone for your crime by meekly going to Siberia in a cattle-car and gratefully accepting whatever the authorities might have in store for you."

The officer delivered his spiel with relish and pathos, but Ebert heard its parodying side. As if the major was giving him a signal: there was something beyond the words to follow.

"Why, you could be pissing blood while mining nickel underground or felling trees. You'd sleep in the open, and vermin would eat you alive. When you died, before tossing you in a swamp they would grant you a plywood shingle tied to your big toe and an inked number on your buttock. And what did you do instead? You grossly aggravated your original sin by making fools of our glorious Crimea branch."

The engine kept chugging in idle. The blanket of clouds somewhat thinned out, hinting at the sun behind it.

The major motioned over his shoulder. "Get to the back."

Ebert changed his seat to keep company with a large plywood suitcase painted in Army green.

"Open it."

Ebert's thumbs slid the rings of the catches and tripped the locks, releasing the accumulated power of the springs. The hinges flipped up and clanged against the plywood. Ebert lifted the lid. A puff of a long-forgotten wonderful smell first stirred his senses. Krakow sausage. Ebert's mouth watered. The smell came from a brown paper package that rested alongside a trench coat and military fatigues.

"Get them on. Put a woolen sock on that right foot of yours. Give your boots a shine. The brush and polish are in. Take care so they walk you to the moon and back without a blister. But start with that sandwich."

Ebert changed in the back seat, ashamed of his threadbare drawers, his long legs stretching out.

The major started backing up the vehicle. "About your family. I'm very sorry."

Ebert looked up. He wondered whether he'd misheard.

CHAPTER TWO

In the morning the major and Ebert awoke to a Siberian winter, amid a snow-clad plain. The train stopped at a station, a stout one-story brick building, where local women offered potato-peel pancakes and white disks of frozen milk with yellowish tops. Passengers picked the tops with their fingernails and licked the fingers, checking whether the yellow was indeed milk fat and not an inferior additive.

When the train started off, Ebert and the major stood on the jerking flat bridge above the coupler between two railway cars. The train rolled, rattling and rumbling. Cold wind pinched Ebert's face, and then the locomotive's smoke was an annoyance, but they did not go back to their four-berth sleeper's compartment. The major wanted privacy.

"Where did you hide from the KGB?"

"In Palai. A village in the Steppe Crimea."

"Why?"

"I was born there. A German agricultural colony. My brother Franz lived there with his family."

"But they were exiled, too, weren't they there?"

"That's for sure."

"So who did you stay with?"

"The Kovners."

The major lifted his eyebrows. "It's a Jewish name."

"There was a Jewish collective farm over there, too."

"A Jewish *kolkhoz*?"

"Yes. *Kolkhoz* Maifeld."

"What happened to them?"

"They're dead."

The major flipped open his grey file, shut it again. Opened and shut it again. A train zoomed by with a deafening rattle. A coal particle must have gotten into the major's eye. He pulled out a handkerchief, but only clenched it in his fist.

"Tell me more about it," he said in a coarse voice.

While Ebert spoke, the major didn't take his eyes off Ebert's, as if every word of Ebert's was being measured and verified against an invisible yardstick . . .

Ebert finished. There was a pause. The major said, "For your information. We're going to the Crimea."

Ebert should have become excited, but he felt only emptiness. The happy Crimea of his youth had been all but erased by pain.

And the major's announcement didn't come as a total surprise. Last night, before falling asleep on his upper berth, Ebert remembered at last where he'd seen those dark eyes and bushy eyebrows. Yes, Hirsh Kovner would've looked that way long ago if he'd parted with his black beard. Now the son wanted to see the grave of his parents. Only they'd said David was an artilleryman. How come he had turned into a dreaded KGBist?

The major narrowed his eyes. "You can peruse this without your watchmaker lens, can't you?"

He handed Ebert a stack of booklets.

Ebert opened one. From the photograph, a lean shaven face looked at him. Pale eyes. Blond hair. A long nose.

His long nose. *His* shaven face. *His* hollow cheeks.

Max read the words inked on the lines, over the wavy pale bluish background. Name, surname, patronymics, age. On line 5: *Ethnicity,* Jewish. A purple stamp: permanent resident of the city of Kuibyshev.

A passport. The regular internal passport of a Soviet city dweller, one Max Aisner, not a pathetic scrap of paper the administratively exiled had to carry at all times.

There was also an olive-green service card assigned to Master Sergeant Aisner.

Ebert inhaled deeply. The passport meant his salvation. Good-bye, Kazakhstan, weekly registrations with the KGB at the station, and waiting for his SMERSH file to marry his KGB file, the sure end of him.

"Your pass to normal life," the major said. "If the life of a Soviet citizen could be called normal at all. No longer the stigma of being German. No taint of staying behind the enemy lines. No special residence restrictions. Welcome back to the freest lot in the world."

He held his hand out. Ebert returned the booklets. The major shoved them back into his map-case. "You'll get them when your task is over. Now tell me about the Lair of Ali Baba." He stared at Ebert, his eyes narrowed to a slit.

Ebert hesitated. He had never, ever before, divulged those pages of his life to anyone except his wife. Should he tell it to this KGB major who was taking him to the Crimea?

"Unload, Max," the major said. His eyes commanded. "How did you first meet Prince Vorontsov?"

There was no point in denying. Ebert's boss had sent him to the palace to repair a clock. The north façade clock, the tower clock with chimes. The Prince had come out and watched him working. Ebert said it and fell silent.

"Go ahead," the major said. "He was in need of a reliable man, wasn't he? Clever with his hands. And you looked both."

Ebert nodded. He made up his mind. He held nothing back. The major threw out specific questions . . . Ebert saw the guard peering out from the sleeper's vestibule and promptly shutting the door back. Over the rumble of the moving train, Ebert could barely hear him fussing with the boiler in the vestibule, making tea for the passengers. The guard checked with them again fifty minutes later, when Ebert was close to the end.

The major let the guard leave before sliding the door open. They stepped into the vestibule, and the door closed behind them, reducing the din to a quieter rattle.

"Hold the door to the car shut." Ebert weighed upon the door handle. The major unbuttoned his breast pocket and pulled out Ebert's yellow ID of an exiled. He placed it between the pages of the grey folder and flung open the little cast-iron door of the boiler. Inside, flames roared over the glowing, shooting anthracite. They reflected from the glass of the entrance door across the vestibule, tinting red the snowy flatland that rushed behind.

The major pushed the file in and shut the furnace door.

"Max Ebert is no longer. Cremated. No paper, no man."

He smiled. Ebert returned his smile. This was the most unusual State Security officer you would ever run into.

CHAPTER THREE

The Crimean steppe began rushing by their window on the forth day. About noon the train arrived at the station. Uniformed men on the platform herded the departing passengers towards the station's door, where a KGB captain checked papers. They took some away. The rest filed through the door under the cracked nameplate reading *Djankoi*.

A KGB major and his orderly encountered no problem at the control barrier. They walked through the waiting-hall two stories tall, stepping over people, sacks and battered suitcases littering the floor, past those luckier ones who crammed two straight-back hard benches. The major and Ebert exited below a full-length portrait of Stalin. The great leader gazed benevolently at bleak women, snotty toddlers, and emaciated old men. His mustached face looked slightly tired. One felt that he had taken the troubles of the whole country onto his tall physique and broad shoulders.

They hitched a ride to Palai in an Army pickup truck and walked out to the barren steppe on the outskirts. The sky was grey and low, and it was drizzling. They stumbled on a clump of dwarf junipers. Ebert walked back to the village and borrowed a spade, leaving his plywood case as surety, while the major weeded last year's tall grass that filled a long narrow depression. They dug out all five junipers and planted them in the rocky soil along the grave, in memory of those lying under.

Afterwards they walked back through Palai. Ebert saw two men fussing in the Kovners' yard about an apricot tree, where Ebert used to steal out in the deep of the night when he hid there. A two-handled saw whined. The major kept his gaze straight

·29·

in front of him, in the street, where three stray dogs fought over the carcass of the fourth one.

They shared a pile of raincoats to sit on, as they rode on the bed of the pickup truck that the major had flagged down. This time the major would not go into the cabin. Their shoulders touched. The driver hurled the vehicle from one side of the unpaved road to the other. Now and then the truck plunged into a pothole, throwing Ebert and the major into each other.

It was now, after the grave and the junipers and the road had brought them closer, that the major revealed what they were up to. It was all right with Ebert. He ventured a question about the major's blue labels of State Security. David Kovner smirked. "I'm an artilleryman, Max. I know the value of camouflage." Ebert felt greatly relieved. The major offered him the passport and service card. Ebert shook his head. "I'll take them when my job is done."

On the outskirts of Djankoi, the major tapped on the cabin's back window. They jumped off and walked in the gathered dusk past low single-story adobe and timber houses, over broken bricks thrown helter-skelter in the mud of the unlit streets, breaking through the thin ice that had seized edges of puddles. Gaping fences sagged and bulged out. From far away, probably from the silver bell of a loudspeaker on the pole at the station, a song was heard; Ebert understood some of it. An august baritone concluded: "You've been listening to the Yiddish folk song from the *Gilgele* cycle. Next up, a news analysis. Now that President Roosevelt has been inaugurated for the fourth time—" The radio gurgled and fell silent.

The major pulled up at a tall palisade fence and fumbled with a cord hanging through a knothole. The latch clicked; the wicket-gate opened. They stepped in a fenced courtyard. A firewood shack flanked a single-story timber house; an outhouse marked the corner of the yard. The major knocked on the door, three short and two long. Ebert scraped off the heavy clay from his boots against a blade on the stoop. The major positioned himself in front of a round spy-hole. A bulb lit up above them and went out. The door opened to reveal a gaunt outline in the dark rectangle.

The man motioned them silently into the dark, tiny hallway. Ebert discerned a shoulder-yoke on the wall. A bucket rattled as he bumped into it.

In the light of the room the host turned out to be bald, skinny, and about fifty, enveloped in a woolen knitted jacket. The major bear-hugged him and slapped his back. Ebert placed his case on the floor, where two Army cots were arranged in an L, rough army blankets immaculately stretched over them.

A door in a sidewall opened; a short man sporting a reddish mustache and a thick green bathrobe with a tasseled belt came in. There was another round of high-fiving. The new arrival shoved his hand at Ebert and muttered his name, Ognev. He had disproportionately long arms, a narrow, sloping forehead, yellow eyes, smallish pockmarks, and close-clipped blackish-red hair strongly touched with silver. Ebert placed him in his mid-sixties.

The major shifted his gaze from Ognev to the host and back. "Well, how have you people been doing?"

Ognev shrugged his shoulders. The other man showed no emotion at all. He covered the table with a checkered oilcloth and set chipped enameled mugs, aluminum spoons, and a preserve jar passing for a sugar bowl. From another nightstand appeared rye bread, knife, and a chunk of salted pork fat. He was serving tea when a knock on the outer door caused his hand to start.

The host whisked away the mugs. Ognev disappeared behind the partition. The major and Ebert followed him into a narrow room, where two cots barely left an aisle between and a window in a shorter wall gave onto the yard. Ebert felt as if he were back in their railroad compartment. They took seats on a cot, Ognev opposite them on a crumpled blanket, from under which bed sheets hung. The stiff air reeked of pipe tobacco smoke.

Steps . . . A squeak of the door . . . Dull voices drifted from the porch.

"Sasha? What do you want?"

"Hey, Misha, just wanna ask somethin'. Won't you let me in?"

"Ask what, Sasha?"

"All them police patrollin' the streets with German shepherds on a long leash."

The cool stream of air across the floor dropped off as the door shut. The voices were now louder, coming from the front room.

"You know why?" the voice persisted.

"You tell me, Sasha."

"'Cause Stalin done come to the Crimea. To see for him how us little fellas live. He walks the countryside. All alone, eh? The other day my neighbor spotted him. He walked down this street, grinnin' under his mustache."

"Stalin is in Moscow, Sasha."

"Stalin's everywhere. He's thinkin' of us. He cares."

"He surely does."

"You're an educated man, Misha. Will you write a letter for me?"

"What kind of a letter?"

"A letter to Comrade Stalin. Wishing him many years of life and the best of health."

"I will, Sasha, and gladly. Come back same time tomorrow."

"You got a pen and ink?"

"I do."

"And some paper?"

"Yes, yes."

The door let in another gust of cool air. The major stared at Ognev, lips tight.

"So you didn't stay put, after all."

Ognev dropped a red slipper and scraped the other ankle with his foot. "How could I? Cooped for three days with this— this fritz. And I don't mean a Fritz Lange. Outside, too, no spa. Utter devastation. Night as dark as a Negro's stomach in a coal mine. They don't even know who they're mugging."

Misha came over and stood in the doorframe.

"What d'you think?" said the major. "That character—who's that Sasha?"

Misha shrugged. "A harmful busybody. Or somebody's spy."

They moved back to the front room, where a kettle hissed on top of an iron stove and the tea sets had reappeared.

"Just as well," the major said. "We're leaving first thing in the morning."

Misha poured out tea. He nodded. "They may shut the roads any time now."

For the rest of the evening they packed. Ebert slept in the back room, sharing it with Ognev. Half-awake, he heard muted voices through the plywood partition. He pressed his ear to a crack.

They spoke in German, and the major called their host Heinrich, not Misha.

CHAPTER FOUR

"A Horch, a real Horch. What a treat, eh?"

The major, clad in a sheepskin coat, appeared from the shack. He pushed a black motorcycle with a sidecar into the yard.

The major walked around the bike. "Well, I don't know." He went to the shack and came back with an ax-hammer. He swung his arm and smashed the shiny front of the sidecar.

He tapped on the bar. "The gentlemen of the public are invited to board."

The morning was dim and grey. Ognev, in a worn quilted jacket, his forehead and cheek bandaged, climbed into the sidecar. Misha, a.k.a. Heinrich, threw a blanket on his lap.

Ebert touched Heinrich's elbow. *"Wiedersehen.* See you soon." He turned to the major. "Let me drive her."

Ebert put on goggles and kick-started the engine. Making a left in the street he looked back. Heinrich stood at the gate, alone in the drab street.

"At last," Ognev shouted over the noise. "Another day with him, and I would've gone crazy."

Half an hour later it started to rain, washing away the dirty patches of snow. Ebert swerved around potholes and gashes that gaped open in the asphalt. The road flew into the Plexiglas of the protecting shield splashed with mud. Pickets flagged the bike down time and again. They mellowed somewhat upon seeing the major's shoulder patches and the injured prisoner, yet scrutinized the papers closely, carping over detail.

The major's team left the road at the exit to Bakhchi-Sarai when night fell. They drove through the Tatar town, silent and empty, past whitewashed, flat-roofed houses, bumping on exposed roots. They hid the bike in the ruins of a manor and sat in, under the protection of a shattered roof. Ognev took off his bandages. He reluctantly threw them away. "One day museums would fight for these rags." Ebert sliced bread, clasping the loaf to his breast. The major took out tall, oval blue cans inscribed in Roman letters rather than in the Russian Cyrillic. Ebert read it in a German fashion—it sounded *shpom*. The major removed the key attached to the top, inserted in it a tab on the side, and reeled a thin metal strip around the key. The top of the can came off. The major shook a rosy, fatty cobble from inside. Ebert wolfed down the meat.

They set out to hike up a canyon.

Ebert led. He was retracing the path he'd walked many times. The last time also at night, with Greta and Elsa in tow, eight months ago. At this cypress they had taken cover, listening to the distressing sounds coming from the Tatar town . . . At that boulder he should take a right. Rain fell harder. Ebert's knees hurt. Cuts, abrasions. Ebert's back ached from his backpack. All his muscles ached. They walked single file. The major brought up the rear, sandwiched between two rucksacks. Even Ognev had a small knapsack on him. What did they pack into it? he complained, his breath coming in gasps. Dumb-bells? *Complete Works* by Marx and Engels?

They bunched together in a small cave to share warmth and slept through the day. After dark they resumed the hike. Ebert was a boy of seventeen when he carried Helena up this trail, his arms crooked under her armpits, her cheek on his shoulder, her crimson fingernails touching his wrists. He'd found no place for his hands until they ended up on her breasts. He didn't know who suffered more, she or he, or Ahmed in front, who didn't carry her legs in Turkish trousers for nothing. Afterwards, in the cave, Ahmed walked away and crouched. The Prince, laughing, crumpled a banknote and tossed it at him. Ebert got his, too. It equaled three months' pay at the fat Greek's shop.

This time, his cargo was no beauty. It was a gigantic backpack, becoming heavier with every step.

It was early morning when Ebert led them into a narrow vertical cave. A huge rock rested snug in the crevice. They slipped out of their shoulder straps. Ebert went into to the woods and brought the trunk of a young oak. They levered the rock off, having broken a frozen cascade that had held it. An opening appeared, about seven feet high. They propped the rock from inside, squeezed in their load above their heads where the opening was wider, and sidled in. Then they knocked the prop off, and the stone eased back into the crevice. They threw themselves to the rocky floor and slept till late afternoon. Freshly fallen snow glowed in a chink, covering their traces.

They set out down a grim underground passage, bumping into slippery rocks. The dancing circles of their headlamps snapped on, now a glittering pool, now a hewn-out step. A stream babbled. The descent lasted forever. Ognev grumbled that he could already hear the Aussies down under singing *Waltzing Mathilda*. Then air became drier. Wooden flooring boomed under their feet—the sounds hinted at the great expanse of a hall. Their lights slid over screens, ottomans, and crates. "Carpets!" said Ognev squatting to feel. "Real Persian carpets! Too bad they're rotting down here."

The major pushed a pile of clothing down off a sofa. "Call it a day."

Ebert fell into a deep dreamless sleep the moment his back hit a fur cover. He hadn't bothered to undress.

In the morning they walked along a narrow, oak-floored gallery. Unlike the passage of yesterday, this one was man-made, hewn through the rock. In about twenty minutes they started to climb up a steep stairway and ended in front of a steel panel.

Ebert examined the hinges. His greasing was still in place. He turned the dial right, left, right again. His hand found a lever embedded in the bedrock. He leant upon it with all his weight. The small steel wall rolled soundlessly to the right.

Ebert ducked. In the opening, a wood panel became visible. Ebert's mouth became dry. He eased the screws and pulled the panel. It gently gave in, carrying along an assortment of brooms and rags hanging on hooks, the back wall of a broom closet. The dim light of electric bulbs seeped through the chinks in a wooden door.

A door banged. Ebert froze. Male voices, young, clipped. Ebert smelled fresh urine. It couldn't be real, at such a distance; it was just in his head. The men spoke a language Ebert didn't know. They chuckled. When they left, Ebert stretched his hand and eased open the door of the broom closet. A blade of bright light appeared and grew into a rectangle. Ebert flushed the door open for a once-over and pulled it back to close. He took in dazzling white tiled walls, two stalls, a tub, a red couch, and urinals.

"Alles klar," Ebert said hoarsely, without realizing that he spoke German. He placed the panel back and replaced the screws and the steel door. Now as before, the steel door, the wooden panel with the cleaning utensils, and the closet door stood between the bathroom and the tunnel.

"All set," repeated the major. "Off we go."

Back in the hall, Ebert found a lamp under the table and poured in some kerosene. The flame lit up upholstered sofas, lamp stands, trinkets, and piles of linen. The *Lair of Ali Baba.*

They unpacked. Ebert lit a Primus stove and quickly cooked a huge omelet from the powdered eggs and condensed milk they had brought along.

The mood was festive. Ognev spied a bottle of wine, its label glistening with eagles and circular stamps above a craggy mountain, which Ebert recognized as Ai-Petri, the local fixture. "Famous Voronstov's port," Ognev said, "discontinued 1916. Believed extinct. There are stacks of it. We're in business."

"I thought Georgian wines would be more to your taste," teased the major. He did the honors. "Here's good luck."

Ognev knocked out his pipe on the top of the oak table and stroked his mustache with the mouthpiece. His voice took on a thick accent. "This major believes that Comrade Stalin is still a Georgian." His eyes twinkled. "This major is mistaken. Comrade Stalin is no longer a Georgian. What is Georgia? A petty ethnical province. No, Comrade Stalin belongs to the Great Russian people. Or, rather, the Russian people belong to Comrade Stalin." He sipped some wine and grinned. "Has become only better with age."

Ebert drank his glass and asked for a refill. The vine was dark and tasted sweet. Not Ebert's choice, actually, but it brought him back to the time of the Prince. As if shadows, which danced on the walls of the Lair of Ali Baba, were thrown by girls in Turkish chalvars and blue-and-red vests, tight-fitting, embroidered in gold. The girls are laughing, their eyes widened by champagne, heels clicking to the beat on the oak flooring, necklaces of sequins jumping on their bosoms, henna-dyed hair falling down their back. The Prince, in a red blouse and baggy trousers over high boots, is sipping from his glass. He's laughing happily, his eyes narrowed by pleasure . . .

The major rolled the empty bottle across the flooring. "Any important visitor to Churchill is bound to take a leak in that bathroom." He turned to Ebert. "Right, Max?"

Ebert nodded. "The only decent one in the house."

"They didn't bother to build many in a last century villa," Ognev said. "Even in a prince's villa. What does the door open on?"

"The hallway between the ballroom and the kitchens," Ebert said. He had told all that to the major back in the train.

The major smiled to him. "So you didn't say anything about Ognev. Looks like—eh?"

"Like who?" said Ebert lamely.

Ognev indignantly shot up his chin.

David laughed. "Don't be pissed off, Ognev. Max was under German occupation. He may've forgotten this universally beloved face of yours."

But Ebert had caught the similarity, of course. Ognev looked very much like the portrait on the wall in the station. Except that Stalin was—taller, his gaze was firm and his face clean.

Ognev said, "Those in the men's room. Who were they?"

"A British decontamination team, slaughtering lice and bedbugs for Winston Churchill's comfort. Felt fortunate to use the bathroom before it turns into a VIP one. Happy with their lot."

"Why not? From gloomy London to a Roman holiday in subtropics."

"Roosevelt is coming on the same day as Churchill. They're flying from Malta. Across the entire Mediterranean and the Black Sea."

"Anything else?"

"The Americans landed in Manila." The major smiled.

"Where's Manila?"

"In the Philippines."

"And where are the Philippines?"

"Come on, Ognev. Don't pull my leg."

They began waiting. The drops falling from stalactites on to the floor made a faint ping, alternating with splashes in the pool.

Ognev milled at the edge of the platform and illuminated stalactites, wasting batteries. The rest of the time he taunted Ebert.

"David says you're Jewish, Max. Is it so?"

Ebert stared at him, saying nothing.

"A blond Jew. Not all that unusual. But he also says you stayed in this cave with your daughter. What's your daughter's name, Max?"

"Elsa."

"And her mother's is Greta, isn't it?"

Ebert didn't reply.

"Back at the Kovner's, that daughter of yours began a diary. A very neat one. On the first page her name, father's name, mother's name. The address. 7 Crooked Lane, Alupka, the Crimea. Everything in German. The whole diary's in German."

"Is it forbidden?"

"No, why? She did everybody's age all right. She even listed ethnicity on the fifth line. Like the internal passport she laid it out. An intelligent girl. And she left it behind here."

"Please, Ognev, stop it," said the major softly. "And give him back his daughter's diary. His daughter is dead."

"Of course, of course. I can understand *that*. A daughter dead. Here you are." He handed Ebert a blue school copybook, from which a sheet of pink blotting paper protruded. "A watchmaker, eh? And your father's family, who were they? Bakers or apothecaries?"

"They were all farmers."

"Those uncounted thousands of German *Kulturträgers*. The culture carriers. Remaking Russia in a German mold. Century after century, coming to teach the Russians how to do an honest day's work. Machinists and ministers, farmers and generals, empire builders and watchmakers. Would the very esteemed Herr Meister repair a Brueget?"

"If you can find one around here." Ebert kept his cool.

"But you wouldn't touch the inferior product of Kirov Clock Works, would you."

The major cut in. "That port—let's have another round."

Wiping his mustache against the back of his hand, Ognev muttered. "Herr Meister would rather have a stein."

Days rolled by, which they knew only by their watches. Ognev sat on the floor crushing centipedes. When he caught the major's glance, he made a wolf's grin. "I'm growing into the role."

Once they awoke to a din. Stalactites sang above their heads, resonating.

The men walked towards the northern exit until they heard the hum of motors. One by one, every ten minutes.

"The vocal chords of history are resounding," said Ognev. "How did you put it, David? The most momentous conference in history? It surely will be the one to be remembered."

His face had taken that dreamy, faraway look.

That afternoon Ognev returned to pestering Ebert.

"The Wehrmacht took all the *volksdeutsche* along, didn't they? Their blood brothers."

"I have no love lost for Hitler."

"So you took cover in this cavern. How about the asthma your daughter wrote about?"

"Had some medications for once. From a German doctor."

"Was it a responsibility of Herr Doktor to certify the death of executed partisans?"

"Ognev, please," the major said leaving the hall. He spent days crouching on the stairs and listening to idiotic coded messages on the security short-range radio through bursts of crackle and static.

When the major came back, Ognev was speaking again.

"And the automobile, Max. The Germans invented the automobile, didn't they?"

"I'll take your word for it."

"Of course they did. But with your thrift—you people are frugal, aren't you? You wouldn't brush off breadcrumbs to the floor. Now, how come that you nearly overlooked one more thing to utilize?"

"Which one?"

"The automobile exhaust, Max! You'd been allowing a valuable chemical substance to go up in the air. Until a German engineer found a use for it. Directed to a van's back. Air-tight. And inside the van—well, they packed people in there, choke-full. Jews on their way to their grave. How do you like this German invention? A mobile gas-chamber?"

Ebert hated the sight of Ognev's smug face. He started to his feet, his fists clenched. He bolted behind the farthest screen and flattened himself on an ottoman.

The major spoke softly to Ognev. The other man answered in angry shouts. The major spoke again. In a while, he called Ebert to come. Ognev sat quietly, without looking at Ebert.

And so it went for two more days, until the major returned from his watch and opened a bottle of brandy. Served a shot to Ognev. To Ebert. To himself.

He held the crystal glass up to catch the light of the kerosene lamp.

"Off we go. Now."

CHAPTER FIVE

Max Ebert and David Kovner had both set foot in the bathroom of Vorontsov's palace at one point or another.

It hadn't changed much since the Prince's time, just another stall and two more urinals added. Ebert had spent hours at the secret door, adjusting and maintaining. He did a fair job, didn't he, if all had held up for twenty-five years without a hand touching it; held up to that fateful day when Greta at the bathtub provided ministrations to the wheezing, coughing Elsa, and Max worked feverishly on the panels, bolts, and lock, until the entrance of the tunnel opened for their escape to the cave . . .

As for David Kovner, he'd gained admittance to the bathroom only once, with Uncle Meir, in August 1926.

Uncle was a big shot in the Communist International, the Comintern, and had lived in Moscow. Every now and then he disappeared. Then some workers' revolt flared up somewhere in Europe—in Hamburg or Vienna, and the bourgeoisie in cahoots with the Social Democrat traitors put it down. Afterwards, Uncle would come back to Palai for a rest with his brother's family.

David had walked the streets of Palai as though through his own backyard. It *was* his backyard.

At twelve, he is running barefoot in the summer heat. The wide road is all dirt and wormwood. Tongues out, dogs press close to the walls, into the near-vertical shade. Their flanks heave, powdered with grey dust. Not the slightest breeze to offer relief.

From behind the wattle-fences he hears grunting. Loyal, progressive Jews keep pigs nowadays. The Jews of the collective farm, the *kolkhoz* Maifeld, have slammed the door shut on the past. They left it behind in the overcrowded, impoverished warrens in the Ukraine. They threw it away along with their striped prayer shawls.

David runs a line to the red speck at the bottom of the street. A flag is hanging dead above the town hall, a two-story timber house and adjoining barn with two holes in the back wall to run movies. The bunting has faded to insipid pink, and so has the banner with three lines of white letters, hanging above the door. The upper lap says in Russian: *Working men of all countries, unite!* The exclamation sign, like a pointing finger, directs David's gaze down. There the line doubles back, right to left. It addresses the Yiddish-speaking part of the world proletariat with the same exhortation. Another dive brings the eye conveniently to the beginning of an appeal in German, which runs left to right. Unbreakable folds of proletarian solidarity. David knows them all by heart. The Yiddish and the German parts sound almost identical to the ear.

This morning a mailman on horseback has brought a telegram. Uncle Meir is coming to Djankoi on the noon train. The kolkhoz's chairman sent a trap to the station. At the last moment Mother remembered that she'd run short of honey. Uncle Meir loves local honey. David volunteered to go and borrow some from the Eberts. They descend from the oldest German colonist families, and they have a brother, a watchmaker in Alupka, whom David has never met. David always volunteers to go to Franz Ebert's homestead.

David makes a left at the town hall. The Germans' colony, Lustdorf, starts here. Behind timber fences German sows grunt just like Jew-owned sows.

He bears down on an iron handle and pushes. The wooden wicket opens. David enters a yard. Stables, sheds. Barns—high-ceilinged, two-floored. At each door stands a pair of footgear.

The Ebert girl of his age with pink freckles on the bridge of her nose is raking a vegetable patch. She shoots him a glance and tosses back her thick chestnut braids.

"*Mutti!*"

Frau Ebert, under a green kerchief redheaded as her daughter, comes out of the cowshed and squints in the bright light.

David relays Mother's request, in German.

Frau Ebert takes off her dung-smeared high galoshes.

She picks up brown shoes from the threshold steps, puts them on, fastens the buckles, and crosses the barnyard to the house.

She unbuckles the brown shoes at the threshold and pushes her feet into clogs painted green.

David spies her shadow moving through the dim lobby. He catches a glimpse of her long frame against a lighter opening to the rooms as she steps out of the clogs and into slippers.

The girl is on the chubby side. Her name is Clara. She goes to the German school in the village. Last winter David's school was invited there for a joint New Year celebration. A pine tree stood festooned in shining balls, glittering tinsel, and little burning candles, next to a shiny black wing of a concert piano. First a girl from David's school read a poem about the galloping Civil War hero, Red Cossack Budyonny, who sliced the Whites in half with his sword while his Maxim machinegun carts, the *tachankas*, sowed death in the enemy's rear; then David read a ballad about a British sailor hanged on a mast because he'd raised the red banner on his ship; and boys and girls from Clara's school sang in German about a young trumpeter felled by a fascist bullet. Then boys from both schools lined the stage in gas masks with elephant-trunk crimped tubes and the girls in red berets ran to them and bandaged their arms, while two teachers said loudly and solemnly, "A war we do not want but we are ready!" and the boys took off their masks, and the girls laid down their Red Cross bags, and all together sang "Lead us, Budyonny, to the battlefield!" Then Clara's class sang a German song about a fir tree, its needles staying evergreen through summer and winter alike, teaching us the values of firmness and steadfastness. The song went on, the silver balls shone, the tinsel sparkled, the face of the boy in blue corduroy shorts to Clara's right blurred, and David saw himself standing in blue corduroy shorts next to Clara, singing *O Tannenbaum*.

Three days later, a black elongated Lincoln auto came from Simferopol, carrying three men in leather jackets. They took away the German school's principal. A brazen ideological transgression, they said. That New Year tree smelled of incense and manger. They also arrested the French teacher, who had been overheard saying French gas masks looked sexier. Another subversive, the Simferopol men said. The French gas mask was just a little bag stuffed with lint and attached to goggles. At a gas attack, the French soldier pissed into the lint and breezed through. The French teacher had held our technology inferior to French urine. It took Uncle Meir to get her released. He went to Simferopol and lectured them on the importance of urine for the Red Army. Told them how the machine gunners in the regiment of which he was a commissar back in the Civil War, when water was in short supply, pissed into the cooling jackets of their Maxim guns to prevent jamming.

The principal never came back . . .

Clara stops raking. She wipes her brow with the back of her hand.

"Why do we Germans work so hard? You people have more fun in life."

"I like your name, Clara," says David and blushes. "After Clara Zetkin, the German revolutionary."

"Clara was my Grandma's name," Clara says. "And Zetkin doesn't sound German."

"She married another revolutionary," David informs. The fire spreads to his ears. "A Russian-Jewish revolutionary."

Frau Ebert comes back from the rooms and goes through the footgear changing in reverse. She hands him a brown earthenware jar glazed with a golden bee.

Clara Ebert resumes her raking even before David has left.

He returns home in time. Well, almost in time. The trap under a striped festooned canvas canopy is departing. The chairman had lent the kolkhoz's best horses, the bay and the dapple-grey. Through the orchard David sees Father carrying two suitcases to the opened door of the whitewashed house. Uncle must have just entered.

The shutters are closed to keep the heat out. The air smells of the wormwood spread on the floor. Like absinthe spills in Montmartre cafés once upon a time, laughs Uncle Meir. David goes through lunch as through a dream. He doesn't take his eyes from Uncle Meir. Uncle is sporting a little wedge-shaped beard. He is short and black-haired, like Father. His bulging eyes behind round metal-rimmed spectacles smile to David.

The door squeaks. The kolkhoz's chairman comes in, big and curly-haired, with mighty broad shoulders. He respectfully shakes hands with Uncle Meir, inquires about the health of Comrade Trotsky. Takes a seat at the table, chases a vodka shot with a pickle.

"And what are the prospects of the world revolution, Comrade Kovner?" he inquires.

The chairman's eyes run over the new leather suitcases with bright foreign stickers stacked against the wall.

Uncle Meir explains the international situation. Europe is a volcano ready to erupt. Germany will, of course, be the first to rise. Soon, very soon, proletarian Germany will lead the rest of Europe into the World Union of Soviet Republics. Elsewhere, the Chinese comrades are doing very well. Great, great, nods the chairman. It's good for the Jews, Father says. David feels uncomfortable in front of Uncle Meir, the Communist Internationalist.

Uncle insists on going outside. In the yard the chairman says to David's father, "I'll mark you a full working day in the field. Of course! Such an honor to all of us. Take good care of your brother." He shakes hands with each in turn, even with David.

The lace of leaves offers little more than an illusion of coolness. Uncle Meir lies faceup on a garden bench, his hands clasped together behind his head, his eyes on the blue sky appearing through the apricot tree foliage, his legs crossed. He rocks his foot shod in a brand-new leather sandal. Frau Ebert's jar stands on the garden table, the golden bee blazing on its side.

Father, barefooted, tucks up his trousers above his knees, and Mother secures them with safety pins. He crushes grapes in a wooden tub. Acid smell reaches David's nostrils.

A German colonist's two-horse wagon rolls by in the street. Alpine scenery glitters, painted on the ironbound walls of the wagon. Tawny-spotted cows swing bells from their necks on a green meadow against the backdrop of snow-capped peaks of strictly equal height and a chemically blue sky. The green of the meadow puts the dusty trees in Palai to shame.

Clara's father is sitting in the box with his whitish faded mustache and brick-red face.

The wagon halts. Springs make it sink and bob. Franz Ebert lifts his round straw hat, removes the pipe out of the mouth. He exchanges hellos with Father. *Vos tutsekh? Nix besondres.* I've heard you have a dear guest? Uncle Meir rises up, waves a greeting and remains seated. The wagon drives on. "I'm a Jew, and he's a German *poer*," Father marvels, "and we need no interpreter."

"Peasant is *bauer*, not *poer*," David says. At his Russian-language school he learns to speak a good, proper German as well. The great language given to the great people, as Uncle Meir never tires of reminding. The language of Karl Marx and the Ruhr smelters.

"Franz never says *bauer*," Father insists. "He says *poer*, just as I do. Why should he say *bauer*? Who is he, teacher Shkolnik?"

"Our ancestors must've passed through Ebert's Bavarian neck of woods centuries ago," Uncle Meir says.

"The German feudal lords kept the Jewish working masses in ghettos and sweat-shops," says David.

"Back in 1918," says Father, "Ukrainians made a pogrom in our *shtetl*. We fled to Chernigov, twenty kilometers to the south. It was quiet in Chernigov. There was law and order in Chernigov. German uhlans stayed in Chernigov. Do you remember, Dovidke?"

David does, if vaguely. After all, he was only born on the day of the Sarajevo shot which triggered the First World War and the German occupation of the Ukraine. He recalls the man in a blue-and-red uniform who'd hoisted him into the saddle. The soldier smelled of leather and horse and tickled the back of David's neck with his mustache.

David says, "They were German proletarians?"

"Why?" Father shrugs. "I didn't ask them to show their calluses."

"At the turn of the century," Uncle says, "the Jews were better off in Germany and Austria than anywhere else in Europe—I mean, the Jewish bourgeoisie was better off. Austrian Germans allowed some Jews to vote in the German curia. Based on the common language, they said. For them, Yiddish was a German dialect, period. A clever maneuver to inflate the German faction in the parliament."

He spreads honey over a slice of rye bread. He chomps off, chews slowly, savoring the aroma. The Palai honey smells different. The bees collect from the buckwheat growing in rocky parcels in the steppe.

Another bite. Meir Kovner finishes his slice. He wipes his mouth with the back of his hand.

"Let me tell you a story. I walked once in the mountains. In the Bavarian Alps, it was. I'm walking like this, and green meadows are around, and sleek cows lie on their side in the grass. Tawny-spotted cows. And snowy peaks loom ahead. The road comes to this village. Regular affair, a single street of fieldstone houses. In his yard a poer's fixing a spout. I say *guten abend*, and could he please sell me some milk from under his deeply esteemed cow. The poer goes to the house and brings back a clay mug and a hunk of fresh bread and spreads it with honey. The clock on the tower starts playing. *Ach du lieber Augustin* playing. Seven o'clock, the poer says. Where's the gracious sir going? Up there, I point up. To the meadow o'er yonder. Your gracious sir intends to lie down on the grass and watch the thin clouds swimming the sky and listen to the birds hammering their racket. *Ach so-o*, the poer says. Will you the same way back *kommen*? By that time, they'll have brought in the cattle from the pastures. I'll give you some of this evening's milk. Pure, untainted health. You'll pay then. *Stimmt*, I said. It's a deal. I did as I said. I wallowed in the emerald grass sprinkled with flowers of all colors—red, white, yellow, blue; I picked my teeth with sweet blades; I sniffed the air fragrant as the Coco Chanel showroom; I counted the dazzling white lambs running across the arching blue sky. The sun rays warmed my cheeks; a little stream babbled. While napping, I heard the bells of Paradise and the mooing over them. Clearly, I've entered the bovine heavenly pastures. I open my eyes and I see a herd pass by. All those cows, tawny-spotted, jingling bells, rubbing flanks with one another. The brick-red roofs down below have turned crimson. I get up, I shake two ladybirds off my shirt, and I set out back. My poer stands in the same spot, sucking on his pipe, and his missus's milking a tawny-spotted cow. That day I understood that in Bavaria all cows are tawny-spotted. I have some fresh milk, and I tell you, it's as good as good can be. And again the chimes are playing. *Ach du lieber Augustin* playing. Nine o'clock, the poer says. And now I think—what's the gimmick? The clock doesn't strike hours. Come on, I say. The tune your clock is playing is the same for all hours, *nicht wahr?* How can you tell the time? The same but not exactly the same, the poer says. The first time it played in C-sharp major, and now it's E-flat major. Just like that."

David demands explanations. Uncle speaks, and hums, and speaks, and hums again.

"And you, can you hear the difference?" David asks.

"Out of the blue? I can't. Most people can't. Even very good musicians can't. But there are those gifted with perfect pitch. Not only can they tell the tune, but also the key."

"Are you saying that the whole village could do that?" David challenges.

Uncle Meir smiles. "Your music education—it should be taken care of."

"And also," David remembers, "you said that all the cows in Bavaria were tawny spotted."

"Well?"

"You could say so only about those Bavarian cows that you'd seen. You can only say that all the cows in Bavaria that you'd seen that afternoon were tawny-spotted."

Uncle's eyes are twinkling. "Oh yeah? I see they haven't yet screwed up your logic at that school of yours. Now, can you one-up this one, you nitpicker? In Bavaria, all cows that I saw that afternoon were tawny-spotted—at least on one side."

Davis shuts up, silenced by the superior logic. Uncle eases off his sandals and stands up. "Let me relieve you, Hirsh." He rolls his pants up and steps into the water in a blue-enameled tub.

The wicket-gate flaps. David's sister Malka returns from the field.

Uncle stops washing his feet and follows the girl with mocking eyes.

"A crazy niece I have, too."

Malka says nothing. She is twenty, large-handed, big-footed, and red-faced. Her sun frock exposes her bronzed arms and shoulders. She stops at a washstand under an apricot tree. She ladles water from a bucket up into the container. The pop-up stopper rattles. She throws handfuls of water into her face and neck.

Uncle Meir's eyes are fixed on her. "No, just look at them. Perhaps they understand Yiddish no more. In Palestine everyone speaks Hebrew, even camels."

"Have more honey, Meirke," says Mother.

"No, I simply cannot understand how a Jewish girl could ever turn her back on the Soviet Union. Is she oppressed? Perhaps my eyes and ears failed me and he wasn't the chairman who dropped in today to share in a vodka but a White Cossack officer with a whip? You want to work on the land? Be my guest! This is your Promised Land. The Party has given land to the Jews in the Crimea!"

"And the Agro-Joint built our houses," Father says.

Uncle doesn't seem to welcome the support, and neither does David. The Joint Distribution Committee is an American philanthropic foundation. A capitalist body.

Malka drinks from the cup of her hands. "Some people would rather work for goyim and speak to the goyim in the language of the goyim."

"Malkale," whispers Mother.

"And you," Uncle Meir bristles, "you're stuffing your brain with that junk of Hebrew. All that we need. The weird, Oriental lingo of rabbis and obscurants!"

"The language of the Song of Songs," Malka says. She takes the towel from a twig and wipes off her face.

Uncle Meir starts, stung by her remark. "And you think—do you think you'll speak like a Shulamite to a Solomon? You and other fanatics down there, fired with an idea? You'll communicate in two hundred words barely oiled with token grammar, as Arnold Hramoy puts it!"

Malka works on her arms. She passes to her shoulders. "We've all heard a thing or two about fanatical experiments for the sake of an idea, haven't we, Uncle Meir?"

Father stops his crushing. His white teeth glint in the opening in his black beard.

"For the happiness of the mankind," Uncle Meir says.

Malka hangs the towel back on the nail. She walks to the house.

Uncle Meir shouts to her back. "Pidgin Hebrew!"

She stops and turns her head. "Again from your friend Arnold's mouth?"

"So what?"

"Nothing. Only Grandpa Osher told me how you and little Arnold and the son of Moyshe Peysakhovich had let cats loose into the synagogue at the time of Shabbat prayer." She disappears in the house.

Mother gapes and covers her mouth with her hand.

Uncle Meir seems to be at a loss for words. He reaches down to a shriveled dandelion that grows near the tub. His fingers hook it at the base. He pulls it up. He shakes the weed at his ear. Little clods of dirt drop into the tab and dissolve at his toes.

Uncle tosses the weed onto the heap of grape rejects. "Their Hebrew? May it rot!"

David feels sorry for his sister, but says, "Yiddish is the language of the working masses. Marxism teaches us that language is a phenomenon of a social class."

"Rightly so!" Uncle agrees, exuberantly. "And a weapon in the class warfare."

David carries the love for the Revolution deep in his heart.

He listens religiously to Radio Comintern on his homemade radio, patiently scratching the crystal for speeches and songs. He daydreams about standing in the barricades, shoulder to shoulder with Uncle Meir. He shields Uncle from a bullet; blood smothers his red shirt and blue corduroy shorts. On the line "social origin" in the innumerable questionnaires that he is to fill out at every step of his life, he will write "of peasant stock." David is a peasant and a son of peasants. A worker would be better, but a peasant is good enough. A poer. *A yiddisher poer.* He only knows that Mother's father, Grandpa Osher, had managed a large estate back in the Ukraine. Now Grandpa stays most of the time in his mothball-smelling room where sunrays never penetrate and striped black-and-yellow tigers run across a Chinese black satin folding screen. He doesn't eat with the family—Mother cooks for him in his own pans. Whenever David comes in, Grandfather is humped in front of a kerosene lamp. He sways back and forth. His forked greenish beard is grazing the Talmud opened in front of him. His gaze glued to the book, he sinks his hand into a jar and hands a marzipan to David.

When David was very small, Grandpa took a bundle from inside a drawer. He unwound a white-and-blue rag, revealing a wooden plaque. Grandpa put the plaque in his lap, then took a silver jar and a spoon from a shelf. He smeared the board with a thick layer of a transparent yellow honey and lifted the plaque to David's mouth.

"Lick it, Dovidke."

David's tongue worked on embossed letters, over pointed tips making lumps and bulges and tapering again, until he licked the plaque clean.

"Feel how sweet is the Torah?"

David came again and again until Malka got wind of it and raised bloody hell. The plaque, the kerchief, the spoon, they hadn't been washed for ages. All kind of filth must've stuck to the plaque, ants crawled over it, and flies left their mark. How totally unhygienic. And what was that all about? As if Dovidke was a baby to train to a teat.

Grandpa said nothing. He closed his eyes and rocked, and his lips moved.

★ ★ ★

The morning after Meir Kovner's arrival to Palai, a blue sedan pulled up to the Kovners'. The neighbors at their gates eyed the chauffeur in a leather cap hauling two suitcases to the car, followed by Meir Kovner in a white linen suit. His little nephew David, face ablaze with excitement, brought up the rear. He wore the striped-breast sailor's jacket which Uncle Meir had brought him from Moscow. He walked along the car, and his hand slid on the smooth running board, starting high at the headlight and sloping under a spoked spare tire. "Peerr-say Ar-rov," whispered the village foreign-language experts, watching the black canvas top disappear down the road.

Towards the evening the auto, sent over by the Crimean Committee of the Communist Party, cleared a mountain ridge. In front lay a wide strip of greenery, now dark, almost black in the mountains' shadow, and beyond it, as far as the eye could take it in, spread the sea, deep-blue and immense, stapled here and there to a lighter sky with a tiny black dash of a coast-guard boat. It was night when they descended into the smells of magnolia and oleander and the mysterious, sensual groans of a large resort spot reluctant to go to sleep, the heart of the Crimean South Coast, Yalta.

They spent long days on the beach, immersed in the shouts, laughter, and murmur of the sea, among sandcastles, tents of stretched bed-sheets, men in black underwear trunks, and women in dark satin bras with four buttons on the back, or in black slips. Skinny Tatar boys with high cheekbones hawked the trays of ground mutton baked in hot dough, oozing fat. Odd tattooed characters offered large cowry shells they said they'd brought from the South Seas. The pink flesh of sinuous crevices strangely aroused David.

On the second day Uncle's skin took on all hues of red, from scarlet to crimson, but he persisted in staying out in the full sun.

"I have to charge myself for the whole year." When dusk began falling, they climbed a long timber staircase with worn steps. Holidaymakers in rolled-up sleeves returned to town with Turkish towels on their shoulders, carrying chaise longues and parasols. Half-way up, Uncle and David took a pathway across a cypress grove smelly with sun-warmed needles to the door of the Sacco-Vanzetti Sanatorium, a two-story unremarkable mansion with a red-tile roof and a tall stonewall topped with barbed wire.

The administrator was an agreeably rounded young woman with sweat beads seeping through the layer of crème-colored powder. She shook her head in an apology. "The next year we'll have a private beach of our own, Comrade Kovner." Guests in slippers and tank tops bore pigmented spots on baldheads and backs of the hands. "The beach," they sighed loudly, and went back to comparing their exalted positions back in Moscow and Kharkov.

In their room Uncle Meir said, "As soon as they get the private beach, I'll start going to another place."

They toured the coastal strip to the west of Yalta in the same chauffeured Pierce-Arrow. The corniche road had bitten into the mountain's flank. The blue sea poked out to their left and disappeared again behind posh greenery and gleaming white buildings. "Oreanda. Koreïz," Uncle muttered the names of the resort towns. Now and then silent men stepped out from the shade, flagged the auto down and bent to investigate. Heavy hands twiddled with Uncle's large, red identity booklet, a golden impression on the hard cover, so imposing back in the Sacco-Vanzetti but looking so helpless here. Intent, unsmiling eyes scanned the man and the boy, and reluctant chins signaled them to pass.

"Alupka," said Meir Kovner.

"Uncle, I need—"

"Oh yes, I know. I'm coming with you. Those plums."

They veered off the road. The wheels crunched over the gravel of a driveway. The automobile pulled up before an iron gate painted blue. On both sides of the steel pipe frame ran a solid iron fence. It took an eternity for the guards in a timber pavilion to examine the documents. The air was scented with unfamiliar flowers. Finally the gate opened. The auto rolled into a paved court and stopped short before a palace with a greenstone façade and a clock up above.

A lank man walked through the high mahogany door. Uncle walked up to him and made a quick half-bow. The man wore a net tank top and navy-blue breeches tucked into top boots. A golden tooth shone in his mouth. He responded by a movement of his eyebrows. Uncle spoke in a low voice. The man listened, sweat trickling from his uniform cap down the pink scar on his left cheek. David held his bowels, hoping against hope. They were admitted into the building and led through a gloomy corridor. The bathroom was to the left . . . Afterwards, David waited on a couch upholstered in red leather, a marble bathtub behind him. It smelled better than the flowerbeds outside, whose aroma also wafted through a window behind David's back, set high, out of reach of a passerby. The stalls were to his right, and then the white tiled wall turned left at the straight angle offering room for three urinals, towel hangers, and a marble sink surmounted by a mirror framed into ornamental oak. The third wall was for service implements. His feet on a peacock rug, David faced a white door, apparently to a broom closet, until Uncle Meir flushed in his stall, setting in motion a noisy Niagara.

The man in the blue breeches escorted them back to the sunlight. "Wanna take a look around?" He smirked, his gold teeth shining. "Be my guests."

Uncle and David walked among trimmed evergreens and flowerbeds and farther on to the green amphitheater of terraced gardens. Two swans spread their wings to the wind and graciously glided over a pond. Down at the sea, the transparent green water heaved at coastal rocks. Not a single bather was in sight. David was hot in his sailor's tunic and uncomfortable with the small pebbles packed in his canvas shoes. A grimace of embarrassment grew thick on Uncle's face.

The man in the blue breeches stood in a vantage position, watching them with a harsh, tenacious gaze.

★ ★ ★

On their way back to Palai, in Simferopol, Uncle Meir bought David a black, shiny upright piano.

They left the sedan in Simferopol and pulled along slowly in a dray, their backs against a huge wooden crate. They jumped off to have a dip in a pond or buy dry-cured herring as hard as wood, sparkling with crystals of white salt. They smashed it against the frame of the dray until it softened, and they ate it with watermelon. Sometimes Uncle gave David a gulp of his beer. He crooned in German—Uncle had a baritone of some quality. In his songs David heard icicles dripping from the roof of an alpine hut, a boy Savoyard beseeching his marmot to perform tricks, the joy of a peasant returning from the field, and the babble of a mountain stream where trout stood against the current, swaying its fins. And then this little song about a drunken tramp Augustin, who lay flat in the street of old Vienna at the time of a plague epidemic. Corpse-pickers had nearly interred him alive, but he'd emerged from the common grave, protesting vehemently. The drunk's resurrection launched the myth that alcohol fought off the pest. The scourge raged, Vienna drank, sang and danced, and the little boozer Augustin waltzed into immortality to keep company with the saint he'd been named after. Uncle laughed.

The drayman cursed his horses in Tatar.

Those two days were among the happiest in David's life.

PART TWO

CHAPTER SIX

I f a Gypsy fortune-teller had foretold his military career, David Kovner would have laughed in her face. In 1938, aged twenty-four, he was preparing for the battles of the World Revolution, but in an altogether different capacity. He was about to graduate from the Philosophy Department of the prestigious Institute of Marxism in Moscow.

He liked the Institute's building, twins with the Factory-Canteen next door. Both were a pile of offset cubes faced with tiling and glass. Enormous busts of Stalin adorned each lobby. Identical *paternoster* lifts ran their cabins in continuous motion. The canteen's hungry customers delivered by the first Moscow trolley line often took the wrong entry from the street and rushed madly between the Departments of Bolshevist Ethics and Philology, craving goulash.

Palai and Yiddish were left behind. Clara Ebert had gone to see her relatives in Alupka and was married there. She had never come back to the village.

David stayed at Uncle's on Solyanka Street. The house of six stories with a granite-faced ground elevation loomed large over the neighbors in its shade. David slept on the sofa in the dining room, where a large table in the middle took up most of the room and books lined nearly the whole expanse of the walls. A steel strongbox, bronze-faced, filled a gap. Uncle stacked his dirty dishes in and on top before carrying them to the kitchen en masse. In another opening, over a set of drawers, hung Lenin's framed photo, the late leader's mouth open to greet the world proletariat. His left hand clasped the edge of a lectern as his upper body followed the forward throw of his right hand into the bright

·59·

tomorrow. Beside him a rectangular spot had faded, but less so than the rest of the wallpaper. Whose portrait had hung up there? asked freshman David, and was told Lenin's. Another portrait of Lenin? Uncle shook his head. No. He'd moved the Lenin to the other position where somebody else's portrait used to hang. Now he could truthfully answer the question about the bare spot: Lenin had hung there. David didn't press as to whose portrait had hung alongside Lenin. Leon Trotsky, with his ferocious wedge of a beard and prickly eyebrows, was exiled from the Soviet Union six years before. Uncle didn't change his wallpaper as often as Soviet Russia her heroes.

A good quarter of Uncle's shelf space was reserved for Comintern publications. *Internazionale Presse Korrespondenz* . . . *Rundschau über Politik* . . . Clara Zetkin's *Kommunistische Fraueninternationale* magazine. Uncle liked to quote from a resolution of the Comintern: "Soviet Russia, joined with Soviet Germany, would at once become stronger than all capitalist countries together." When freshman David walked past the German Embassy in Leontiev Lane, his heart beat faster: soon the black-red-golden flag of the bourgeois republic would give way to solid red. David took the Institute's seminars on German History. He learned that in sixteenth-century Germany the emerging progressive classes clashed with the forces of feudal reaction. The towns demanded economic liberties; the peasants, the abolishment of serfdom. Professor Zarnitsyn explained that the rebellion of Martin Luther against the papal authority was a manifestation of the conflict between the new productive forces and the old relations of production, which blazed up in the Great Peasants' Revolt.

Uncle Meir concurred, but Uncle's friend, the linguist Arnold Hramoy, laughed at the "meaningless clichés." David couldn't help being impressed by Professor Hramoy's extraordinary tall stature, the shaved, knobby cranium, the bony face, the animated, clever eyes behind extra-thick lenses. Arnold Hramoy never parted with a cigar. "That thing of yours!" jibed Uncle Meir. "The very symbol of the Yankee capitalism! You're the only man in the Soviet Union to smoke a cigar and get away with it!" Arnold Hramoy was ironic, encyclopedic, sparkling. He could open any dictionary on first try within two pages from the sought-for word. "My putting," he laughed. Hramoy made the past come to life. When he spoke, David heard horses neigh, wagons squeak, the wounded moan, Luther's hymns thunder over revelry and blasphemies; he saw hordes roam the roads, armed with pitchforks, scythes and muskets, brandishing the standards of revolt, sky-blue and white, and a wooden peasant clog, the *Bundschuh*—Hramoy was there himself and took his audience along. He spoke to David as an equal, inquired of his interests, commended his German and his translations from Latin. When Hramoy left, Uncle said, "Arnold was ten when he came up with an explanation for his family name. It had something to do with the Roman Emperor Claudius, no less. An ancestor of Arnold's was Claudius's freedman, you see. A revolutionary. The cross of Spartacus and Bar-Kokhba. He came within an ace of overthrowing the Empire. Arnold hinted at some secret pages authored by Josephus Flavius, the historian. I don't remember, though, exactly how Arnold charted the way from Claudius to Hramoy." "Must've been through the Latin *claudus*," said David, and hobbled a couple of steps, limping in dumb crambo. "It translates into Russian as *khromoy*." He was still basking in Hramoy's compliments. Uncle humphed.

Another civil war became a painful reality three years into David's studies. When the Nationalists in Spain rebelled against the Republican government, Uncle Meir slipped on his secret agent's gloves and made himself scarce. Uncle's assistant, Andronikos the Greek, would drop in with a bottle of *retsina* and a bag of olives to report Meir safe and sound. Anything beyond that? Andronikos laughed and asked David to sing the *Bandera Roja* once more for him.

Two years into his disappearance, Uncle Meir returned to Moscow in the middle of the night, thin and tanned. In the morning he rested in bed but promised to join David for lunch at the Factory-Canteen, next door to David's Institute.

They stood in a long line on the first floor, under slogans on the walls extolling the efforts of the Party and Comrade Stalin in securing tasty and healthy food for the working masses. They paid at a teller's window, got their set of coupons, and walked towards the *paternoster* lift.

Two files of boxes devoid of a front wall ran nonstop in slow motion—one upward, another downward, like rosaries. As a moving bottom came level with their feet, David and Uncle Meir stepped in. Presently the light of the second floor appeared above. The opening grew, exposing top boots and high galoshes. Then skirts and jackets became visible. The floor of the cabin was coming level with the second floor. A flurry of activity followed: some in the cabin were stepping out, and those outside hastened to enter before the cabin had risen away from their step. David and Uncle Meir alighted on the fourth floor reeking of cabbage. Dumbwaiters to carry humans, Uncle growled up. But David was rather fond of the American-made *paternosters*, the only two in Moscow, so progressive and democratic.

They stepped up to a conveyer belt, exchanged a coupon for a plate of soup and a piece of bread, and consumed it all in the large colonnaded hall, standing at round aluminum tables upon which the sallow-complexioned customers extinguished their cigarettes. From the ceiling hung sticky spirals, which flies had learned to shun.

Uncle said precious little about his adventures. David related his news. Arrests in Moscow—Uncle cut him short. How about the family? A letter had come from Malka, David said. What was she doing down there, Uncle asked as they walked down the stairs to the third floor. Raising chickens in a kibbutz, David said. And she wouldn't call it *down there*; to her, it was *up there*. The Jew who went for good to the Land of Israel rose up to the heights of the pioneer spirit, and therefore the only appropriate way to put it was that he *made aliya*, ascended. David thrust his hand into his pocket and offered the letter. Uncle shook his head.

They talked against the clatter of aluminum plates on aluminum tables and aluminum forks on aluminum plates.

"She says they have a new immigrant in the kibbutz. From Nazi Germany. He started working as a bookkeeper. A funny man. He sits in his wool jacket and starched collar over his ledgers in his corner. And hens clack and cackle and the kibbutzniks run about in short sleeves if anything at all from the waist up. They branded him *yekke*, the Jacket. He had to discard his silk necktie, though. Not for the heat, but because that symbol of the hypocritical rotten bourgeois civilization is prohibited in her kibbutz."

Uncle Meir remained absorbed in his efforts to cut meat on his plate, but the blunt blade kept slipping off. David read aloud about the yekke who worshipped German values. He hadn't made spiritual *aliya*—he'd come because of storm trooper thugs. He would gladly have stayed forever in his beloved Berlin, running a furniture shop and speaking the proper German he's so proud of. Goethe couldn't be blamed, the yekke argued, for Dr. Goebbels's mutilation of the great language. And the yekke had the nerve to point out that it was in a very proper German that Theodor Herzl had written Malka's bible, the *Judenstaat*. And what did they sing over here, in Palestine, the yekke asked. To what song did the kibbutzniks march? "From Metula to the Negev, from the desert to the sea." The yekke said something that made Malka's blood boil, and she refused to speak to him for three days. He'd said he'd heard something like that back in Germany. "From the Meuse to the Memel—"

"—From Tyrol to Northern Straits," Uncle Meir crooned, upon which two characters who stood behind David and Uncle, biding their time with plates in their hands, remarked rather loudly that some people might think they'd come to a choir rehearsal. Uncle Meir smiled apologetically and started to rise, but one of the waiting men stared close into Meir Kovner's face, and his eyes went wild. He whispered into his companion's ear, and the two vanished instantly, dissolved in kitchen fumes and tobacco smoke. Uncle Meir shrugged.

David resumed. Every now and then Malka had seen the yekke pull out a drawer and stare into it. When she came in, the yekke would push the drawer back. She wondered what was inside. A snapshot of a ladylove? (His poor wife was very sick.)

Dirty pictures? Not that it mattered to Malka, but the kibbutz needed to know about their new candidate, right? One day, he didn't lock the drawer. Malka opened it. There lay two German military medals. (Crosses, compounding that.) The yekke explained. Those were his medals for the war of 1914. He had volunteered at seventeen, passing himself off as eighteen.

Uncle sputtered onto his plate. "Serves him right. Offered himself for the imperialistic war!" He threw his knife on the table, disgusted. "I can't cut through this—what's this, a windpipe?"

"The menu said backside."

"A length of the backside's windpipe indeed."

Uncle pushed his plate aside. He still fumed as they left. On the second floor they had some compote in thick pressed-glass tumblers, round within and eight-faced outside. A dried plum and several sleazy apple disks with tough skins and prickly centers lay drowned in the brown wash. Uncle worked his fingernail to dislodge apple core splinters from between his teeth.

They walked down the stairs. In the lobby, Uncle Meir pulled up before a slogan on the wall. "Yes, we do," he firmly said to the banter: *All Soviet People Approve of the Execution of the Saboteurs Responsible for Meat Shortages.*

Once in the street, Uncle said, "Now, I'm coming with you to the Institute."

"What for?" shouted David. "To pull strings for me?"

"I want to look up a quotation in your library."

"Couldn't your staff do it for you? Couldn't I?"

They had already entered the Institute's lobby. David left Uncle right away. Or rather he made an attempt to leave, but a powerful arm came round his shoulder, pulled him in reverse, and pressed him close to a brawny flank clad in light-grey soft worsted.

"Comrade Kovner! What an exceptional honor to the Institute!"

The squeaky voice belied the corpulent body. Both belonged to the Deputy Rector, Professor Zarnitsyn, smelling of aftershave.

"Which happy occasion has brought you to us?"

"Your library," said Uncle Meir.

Zarnitsyn bobbed light-brown hair, neatly parted. "Of course, of course. I'll be happy to act your cicerone through our collection of Marx's manuscripts. Naturally, we don't show the early Marx to students. Too provocative at places."

Meir Kovner shook his head. "I hate to take up your valuable time on a trivial matter."

"Not at all, not at all. But I understand. Young David will show you around. He's our pride. The *crème de la crème*. I'll make the collection available for him. Also, I'll let him speak at my colloquium on current German affairs, and I'll invite the whole Institute. A great honor."

Uncle must have taken pity on David. Or decided that he had attained his objective. He looked at his wristwatch. "I don't have time left for the library, after all."

A crowd gathered around, excited and curious, dressed in shabby jackets or dull dresses. "*Red Front!*" called two students and saluted with their fists. "Good afternoon, Comrade Kovner!"

"You are dearly beloved here," said Zarnitsyn.

But not nearly as much as Stalin when he came to the Institute.

He'd walked along the proscenium, a short man in yellow-top boots. Amid the rattle of released seats, the students greeted him with thunderous applause. He settled down modestly into a side chair between the lectern and the presidium's table, his grey field tunic jacket buttoned up to the chin. Turning towards him, the men and women standing in the presidium kept applauding. And the audience roared. "Long live Comrade Stalin! To Comrade Stalin—hurray!" A storm raged through the rows, from the front seats up the amphitheater. Stalin stepped behind the lectern, held up his hand, and the hysterics of loyalty and admiration gradually died down.

Stalin didn't look much like his portraits where he was a benevolent father, squinting good-naturedly, or a Roman emperor of granite sculpture quality. This man was neither. With his thick hair over the narrow sloping forehead, he looked prosaic and unassuming. But when their eyes met, David shuddered. The yellow tiger eyes pierced him.

Stalin's speech was brief. He spoke slowly, as if dictating to little children, in a muffled, guttural voice, with the thick accent of fruit merchants in Moscow's open markets. He asked questions and answered them, as in a catechism, an undying habit of a former seminarian. Was there such a notion as an undivided national culture? No, there was no undivided national culture; there were two cultures, bourgeois and socialist, within every nation. Who stood behind the slogan of a national culture? The slogan of a national culture was a reactionary slogan of the bourgeoisie, which did their best to poison the conscience of the working people with the venom of nationalism . . . When he finished, he won another roaring ovation.

David looked along his row of ecstatically clapping young men and women. Many a male student's breast welt pocket was cut open on the wrong side of the coat, betraying the fact that his mother had turned the fabric of his coat inside out and set it in to a new lining to give the worn wool a new lease on life.

Not so the coats of those brawny men seeded throughout the auditorium. Their faces were unfamiliar to David, and their double-breasted grey business suits cut from Polish wool passing for English bulged on the left side . . .

The next day Uncle brought home Stalin's portrait shining of fresh paint. He sighed audibly as David hung it to cover the darker spot above the chest of drawers. After David jumped down, Uncle took time to observe the result. Stalin had arrogantly turned away from his neighbor on the wall. His mustache bristled. Every golden button on his tunic has painstakingly been drawn up.

Young voices filtered through the ceiling, laughter and sounds of a piano. Uncle said, "You know what? If I ever need to refresh his adored features in my memory, I can mount two flights of stairs. The Ognevs just moved in above us. He's an actor fabulously resembling Stalin. Climb the chest again, will you, Dovidke?"

The portrait ended up buried in the crack between the chest and the wall. And Uncle Meir made good on his words. He went to see the Ognevs that very evening.

He came back and walked to the kitchen, forgetting to close the apartment's door.

David was boiling water on a portable electric range. On seeing Uncle's face he started and his hand missed the pot. Some macaroni fell on the open spiral sunk into ceramics. A whiff of smoke streamed upward. "What happened?"

Uncle Meir slumped down on a stool.

"You know what Ognev says about the Nazi persecutions of the Jews? It may be for the better, he says. Turning his wrath against German Jews—that will take Hitler's mind away from making war against the Soviet Union."

David gasped. "He—does he mean it?"

"I don't know. He's a man of paradoxes. A gadfly of sorts. But what makes me sick when I'm hearing it from him—he's a Jew."

Uncle sighed.

"And there's more to wonder. He has an uncanny ability to get into Stalin's mind. Sometimes he thinks like Stalin."

That night David tossed and turned in his bed.

Germany had turned against its Jews . . .

Back in the Ukraine, when the household was in turmoil packing for the move to the Crimea, little David had treaded on a little picture lying on the floor. He stooped down and picked up the postcard. David eyed what seemed to him a magnificent palace . . . Narrow windows rounded at the top . . . Carved cornices . . . An enormous ball on the roof . . . A lofty hall hinting at by the tall, narrow windows in the recessed façade.

Above the picture ran an inscription in unfamiliar letters, neither Yiddish nor Russian. David, then six, asked Malka about it. She unpacked a German alphabet to him. With its help he deciphered: *The New Synagogue in Oranienburg street, Berlin.*

That was the first German text he'd ever read.

On the back of the card marked December 1911, the unknown Berlin correspondent of Grandpa Osher wrote in Yiddish:

"In France, it's the Dreyfus affair. In Russia, the charges of ritual murder. God bless Germany, where the Jew holds his head high!"

★   ★   ★

David Kovner reverentially sorted out the Early Marx Collection at the Institute's library. Drafts, jotted notes, letters, abstracts . . . Professor Zarnitsyn had suggested that David pick a selection of Mark's notes on German history and prepare a synopsis. David chose the German expansion into East Europe, the medieval *Drang nach Osten*. One especially bloody chapter was the conquest and colonization of Baltic lands by the Teutonic Order, semi-warriors, semi-monks. Those Allied Knights, *the Reitersbund*, brutally subjugated the locals in the name of their Christianization. David's task was no piece of cake. The subject matter required a solid background. An added challenge was that young Marx had written his notes in Old German Gothic cursive, a puzzle for an untrained eye. For instance, seven consecutive bars connected into a seesaw were supposed to mean the word *einen* . . . David handed his synopsis to Zarnitsyn, who glanced over the first page on the spot and promised to publish it in the Institute's *Transactions*. But when they ran into each other in the library and David asked about his paper, the professor looked aside and abruptly left after reminding David about tomorrow's colloquium.

And now, in the fan-shaped Main Auditorium, the students raised their hands unanimously for the Honorary Presidium to be headed by Comrade Stalin, with Meir Kovner second in the list. Then, also unanimously, they voted for a presidium. A small herd of assistant professors in navy blue suits trooped to the dais to join Zarnitsyn. In their wake marched a student with coarse red tufts of hair sprinkled with dandruff. He placed himself modestly near the door to the hall, as they took seats behind a long table draped in red broadcloth. Invisible specters of the Honorary Presidium hovered above their heads.

David climbed the steps to the lectern. A Lenin badge adorned his smart corduroy jacket with a zipper lock, the latest Parisian fashion, which Uncle Meir had brought from his travels. When he raised his eyes from his notes, he saw only the sea of faces in terraced rows. He anchored his gaze on the prettiest among the audience, the blond, red-cheeked girl in the second row, a bucolic shepherdess dressed in a blue satin blouse.

As David expounded on the misguided German proletarians who had channeled their dissatisfaction with the Nazi regime into the smashing of Jewish businesses (his topic was *The lessons of the Kristallnacht pogrom)*, Professor Zarnitsyn's neatly cropped head nodded rhythmically in approval. The shepherdess's blue eyes were wide open. Yes, she was dying to learn more about the racist Nazi legislation.

David passed to the German poet, Heinrich Heine, an enemy of all obscurantism, and read Uncle Meir's favorite lines. Professor Zarnitsyn smiled, and those in the audience whose German was adequate for getting it that a monk and a rabbi farted equally foul chuckled and giggled, happy for a diversion. Those who hadn't understood masked it by laughing louder. Heinrich Heine, David said, had called the Jews and the Germans two ethical nations, the People of the Book and the Nation of Poets, Composers, and Philosophers. Heine had forecast that, through their common efforts, a home of philosophy, the new European citadel of lofty spirituality, would rise on the shores of his beloved Rhine. David saw that synthesis personified in the shining figure of another Rhinelander of Jewish extraction, Karl Marx.

The door from the stage to the corridor opened a crack. First a folded newspaper crept in, and then a sweatered arm emerged. The invisible man cleared his throat. The red-tufted student turned his attention to the sound. He reached out for the paper, spread it in front of him, and scanned the first page, finger-combing his tufts. Then he started to his feet. He grabbed a pencil and slashed, back and forth, in the paper. He walked behind the backs of the assistant professors to Zarnitsyn. The student reached over

Zarnitsyn's shoulder with the paper, placed it on the table before the professor, and pointed to something in it. He remained standing behind Zarnitsyn's back while the professor read.

Zarnitsyn looked up, and his face broke into a grin.

David meanwhile reached the end of this passage.

"Such an enterprise, a teamwork of Germans and Jews, is an abomination to Hitler. Rather than sharing with the Jews, he is set on their annihilation. To him the chosen people are the Germans. The Teutonic tribe has wrenched the baton of exclusivity from the House of Judah. The previous bearer's very existence is a threat to Hitler's legitimacy. Its every trace should be wiped off the face of the Earth."

Professor Zarnitsyn rang a bell. His hands firmly on the red fabric, he leaned forward.

"We have just witnessed, Comrades, a dangerous attack against our values."

He pushed against the table. Now he loomed tall. His breast swelled. His shaved chin pointed forward. He shouted.

"'Lofty spirituality' indeed! Where is the speaker dragging us, to which morass of clericalism? He presented us with no semblance of a class approach! He demands that we renounce the class warfare, the moving force of history!"

"I said nothing of the sort," David protested. "And I haven't finished yet."

Zarnitsyn spun his corpulent body around.

"Are you still there, Kovner? Clear the lectern. Now."

David, aghast, walked down to the rising hoots and took his former seat in the first row. Immediately, both his neighbors rose and walked to the back of the Auditorium.

Zarnitsyn brandished a scarlet pamphlet, the *Communist Manifesto* by Marx and Engels, wherein the classics had proved mathematically that national differences were irrelevant and class antagonisms alone made the locomotive of history chug along. And it made not the slightest difference that Marx was born into a Jewish family and Engels wasn't.

His little polecat's eyes scanned the rows. In his squeaky voice—wags liked to say that Zarnitsyn's voice was as a hair in your asshole, thin and dirty—he invited the student body to show high political vigilance and rebuff the enemy's provocation.

And so they did. Young men and women rose to the podium in a steady procession. Incantations bombarded David's ears. Militant nationalism . . . We won't let . . . The whole world knows . . . Petty-bourgeois objectivism . . . Ism . . . Ism . . . They'll never pass . . . Crafty designs . . . The red-tufted student, Secretary of the Institute's Young Communist League, led the pack. He pounded his hand on the lectern. "Annihilation of the German Jewry?" Laughter on the stage, catcalls in the audience. "Look at Italy where Jewish capitalists helped Mussolini come to power. Look at the Jewish functionaries in the Italian Fascist party. At Spanish Jewish capitalists who supported Franco's revolt! Surely the German Jewish bourgeoisie will also find a common language with Hitler." Ism. Ism. Root it out. The blue-bloused shepherdess, getting harsher by the word, lashed out at class enemies who were using any crack to slip into our ranks.

David staggered home, blind to his route. Snowflakes gathered on trolley cars to form shrouds.

Outside his uncle's house somebody separated from the wall and took David by the elbow. He started and swung about.

Clara Ebert smiled at him, thinner and prettier than he'd ever imagined, even in a man's suit coat over a thick wool turtleneck and a woolen skirt.

"Do you still remember me?"

David grinned ear to ear. "You—you've cut your braids!"

She took off her knitted green ski cap and tossed her red curls. "One headache less. Gives no trouble at a construction site. I'm a plasterer."

They walked through the doorway.

"And your husband?"

"We've split."

"Oh. I'm sorry." But he pushed the elevator's button with vigor and joy.

"Don't." She smiled again. "I waited there for you."

"Waited? Why today?"

"I read in the paper."

"Read what?"

They got out of the elevator's cage. On the landing, a neighbor clad in bedroom slippers and a blue silk dressing gown with scarlet roosters on the back was dumping garbage into a collecting chute. He turned his head to the sound. His small eyes in his fleshy face went wide. He dropped the little trapdoor open and ran back to his apartment without uttering a word. The entrance door slammed.

Clara kicked the trapdoor closed.

David took out his keys. He was searching for the keyhole when he realized that the hole was no longer there. A piece of tin sealed with wire and lead had covered it.

Clara tugged him by the cuff . . .

In the street she nudged him towards a showcase on the wall, glazed and padlocked. Snow had fallen on the frame's top to form a bar. On page one of the morning *Pravda,* David read that his adored uncle, famous Meir Kovner, the patron of their Institute, had been unmasked and arrested as a Trotskyite enemy of the people.

CHAPTER SEVEN

C lara made him a bed on the floor. There was nothing but a
pallet bed and an upturned wooden crate in her tiny
windowless room. Behind the wall, girls shrieked. Residents of
the builders' dorms in Mytishchi, near an armament plant in the
northern outskirts of Moscow, shouted drunken songs.

Later in the night she came to him. She didn't smell of milk and
bread as he'd expected, back in Palai. She smelled of fresh plaster.

In the morning David walked into the Institute's lobby. A
small bunch of students crowded at the stuck *paternoster*.

Deputy Director Zarnitsyn appeared out of thin air as if he
had been waiting for David.

"Ah, Kovner."

Zarnitsyn stood where he had hugged David in front of Meir
Kovner. His small eyes were shifting.

"I thought you'd have sense enough to stay away from this
place."

"Nothing like good advice," David remarked. "But why should
I? I'm a student here. Graduating this year."

The students at the elevator turned to see.

"You aren't. It is my duty, grave but not altogether unpleasant,
to let you know that you have been expelled. Squads of Red
Professors, the kindlers of the World Revolution's fire, graduate
every year from this distinguished place. Into their ranks, the
Institute cannot allow" (Zarnitsyn's lips curved in disgust) "a deviant
and the nephew of a wolf in sheep's clothing."

"Aren't I?" David said. "But why don't you go and wash your
face, Professor Zarnitsyn? That brown stain on your nose. You got
it on this very spot."

·73·

The little crowd at the elevator melted away.

Regally, David stalked out.

In the street, a rushing man nearly knocked him down.

"What are they serving today?"

"Stew," said David. "Stew of bullshit."

He went straight to a rival institution, the Marxist-Leninist Joint School. Its Party boss had been boasting of his friendship with Meir Kovner to anyone willing to listen. It started, he would say, when he escorted Meir's nephew through the Government villa in Alupka, as the said nephew was full of prunes, ha ha.

At the sight of David, the secretary whisked behind a wide door soundproofed with beige leather. David waited, counting the flower-shaped brass heads of upholstery nails, arranged into five-point stars.

When the secretary returned, red spots speckled her face, a minute earlier white and mealy.

"Go away with you!" she spitted out. "How cruel of you to come!"

She stood leaning against the door, spread-eagled, protecting her boss with her body, the red spots an extension of the upholstery pattern. "You have no consideration!"

She would make a poor audience for a grand departure. David left quietly.

In the course of the following days he gradually descended the ladder of prestige. Everywhere a mixture of fear and malicious joy met him. At the School of Confectionery he heard someone say loudly behind his back: "Odd that he should still be walking around." David ran into Uncle's cadre Andronikos in the street, but the Greek looked through him and walked by.

When a second week came and went, Clara said, "I've talked to my foreman. You'll learn masonry."

"I know some. Your father showed me bricklaying."

The stocky black-mustachioed foreman looked from him to Clara and back. "Ever held anything in your hands heavier than a pen? Or your little dummy doin' pee-pee?"

"I'm a farmer's son."

"Farmer? A Jewish farmer? You must be kiddin'."

Clara said, "Shut your trap, you. Think you own the title to my room? The lousy three yards of the corridor that you partitioned off for me? Thanks a lot, but that's where it'll end."

They worked at a lakeshore construction place in Moscow's northwest, where the gurgling orange sewage from an adjacent chemical plant kept the pond surface from freezing. David was bringing up mortar and bricks under a lazy gentle snowfall when the personnel man came up, dragging his left leg. As he watched David, a huge brown wart twitched on his cheek. He said nothing and left.

The next morning the foreman looked past David. "Ain't got no need for a bricklayer after all."

"I can continue as a laborer."

"Ain't got no need for that either."

Now David unloaded barges in the Moskva River harbor. The spring sun was eating through the thin ice beside the crazy gangway he walked with timber on his shoulders.

He counted his steps. Nineteen, twenty, twenty-one.

Ruddy fog misted his eyes.

Hope I don't fall down.

He came home with aching back and stiff legs. He peeled and boiled potatoes in their room, waiting for Clara.

They sat on the floor mattresses, hugging each other's shoulders and listening to the song of the Primus stove. The narrow trestle bed was gone. Three walls glistened with oil paint. On the fourth one, the half-glass partition, Clara had drawn plain cotton curtains.

"Your husband—was he a German?"

"No way. A Ukrainian vacationer. I hooked up with him on a beach."

"Were you happy?"

"Not a single day. He boozed like a sponge."

"But you dropped out of school to marry him!"

She shook her head. "Not to marry *him*. To bail out of Palai. Away from my family."

"Why?"

"My mother. The shit she did to me."

"Like what?"

"Like beating me."

David opened his eyes wide. "Beating you?"

"No malice—educational. If she disliked something-anything, she smacked me in the face."

"But your father—"

"He wasn't gung ho about it, but he dummied up. His mother'd slap him in the face, too."

"Who did you stay with in Alupka?"

"Uncle Max." Clara smiled.

"I never met him."

"He never visited. Mother was allergic to him 'cause he wasn't like his parents or us. Became a watchmaker. He's tops. Been places. In the old days, rubbed shoulders with Prince Vorontsov."

David laughed. "Really? I've gotten on with the Vorontsovs too—I dropped by at their former palace in Alupka. Once."

"The banquet hall?"

"No, a bathroom."

A loud knock on the plywood wall made them start. Kovner to the phone.

David took the call at the front desk, where a concierge darned the heel of a sock stretched over a tea glass. "You can't stay here," she hissed. "Got no residence permit."

"David Kovner?" The low baritone had a haughty tinge in it. "Submit your papers to the P— military school . . . You won't get any reply? Oh yes, you will, and you'll like it. Don't mail the papers. Bring them over—now!"

David heard the rapid beeps of a disconnected line.

"The police comes tomorrow to kick you out," the concierge went on. But David didn't listen.

The caller hadn't lied. In the provincial town of P— dominated by the artillery school and a gigantic gun plant, David plunged into ballistics, strategy and tactics. He spent hours behind the arithmometer *Felix*, processing data from ballistic tests. He pitched little levers in vertical slits; they clicked into position; he cranked a handle; entered another number. The levers formed a ragged line reminding him of the notes on sheet music. Sometimes David read the improbable cacophonic tune from the line and hummed it to relieve his boredom. And it reminded him of the safe in Uncle Meir's dining room, whose face, too, was cut with vertical slits through which—up and down—ran little levers . . .

A clerk spilled the secret about David's previous academics, so the fellow cadets, after hoisting one too many and spotting no informer, cracked for him the same hackneyed one about this meat shop where price tags read: workers' brains at 3 rubbles and 40 kopecks a kilo; engineers' brains at 4.20 a kilo; Marxist-Leninist philosophers' brains at 26.50 a kilo.

Why the pretty penny?

It takes heaps of Marxist-Leninist philosophers to raise a kilo of brains.

David often wondered whether he would be allowed to graduate, yet so far so good. His superiors even assigned him to serve as interpreter to the German military attaché visiting the school—the new partnership with Hitler's Germany was in its peak. Soviet military wives flaunted silk, furs, and perfumes plundered in Lvov, Vilnius and Riga, as the USSR and Germany carved up Eastern Europe between themselves. The cadets were shown the documentary—not for general distribution—of Soviet-German joint parade at the troops demarcation line. In class they scrutinized Hitler's blitzkrieg. The tactics professor relished the calamities befallen to the inveterate warmonger, Winston Churchill, and his French minions. He gloated over the fall of Eben Emael deemed the world's strongest citadel. Nine German gliders had landed on top of the flat-roof forts; eighty-five men hopped out, thrown grenades, and blinded the gun ports with flamethrowers. The fourteen hundred Belgian defenders could have overwhelmed the Germans by sheer numbers, but instead, badly shaken and demoralized, they did as they had been taught and remained inside the impregnable fortress. But impregnable it wasn't. When they threw in the towel, the whole Belgian front collapsed. Revolutionary derring-do, the colonel lifted his finger. German inventiveness! Prussian efficiency!

Clara came for visits. Their nights were in the barracks' Lenin Room. They pushed off papers and magazines and the red wool cover, and made a conjugal bed on the table. She was going to have their child down in the Crimea.

When in June 1941 the German army invaded Russia, the senior and junior classes of the school graduated at once, before their time. David entered the new war as lieutenant.

In Palai, his parents wrote, most of the Jews shunned their German neighbors. Rumors were awash that the fascists dropped parachute saboteurs and German farmers gave them shelter and help. Clara's father advised her to keep away from the family, drop her German family name, and become lost in the human ocean of Moscow under Kovner's name. Why not? David said. After all, Clara Eissner, the German Communist militant with a thick, tight, blond braid, had done exactly that. She'd become Zetkin and made famous her husband's name; and David was looking forward to become famous through Clara Kovner. She kicked him in the chin for somebody else's blond braid. But she dug in her heels about that stinking letter of her father's. She'd stick with her family name. She found it shameful to hide her ethnic belonging when her tribe was in trouble. Clara gave birth to little Karl Kovner in a Moscow maternity ward in November, when David was with the fighting troops east of Rzhev.

His father's letter came in the same mail. It was drawn in a hasty hand on two pages raggedly torn from a school exercise book. Father asked David's advice: should they go east with the rest of the villagers or stay put?

David folded the letter carefully and eased it into the back slot of his briefcase. The Steppe Crimea had been under the Germans for four weeks now. He never again heard from his parents.

Two months after Karl's birth, Clara's foreman wrote to David before the builder, too, left for the frontline. A German bomber plane had dropped its load on the Mytishchi armament plant. One of the bombs leveled the hostel where David used to stay. Clara and Karl were killed in their sleep.

CHAPTER EIGHT

Although David had shared a doorway to a Moscow house with Joseph Ognev, he first laid eyes on him at a frontline concert in June 1944.

Standing troops packed a forest clearing. Artillery Major David Kovner made his way through the crowd, treading on the enlisted men's cigarette butts of coarse tobacco rolled in newspaper scraps. Those gave way to the officer's cardboard-tipped *papirosas*, as he reached the rows of backless benches in front. David took a place next to a woman in medical captain's shoulder loops, whose abundant flesh burst open from her tunic.

The beds of two aligned Studebaker pickups, flaps down, served as an improvised stage. An actor in dog's clothing, flaunting a long, pointed nose and a Charlie Chaplin mustache, hopped about on his hind legs. He spluttered spit and abuse until another actor in Red Army fatigues with the face of an aged Hamlet cut off his cardboard nose with a glittering sword, which prompted loud cheers. Then a uniformed male-female couple crooned a syrupy song about a soldier dreaming in his dugout about home. The woman captain beside David clapped hysterically. Afterwards, the man draped himself in the *Stars and Stripes* and the girl placed a headset on her head, and they sang about a plane barely making it home after a bombing mission. The words sounded fresh even in a Russian translation, and the beat was different, and the whole song was like an exotic bird that erred through the open window into a stuffy room. David loved it instantly.

The emcee announced the People's Actor of the Soviet Union, Joseph Ognev. A man in a peak-cap thrust deeply down his forehead walked across the stage and stopped short at the edge, looking at his boots. Then the actor took off the cap, lifted his head, and David gasped with the rest of the audience.

Standing before him was the short man in top boots, whose face every man and woman of the Soviet Union knew from omnipresent portraits and newsreel clips. Once a privileged youth, David had seen Stalin close by, on the podium of the Institute of Marxism waiting modestly for the storm of applause to die down. Compared to him, the man on the scene had certainly gotten on in years, his jowls pronounced and his hair rather grey than reddish-black.

Quelling the murmur in the rows, the actor lifted his forbidding hand and spoke. The text came from Stalin's radio address after Germany's assault on the Soviet Union. Stalin's address had lacked inspiration. The actor's voice carried the same undertones of hesitancy, even perplexity, which many had discerned in Stalin that July day, three years before. The cap in Ognev's hand added to the impression that the man on the stage came to beg for a favor of trust and patience. David felt anxiety grow and become palpable. The intense breathing behind his back produced a soft, high-strung hum. In front of David, a stout lieutenant colonel cleared his throat.

The words that David heard now were the same as spoken on the radio three years ago, and the voice was the same. But somehow they impressed David differently, even if he didn't know why. The voice from the stage promised, assured, led. The mood changed around David. He heard it in the altered pitch of the humming, in the beat of breathing. Clouds of tobacco smoke rose to the skies like incense. Suddenly the lieutenant colonel uncovered his head, and many followed. When the actor finished with a "we'll win the day," the clearing in the woods became one clapping, yelling, roaring mass. The woman captain—her lower lip bitten over, thighs tightly pressed together, hem of her military skirt gone above her round knees—clutched David's wrist. She quivered in orgasmic waves.

Afterwards, complying with the orders received through the lieutenant emcee, David dozed in the bunker of regimental headquarters, enveloped by dampness, the stench of kerosene lamps, and the mumble of the girls with headsets. The door opened and Ognev appeared in it. Obeying his beckoning, David walked out to the dusk.

The actor held out his hand. "Your former neighbor, one floor up."

David felt this was surreal. At his side walked Stalin incarnate, complete with the leader's porous nose, wildcat eyes, and a smoked-through mustache.

"You know English?" Ognev asked. Without waiting for an answer, he sang, *"Comin' in on a wing and a prayer.* What exactly is that?"

"But you speak a perfect American English."

Ognev laughed. "I understand not a word. Just parroting a record."

David translated. Ognev grimaced. "A prayer, eh? But tell me how you're doing, Major." His voice fell to a lower timbre. Now it rang with the lordly overtones that David had once heard on the phone in the Mytishchi hostel lobby. "Tell me whether you liked the town of P—." He laughed.

David gasped. "Did you get me into the school?"

Ognev snorted. "Their commanding officer was at a reception in St. George's Hall. The banquet for the top brass of military schools. A usual drunken revel. Waitresses dancing on the tables. Crystal glasses flying. Top boots smashing shards on the unique parquet floor. I confronted your general in his way to a man's room. The flaps of his tunic were buttoned on the wrong holes, the collar unhooked."

Ognev switched to Stalin's voice, which made David shudder. " 'Having a good time, don't you, Comrade Pavlov?' " Ognev went back to his voice. "I waited, and he stood rigid, paralyzed with fear. 'Now,' " Ognev returned to Stalin's voice, " 'do you remember that exemplary communist turned a dirty Trotskyite traitor, Meir Kovner? You must remember him, mustn't you? He spoke at your school shortly before his arrest.' "

David laughed nervously.

Ognev went on, replaying the conversation. " 'Kovner had a nephew. A nice young man. Don't you think we should allow a measure of Soviet humanism for the nice young man?' I puffed at my pipe, and the general just trembled, speechless. 'I think we should,' I said finally. 'We'll give the nice young man an opportunity to prove himself. You'll accept him to your school. But not a word about it!' "

"Now I know why the general never looked straight in my eyes. But you—you probably saved my life." David felt warm surge of gratitude.

"Ah," Ognev brushed it aside. "I was glad to do something in memory of—I mean, something for Meir."

"Have you heard anything about him? I've received no answer to any of my inquiries."

Ognev shook his head.

David asked. "Do you often make appearances like this?"

"Permissions for each performance come only very reluctantly." Ognev spoke now in dry, cut voice. "But I wanted to be nearby. I can barely wait for you to drive the Germans out of Vilnius."

David nodded. "It's coming. Why?"

Ognev broke a twig in his fingers.

"You see, my family was stuck in Lithuania at the start of the war. Vacationing. All three of them—my wife, son, and daughter."

He lifted his head. His voice grew harsh.

"My wife's name is Nadezhda Mikhailovna. My children are Volodya and Tanya. All-Russian names, nothing Jewish in them. They don't look Jewish. It's just in their passports. The Fifth Point—" His voice trailed. "It's unfair. There was a saying in the time of my youth: they strike in your Jewish nose, not your baptismal certificate. Now it's sort of the other way around. My family doesn't have the Jewish nose, and yet—Do you think they stood a chance to survive?"

David took him by the elbow. "It's possible, of course." He added a lie. "I've seen hundreds of Jewish survivors."

A Wyllis caught up with them and stopped. Ognev climbed in. David watched the ruby taillights vanish in the thickened gloom.

COMRADE STALIN CHANGED HIS HAIRCUT

★   ★   ★

Four months later, the battles of Minsk, Vilnius and Kovno behind him, having crossed the river Pissa into Germany, David Kovner walked the streets of a little East Prussian town through the wreckage caused by his battalion's fire, past the infantrymen tearing open the doors of spared buildings with their boots and rifle butts, giving way to pickup trucks piled high with carpets, grandfather clocks, accordions, and even an upright piano. Plumes of thick smoke rose above the roofs. Bursts of gunfire erupted spasmodically at a distance.

A side street had been spared destruction. It was quiet, almost peaceful. David trod on the row of grey granite slabs in the middle of the sidewalk, polished to shine as if they had been in place since the Knights of the Teutonic Order reclaimed the newly conquered land from swamps, marshes, and Pruses . . .

The Knights of the Cross. David remembered episodes of their conquest of this land. Once they caught a renegade, a baptized Pruse who lapsed back from Christianity. The Knights ripped open his abdomen, got hold of his intestines, and nailed one end to a tree trunk. Then they chased him around the tree so that his guts got wrapped around. How could those very people transform themselves into exemplary burgers?

And now David walked their country, vanquished and doomed.

On either side of the slabs ran neat rows of cobblestones. Where they couldn't fit a doorstep, or an undisciplined grill protected a window pit, or the circular perimeters ran around trees at the roadside, tiny mosaic had neatly patched the triangles and segments. A stately counterpoint in stone, a choral played in a temple where order was worshiped. The tamed rainwater ran across the sidewalk towards the gutters in shallow depressions marking bars in the score.

A sign told the passerby which street numbers would be encountered on this block up and down the street. The wasp-waisted, bulging Gothic letters made David's tongue tickle again, driven by the memories of Grandpa Osher's honey spread over the Torah plaque.

David experienced a strange feeling, something like recollections of the time before being born, of another reincarnation, perhaps. A kinship of sorts. Perhaps, perversely it was also felt on the other side. Otherwise, why had such a flood of hatred erupted from this seemingly peaceful world towards David's tribe of men? So strongly you could only hate a blood relative of yours. Your sibling. The two brothers. Brother Cain had murdered Brother Abel. One day, in a cemetery, Brother Cain would say to his children: look here; your uncle was in luck. Didn't I give him a plush funeral and set up a beautiful tombstone? I even added a layer of special paint so that no bird would sit on the stone and smear it. He would've never gotten treatment like that on his own—

Howls tore through the calm. David heard female screams coming from the second-floor windows. He walked through the gaping entryway, quickened his steps up the stairs, opening his holster as he ran, and burst into the chaos and violence of overturned plants and scattered chairs and a girl about ten lying on the floor at the fireplace, pink ribbons in pigtails, red freckles on the bridge of her nose, naked gory flesh thrust open, and another woman who stood bent forward, stripped naked below her waist, face pressed hard to the dinner tabletop, a figure with dropped trousers swinging rhythmically behind her; and David yelled, and trained his gun on forage caps and pug noses and enormous nostrils, and shot above their heads, until the two privates retreated through the door.

When the sounds of the rapists' steps died down the staircase, David, too, descended to the street.

Wind had drifted a pile of mortar dust against a bench's heavy armrest. *For Aryans only.* He sat down. His heartbeat was returning to normal. Dusk was falling. Someone tortured an accordion and guffawed loudly. To his left, the riverbanks flamed with autumn colors. The Pregel snaked away, towards Königsberg and the Baltic Sea. David had first heard the name of the river from Uncle Meir as they traveled in the Tatar's dray in Crimea. In Königsberg, Uncle had said, the river broke in branches to skirt two islands. Seven bridges connected the islands and various parts of the city of Teutonic Knights, Hanseatic merchants, Lutheran burgers. In the sixteenth century, Prussia's first secular ruler, duke Albrecht, founded the university, whereat Immanuel Kant later taught. There was a tradition among the students of the Albertina to stroll across the bridges in search of a route which would take them over each of the seven bridges only once. For some it became an obsession. From other towns students came to challenge the famous seven-bridges puzzle. All in vain. One day in the eighteenth century, they wrote to the first mathematician of the day, Leonard Euler, the German Swiss in Russian employment. Euler did solve the problem once and for all, but in his own way. He rigorously proved what generations of the students had discovered with their feet: such a route didn't exist. You either left one bridge uncrossed or walked some other twice, Uncle had said. With that solution, Euler inaugurated a new mathematical discipline, but don't ask me, Dovidke, about it.

Tomorrow David's battalion would resume its push, and he would do his best that they reach the doomed town . . .

The Germans must have regained some ground, because their mortars started to produce sibilant noises above. Three officers walked David's way skirting a dead tawny-spotted cow. A blue rag fell to David's feet from a window. Blue corduroy shorts. The recollection of a New Year school party and Clara came home like a sharp pain in his chest.

He heard the crescendo of the whistling and knew instantly that it was coming up to get him.

CHAPTER NINE

On the day paramedics loaded the stretcher with David Kovner on a hospital train, Arnold Hramoy, Corresponding Member of the Soviet Academy of Sciences, a distinguished linguist, popular speaker, and newspaper contributor of repute, set off to the United States with the delegation of Soviet Jewish public figures.

Arnold had long been allowed to rub shoulders with intellectuals in the West. A non-Party fellow traveler with cosmopolitan airs, he spoke at antifascist congresses and in the League of Nations committees at the time of the Spanish War and the Popular Front in France. He defended the common humanist values of the Western civilization against advancing Fascism.

Humanist values shared by Lincoln and Stalin? Arnold had wondered what they might have been. But speak he did, and he did his bit willingly, because Nazi Germany embodied the evil that Arnold Hramoy hated with a passion.

All Arnold's antipathy didn't result from Germany's Nazi present gutter quality. He'd never been anything like his unfortunate old friend, Meir Kovner, a dyed-in-the-wool Germanophile. What a hodgepodge of images, sounds, ideas had Meir gathered in his Teutonic Pantheon! Meir's naïve admiration of Germany could only result from his narrow-mindedness. Marxist blinders plus the parochial East European bias. Arnold had never cared about Marxism, the boring creation of a second-rate German journalist and his swarm of epigones, also predominantly German. Naturally, he held his tongue about it, even with Meir.

And Arnold had long overcome the limitations of those Russians whose vision was blocked by the proximity of Germany.

They could not see beyond an uncertain, distant glare edging the snow-capped mountain ridge called the German *Kultur*. A true European, Arnold could only squint at the optical aberration. He knew that the genuine civilization started on the far side of the Rhine. Long before German storm troops and German Communists raised arms in like salutes, Arnold was sick of geraniums in the window, sing-alongs in the *biergarten*, and well-behaved children in corduroy shorts. He would forsake all that for any picturesque street in Marseilles slums. Provided you didn't have to live in that mean street, Meir Kovner would retort. Poor Meir. Such a middle-class sentiment from the sworn revolutionary.

And then the language, of course. Arnold believed that the language was soul of the people. Whereas the French created a beautiful cascade of sounds clinging to one another to the exasperation of the uninitiated, the German language sacrificed grace for intelligibility. The Germans interspersed the speech flow with a characteristic quasi-pause to mark the initial vowel of their long words. They even carried that glottal stop into the word's interior to mark the border between the prefix and the root, God forbid confusion. How typically German. Pedantically German. Too bad that some speakers of English did the same to the phoneme *with'out*.

And the nerve of German linguists! To listen to them, history and geography had conspired together to place the German language right in the middle of the European stage and bestowed upon it a special role. To the east resided the Slavs, ever churning out new word forms through declension and conjugation, whereas the English, on the western extreme, knew very little inflection and relied heavily on syntax. To listen to German linguists, the German language was both and much more. The natural order had made the German ear and brain tuned to the East and West alike, which was why it was the Germans who had built the body of comparative linguistics. Arnold's blood boiled. What a pretense! A Grimm Brothers' fairy tale!

Here lay, Arnold reflected, an archetypical Russian problem. The French and the German fought in the Russian soul—that's to say, for whatever room in the Russian soul remained unoccupied by the Asiatic. The great French vs. German dichotomy sorted individuals in accordance with their temperaments, ideologies, weltanschauungs. *Tell me who your European is, and I'll tell you who you are.* And Germany was closer. The German myth prevailed. The Russian czars took German brides; German material culture fascinated the middle class; the vulgarized German philosophy reigned over the minds of the Russian intelligentsia; Teutonic spirit appealed to both Russian aggressiveness and sentimentality. Those forces successfully challenged the notorious Frenchiness, short-lived and skin-deep, of Russian aristocracy. Arnold conceded grudgingly that French words and French ideas often came to Russia in German packaging.

But even in his worst nightmares couldn't Arnold foresee the current, bizarre chapter in Russian-German relations. The Soviet-Nazi alliance. It came like a bolt from the blue. Arnold blinked in disbelief at newspaper photographs of Soviet and German officers shaking hands over the friendship cemented with Polish blood. Arnold's country became a partner to Hitler's Germany! England and France declared war on the latter and came damn close to outright warfare against the former. When in 1939 the League of Nations expelled the Soviet Union, all of Arnold's eloquence couldn't prevent it. His country became an international pariah, because Hitler had seduced Stalin with an offer of group rape of Eastern Europe.

It was, perhaps, to shake off his frustration that Arnold got embroiled in that silly bickering at his Geneva hotel foyer, his suitcases ready for a taxi.

Arnold was there with his French colleague, a professor of the Sorbonne. Arnold was telling him about his recent visit to a mutual acquaintance, the German professor in Göttingen, who would get very angry when foreigners pronounced his name without the sacramental catch in the throat. "*Schwarzen'egger!*" he'd shouted. "Black Plowman! I'll have nothing to do with a black Negro!" But, *mon ami*, countered the Frenchman, the vaunted clarity of the German language was history. In Nazi usage, it had dissipated in a sea of amorphous, pretentious compounds and repeated clusters, whereas the rudeness and harshness were allowed to develop to the full. Perhaps, it served to expose the deficiencies of the German national soul. What a peculiar fusion of tactlessness and touchiness, of arrogance and docility!

Arnold noticed a German guest at the bar straining his ear to the conversation. In spite of his striped brown business suit with a double-breasted coat, his straight back and monocle betrayed a military man. Arnold raised his voice. The Germans were proud of belonging to the Chosen People, the Nordic race, he said, but it was only the reverse side of their self-contempt.

The German loudly objected to the "caricature."

"So this German isn't touchy, is he?" Arnold said. "And this Jew isn't tactless, is he?" retorted the German. "You're right," Arnold said; "similar shortcomings are intrinsic to the Jewish character as much as to the German."

The German wasn't pleased. His pedigreed aquiline nose jerked.

Arnold developed the theme. "The merits are similar as well. Diligence. Perseverance. Thrift. Respect to learning. Sometimes the German and the Jew look like a family."

"The Jew is the exact opposite of the German in every respect—"

"—and yet is as closely akin to him as a blood brother."

"Disgusting rubbish." The German's voice was icy.

"But it was Herr Hitler who said it," Arnold said, pleasantly. "In so many words."

The German's immaculate hair parting turned crimson. "Lies! The Führer of the German nation could never tell such a—, such a—"

"Disgusting rubbish?" Arnold helped. "And yet he did. To a senator of Danzig."

"The turncoat invented it all!" From the look of things the German was going to flush his schnapps into Arnold's face. Instead, he pivoted and left.

Arnold and the Frenchman rode in a taxi to the railroad station. Behind the window, the Calvinist Geneva, coldly contemptuous of idolatry and pageantry, had barred Christmas from its frozen streets. The Sorbonne man congratulated Arnold on defeating the *boche*. But did Professor Hramoy really give any weight to the stretched analogy the Führer had unexpectedly endorsed? Arnold shrugged. He'd done it only for the sake of the argument. Jews versus Germans—that wasn't what Arnold had thought much about. It was rather Meir Kovner's theme. What would his unlucky friend have said about that quotation from the controversial book. And what would Meir's nephew, with his naïve German-versus-Jew fantasies? His unusual colloquium talk had reached Arnold through the grapevine. The young man seemed to have had a crush on Arnold. Where was he now? After Meir's arrest Arnold had played with the idea of reaching for David, but was relieved to hear that Meir's nephew had left Moscow, destination unknown . . .

In Dijon, the express Geneva-Paris train took a load of fresh Burgundian victuals. The Sorbonne professor, youthful, thin-lipped, carrying golden round-rim spectacles glasses on the bridge of his straight nose, exalted over superb *foie gras*. Arnold remembered another train, a half-life back, that had rushed three teenage runaways—Meir Kovner, Joseph Ognev, and Arnold— from the little town in the Ukraine to a new life in Moscow. Arnold, at that time still Aaron, had sported a long belted blouse *à la* Tolstoy and a shock of black hair. He'd perceived a providential design in his name's roots. Coming from *khromoy*, lame. Modeled upon the bright hope of the Russian culture, Gorky, meaning *bitter*. The thinker at odds with the establishment. The intellectual giving voice to the plight of the underprivileged and he himself an underdog. Arnold and Meir talked excitedly, nonstop, as squat redbrick stations and gold-domed churches flew by. What about? The startling new production of *Swan Lake* in Mariinsky Theater; the death of Friedrich Engels; the new marvels of science, the X-rays and Marconi's experiments with the wireless—all in rapid German, for self-importance, to impress the fellow passengers. Ognev, of course, couldn't follow. His German was halting . . .

Arnold's barroom speechmaking was a tribute to his old friend, Meir Kovner.

Arnold Hramoy felt braver when outside the Soviet Union. Paris shivered between the leaden skies and ice-plated asphalt. The large, elaborate crèche in front of Hôtel de Ville was an embodiment of kitsch. The Sorbonne professor called the next day. He'd secured funding for Arnold to pursue research in Paris for eight months! The area? Old North French. Arnold understood. Now that France was at war with Germany, Arnold's long-standing denial of any significant German influence on the *langue d'oïl* came very handy indeed. And his confrontation with the German military attaché in Geneva hadn't passed unnoticed, his friend intimated. Arnold advised the Soviet Embassy on the rue de Grenelle of the offer and set to waiting. Had his childish attack at the officer of the friendly nation been reported back to Moscow, too? Apparently it hadn't, because five days later the Soviet Foreign Office telegraphed an approval. Arnold remained in Paris. The funds were barely sufficient for living. When he bought cheap, pungent cheroots under the tobacconist's *carotte* in rue Gay Lussac, straight, devoid of any green except for the awnings of street cafés, he noticed police surveillance. His mail was being opened, and not that discreetly. Arnold was still regarded as a pro-Germany suspect! He shrugged it off, but it hurt.

The German blitzkrieg and the Wehrmacht's triumphal entry into Paris caught Arnold unawares. The occupying authorities cordially cooperated with the Soviet Embassy, but Arnold was worried. The Embassy also thought it best not to tempt fate and leave now. For Arnold's travel back to Moscow they provided him with a better identity. He was Nodar Kupradze, an accountant from Tbilisi. With his knowledge of languages (Arnold never disowned his admirers who claimed that he mastered a hundred), he would pass the chance encounter with a Georgian with flying colors.

The Embassy booked a room in Hotel Adlon in Berlin. Arnold tipped the bellhop and descended to the street gay with officers and their ladies. His topcoat of fine straw-colored wool slung over his arm damp with the August sweat and his heart wrung with loathing, Arnold strolled the Third Reich's capital. *The Third Kingdom*, he thought as a brass band thumped a marching tune— *the Nazis had hijacked the name*—past the Soviet Embassy pleasantly festooned in red—*stolen the Christian symbol to ingratiate themselves with the German Protestants and borrow from the longevity of the Millennium*—past the spot where five years ago student fraternities built a scaffold, loaded it with armfuls of books, and set fire to the writings of the enemies of the German nation, such as Jew Hramoy.

The grand billboard in front of the Cathedral featured Hitler in the sparkling armor of Wagnerian Parsifal. The Führer stretched his hands to the Holy Grail mounted on a swastika. Behind him, under red banners, marched row after row, their faces shining with joy and hope . . .

Arnold came to a scorched building, the tall façade blackened by smoke, the spherical dome and four turrets still with shards of glass on their girders, the blue sky showing through their spider legs.

Beasts. He turned back and walked away from the scar of the Kristallnacht.

His Jewish roots played little if any role in Arnold's identity. He had simply shrugged them off, unlike Meir Kovner, who in spite of all his Marxist internationalism had fussed a great deal about his Jewishness, which, of course, had nothing to do with rabbis' Judaism. But much as Arnold was alienated from that silly little religion, the gutted synagogue was a powerful reminder of his vulnerability in Berlin.

In Alexanderplatz, a group of youths swaggered singing to a tune of a popular Russian revolutionary song. They drew closer. Arnold made out the words. No, they were Nazi. The red was spliced with the brown, Rot Front replaced with the SA, the remaining fierce rhetoric fit to the word. He wandered in narrow alleys behind the Red Town Hall when he spotted two characters in fedoras, raincoats, and rubber-soled walkers. Twenty minutes later, near Nikolaikirche, he saw the men again.

Arnold pressed down the brim of his straw canotier. His heart beat faster. What should he do? Pretend that he didn't see? Hurry back to his hotel? Finally, he decided. He'd make sure whether they really tailed him.

He took a seat on a bench facing a rococo palazzo of marble, bronze, and curved forms. Presently the two men beneath fedoras landed on either side of him. Speaking to one another over Arnold, they took turns telling the story of the house's first owner, King Frederick's Jewish financier, who had built it on the lighter silver thalers he'd minted. Arnold felt the prickle of sweat under his collar. He made an attempt to get up, but the man to his left pressed his thigh, and Arnold's feet gave under. When he finally gathered enough strength to rise on his wobbly knees, the man to his left said, "Have a good time in Berlin, Herr Hramoy."

★　★　★

Ever since that Berlin afternoon, Arnold Hramoy carried the sting of humiliation in his heart. The deep, animal fear he'd felt. The indignity of using your enemy's—what exactly? indulgence? contempt?—bore down on him. Or was it commonality? The thugs had let him pass, in full knowledge of who he was, because Arnold enjoyed the protection of another criminal boss who had befriended theirs. Their helpfulness stuck to him like dung to the bottom of his English shoes.

He told nobody back in Moscow. Here too many things had changed. The word "fascist," previously bestowed generously upon anyone and anything evil, from Mussolini to Hitler to Franco to Trotsky, was no longer permitted in reference to National Socialist Germany. At the annual November rallies, thousands of Muscovites paraded in front of Lenin's Tomb, the Mausoleum, and on the very next day pageants in Munich glorified the martyrs of the German national socialist revolution. The May Day was celebrated in Moscow and Berlin simultaneously. The pride of scarlet banners stretched uninterrupted from the Pacific to the Rhine. And solid red was the flag at the German Embassy, when it draped in no wind, concealing the black-and-white spidery swastika that lurked in its folds.

The German invasion of the Soviet Union meant liberation for Arnold Hramoy. The country's enemy was defined unequivocally, and that was Arnold's enemy as well. Never before a journalist, Arnold embarked on writing for newspapers. He found a language appealing to any reader. Whereas some in the élite still clung to the hope that the German workers in trenches would turn their rifles against the enemies of the world proletariat, Arnold Hramoy advanced but a single message: "Kill the German." And he elaborated it tirelessly.

At a meeting in the Press Club, a correspondent of the *Chicago Tribune*, burly, bearded, and thick-necked, asked whether it was Soviet or Russian patriotism that drove Professor Hramoy. Both, Arnold told him. He drew on the Russian tradition of repulsing an aggressor invading from the west. His heart and soul belonged to the Soviet Union, the happy family of nations, the bright hope of the humankind. He added, on a hunch, "And another point to make. At the time of unheard-of Nazi atrocities, I can't help but remember that my mother's name was Sarra."

He meant it; and he also caught the right wind, as was usual with him. A renowned Yiddish songwriter came to see Arnold in his high-ceilinged office at the Division of Linguistics, in a rundown eighteenth-century palazzo.

The writer was a jovial potbelly whose bushy left eyebrow dropped at the bridge of his nose a half inch below the tip of the right eyebrow. He mastered them as a military orchestra conductor used his batons. He told the news. A delegation of Soviet Jews was to leave for a grand tour of the United States. What for? Pressure, Arnold. Pressure for American war efforts, for credits and loans. Giving a human, civilized face to the mysterious Russian ally. Opening hearts and wallets. Raising money in the land of Mammon. The jovial writer would head the delegation. "Your candidacy has, of course, been cleared at all levels."

As the train Moscow-Vladivostok rumbled across Siberia, Arnold replayed in his mind the stormy events of the last day in

Moscow, until in Petropavlovsk a folk poet, Abay Kunayev, barged into his compartment with grapes and melons. Abay was heavyset. His broad face glistened with fat. He was clad in a coat of fine grey cheviot and a blue polka-dot necktie. At their first meeting twenty years before in Abay's native village, the poet answered calls of nature by squatting in the middle of the street under protection of his quilted wadded robe. At that time, Moscow took on the role of nation builder for dozens of Asiatic ethnic groups it had inherited from the Czarist Empire. Hordes of hacks created phony history and folklore and wrote grammar and dictionaries for the new languages fashioned from local dialects. Arnold put Abay's nation on the map and styled Abay steppe Homer. Ever since, Abay had kept in touch, bringing over to Moscow now a basket of roses, now the back of a lamb. The success launched Arnold's meteoric career . . .

The Japanese men of war followed the Soviet ship on route Vladivostok-San Francisco but didn't interfere. The hectic American tempo quickly ousted everything else from Arnold's mind. The delegation appeared at union clubs, civic centers, synagogues; they met senators and journalists. With his speaker's talent, his easy worldly ways, his gloss polished at the Sorbonne, Arnold Hramoy found himself an ideal fit for the role of cultural ambassador. He did not preach solely to the converted. His voice's velvet modulations brought tears to the eyes of the doubting and won them over. And he knew how to destroy the hostile or misinformed. Some measure of good-natured humor, a dab of sarcasm—the audience did the rest. They shouted down the dirty fascist mercenary, the slanderer of the heroic Soviet Union, the people who made incomparable sacrifices on the altar of the victory.

And everywhere on his route, having taken notice of Arnold's un-Soviet smoking preference, they gave him cigars. Arnold accumulated a three-month supply.

Sometimes Arnold was asked to present his linguistic theory in a nutshell. He obliged. At the dawn of time, a tribe of hunters-gatherers had lived in the Middle East. For reasons unknown but momentous they had embarked on eastward migration. And so did their language. Every single word and every minute grammatical feature had drifted like pebbles dragged by a mighty river current, changing shape, smoothing sharp angles, agglutinating under pressure, or crushing into pulp with loud rumbling . . . Arnold went to a wall map—those were ubiquitous, what with the American armed forces straddling the oceans. The long-armed ape, he charted straight lines and horseshoes, using his cigar for a pointer. Streams branched and collided, produced whirls and maelstroms, filled riverbeds, flooded valleys. They blended into the local landscape, filled mountain lakes. The torrent poured up the Trans-Caspian and streamed due westward, to Europe.

Arnold screwed up his eyes, peering into the distant millennia. Following his glance, the listeners turned their heads. They, too, seemed to see the streams rolling through the interminable steppe or stagnating in northern swamps, leaving fragments—now a piece of green malachite, now a sprinkle of red rubies or a vein of glittering quartz—amidst the plain clay sediment, dull as the landscape it traveled. The great family of Indo-European languages stretched throughout the immense region from the Ganges to the Atlantic. Sanskrit and Russian, Greek and English, Gaelic and Spanish—you name it. In good time they followed Columbus across the ocean to put down roots—Arnold tapped at his lectern— in this soil.

Applause.

Question period.

Regarding Professor Hramoy's tribe of men: did they start their wandering before or after the Lord confounded the language at the Tower of Babel? Arnold chased away the devil instigating him to say that his theory didn't require the hypothesis of the Lord. Too bad he had to waste his talents here. If only it were Paris, where he could have sparred with those on an intellectual par!

But when he tried the same manner of presentation in a university faculty club set with deep mustard leather chairs, he met with polite but highly professional questioning, so he had to get to nuts and bolts, mixing embarrassment and pleasure. He stayed overnight to spend more time with his hosts, those nice and—yes, knowledgeable and gifted men, who were, sadly, steeped in fallacious Indo-Germanism, which they had adopted from Arnold's sworn enemies in Berlin and Göttingen.

Christmas interrupted their discussions. As the rest of the delegation toured the Chicago Loop, Arnold remained in the sleepy midwestern town. He wandered about, listening to carols on street corners, occasionally being treated to hot eggnog, wassail, and a warm smile, while the spirit of two-story America slowly oozed into his blood. After the dinner at the department chairman's clapboard colonial, at the coffee and bourbon in the living room overstuffed with heavy furniture, a guest sociology professor from the East Coast, robust and freckled even in the middle of winter and a staunch supporter of progressive causes, expanded on chiliasm, the Christian millennia which was supposed to arrive after the Second Coming of Christ, the Advent, and didn't Professor Hramoy find it remarkable that the theological name for Advent was *Parousia*, pah-ROO-see-yah, which rhymes perfectly with PROO-see-yah as the Russians pronounce Prussia? And he stared at Arnold, who found nothing remarkable but smiled and nodded to the dancing reflections of the fire in Professor Gibbs's spectacles rimmed with tortoise shell. Arnold was rewarded for the tedium of the dinner with a king's present, a twelve-cigar cedar-lined humidor filled with *Habanos*.

Back in his hotel, he unloaded his swollen collection onto his desk. Like Romance dialects, he thought. Changing ever so gradually, almost imperceptibly, valley by valley, village by village, until the accumulated change called for the recognition of a new variety . . . Arnold spread a map of Europe on his bed. He picked the darkest cigars and placed them over Sicily to represent the local speech. He went up the Italian peninsula, humming *Funiculì Funiculà* and laying his gradually lightening stock of *maduro* cheek by jowl. *Nel mezzo del cammin*, amidst the sweet dialect of Toscana ringing like silver bells, the color graduated into a perfect *colorado maduro.* Arnold paved Piedmont with brownish corduroy all the way over the snowy Alpine peaks, in which process the coffee-color cylinders brightened to shadings of *colorado* Occitan. Along the littoral, Provençale accents morphed to Catalonian and—-farther, lighter, into the blistering sun and lisping winds of Castilian *colorado claro*—until the pounding Atlantic waves completed the bleaching of Galician into the fawn *claro.* That last cigar he immersed into the twang of oblong Portugal.

Nobody had given Arnold a single cigar back in Paris . . .

He caught up with the delegation at Cleveland. Their KGB shepherd made an audible sound of relief. The tour ended in New York. As they were leaving the hotel lobby on 56th Street, a haggard man approached Arnold. The man wore a faded scar across his cheek and a thick German accent. He wanted to know what happened to an old friend of his, whom he had last seen eight years ago. An associate. A comrade-in-arms. The incomparable Comintern hand, Meir Kovner. Was it true that he had perished in Siberian slave labor camps?

CHAPTER TEN

D avid hadn't fully recovered after the surgery in the Minsk Army hospital when marching orders came. Major Kovner was to report to the Kremlin Hospital in Moscow.

A singular summons.

Doctor Petrov, who had operated on David, thin-lipped, lisping, blond, and bespectacled, said, "While you lay unconscious, an interrogator came to see you. A SMERSH man. Looks like they have something on you."

They spoke in the chief surgeon's tiny office behind a whitewashed glass partition.

"They do indeed," David told him. "An assault on the gallant Soviet troops sweeping the town clean of those entrenched Hitlerites. Never mind that the Hitlerites in question were a mother and her pre-teenage daughter. And the sweeping—well, the bastards performed it on their vaginas and anuses."

The white-coated chief surgeon took off his glasses and polished them on a flannel shred. Breaking the racial pride of the German woman they call it, he said. The just revenge. He had treated some of the raped. Lacerations and fissures at just about any feasible entry. Bladder ruptures. Broken ribs. VDs. Concussions. A foot-wrap thrust into the uterus. A potato rammed up the anus.

He hoisted the glasses back onto the bridge of his nose.

"What surprises me—your interrogator never came back. But you never know with them, not with those—Once a patient of mine was recalled to Moscow in a similar way. They tailed him in the train and arrested him on arrival. I wanted you to know."

David silently shook the good doctor's hand.

·99·

The Moscow train left that very night. David stood in the car's vestibule. Gloomy single-story timber houses rushed backwards in the blue snow. He had twice crossed this land with the army, first retreating eastwards, then regaining the territory, until in a small German town he challenged the system.

During those years in the Army nobody had bothered him about his uncle. Now it was different. What could have been forgiven somebody else portended a sure end for the nephew of Meir Kovner . . .

The night grew lighter. The train rumbled across a viaduct. A great city began being sensed, an immense transport nexus. Maneuvering started, back and forth in marshalling yards. For hours the car jerked on frogs and points. David was in luck: the train dragged through Mytishchi. He jumped off. He didn't notice anybody following suit.

CHAPTER ELEVEN

The scorching August sun began descending on Alupka from high above the lilac mountains. It had just crossed the axial line of the tall, sprawling former Vorontsov's palace. The little wedge of shade at the northern façade was no more. The rays stung the crowd packing the courtyard. They sat on their belongings, motionless, passive, with the same stunned expression on their faces.

Ebert stood in front of a heavy mahogany door recessed in the façade. At his shoulder brown ivy stems climbed the green stone wall like veins on an old man's legs. He held ten-year-old Elsa in his arms, who was shaking in a fit of cough. Tears of exhaustion rolled down her cheeks. Greta, herself on the brink of collapsing, was patting her hand.

The sentry spat onto the ground. His heavy gaze shot past Ebert.

"Could we go to the bathroom?"

The thickset sergeant motioned to the alley leading to an outhouse.

Ebert's palm touched the sentry's dangling hand. He said softly, "In the outhouse, my daughter will choke. The smell of carbolic acid—it burns in the throat and stings the eyes. And she needs running water. Listen, we can't possibly run away. All the exits are manned, right?"

He pressed on the sergeant's palm.

The sentry's face remained blank. His hand disappeared in a pocket of his army tunic. Reappeared empty.

He waved Ebert and Elsa in.

"Your woman stays."

"It takes two of us to look after her. Please."

It also took another hand contact.

At that very hour in Palai, troops with semiautomatics stood over the perimeter of the town hall's courtyard. Inside, the ethnic German villagers boarded pickup trucks, one sack per person, clutching toddlers and babies.

The trucks rolled out of the gate, past the Jewish farmers, who stood in silence. The hostler Borukh, the one who had been mongering rumors of German paratroopers, shouted:

"Say hello to Hitler!"

Hirsh Kovner muttered, "We Jews are a smart people, but when you have a stupid Jew, he is a very, very stupid Jew."

The last truck cleared the gate and dragged on the road to Djankoi.

Max Ebert left his wife and daughter behind, in a gully outside Palai. The night was warm and dry. An August steppe night, a week after the roundup. The air smelled of dry grass, wormwood, and cow dung.

Ebert made it over the wicker fence. The Kovners had no dog—few Jewish villagers had pets.

The windows gaped. Ebert scraped at the windowpane.

A bed squeaked; a soft whisper wafted out.

Ebert scraped again.

A pale forehead and a dark beard appeared in the window frame.

"Hirsh, it's me, Max Ebert. Franz's brother from Alupka."

Hirsh Kovner stared at him. Then he said, very softly, "Franz is gone. And Hilde too."

"I know. Is Franz's place empty?"

"No. Some refugees moved in."

"Could we—you think there's a chance we could stay in the village?"

Hirsh Kovner said, after a moment, "You'll stay in Osher's room. He's dead, Osher. And my son's room is vacant too."

"Thanks, Hirsh."

"Ah, no big deal."

Ebert went to fetch his wife and daughter. Hirsh Kovner waited at the wicket.

Greta and Elsa spent most of the time in Osher's room, where the tigers lurked on folding screens, and the smells of cinnamon and mothball lingered. Rachel Kovner took food to them and their night buckets to the outhouse. Greta had calmed somewhat. Her elongated face relaxed from the permanent grimace of pain that it had taken on the Vorontsovs grounds. Elsa had had no asthmatic fits since they left the cavern with its peculiar air. She itched to play the piano in David's room—"very softly, Mutti!"— but Greta didn't allow it for fear of the neighbors. A distant cannonade rumbled in the north. German planes flew over to drop bombs on the Soviet Navy bases down south. Hirsh Kovner went to the buckwheat field every day, mobilized to dig trenches. In Osher's room, the pendulum of a cuckoo clock swung on the whitewashed wall. Ebert strove to return permanence and stability to things around him. He revitalized an alarm clock, the glass-faced disc on three legs with a nickel-plated cap of a bell on the top. Every day, thrice a day, he took it apart and put back together with the sole help of a little screwdriver, which he always carried tucked under the black leather strap of his wristwatch. He fixed all locks in the household, sharpened and tuned shears, oiled hinges. Now and then, the Eberts had to raise a trapdoor in the kitchen, tiptoe down a ladder to the cellar, close behind them, and sit out a visitor. The air was cooler and smelled of bare earth, sprouted potato, and mold. He sat there and prayed that Elsa could take it without coughing.

One night the Kovners left for the community center. The kolkhoz chairman would speak on an important matter. Ebert took a risk and stole his way through the village. The meeting was in the converted barn adjacent to a two-story office. Ebert stood behind the men who sat on the open windowsill, legs dangling into the room. He'd drawn the visor of his cap deep down—perhaps, needlessly, because the electric power was down and the light of two smoking kerosene lamps didn't spread out. No one was paying much attention to him. Many strangers walked around in the village nowadays, war refuges from the Ukraine.

The room was packed with men wearing baggy pants and soiled top boots, and women in kerchiefs around their heads. They sat on long backless benches. An immense brawny man stood behind a table. He kept filling his glass and drank from it in large, audible gulps. Ebert could follow the chairman's Yiddish. Words the chairman inserted above and beyond the Germanic core were mainly Russian. One came up over and over again. *Evakuatsiya.* The chairman finished and all hell broke loose, but he tapped his pencil on the table and smiled as if dropping everything and leaving in the dark was the most natural thing to do. A young woman climbed onto a back bench and shouted yes, go they should, because the German fascists herded Jews in ghettoes, clamped on a yellow star, and assigned them to grueling work. They'd driven out their own Jews to Palestine, was what they did, and they would do the same to us. Wait a moment, the chairman said, and his forehead under a low hairline gathered into wrinkles; the fascists mistreated *all* Soviet people, regardless. And if he was calling for the evacuation—But the people didn't listen anymore. Everybody shouted. Ebert left.

The Kovners came back after midnight. Ebert walked out to the backyard and sat on the kitchen stoop. Soon Hirsh Kovner came out, too. Ebert scooted over for him.

"You want to hear about the meeting, Max? I'll tell you. May my enemies have many a meeting like that one."

Cicadas sang on the far side of the little vineyard. Overripe apricots fell soundlessly from the trees. The darkness seemed to be deeper because of the twinkling insects. Hirsh spoke in a fierce whisper.

"Where should we go now? To Siberia? What have we lost in Siberia? If the Germans chase us away, go away we will. But! Why now?"

He waited, but Ebert said nothing.

"And the yellow star—who has ever seen a yellow star? For two years we've heard no single bad word about Hitler. But I don't need them educating me on the Germans, Max. I know the Germans. I know how to reason with the Germans. I'd rather trust them than the Bolsheviks, and may my chairman and my brother Meir forgive me and where his love to the revolution has gotten him. What do you think, Max?"

Ebert shrugged his shoulders. "I don't know, Hirsh. I'm just a watchmaker."

The wind brought down the rotten smell from the northern marshes and mixed it with Hirsh's hot whisper.

"It's like in the Czar's war, one war ago. The Russians deported all the Germans from the frontline area and all Jews in the bargain. They took us for German or Austrian spies, because of our Yiddish! And you know what, Max? Spies we wuzn't, but for a German victory we did pray."

Hirsh Kovner sighed and got up.

"Life is such and getting sucher and sucher."

★ ★ ★

On the day the Jewish villagers departed, dresses flapped on the porches of Djankoi like multicolored flags. Puffs of steam drifted about. Their hair in curling pins, local girls readied their wardrobes for new wooers. They blankly regarded the Maifeld kolkhozniks boarding the train to the Kerch ferry. Hirsh and Rachel Kovner weren't at the station. With ten others, they had chosen to stay put.

The Red Army didn't make a stand in the buckwheat field. The Wehrmacht's Eleventh Army in field-grey came and rumbled by, towards Sevastopol. Then *sonderkommandos* rolled in on motorcycles. Ebert was in the fields, collecting occasional corncobs. As he walked back in the street, he heard in a courtyard *raus, du Judenhure*! Get out in the open, you dirty whore of a yid. You and your little bastards. Ebert thought bitterly that the thugs needed no interpreter.

At the Kovners', the faces of Greta and Elsa told him all. Ebert walked to the town hall. In the courtyard, men dressed in black fussed with the machinegun fixed to a Horch's sidecar. The Obersturmführer, a ramrod seven-footer with slanted cheekbones, protruding nose and receding chin, watched them, tapping with a stick at the top of his shiny boot. Ebert came close. The Obersturmführer smelled of heavy sweat and shoe polish. Ebert said those people saved his family. Could they possibly be spared? The Obersturmführer said, what kind of a German you are. Smeared in *Judenscheisse*. Jewish shit. Ebert said the Kovners were his in-laws. A German's in-laws. Doesn't it call for leniency?

Your Jewish in-laws?

They arrested him. Detailed investigation, though, cleared Ebert from *Rassenschande*, the race defilement committed by his niece.

Beat it, Jewish lackey.

The *sonderkommandos* lined all the Jews at the entrenchment Hirsh Kovner had helped dig. They set out sentries. Ebert could only hear the rattle of the machine gun.

As a *volksdeutsche*, Max Ebert could have taken a post in the administration, but his disreputable family connections had cast a shadow over him. He was thankful. He lingered in Palai, for Alupka was a war zone. Down the coast, the Soviet Navy base, Sevastopol, barely held. The frontline lay roughly on the same hills as eighty-seven years ago, at yet another war in the Crimea, when the British and the French had besieged Sevastopol.

The German soldiers in Djankoi—some were scum, like that Obersturmführer, others decent men. Those were in a majority,

Ebert felt. He repaired their watches—step by step he acquired some tools, or what could pass for tools. The old fart Stavraki back in Alupka was an *arschloch,* asshole, but he was right about one thing: the real master can do anything with just a screwdriver. The soldiers gave Max food and schnapps. The food he brought back home, the schnapps traded for more food. They spoiled little Elsa. But they treated Ebert with thinly concealed contempt. He, a *volksdeutsche*—was he a *deutsche* for them? Hardly. Something on the level of a nightmare trying to pass for a mare. And his country was not the Germany they'd come from. His was the Crimea, with its sun and sea and cicadas and his folks and Tatars and Russians and Jews.

The ground settled down in the trench that had accepted Hirsh and Rachel Kovner . . .

It was in July 1942 that Sevastopol fell to the Germans. Ebert settled back to Alupka, doing what he loved second only to his family, which meant repairing watches. The bittersweet scent of dried manure, *kizyak,* burning in Tatars' stoves wafted into the shop. On the walls, pendulums swayed and clocks ticked away, striving to catch up with one another. Cuckoos made bows to grandfather clocks: the world's turned kooky, gramps.

The Vorontsov's palace was heavily guarded and there was heavy traffic to and fro, high-ranking officers in important-looking vehicles. It was rumored that Hitler had given the palace to Field Marshall Erich von Manstein, the "Conqueror of the Crimea."

In the spring of 1944 the frontline came back to the Crimea. The Germans and Rumanians abandoned the steppe. The occupants of the palace left. Gone were the generals and their staff. Retreating troops clogged the roads. The street monitor came to the Eberts to say that, as *volksdeutsche*, they were scheduled for relocation to the Reich the following morning.

At night, Max, Greta and Elsa skulked off to the grounds of the palace, stepping on the white cover of acacia petals. The doors were unlocked: locks wouldn't keep the Red Army away; they would only provoke violence and destruction, and von Manstein counted on returning to his property.

Once more in the familiar bathroom, Max Ebert let his family and himself through the cupboard passage. The Eberts stayed in the cavern as a battle rumbled on the surface. At last, the sounds of guns died down. The Soviet Army was in possession of the town. The palace remained occupied by a military unit, rather large by the sound of it, twenty-four hours a day, and there must've been night patrols as well.

The Eberts decided on the northern passage. At night, perched above Bakhchi-Sarai, they heard commands bark, children and women cry, truck engines roar. When they descended in the morning, the Tatar town was empty. Dogs alone roamed the alleys.

They stumbled onto a Soviet road patrol. The pimpled lieutenant of the military counterintelligence, the SMERSH, looked, bug-eyed, from their passports to their faces and back to their Soviet passports, where on the fifth line, ethnicity, he read *German*.

The patrol locked them up in an adobe hovel that smelled of Tatar sheep cheese. Ebert caught snatches of a conversation outside. They awaited instructions on whether to send the spies to Simferopol or shoot them on the spot. He took his Longines wristwatch, black-faced with luminescent hands, off the leather strap and managed to slip it over to the clerk, a thin-lipped, skinny girl in uniform. At noon, a pickup truck loaded with Tatar deportees pulled up at the post. While the driver changed a flat addressing the road and the Tatars in unflattering terms, the lieutenant came into the hovel. He collected Greta and Elsa's watches. A private led the Eberts out to the truck. The lieutenant waved them through. Ebert placed Greta on a truck's tire and heaved her up by the hips. She received Elsa in her arms, over the flap. Then Ebert climbed up. The Tatar women in motley shawls made room on the bed. The driver loaded firewood into the belching cylinder producing gas for the engine, and the truck went on.

The train stood in a sidetrack at Simferopol. It set out on the day the Allied troops landed in Normandy. The following five weeks the wheels clattered, then rested, then clattered again under the forty-two women, old men and children on double-deck plank-beds of the cattle car. There was a tiny grill window in the wall and a round hole in the floor to squat over. Once the train remained standing for eight days. The smell of excrement hung heavily in the steamy heat of the car. Elsa was coughing at the window, her eyes ready to pop out, her breath whistling and wheezing, and Greta desperately comforting her. The medication given by the German doctor was gone. Hoping against hope, Ebert banged on the doors. Normally, it would bring a guard, a threat "stop it, you fascists; wanna get a nine-gram candy into your dirty guts?" and a muzzle in a crack, sweeping the wagon. Now nobody even bothered. Ebert pounded on the doors, on the walls. Some men joined him; others murmured, "Don't make them angry."

Ebert banged and kicked, smashing his toes . . .

The guards didn't remove Elsa's corpse until the following morning.

Two months later, in a squalid room at the Kazakh settlement, Greta hanged herself on a length of clothesline.

Behind his barrack, Ebert spied a discarded prison's window grate. With a hacksaw blade, he sawed out a little cross and put it into Greta's hands.

CHAPTER TWELVE

Having jumped the train in Mytishchi, David stood at the edge of a water-filled crater. Here was once a wing of the former builders' hostel. Ice had bound the surface. Two boys shared a pair of skates between them, skating on a single blade. A skate tied with a length of cord to his felt boot, the boy pushed off with another foot. The blades swished. David gave the boys two hospital biscuits he still had in his pocket.

Afterwards, he stood squeezed in frozen streetcars and hung at the railings of a bus, one foot on a running board, in a bunch of passengers that kept the door open. The bus waited for a trolley car which crossed their way sending off fireworks of blue sparks from the catenary wires. Muscovites in thick baggy overcoats made haste to cross. Some carried a fir tree on the shoulder. Oh yes, today was New Year's Eve.

In downtown Moscow, white strips of anti-shock protection crisscrossed empty shop windows. Occasional automobiles passed the *Lubyanka*, a turn-of-the-century building with rusticated Renaissance ground floor elevation. David shunned the sidewalk at the KGB headquarters, where sentries did their beat.

He still didn't know what he would do.

Downhill, in front of the Bolshoi Theater, portraits festooned with electric lights around the fringes spanned the gaps between the columns. The Vandykes of the Party founders had long given way to the solo mustache of the newer cohort. Dwarfing the others, a full-length Stalin at the center prescribed the current standard of facial hair. Defying it, the clean-shaven upper lip of Lavrenty Beria stood out.

Take Budyonny's enormous mustachio, David thought. Sprawling, bristling, like fir-tree boughs. Yes, the lower boughs of a fir tree. Suspend Stalin's handlebar above them, full and stiff. Still higher, hang up Hitler's short strip. Why, you'll get a Christmas tree, won't you? Trim it with morsels of flesh and specks of blood strained through the mustaches, and crown it—with what? A star, or an angel? No, with a demon. The wriggling, grimacing, rat-tailed imp . . .

A patrol checked David's service card and the summons to Moscow. The sixth control for the day. His papers were all right, and he was still moving in the general direction of the Kremlin Hospital in Granovsky Street, a couple hundred yards from the Kremlin.

He stopped short of the History Museum, as far as the public was allowed nowadays near Red Square. The terrain allowed him to see only the top of Lenin's Mausoleum looming outside the Kremlin walls like a barbican. Long ago, in what seemed to be another life, David marched twice a year with throngs delirious with love and admiration, past the walls where the remnants of revolutionaries had been enshrined. Dignitaries, Uncle Meir among them, packed the temporary stands flanking the red granite cubes of the Mausoleum. They shouted greetings and waved their hands, but the marchers eyed only one man. Afterwards, strolling on past St. Basil's and down to the bridge, people spoke to one another: Did you see him? I surely did. He was smiling at me. He had his pipe in his mouth. No, he didn't. He smiled at us all right but he had no pipe. He had a peak cap on, green with red band. What are you talking about? His peak cap was plain white, what with the May Day heat . . .

Major David Kovner smiled at young David and turned back, towards the American Embassy. The Soviet Union's war allies enjoyed prize locations—the Brits behind the Kremlin, on the far side of the river, and the Yanks right across the Manege square. Positioned between David and the Embassy guards, two Soviet police stared at him, and a couple of characters in civvies moved casually his way.

David walked by the Embassy without breaking stride.

What could a fugitive in the most strictly policed state on earth do, with no one to confide in, without family to lean on? Clara's parents were somewhere in Siberia, and Malka as far away as if on Mars.

David swore a heavy trooper's oath. After all, he was innocent! He'd done what his duty as an officer demanded of him . . .

At the Kremlin Hospital a message waited for David. Major Kovner was to present himself at once to an office building in Old Square.

Old Square? That wasn't the KGB or SMERSH. Old Square housed offices of the Central Committee, and David wasn't even a Party member.

He walked over, a twenty-minute stroll. In a street recess, he stuck his arm with his service card into a tiny semicircular window, and the card was pushed back to him through a tunnel, the pink slip of a pass sticking out. A revolving door pushed him into a grey-marble lobby. An elevator coughed out a three-hundred-pound peroxide blonde. High on her forehead, a perfect ringlet hung like a length of platinum pipe. He followed her down long, brightly lit corridors where thick carpet runners swallowed the sounds of their steps and brawny uniformed men at vantage corner positions ran their stares all over him. She showed David into a palatial office dominated by a running-track-long conference table under green broadcloth. It abutted a massive desk. There sat Uncle Meir, his elbows on the desktop, his eyes laughing.

Behind him, another Stalin gazed from the wall towards an imminent victory. His grey coat seemed cut of painted steel, the right hand concealed in the bosom. The great leader's face had the hard, imperial quality of granite.

CHAPTER THIRTEEN

B linking back happy tears, David hugged his uncle. But how thin and frail Uncle's body had become! Holding his shoulders, David pushed him off to have a better look. The pathetic remnants of Meir Kovner's hair had turned into snow-white wisps. His little beard was gone; the Adam's apple protruded from his thin neck. But the razor had revealed something new in his face, a dimple in his chin, which supplied a youngish dash to his otherwise crumpled face.

The peroxide secretary brought tea and Spam sandwiches. The windowpanes grew grey and then black while David and Uncle caught up. The secretary came again and drew the curtains before turning lights on—the blackout was still in place, albeit not as rigorous. They reflected in the thick beveled glass plate on top of Uncle's desk.

Uncle wouldn't talk about the past; no, he wouldn't. The camps. Yes, hard labor. "Mistakes do happen, Dovidke. They" (he pointed his fingertip to the ceiling) "looked closer into my case. But the truly important thing is that you have survived. I dreaded dragging you over the cliff."

"A miracle saved me. The miracle by the name of Ognev."

Uncle Meir nodded. "He told me about it, on my first night back in Moscow. Arnold left to catch his train, and Ognev stayed on. He said he'd done it as a bunch of chrysanthemums onto my grave, much as I was difficult at times." Uncle chuckled with a strange, cackling laughter, which David hadn't heard from him before.

"Why did Ognev stick his neck out?" said David. "He'd never even met me."

·113·

"He's far from your ordinary man. But let's set the past aside and look ahead. We're up to something new and exciting. When the war's over, we'll blow up the capitalist Europe!"

The former enthusiasm burned behind the lenses of his glasses.

"Wherever the working class takes power in the aftermath of the war, it will never give it back. General Markos in Greece, Italian Communist partisans—*avanti, poppolo!*"

"A reanimation of the Comintern?"

Uncle shook his head. "Those were romantic years. Now the Party backs national aspirations."

"Something new to hear."

"Nothing new. The Soviet Ukrainians had always dreamed of embracing their blood brethren in what used to be Eastern Poland. Similar to the aspirations of the Bielorussian people. The Poles have no choice but direct their ambitions westward. Theirs is a yearning to liberate *Polonia irredenta*. The Slavic lands lost to the Germans."

"When did it happen? A thousand years ago? Should there be a time limit for the claims like that?"

"Tell this legal principle to Malka—she'll love it."

David let it pass. "What do you mean, Pomerania or Silesia?"

"Both, and a good deal of Brandenburg." Uncle made a wide sweep against the wall map.

David whistled soundlessly. "Quite a wrenching to the West. Now, the German exclave of East Prussia will fall far behind. Is it to the Poles to boot?"

Uncle's eyes shone triumphantly. "It will return to the rightful owners! To those who lived there before the Teutonic Knights. But we'll talk about it later. You don't have to go back to the hospital tonight. We're expecting guests."

A stone's throw from Uncle's work, David opened the door to the familiar apartment.

He closed his eyes before stepping into the dining room. Then he reopened them and laughed. Little seemed to have changed. The same shelves lined the walls; the same rows of red-cover Lenin's *Collected Works*; *Das Kapital*, black and smug, occupied the same place on its shelf; the same bronze safe with its face cut with a row of vertical slits. The familiar open-mouthed Lenin reached for the land where the lion would lie with the sheep but never a Communist with a Social Democrat. Now the portrait shared the wall with a Stalin. The Comintern publications had disappeared to make room for the glossy backs of Stalin's works. They dominated the entire section between the sofa and the chest of drawers, on whose top stood an alarm clock shaped into a Kremlin tower.

David put books all around himself and stretched out on the sofa, blissfully immersed in the intrigues of crafty Aramis.

Uncle came in late, laden with a bloated briefcase and neat packages. He set them on the end of the table: meat and fish cans, tangerines, American chocolate, and jars of Nescafé. In his previous life, Uncle proudly carried potatoes, onions, and black bread exposed through the cells of string-bags, the same as other Muscovites. David suspected that Uncle Meir had fallen from grace partially because of his early-revolutionary democratism, an eyesore to the others. David lifted the free end of the laced tablecloth and rolled it halfway to the center. They transferred the goodies on the emerged oilcloth and disposed of the tablecloth. "Uncork the bottles, will you, Dovidke? I've got to caution you: Ognev has just come back from Vilnius, and he doesn't speak of his trip."

The first guests to arrive were Comrade Vicente, Uncle's old hand from the Communist International's time, and a younger Englishman, Jim Hathaway, attached to the British Military Mission in Moscow. Hathaway, tall and lean, with close-cut dark hair and brown eyes, set two bottles of Johnny Walker Black Label on the table. He thrust his hand into a pocket of his neatly pressed Royal Navy dark uniform with anchors and laurels sparkling on the buttons, extracted a bluish oblong envelope, and handed it to Meir Kovner. "Came care of the Embassy."

Uncle Meir hesitated, but took the envelope and slipped it in his pocket. All settled at the table. Hathaway joined David on the sofa, Uncle and Comrade Vicente landed on the other side of the table, the head chair unoccupied. Hathaway and David compared their ranks, which turned out to be equivalent. The Englishman admired the martial prowess of the Soviet artillery, which would be bombarding Berlin very soon indeed. All four drank the first little one to that. David lauded the gallant Royal Navy that had kept Russia alive with its Arctic convoys. Credit accepted only partially, Hathaway said, inasmuch as the true heroes were the merchantmen flying the Red Ensign. All drank the second little one to those on the sea. "Keep talking, young men," said Meir Kovner and left for the kitchen.

He came back with a jar of pickles, pushing Ognev in front of him. That drew the shouts: "A penalty! The last arrival's penalty!"

Ognev, in an olive-green turtleneck, acknowledged the acclaim with a quick smile. He gave a curt nod to David and watched Meir pour drinks for all. He flicked his finger up when Meir came to his glass, knocked back a tall measure of vodka, and hooked a bunch of sprats with a fork right from the can.

His cheeks pinked. He stopped chewing and said with a thick accent, "I wonder, Comrades, whether you drank the first toast to me. Bear in mind that Lavrenty keeps a record of your transgressions."

Amidst the nervous general laughter, David asked, "Will we see you soon in a Stalin movie?"

Ognev sneered. "The blockbusters—these I can easily do without. Let others fight over the roles. They aren't altogether without talent. I'll be the first to admit that they don't owe their Stalin Prizes solely to patronage."

He pulled up at the safe to fiddle with the lock. He pitched little levers up and down, humming a tune, and pulled the handle. The dor resisted. "What song does it open to, Meir? *The Internationale? The Yiddishe Momma?* The new State Anthem? Anyway, it's out of style at your place, this thing of yours. You should give it to me."

He scanned the table. His voice slipped back to Stalin's mode. "The comrades from the motion pictures may call it a good film set. I disagree with the comrades. I believe this is an excellent film set."

Jim Hathaway laughed. "Fantastic. Like two peas."

"Ever met Stalin?" Ognev asked. His eyes twinkled.

"No," said Hathaway, "but I saw a documentary they had sent to the Mission."

"Which one?"

"Him devising the Stalingrad operation."

Ognev smiled.

"Here's to the mighty British Navy," Meir Kovner said quickly.

"We have drunk this one, Uncle."

"No, that was to the Merchant Fleet. Now the Royal Navy. In complete command of the Mediterranean." Meir pulled the envelope out and studied the postal imprints on the stamps. "No longer a roundabout trip around Africa, eh? Great Britain has regained its positions in the Middle East."

"I wish it were so," said Hathaway. "In this war, the Arabs went largely to the enemy. Met Rommel's troops as liberators. As they see it, the Jews dispossessed them in Palestine while we British sat on our hands."

"The moment the war ends," said Ognev, "Arab proletarians and Zionist socialists will be at one another's throats." He rubbed his hands and grinned.

"They might, for all we know," Hathaway said. "The Jewish colonization of Palestine threatens to blow up the Middle East. Winston Churchill has only realized it belatedly. Ironically, he used to be a champion of Zionism."

"Of course," said Meir Kovner. "A safety valve, that's what Churchill wanted. Providing Jewish firebrands with an alternative to class struggle. A clever plot to siphon them away from Europe." He smiled at the Englishman. "Will the Americans step in?"

Ognev chuckled. "You bet they will. Filling the void, Yanks the grabbers."

Hathaway's face clouded over. "Roosevelt's planning to see King Ibn Saud."

"For Saudi oil," Meir Kovner said. "Of course. Turning the desert sheik into the attendant at a petrol station, with an American cop as a guard."

Hathaway nodded gravely. "They're likely to discuss the Jewish immigration, too. There is a broad sense in the air: now that the Jews have suffered terribly in Europe, they are entitled to their own state. To become a nation."

"A nation," Ognev said. "Have you ever met Arnold Hramoy? No? A clever piece of a geek. He says nation is a group of people— what was that, exactly? Yes. A group of people who share twisted notions about their past and hatred of their neighbors. Jews down there in Palestine will qualify instantly." He guffawed. Nobody joined him. He set off pacing behind Meir and Vicente's chairs. Meir Kovner shuddered uneasily.

Hathaway's eyes followed Ognev's movements. "President Roosevelt's going to drum up the Saudi king's support for Zionism. Roosevelt's envoy in Riyadh, Colonel Eddy, sounded it with the king."

"Aye-aye-aye," Meir Kovner shook his head, and his friend, gaunt and bald Comrade Vicente, nodded. "Aye-aye-aye. Just to think about it."

"Ibn Saud nodded politely to the tale of Jewish sufferings. Then he said he didn't understand one little thing."

"Just one?" Ognev butted in again, still on his feet. "That was the raghead's lucky day." He stopped, poured from a bottle, and downed another glass. Then he resumed pacing.

"One little thing," Hathaway repeated. "Why the Arabs should make room for the Jews if it was the Germans who wronged them. Couldn't the Great Powers award some choice real estate in Germany to the Jews and thus settle the matter?"

"I would gladly share my homeland," said Comrade Vicente quickly, "with the maltreated Jew."

"Your homeland," said Ognev. He stopped pacing. "Whereabouts is your home, if I may ask?"

"Used to be in Thuringia. About where Martin Luther hurled his inkpot at the devil."

"You bet he missed," said Ognev. He drew close. "And what's your real name, Comrade Vicente? You don't look Spanish to me." He stopped short behind his chair at the head of the table.

"There are Basques like him," said Meir Kovner, slightly inclining forward in his chair, as if to make a barrier between Vicente and Ognev.

Comrade Vicente said, after a moment, "Heinrich. Heinrich Schulz."

His hands on the back of the head chair, Ognev glared from Heinrich to Meir Kovner. "I should've known. It's you all over, Meir, inviting a German to your party."

"Relax, Ognev," Uncle Meir told him. "This distinguished comrade is a communist."

Ognev pushed the chair away. "So what! Piece of cake, turning a good communist into a born-again Nazi. Done on many occasions."

Uncle sprang to his feet. "You're talking nonsense!"

Ognev pointed the stem of his pipe at Meir Kovner, two inches from his face. "Not at all. For a true believer, the fact of faith is what matters, not the subject."

Vicente-Heinrich unbuttoned his grey wool jacket with yellow leather elbow patches. His fingers quivered. Then he buttoned it back. "Unfortunately, Comrade Ognev is right. The Nazi silver tongue, Joseph Goebbels, understood it too well."

Ognev snorted scornfully. "Thank you, Herr Schulz. Doktor Goebbels and me in exclusive company. How big-hearted of you. So neat. German-like neat."

"No, what's wrong with German neatness?" David asked, and sighed. His head was light from the whisky. He flashed back to the five pairs of footgear in the yard of Frau Ebert.

"Nothing if you don't overdo it," Heinrich said.

"We have our Jewish obsessions too," Uncle said, mollifying. "Even if of a different sort."

Ognev's fork, with a dead sardine hanging on, poked air from Meir to David to Heinrich. "Here you go again. On the same footing, Herr Schulz folk's anti-Semitism and our good old Jewish self-hatred."

Heinrich said, "It wasn't self-hatred that destroyed those Jewish Commissars. It was somebody else's hatred."

Meir Kovner frowned. "You'd rather stick with the Germans, Heinrich." He shot a glance at Jim Hathaway across him. The Englishman was engrossed in the book David had put aside on the sofa when the guests came.

David chuckled inwardly. Sharing the sofa with him, a representative of the imperialist camp was witnessing the squabbles of communists!

The pause hung. Hathaway put the book off and looked at his watch. "Unfortunately, I have to go. Good to meet you all."

Uncle Meir walked Hathaway to the hall. He spoke there softly for a while.

In the room, Ognev hissed, "If you're ashamed of your name—" He bent over the table to Heinrich. "Are you ashamed of your name? But of course you're ashamed of your name. Why else would you hide it?"

Heinrich sprang to his feet. "How about yourself?" He clenched his fists.

David heard Jim say, "Absolutely. Completely off the record. I understand."

The click of a lock gave the signal to an eruption. Ognev yelled into the face of returning Meir Kovner. "Of all things! He hid behind a Spanish name! Why did you do so, Heinrich Schulz?"

"I wonder what's *your* real name!" countered Heinrich.

"None of your pork-guzzling, beer-swilling business!"

Uncle also shouted. "A bit of fairness, you two! Vicente is Heinrich's *nom de guerre*. Under that name he fought Hitler in Spain. Show your scars, Heinrich! And Ognev is a stage name! How could he possibly win the Russian people's acceptance and love as a Peysakhovich?"

Heinrich yelled to Ognev, "Bad memories about Germany? Then why have you people been holding on to a German dialect? Centuries away from Germany?"

"Rest assured it's over!" Ognev shouted back. "No Jew will ever smear his mouth with anything resembling German! And I—I never cared about Yiddish; you remember, Meir, don't you? My children understand—understood some Yiddish only because of the bit of German they'd learned at school!"

"And why did they study it? Why do Russian schoolchildren recite *Wir fahren nach Anapa*?"

Meir Kovner hugged their shoulders. "Now, you, whom I love. Both of you. What can't you divide between you two?"

Ognev threw Meir's hand from his shoulder. "And you, Meir? You make much ado about your Yiddish language. You fantasize about Yiddish as a certificate for the Jews of their Germanism—"

"I don't," said Meir quickly.

"Oh yes, you do! But the Germans laugh at your pretense! This German pal of yours—doesn't he chuckle behind your back?"

Heinrich's breathing was returning to a normal rate. "That's all right, Meir. We Germans are in for a long bout of ostracism. Of blind, irrational hatred. Many generations will pass before we're allowed to forget our shame."

Ognev laughed loudly. He circled a finger at his temple, pointing the pipe in the other hand at Heinrich. "Irrational hatred? Did you say irrational? My loathing of your crimes—is it irrational?"

Heinrich stood still, his face red.

Ognev's heavy eyes swept the room as he intoned in his thick Stalin accent.

"In the dark night of the first war-month, I pledged to you, brethren and sisters, that our day would come. The day of reckoning is breaking as I'm speaking. And it's colored in blood."

He pivoted and was gone. The outer door slammed, and presently a door banged upstairs.

A sudden ringing made them start.

Meir Kovner gripped the left side of his coat.

The bell went on nonstop.

"No, it's the clock!" shouted David. He tapped down on the Kremlin tower, and the ringing stopped. "I set the alarm at two minutes to midnight! I'm sorry, Uncle."

Color slowly returned to Meir Kovner's face.

"The alarm clock, eh? The New Year?" He unclenched his fist and let his coat go. "Let's drink to the New Year. To the year of our victory."

They did so and sat in silence. Heinrich kept his eyes closed. When he opened them, they glistened suspiciously.

"Where are the old days of our innocence, when we were all brothers? *Alles ist hin*. Gone with the wind."

Uncle Meir put his hands on Heinrich's shoulders. "In my home, I shall treat any anti—any ethnic hatred as firmly as anti-Semitism!"

"Any? Nazi Germany included?"

Uncle's voice lost some of firmness. "Any improper generalization."

Heinrich sighed. "Whoever picks this fight, his will be a very deserted road."

They sang softly the defunct Comintern's oldies. *Die Moorsoldaten. Der kleine Trompeter* . . . They sat, tears in half-closed eyes, arms on each other's shoulder. The lights suddenly died. David lit candles. Empty bottles on the table among saucers and conserve cans resembled stalagmites. Plates of meat-jelly glittered like pools of dirty water in the cavernous room.

CHAPTER FOURTEEN

Heinrich left after much hugging and whispering in the hall. The bulbs passed slowly through yellow, then orange and red to the original brightness. David took the envelope, which Uncle Meir had left on the table for him. The stamps carried a profile of the British king and the inscription *Palestine* in three languages. How different it was from the three-language slogan of his childhood! He opened the envelope and read Malka's letter while collecting dirty glasses, saucers with thin slices of dried cheese, cigarette stubs, and a little heap of ash from Ognev's pipe.

Uncle came back.

"Leave them on the table. The cleaning woman will come in the morning. I've indulged myself with a cleaning woman. I'm a capitalist in New York." He moaned. "Poor Heinrich."

"He's got quite a problem on his hands," said David.

"A problem? A tight squeeze! He's against a wall of hatred, albeit well earned by association. You read Malka's letter? How about her yekke?"

"He dumped his German war medals into a dustbin. His European clothes, too. His wife is dead, and Malka married him."

"Married? She kept mocking him!"

"She still does. That's why she's married him, I'm afraid."

Uncle snorted. "Good for her. What else? How does she cope with the weather? That suffocating wind—what's the name? Khamsin?"

"The khamsin, yes. She adores khamsin—it's Jewish khamsin."

Uncle Meir served himself a shot of whisky and pushed another serving towards David, who shook his head. Uncle had

·123·

his scotch straight, and flinched. Upstairs, pacing was heard: Ognev didn't sleep either.

Uncle glanced at the ceiling and frowned. "Ognev's working out his guilt. Back in forty-one, he took it into his head that his family should visit Vilnius. His wife was born there, you know. Then for twenty years Lithuania was a foreign country, out of reach. All of a sudden, our troops were there!"

"By Hitler's permission."

"David!" Uncle nervously looked around. "Still, Lithuania remained a special regime zone. Ognev pulled all strings and procured a pass. Vilnius, he said, a little piece of Europe; go get some touch of it while it lasts. See your folks, do some shopping. His wife wouldn't listen to it. Vilnius? What a ridiculous name for a city. She knew no Vilnius. She was born in Wilna. He pressed. Stay in nice hotels; sip good coffee. Take vacations. Put some color to the drabness of our life. Now that he's back from his trip he doesn't tell, but you can guess it."

"I saw him play. He's a great actor. But he takes the bear by the tooth. To read Stalin's address the way he did!"

"A hell of an actor. He was an outstanding Hamlet, until I brought him over to see my bosses. They fell from their chairs. Since that, they haven't let him play anything but Stalin."

Uncle Meir walked to the hall, came back with an armful of bedding, and threw it on the sofa. He picked a large pillow and placed it on the telephone. Still, he lowered his voice. "The others don't play Stalin. They play his state function. Their Stalin is tall, articulate, handsome. No Georgian accent. Forehead larger. Nose shorter. Face clean. As in his painted portraits or retouched photos. Socialist-realist icons of Stalin. All what the Soviet audience is allowed to see."

"Then I don't see any role for Ognev."

Uncle reduced his sound volume another notch. "Ognev's taking part in a sensitive project in the making. Two dozen films. A quasi documentary, *The History of the Great Patriotic War.* Stalin for posterity. Ognev there is indistinguishable from Stalin. Complete with Stalin's mannerism, Stalin's vocal intonations—

he imitates Stalin to perfection; he's got absolute pitch. And Stalin's presence, when he wants. When tonight he paced behind my back in Stalin's stealthy gait—" Uncle Meir shuddered. "The only difference, Ognev has no pockmarks. Stalin ruled them out."

Uncle Meir imparted some semblance of Stalin's Georgian accent to his voice. "Why should we blemish the healthy skin of the People's Actor Ognev with ugly marks?"

"He said so?"

"In so many words."

"Doesn't bode well for Ognev, when his job's done."

"You're telling me."

"But the nitty-gritty of Stalin's manners, behavior, habits— where does Ognev get it?"

"They let him watch Stalin from the wings, a security man at Ognev's side. Those frames that they shoot with Ognev—they will be played over and over again for years to come. They're very convincing. They portray Stalin in a jeep jolted by bumpy roads as ordnances explode nearby. Stalin in trenches, inspiring troops. In hospitals, comforting them."

"Does he ever?"

Uncle squinted at the pillow on the phone set and shook his head. "Those images will replace the real history. At some point, virtual reality will have become *the* reality, period. They will establish him in the people's consciousness. And perhaps even more important, in his, Stalin's, subconscious. He wants to see himself wise, decisive and articulate—and believe he was. Ognev can do it for him. He's capable of total identification with his role."

"Including Stalin's infatuation with Hitler before the war?"

Uncle sighed. "Unfortunately, some of that—some anti-Jewish feelings of Ognev weren't borrowed. He has that streak in him. You see, when he has to sign with his real name, Peysakhovich, as for a payroll, he suffers the indignity of it."

The pacing upstairs went on nonstop.

David frowned. "Well, he's paid dearly, hasn't he?"

Meir Kovner stood up.

"Sleep well after your long day. And come to see me at my work, will you, Dovidke?"

He walked to his bedroom and returned with a large sealed envelope. "I want you to read this first."

"How about the hospital?"

"You've been released to my care."

He was on his way to his room when David called him.

"Uncle?"

"Yes?"

"You never told me what the wife of the Bavarian *poer* said."

Uncle Meir blinked. "What's that?"

"The thing she said to her husband as she milked her cow."

"And what was it?"

"C-sharp major, C-sharp major—whoosh! swish! whoosh! swish!" David pulled at a virtual teat, and a white stream hit the bottom of a virtual bucket. "Who are you—a Johann Sebastian Bach? Why don't you say D-flat major, like all good people?"

"Same thing," said Uncle sheepishly. "It's like thirty-five after the hour or twenty-five before."

"If you care to mess—whoosh! swish!—with seven sharps in the signature key—whoosh! swish!—instead of five flats."

Uncle's envelope contained a thin pamphlet in a pink cover, marked *Confidential* in the upper right corner. The title page announced, *Who were the Pruses?* Subtitle: *Basic Memorandum.*

Faceup on the sofa, David turned the pages over.

He read:

> In 1226, the militant Order of Teutonic Knights obtained a Golden Bull from the German Kaiser and the Pope's blessing for a crusade. Normally, crusaders went to fight the infidel in the so-called Holy Land. But the Order's colonial adventures in the Middle East had just come to grief. The locals had thrown the invaders out of Jerusalem.

The Mounted Hounds took the defeat hard. They redirected their hatred to the north. Their new campaign was aimed at the people living next door to Christian Europe, the Pruses. At the time, the name Prussia applied to the land wedged between Poland, Lithuania, and the Baltic Sea, which we know nowadays as East Prussia. The German Knights in white cloaks with black crosses over their armor laid Prussia to waste with fire and sword. Few Pruses escaped to the neighboring countries or farther to Russia. Still fewer survived in Prussia.

On the occupied land the Knights founded a robber state. From there they launched their plundering expeditions to Russian principalities. The Order's heirs, the Prussian militarists and Hitlerites, used the country as a springboard for their aggression towards the east.

Who were the Pruses, the legitimate owners of the land that the Order snatched?

Benefiting from incessant attention and guidance of the Party and Comrade Stalin, the Soviet historians in cooperation with progressive scholars of the world have solved the mystery. Unimpeachable material evidence, reinforced with linguistic attribution, attests to the fact that the pre-Teutonic inhabitants of Prussia were Jewish working masses.

Stop! David blinked. Incredulous, he reread the latter paragraph. The typewriting was clear, as the first copy should. *Jewish working masses.*

David flipped towards the back. The heavily footnoted text was followed by several pages of references. He leafed them back, to the end of the main text.

Here you are.

Signed: Director of the Project Prusa,
Corresponding Member of the Academy of Sciences
of the USSR,
Rector of the Institute of Marxism,
Professor
Zarnitsyn

His old nemesis. The squeaky hog who'd wrecked his colloquium talk and thrown him out of the Institute.

From Uncle Meir's bedroom, David heard rhythmic snoring. Any questions to Uncle had to be delayed until the morning.

Back to the first pages. David read of Judea / Palestine about the time of "the mythical birth of certain Jesus." The poorest of toilers were the Pharisees, in their language Paruses. The Paruse, pah-ROOS, derived his name from the same root as *pros*, a half of a round pita bread. This was the farm laborer's share, his *prusa*, pru-SAH, with which he was paid for his backbreaking day's work. What made these three words closely related? They had the same set of consonants, the consonant root, P-R-S. In Semitic languages, whether Hebrew, Arabic, or Aramaic, the root consonants made a stable framework, which passed unaltered through the word's forms and derivatives. In contrast, vowels were rather circumstantial. As often as not, they didn't even appear in writing.

Next followed an analysis of Judea's political and economical life. David learned that the foreign imperialist occupiers, the Romans, had held the Jewish working masses in bondage. The Judean upper class of feudal landowners and corrupt comprador bourgeoisie—the Sadducees, those precursors of the Rothschilds, the Brodskys, and the Rathenaus—had kowtowed to the Romans. The working men, misled by opportunistic rabbis, did not rise to their class interests above the economic demand, "his daily *pros* to each Paruse!" Even the amendment "stuffed with humus" was defeated as extremist.

At that time, David read, a man named Mark had appeared in Judea. Fueled by hatred for oppression, Mark had set to organizing the Jewish proletariat for armed struggle.

In his recently discovered *On False Friends*, Mark had denounced former comrades, Mattheas, Lucas and Johannes, turned traitors, and called for a national revolution. It would put an end to the subjugation of a people by another people. In the new society, everything would be the other way around. "Raise your left fist, Paruse! And never doubt—the doubting Thomas is Johannes' fib!"

Zarnitsyn quoted the newly found copy of the *Judean War* by Josephus Flavius, which had escaped doctoring by medieval monks. The illustrious Roman historian had observed Mark— eyes burning, hair touching shoulder, preaching in the squares and gathering throngs. The words of the aging prophet as their great inspiration, the Paruses rose up in a heroic revolt. The arrows from their *tachanka* chariots rained death upon the ancestors of Mussolini's fascists. If only it weren't for the Mattheas-Lucas-Johannes traitorous ring!

Betrayed but defiant, the Paruses tore through to the coast, some still in chains and shackles. Mark led their galleys to an island in the Greek Archipelago, a single gigantic marble mountain rising from the sea. There, after a forty-day solitude at the summit of Mount Marpessa, Mark descended to the awed Paruses.

"Precisely," said the man with small, piercing eyes, sitting in Uncle Meir's chair. His long, white beard rested on his breast. David, lying as he was on the sofa, could see his loose robe touch sandals under the table.

The visitor placed his hand on the pile of stone tablets on the table. "I brought the Law to those unworthy." He waved derisively away. "They are human dust blowing in the road and never belonging to the soil. I'll compact those loose crumbs into a nation. And when I say nation, I think of a sacred community of the alive, the passed-away, and the yet unborn, bound together by blood, soil, and myth."

David, alarmed, straightened up into a sitting position. "Just what we needed."

Mark the Lawgiver wagged his finger at David. "I know what you are sneering at. But all true thinkers subscribed to the primacy of blood, from the Book of Genesis on. Blood is a deep-rooted nurturing force within individual man. The profoundest layers of our being are determined by blood. It's the most fundamental precondition of belonging, and belonging to a nation is stronger than any other human need."

"And how does one get into this exclusive club?"

"Through one's maternal bloodline," Mark said quickly. "Here I stand firm." He shuffled his tablets, picked one, and shoved it toward David. "Read here. You will understand the history of mankind as the history of struggle between nations. See nations emerge, clash, devour one another. Like men, they strive for their place in the sun. National selfishness is a norm."

"Not cooperation?"

"No. Universal brotherhood is not even a beautiful dream. Antagonism is essential to nations' advancement."

"Your mantras sound strangely familiar."

"Oh, those scavengers. They pilfered my *Manifesto* line by line for sound bits. Distorted them to fit their pathetic little lies. But I hold no grudge. At that price, my masterpiece escaped extinction after the original became lost."

"Destroyed by fire, wasn't it?"

"Don't play a smart aleck." Mark lovingly stroked the stone tablets. "Hereby, I'm giving the Paruses their cut of the world, their patrimony, their Prusa."

Mark the Nation's Father sprang to his feet. He shouted over David's head, addressing the invisible multitudes. "Your Promised Land lies due north and abuts a sea. There the rocky hills drip with honey. There, away from the Romans' vengeance, you will have no more enemies. Peace and tranquility will reign. This will be your safe haven, your Earthly Paradise, the world without evil. There you will establish a Thousand-Year Kingdom. Verily I say unto you: a Parusian policeman will arrest a Parusian harlot, a Parusian judge will sentence her to public birching, a Parusian executioner will administer the rod—and the nation of Prusa will be born!"

The squeaky tones in his voice growing with every minute, Mark yelled on:

"Beside my gift, you shall take along a single book, the Book of Esther, because the Book of Esther never mentions that old deceiver, God the Sham Father, under whichever name or alias: you have no other Father but Me. In your new home dialectical nationalism shall rule. You may call it Markism if you wish. Needless to say, your currency unit shall be the mark, and one-hundredth thereof, markette. But beware of the Idols of the Market. They are the fetishes of those schismatics back in Judea, the servants of the Mammon who didn't go with me."

His eyes burned with the flame of idiocy. "And fear not: I will always be with you. *His daily* pros *to each Paruse!"*

Uncle Meir muttered something in his sleep.

The lights went out again.

When David lit up a candle, the visitor was gone. Something bulky rested on the table, a long, narrow box; of stone, as David found out when he tapped on it. He raised his candle; its light reflected from the gooey, glossy substance inside, through which the outlines of a bundled body and the white beard barely showed. Shadows glided along the table, men and women in robes, chitons, tunics, and plainly in rags smelling foul. Some dropped their jingling chains at the Invincible Captain's feet, and an immovable shadow at the head of the casket, apparently Mark the Second, pronounced solemnly each time that they had nothing to lose from now on. They had a Prusa to conquer.

Off they sailed from the island, which would carry the name of Paros. The peak of Mount Marpessa, pinked by the rising sun, was slowly dissolving in the cloudless sky. What a day to launch a quest, Zarnitsyn exalted before giving the floor directly to a chronicler.

> The Parusian galleys made it to the very top of the Black Sea. They
> landed into an abundance of watermelons, grapes, and sheep's
> cheese. Who are you? their leader asked the locals. We are
> Moldavians. What's the name of the land? Bessarabia. Bessarabia,
> marveled the Paruses. See what a Moldavian accent can make out of

the phrase *Prusa, rabbi!* And you, asked the locals, who are you? We are P'ruses, the newcomers answered proudly. They had been away from home for quite a while, and their vowels began blurring.

They resolved to stay.

That didn't sit well with their neighbors to the west. Organized crime was the only area where Rumanians didn't lack organization. They invaded Bessarabia and explained to the Pruses their mistake, wielding bludgeons, spades and rocks for an argument.

Bessarabia wasn't Prusa, after all. The Pruses took their wagons up a river known since as the Pruth. The Long March to the North began. The Pruses beat the roads of Eastern Europe. Their flocks and herds raised clouds that hung in the air, the dust becoming the light unto the nations right before their eyes, as the airborne particles glittered in the sun shafts. Now and then, a far-away glitter promised a sea only to introduce a fishing pond or a vein of mica. The Pruses walked on, and their open breasts inhaled freedom's alluring air.

A bunch of notes referred David to the recent findings of Soviet archeologists, mostly in the form of internal reports of Zarnitsyn's Institute, classified.

David laughed. One day Zarnitsyn would reveal his *Basic Memorandum* to the world, but the sources would remain unavailable for the general public to verify, wouldn't they?

David needed a break. He went to the kitchen and drank some water from the tap.

What was all that about? Why had Uncle Meir, on the first night of their reunion, given him Zarnitsyn's bogus historical opus for perusal?

David dropped the mug in the sink. Gaping holes had pierced the kitchen walls and ceiling. The building was being readied for gas, the first utility gas in Moscow. He heard Ognev's pacing upstairs as if at his elbow. Soundproofing was even poorer than in the old days before the war, when Ognev's children practiced piano.

David called out, "Are you all right?"

The pacing stopped. Then a furious voice shouted, "Go to hell, Meir, you and your Germans!"

"It isn't Meir," David said. "I'm sorry for the—for the unpleasantness."

After a pause, the steps moved away.

Too bad. David returned onto the sofa and plunged back into the text. He picked the story up on AD 255, when the Pruses had slogged across Lithuanian swamps and gained the edge of the Promised Land.

The virgin Forest Primeval lay before them, a vast waste of verdure, overhanging, prohibiting, and threatening. Twelve picked men had gone off, and a camp harlot tagged along. They walked in, and the forest took them up . . .

Zarnitsyn had piled up a standard set of romantic props: thick leafless serpents of ivy twining over the trunks . . . deformed branches, twisting and gnarling . . . the gloom of perpetual night . . . rustling noises underfoot . . . eyes burning in the darkness . . . invisible wings whooshing through the air . . . Zarnitsyn's Department of Folklore had purportedly interviewed dozens of men and women for their legends, myths and songs.

The scouts advanced slowly, day after day, the twelve brave men with clubs and knives at the ready and one frightened girl. At last, a light glimmered ahead. Their hearts beat fast.

The Pruses came out into the open. The sun was quickly eating into the mist. A river bent in a marshy plain seeded with boulders; beyond, green meadows rolled to either side as far as the eye could see, which betrayed no sight of human habitation. And farther across lay the sea! It spread out, Prussian blue, fading into the sky. Although milk hardly flowed in the fens, the heather did smell of honey. The Pruses took the sweat odor mixed with the rotten steam of swamps for an omen. The body of Comrade Mark must have smelled thusly when their forefathers downed it into the honey bath. Comrade Mark was with them! There was no doubt in their minds, not this time. Around lay Prusa, seductively rotten. The people without bogs came to the bogs without people.

Here, at the edge of the forest, it was the right place and time to make good on an old prophecy.

Their leader was a spare, stern man with a wrinkled, weather-beaten face.

He invested himself with the office of judge.

The first Prusa's judge meted out the sentence: *pirgul!*—which is the Hebrew for whipping.

Then he appointed the executioner.

The first Prusa's executioner rolled up his sleeves. He tied the whore to an oak trunk and tucked her motley skirts under the straps. With the last swing of the forearm grown thick with red hair, the last thwack of the whip, and the last yelp of the girl, in the sanctity of the *pirgul* the Prussian nation was born. With joy and love, the twelve pioneers grasped the eternity of their nationhood.

The Pruses' collective mind has chiseled the consonant frame P-R-G-L of the *pirgul* into the deepest level of the national consciousness. It has survived to our time in the river name, the Pregel, on whose bank the high drama of nation-building once played.

The Pregel. The river flowed at his side when the German mortar round found David . . .

Uncle's snore kept coming from his room . . . David returned to the pamphlet.

On the night the First to Prusa came back with their report, the entire people didn't get a wink of sleep. In their tents, the old and young sang hymns, celebrating Comrade Mark and His Manifesto. In the morning the Pruses set off. They crossed the forest and the Pregel and continued to the sea. There they washed their feet in the salty water, and they felt good about it. They followed the shoreline to the mouth of another river. They named it Gilgele after the Great Metamorphose, the *gilgul*, G-L-G-L, the affectionate

Gilgele of Yiddish songs and legends. "The butterfly has spread its wings, the graceful butterfly emerging from the pupa. It lets them dry, and strikes, and flies away, to life. O glorious butterfly, with wingspan of an eagle!" Such was the anonymous poet's rendition; in these words a Baltic Nawadaha, a Prussian Ossian, would glorify his nation's nascence. The prophecy had come true! The fanny of the brave girl who had sacrificed her virtue and flesh for her people would come emblazoned onto the proud national flag: two golden discs on blue and red background, like prize medals on a wine label. The scarlet scars across the orbs symbolized Pruses' sufferings prior to the redemption. Those banners would soar over the multitudes gathered annually for the national holiday week, between Pirgul and Gilgul.

The next section dealt with the happy life of Pruses in their Promised Land. Well protected behind moats, swamps, and prickly hedges, Prusa bloomed by the year. Prussian women lent their wombs to the service of the state for the great task of peopling the land. Prussian victories at the World Marpessaic Games on the Isle of Paros proved the superiority of the Prussian system over the transpaludal world.

Then came the German Order and the Catastrophe. On a hunting license from the Pope and the Kaiser, the Mounted Hounds rampaged through the land.

The Mounted Hounds? Zarnitsyn again attached this strange label to the Knights of the Teutonic Order. Why?
One more *why* among many. David read on.

Many Pruses were killed, "by death delivered," as the poet said, and others took their "flight from Prussia's timid region." On a sad day in 1255 the Knights captured Tel Hamelekh and renamed it Königsberg. In Rome bells rang non-stop for three days and monks rejoiced, whereas down in Judea Sadducee rabbis ruled that Prusa had fallen under the crashing weight of her sins.

The outward appearance of Prussia thriving under the German occupation was deceiving, its cultural achievements arguable. The obtuse sausage-eaters couldn't care less for the treasures they had inherited from the Pruses. In the river name, Pissa, their primitive senses felt only a malodorous hint, an affront to their neat plumbing habits. Repeatedly, the good townsfolk of Gumbinnen petitioned their rulers for the name change. Finally, King Friedrich-Wilhelm IV granted their request. He recommended a new name, the Urinoco. Neither the king nor his subjects remembered that the stream, the Pregel's tributary, owned its name to the Hebrew verb *pis*, to apologize, for it was on this banks that the chastened wench had publicly denounced her dissolute way of life, embraced her whipper, and they had walked hand in hand to the woods.

Not only did the German conquerors rob the Pruses of their land—they lived upon the established reputation of all things Prussian. In the process, they distorted the noble Prussian traits and turned them into a caricature.

Renowned Prussian orderliness became Prussian regimentation.

Prussian efficiency lapsed into Prussian automatism.

Prussian cleanliness degraded into Prussian fastidiousness.

Prussian directness grew into Prussian tactlessness.

Prussian honesty slipped into Prussian rudeness.

Prussian scholarship reduced to Prussian pedantry.

Prussian mental sobriety sank to Prussian philistinism.

Prussian faithfulness degenerated into Prussian blind obedience.

Thus contrasted the shiny virtues of pioneer Prusa with the vices of Prussian Junker militarism . . .

The gist of the verbose *Conclusions* was as follows. Now that the gallant Red Army under the wise command of Comrade Stalin, the unsurpassed Captain of all nations and centuries, was poised to liberate Prussia, every honest scholar's sacred duty was to facilitate restoration of the historical truth.

Zarnitsyn's signature.

Commentaries.

References.

On the margin, against the scene of Mark's body being submerged into the honey bath, David found a note penciled in Meir Kovner's scraggy hand:

And the honey scented of buckwheat blossom!

CHAPTER FIFTEEN

From behind his desk in the Party Central, Uncle Meir gazed serenely at his nephew.

David laid the pamphlet in front of him. "Incredible."

"Have you read it all?"

"I have read it all. Not too bad for Zarnitsyn's level. Even remarkable. But of course he didn't do it on his own. He's got the whole stinking Institute behind him."

Uncle leaned back and crossed his arms. "You sound definitely nostalgic, don't you think?"

David sank to a chair. "But since when has Zarnitsyn backed nationalism? Quite an about-face, away from class warfare!"

Uncle Meir narrowed his eyes at the bust of Marx crowning a bookshelf. "Nothing of the sort. If you dig deeper, you'll find out it's one and the same. When one people enslaves another, the conquerors evolve into a noble class. Indian Brahmins, Viking warriors, Spanish conquistadors—it has occurred ever since the world began."

Uncle Meir had done his homework.

"But this—this memo is an outrage!"

"No more so than any other historical research. History is politics projected on the past. The historians glorify their country and belittle its foes. Now they derive all the greatness in the world from their nation, now they assert that their people have always lived in this or that land. Where have you ever seen an unbiased historian?"

Uncle Meir grinned smugly.

"You cannot deny the basic facts, David. In the wake of the grand revolts known as the Judean Wars, Jews were forced to leave Palestine. Some settled in the Roman Empire, some elsewhere. The strongest community formed in Germany, right? Acquired the name Ashkenazim, after the biblical name for Germany, Ashkenaz. Now, the Basic Memorandum narrows the biblical Ashkenaz to Prussia. You can consider it a bold, uninhibited interpretation of historical facts. With some—well, flourishes."

"*Some* flourishes! And Zarnitsyn isn't above stealing from the Zionist myth! Those allusions—"

Uncle Meir shrugged. "Well, what's wrong with borrowing tricks from the enemy?"

David's suspicions seemed to be confirmed. "Uncle, you aren't just talking for the sake of argument. You're behind Zarnitsyn, aren't you?"

Uncle Meir smiled self-importantly. "Well, the guidelines came from here."

He pressed his hands on the glass top. When he lifted them, two damp imprints of his palms remained on the glass, like stamps of a State Seal.

David watched the marks dissipate revealing mementos, phone numbers, useful quotations, and a snapshot, the sepia print faded, of a girl in a cavalry greatcoat and a peaked felt helmet emblazoned with a red star, leaning against a machine gun mounted on a wagon.

David brought his gaze back at Uncle Meir's face. "Uncle, what's going on?"

His eyes shining, Uncle Meir declared in a stage whisper. "This February the Big Three will hold a meeting in Greater Yalta."

Uncle waved his hand towards a wall map, where the clawing lemur of the Crimea hung, back down, amidst the Black Sea's azure. Black strings of place names—Yalta, Koreïz, Alupka, Phoros—protruded into the blue, resembling elongated bodies of dragonflies whose heads rested on lemur's withers.

"The Big Three? You mean—"

"Yes. Stalin, Roosevelt and Churchill. They will chart a post-war world."

"What does it spell?"

"Is it good for the Jews, as your father used to say?" Uncle Meir smiled triumphantly. "Now for a change it is so, Dovidke. East Prussia will make a Jewish state."

The lemur unclasped its claws and plummeted into the blue. The promontory of Phoros hit the bullock's hump of Turkey. The lemur bounced back and snatched again at the soft underbelly of the Ukraine. Uncle's spoon squashed a lemon slice in his tea glass.

"A Jewish Soviet Republic?"

"No need. The new socialist entities beyond our western borders will be known as People's Democracies. They will possess all the outer trappings of sovereignty. Three million Soviet Jews will inhabit the People's Democratic Republic of Prussia. You want an Academy of Sciences? Instantly. Actors, performers, composers, singers? Help yourself. The Soviet railways will motor their best locomotive, Lazar Kaganovich, into the prime minister's office. Now, a million foreign Jews have ended up in the Soviet territory during the war. They don't want to remain in the Soviet Union, regrettably. Where will they go? Back to Poland and Rumania? No takers. America? Sure, but the American government isn't that hot on the idea. So the Joint—remember the American Joint in Crimea, Dovidke? They want to channel the refuges to Palestine. The British object, naturally. The Arabs riot. We'll offer the refuges something better, their own new state. Then from Argentina and Australia, from New York and Los Angeles, Jews will sail to the ancient haven of Tel Hamelekh. We'll invite Einstein to serve as the first president!"

"And what will the Allies say?" David pressed a lion's head carving on the chair's arm till it hurt his palm.

"Ha, the Allies!" Uncle Meir scoffed. "Winston Churchill thinks it was his idea. Remember what the Britisher said last night about the American gambit with the Saudis?"

Uncle produced a typed page from a drawer.

"My man in Washington had perused the ambassador's report before Roosevelt had a chance to see it. And afterwards, my man in London had read it before Roosevelt's letter ended up on Churchill's desk. Have a close look at these lines."

His finger traveled across the page as he read aloud, in his strongly accented English: "Then King Abdul Aziz ibn Saud said, 'Make the enemy pay; that's how we Arabs wage wars. The criminals, not the innocent third party, should make amends. Why wouldn't the Great Powers carve a state for Jews in Germany?'"

"Take it to the window," Uncle commanded.

David did. A thin brown pencil line under the last sentence looked as if somebody had tried hard to erase it.

"That was a sure thing. Knowing Winston Churchill, one could rest assured that he'd be intrigued. What had attracted Roosevelt's attention? Churchill didn't know that it was my man's unseen hands that had first drawn the brown line and then erased it. Friend Churchill is a man of vivid imagination. You have to hand it to him. He saw it right away. A Jewish state in Europe would take the immigration pressure off the British Middle East. The new project would compete with Palestine for the prospective populace. Considering the sour realities of the Middle East, it would sound a death knell for a Jewish state down there. Churchill swallowed the bait. He sent the report to Stalin. The same copy with the brown pencil line. Soon Stalin and Churchill began talking in words rather than in hints. At the moment, as our allies put it nicely, the ball's in Stalin's court—why are you laughing?"

"Forgive me, Uncle. I imagined Stalin—"

He caught Uncle Meir's eyes bulging in horror and stopped short. David swore inwardly. Bugs, even in the Central Committee? And actually, why not in the Central Committee? Precisely in the Central Committee! He finished with a swing of his arm, as if serving the ball over a tennis net.

Uncle Meir didn't smile. "That was the mistake his enemies made," he mouthed. "They laughed at him, but he won the game." He penciled on the paper scrap: "and took their heads for prize." He pushed the paper towards David, waited for him to read it, and said, "You won't know till the ball's in the air as to which sideline it is served. We count on calling the shots for either of the two Jewish states in the making. Many old comrades of mine have gone to the Middle East. They'll do their best to turn Palestine into a communist Vilnergrad. Unless that damn Ben-Gurion steps in their way."

David wrote on the same scrap. "I hope he will."

"David!" Uncle sounded shaken. He crumpled the paper and threw it in the basket, but changed his mind, dipped his hand into the basket, fished the ball out, and stuffed it into his pocket.

David watched these manipulations, amused. "And Roosevelt? How does he feel about this idea?"

"Roosevelt will go along. If Yalta fails to endorse a Jewish state in Europe, Palestine will face massive Jewish immigration. Any Jewish soul that has survived the Nazi onslaught will strive to get down there. In this emotionally charged atmosphere, Roosevelt cannot possibly place himself in their way. Nor can he remain passive. On his way back from Yalta he'll stop over at Cairo. He'll meet Ibn Saud. He'll raise the issue. Enlisting the king to the great challenge of Zionism? I wouldn't be in Roosevelt's shoes. He's facing a hard sell. We'll make it harder still. We'll preempt it with the Project Prusa!"

David smirked. "Sure, a grand objective. And a piece of research to back it. For all I know, next you discover that the German language came from Yiddish."

Uncle blinked, and blinked again. "I beg your pardon?"

"That the Paruses took their Yiddish from Judea to Prusa." David put as much sarcasm as he could in his words. "And taught it to the Germans. The Knights included."

Uncle Meir sprang to his feet and paced between the table and the windows. Once; the second run; the third . . . He pulled up in front of David and jabbed his index finger at David's chest. Uncle's nail was hard and sharp.

"You know what? A brilliant idea. *A yiddisher kop*, you Dovidke. A truly Jewish brain."

David gasped. "Are you serious?"

Uncle Meir had stopped listening. He held his finger on a

button until the secretary appeared in the door. "Zena, I want you for a stenography session. Now."

When the secretary with her pad settled down next to his desk, Meir Kovner was firmly back in his seat. "Thesis: *On the Origins of the German Language*. Re: Project Prusa.

"Our great leaders, Lenin and Stalin, teach us that within every nation there are two cultures—one, of the exploiters, and another, the working masses, the latter developing democratic, socialist trends. It is in the light of these wise teachings that we regard the society of ancient Judea, where the ruling class used the moribund language of the reactionary rabbis, Hebrew, whereas the thriving tongue of the toilers was Yiddish.

"When Jewish Paruses relocated north, their proletarian Yiddish became the national language of Prussia. Yiddish spread over the territory of present-day Germany. Wherever the Prussian mark went, the Yiddish language followed. The barbaric Germanic tribes adopted Yiddish as their own. It gave rise to the manifold of German dialects."

Uncle Meir lapsed into silence. His face revealed a brain at work. Zena rustled through the pages, making pencil marks.

Then Meir Kovner perked up again.

"The last and most dramatic act played out at the close contact of Paruses with the Order, the Latin-speaking—"

Meir threw a glance at his glassed desktop.

"—*Domus Sanctae Maria Theutonicorum*. Their Latin kingdoms in the Middle East crumbling, the Mounted Hounds fled north. Yes, they defeated the peaceful Paruses, but did they defeat their culture? Great Lenin laid down the rules for such historic clashes as he spoke to the Eleventh Party Congress."

Meir sprang to his feet. He crossed to the bookcase and flung open the glazed door. He hesitated no longer than a second before pulling out a red volume with Lenin's black profile impressed. Meir leafed violently through it. "Now . . . aha!" He cocked his head and grinned triumphantly.

"I quote: 'It happens that a people conquers another people, and then the conquerors are the winners and the conquered are the losers. This is very simple and self-evident. But what occurs to the two peoples' culture? If the conquerors are of a higher culture than the subjugated, they ordain their culture. But if the case is opposite?'"

Uncle pointed his finger up, calling for attention. His reading slowed. His voice acquired solemnity. His finger swayed in the manner of a metronome. "It happens sometimes that the vanquished impose their culture upon the conquerors."

Meir Kovner shut the book close and thrust it back into the gap.

"Examples, David?"

David kept silent.

"Please?" Meir Kovner walked back to his deck and sat down, elbows on the top.

David said, "Well, when the Franks came to what would become France, they dropped their German for the Romance dialect of the natives civilized by Antiquity and Christianity."

"Put it down, Zena. Any more?"

"Nor did the Norse language of another invader people, the Viking barbarians, outlive their victories in France."

"Did you catch it, Zena?"

"Just a couple of generations later, the same Normans, now French-speaking, conquered England. They would switch to Saxon—"

"—the language of the English peasantry," Meir Kovner took over, "the tongue of the progressive masses. That's the model we are taking for Prussia, where a similar experience befell the Teutonic Knights. The truth of the vanquished overwhelmed the Mounted Hounds. The Order shed off its vulgar Latin—with a small v, Zena—the language of papal imperialism. From then—hold on, Zena. What's bugging you now, David?"

"You won't get away with it. The Pregel—"

Uncle Meir pointed to the wall map. "Look for yourself."

"I need no map. I was wounded on the bank of the Pregel.

But those river names in Prussia—the *Basic Memorandum* asserts the Hebrew origins of them. If Pruses spoke Yiddish, where did the Hebrew names come from?"

Uncle Meir stared at him.

"Ha! Why shouldn't they come from Hebrew? *Pirgul!*—you think Sadducees bothered to translate the ruling as they took a sad sack to whipping? Back in Judea, the Paruses' Yiddish had gotten contaminated with Hebrew. The centuries of slavery under Sadducees did show! And the river Gilgele—don't you hear the Yiddish ring of it? The endearment suffix *le,* toning down the current name of the river, Gilge?"

David couldn't help it. "Why don't you recast their German measles into Yiddish rash?"

Meir Kovner disregarded his nephew's impertinence. He tapped at the steno pad. "Signed: David Kovner."

David sprang to his feet. "No!"

Uncle chewed his lip. "All right. Scrap the byline, Zena. You can go, and get right on to it."

When the door closed, Uncle Meir walked around his desk to David. He laid his hand on David's shoulder, urging him back to the chair.

"Why protest? I want you to work for me. I'll obtain your transfer from the Army."

David shook his head. "I'd rather stay in the Army, Uncle. You people are too creative for my taste. Your claim about the German language—"

"*Your* claim!"

"—is pure gibberish! A joke! What are you going to do with it?"

Uncle Meir seated himself on the hard arm of David's chair. "I'll bring it to the top. To the utmost top. You don't realize the power of your idea."

His eyes shone. He hugged his nephew by the shoulders.

"Give me a hand, Dovidke. Don't say no; give it a thought." He lifted his behind, felt the lion's head below him, and lowered his weight back. "Tell you what, why don't you do some reading in the interim? Special libraries, archives—Zena will cut red tape for you. Any place you want, the Lubyanka included." He chuckled. "Nowadays, I carry clout with my former jailers."

David paused. "Could you tell me why you're calling the Knights the Mounted Hounds?"

Uncle Meir averted his eyes. "I follow the established terminology."

"Established by whom?"

Uncle cleared his throat. "You remember Marx's term for them?"

"Sure. The Allied Knights. The *Reitersbund*. I put it into my syllabus on early Marx, which I gave to Zarnitsyn."

"Well, he happened to stumble on that particular note of Marx before you did. And he misread Marx's Gothic longhand as *Reitershund*."

"What?"

"An *h* instead of a *b*. He translated his hybrid as *riding hound*, or m*ounted hound*, published his discovery, and earned the reputation of the utmost Marxist authority on medieval Prussia. Now you know why he blocked your paper about the Allied Knights. Your innocent discovery spelled his ruin. So my fall from grace was doubly sweet to him. A license to make short work of you."

David was stunned. "And you—you deal with him! And keep using that illiterate cliché."

Uncle Meir chewed his lip. "Illiterate it may be, but it's canonized. The other day they showed Zarnitsyn's paper to—"

Uncle made the thumbs and forefingers of both hands converge under his nose. Then he slid them outwards along his upper lip, as if grooming invisible mustaches. A metaphor for Stalin.

"He endorsed it. He put the quotation into his writings—he said Marx had branded the Teutonic Order with the scathing moniker, the Mounted Hounds. The German invaders of today are the heirs of the *psy-rytsari*, the Mounted Hounds. They are being destroyed just like their ignominious ancestors . . . In the wake of Stalin's recognition, Zarnitsyn was made a Corresponding Member of the Academy. Amen."

In the anteroom, Zena smiled at David from her typing. "I'm so glad. You're going to get your own state."

A scarlet rosebud popularly known as the "little heart" burned on her lips: it was to make them look shorter and thicker.

"Who is?"

She became shy. "Your people."

CHAPTER SIXTEEN

A couple of days later, Uncle Meir said in a triumphant tone, "*They* liked your Yiddish-to-German thing. It's a go-ahead." They were breakfasting in Uncle's kitchen. As was customary when Uncle Meir spoke speaking of his bosses, he started pointing up, but stopped short: the only *they* above was Ognev in his sixth-floor apartment. So Uncle's finger made an evolution and ended up pointing at the window. There in the distance, behind lower buildings of Kitai-Gorod, lurked the Kremlin towers.

David blinked. Who gave the green light to his facetious remark? Didn't they see what they faced? At the moment, the Project Prusa was protected by secrecy. But when the time came to reveal it to the world, the absurdities would be for all to behold. And Stalin was no fool . . .

David sipped his hot tea. "Good luck with your Pruses—or are they Paruses?"

"Same thing," Uncle Meir said, spreading butter over a slice of rye bread.

"They may've swallowed the *a*-sound on the Isle of Paros, poor starving things."

"Why should they be starving?" inquired Uncle Meir, dryly. He blew air at the surface of his cup, chasing small black waves towards the rim.

"Oh, a very simple *why*, forty days on the barren island. After they had eaten all clams and lizards."

Meir Kovner didn't give up. "They could always resort to fishing."

"I'm sure Mark had hidden their sails and paddles before ascending to his highland office, no risk taken, no sir. Coming down with the Law and having nobody to give it? And he, what did *he* eat up there?"

Uncle Meir shrugged. "Ask Zarnitsyn about it."

"Oh, I know," David mocked. "Buzzards brought him bread and flesh in the morning, and bread and flesh in the evening; and he drank the dew from puddles.

Uncle Meir grimaced. "You took your page from the Bible."

"Not me—Zarnitsyn. The parallels are obvious: the Exodus, the Mount Sinai revelations, the wandering, and the Promised Land. And earlier, still in Judea, those evangelists. All this coming from the citadel of atheist Marxism? Remember, Uncle, the New Year in Palai, twenty years ago? The trouble Clara's school principal got into and you tried to rescue him? How did they put it, those men from Simferopol who arrested him? His fir tree, they said, scented of incense and manger. A capital offense. And now the smell of incense is emanating from the Institute of Marxism in Moscow."

"The Memorandum *is* anti-religious!"

"Only on the surface, but not in the method. Isn't it weird?"

Uncle Meir looked away from his nephew. He was obviously holding back something.

They left home together and parted in the street. David had been spending entire days in places far beyond reach of your ordinary Soviet citizen. Sentinels stepped back to let him in. Reinforced doors clanged and rolled back. David rummaged in catalogues, ran his fingers over spiked cards in long wooden boxes, turned over dusty piles. They arrived from rooms filled with stacks and folders that looked as workaday as any public records' room of yours. David read, his back bent from dawn to dusk and far beyond.

It was Uncle's bait. Uncle Meir, the clever operator, had lured him with an offer that David, always a political animal, couldn't turn down: access to privileged sources of information. "Red" bulletins of restricted circulation, foreign newspapers . . . At the Lubyanka, under observation of an archivist in the reading room, David read protocols and confessions.

He requested the files of Franz Ebert and his wife. Clara's parents had ended up in Siberia, dumped in the Vasyugan region in the midst of swamps and marshes.

Next came the dossier of Franz's brother. It was actually two files—the KGB's and the military, SMERSH's—joined into a common folder. A note in red pencil ran across the jacket: *How come this trickster is still walking around?* Ebert's Kazakhstan exile looked an oddity indeed, given his offences and the murderous habits of the two services.

Clara had said her Uncle Max had known Prince Vorontsov closely. Whatever it might have meant, there was nothing of the sort in his file.

The archivist dozed behind his counter, his false leg splayed out in front of him . . .

Back at his uncle's place, David was unbuttoning his trench coat when a door banged upstairs. He heard the elevator cabin whine its way up, to the top floor. David left the apartment and ran down the stairs, two at a time. The cabin whooshed past him on the second floor.

In the lobby, a man enveloped in a wide-belted brick-red overcoat was emerging from the elevator. Ognev looked up at David from under a red muskrat fur hat, earflaps down.

"Can I walk with you?" asked David.

Ognev nodded assent.

At the door he buried his face in an orange woolen muffler and raised a red fur collar.

Biting snow lashed at David's face. They turned uphill, into crooked lanes. David said, "I'm sorry about the other night."

Ognev shrugged. "You people went on with that New Year celebration turned Oktoberfest, didn't you? How can Meir put up with it?"

The climb became steeper. They walked past the tall ancient walls of a former monastery. Ognev lumbered along, a rare bird in uniformly grey or navy-blue Moscow . . . They debouched to a wide boulevard and bode their time while a streetcar rang and rattled on a sloping traffic lane.

David heard a greeting. A sleek grey Rolls Royce with a Union Jack on the radiator pulled up at the curb. Smiling Jim Hathaway waved from the passenger seat. "Could I have an interview with you one day, Major? I'd like to hear more about your battlefront experiences."

"You could indeed. Call me at my uncle's."

Hathaway motioned towards a huge box that encumbered the car's back. "The birthday present for the son of my boss." He made a comic horror gesture. "Got to make haste."

The window rolled up. The auto shot a bluish puff and surged ahead, towards a bridge and the British Embassy. David and Ognev crossed to the deserted boulevard's garden and turned left.

Ognev kept his clenched fists in his pockets. He spoke to his feet.

"A small town near Vilnius. A German pilot project of sorts. The automobile looked like a bread delivery van. Might've been a bread delivery van before the Germans had worked a change or two. Redirected the tail pipe into the load space."

Ognev turned his head away. "It took a twenty-minute drive to a pit in the outskirts. What hellish scenes were in there, while women and children—"

He choked on his words.

"But damn efficient, the whole racket. And humane. Spared nerves of the SS and their homegrown helpers—they may've been on edge from endless executions. One prisoner lived to tell it. He'd pissed onto his handkerchief and breathed through the cloth. As they unloaded the van, he played dead. He heard the Germans speak. The consensus was the project might fly, but the van's bed ought to tilt, like a dump truck. More practical. Never laying their hands on cadavers befouled with vomit and excrements. Just back the mobile gas-chamber to the pit and pitch the floor."

That's how they started their nightly walks.

More by instinct than reason, David kept them secret from his uncle.

PART THREE

CHAPTER SEVENTEEN

The blinds in Meir Kovner's office in Old Square were drawn, shutting out light. An 8-mm projector hummed, manned by the dark lump of a technician. At his desk, Meir watched a color movie on a screen unfurled on the wall.

A village street. A house of yellow stucco. Flower boxes underscore two rows of windows. Another window looks down from the steep gable . . . In the court, a group of tourists with a guide are walking through barns, pigsties, stables.

Close-ups . . . Captions . . . The guide names the articles of harness in the primal, earthy Yiddish of Galilee, transported here by the first immigrants along with their herds.

The group enters the house through the back door and walks across the ground floor. Souvenir booths . . . Glass displays . . . Exit.

Countryside . . . Fields . . .

"Stop," Meir said. "Back to that brick."

A sunny, open field. Dozens of volunteers, youthful and sun-baked, work spades, picks, and pallets in a pit. They sing from the *Gilgele* cycle. A burst of merry excitement: a thin, chipped brick changes hands.

The guide brings her group over.

Close on the brick. It bears the carving ♥ = א ⊥ כ. The guide intones: "Sixteen hundred years ago, in pristine Prusa, one Caleb and one Abigail declared their love. This artifact makes you feel as if it were yesterday. It *was* yesterday! The 700-year gap never happened! Did that old house imbue you with the feeling of generations' continuity? Did you smell the Prussian horse manure in the Prussian barn? Caleb has just mounted his horse and galloped to a seminar for the propagandists, and Abigail, their first baby in her lap, is waiting for him upstairs, reading the classics of Markism."

The imagery changes. Now it's primeval forests . . . cave-ridden slopes . . . tents . . . a castle . . . a sea . . . a stone bridge . . . The male voice takes over.

"With Prussia liberated and the German occupiers gone, those towns and villages spared by the war will stand like ghosts of the past. We propose setting aside a number of farmsteads and windmills for the Old Prusa Foundation, the custodian of Prussia's glorious past before the Catastrophe. The ancient nation will reach back for her fountain of youth!"

The voice pairs up with a man. He stands before the door upholstered in yellow leather with nails patterned into five-pointed stars. He reads from the page in his hand.

Close-up on the face, a pink scar on the man's left cheek. A gold tooth flashes.

"Every immigrant to the People's Democratic Republic of Prussia will pass through the orientation program that we have sketched above. He will absorb love for his historic motherland through his connection to its landscape and artifacts. The program will bridge the hiatus in the national psyche that burst open seven hundred years ago. It will provide the nation with a cathartic effect. It will restore the man's mystical bond with the soil. It will enlist the girl for the glory of motherhood. It will infuse the boy's soul with the enchanting mixture of forest odors, lullabies, and swords' glitter, destined to explode in the man with love, glory, and fury."

The director raises his eyes from the paper.

"The Party will appreciate the soundness and practical sense of our proposal. It sets us apart from Zarnitsyn's dilettantes. The Project Prusa should land where it rightly belongs—"

"Herder-merder," Meir Kovner muttered. He waved the technician to stop. The lights went on. The man in a thick red sweater rolled off the screen and retreated. Meir scooped typewritten pages and thrust them into his morocco briefcase. Zena came in and offered to help him into his overcoat of dark-grey padded ratteen and astrakhan, the product of the best Kremlin atelier, but Meir declined. He thrust his arms into the sleeves slippery with grey satin lining, upon which black embroidered autos were scattered. He felt young and dapper beneath a matching fur cap. A general's *papakha*. Meir Kovner felt like a general marching his troops.

★ ★ ★

That morning, David had been working in a redbrick pseudo-Gothic building, in a room with windows carefully boarded up: the fifth floor of the History Museum had offered a generous view of Red Square. David researched the Vorontsovs. The family boasted an aristocratic pedigree dating to the eleventh century. A hundred years ago the Alupka manor became their entailed estate.

The reference to a book in the Kremlin library caught David's eye. He was copying its definition when the balding, paunchy library director came running to his nook, bug-eyed with curiosity. "You're wanted on the phone, Major Kovner. From—from Comrade Kovner's secretary." He looked from David to the letter David had left with him, apparently making the names' connection for the first time. "If you'd come through here."

David took the phone in the director's office: Zena informed him that his uncle had just left the building and would pick him up.

Four minutes later, in the rear of a slick auto, Meir Kovner smiled at his nephew, who took a seat beside him.

"The Institute of Marxism," Meir ordered.

"Really, Uncle!"

"What's the matter with you? You don't want to pay a sentimental visit to your adored alma mater?"

They said nothing more until the auto pulled up at the cubist building. A waiting assistant professor rushed to them in the lobby.

He showed them along a corridor, through a spacious anteroom where they draped their overcoats, to an office rivaling Meir Kovner's in size and almost a copy of the above: glazed bookshelves, wall maps pinned with little flags, a twelve-meter long conference table under a green wool cover set with ashtrays and water carafes, and a vast desk completing a Т, with Professor Zarnitsyn atop like a diacritic sign. A dozen or so men and women lined both sides of the table, one man standing at the corner formed by the table and Zarnitsyn's desk. They turned to see. As if at the command, they looked back at Zarnitsyn, who rose to his feet. The audience followed suit.

Zarnitsyn ceremoniously bowed, and so did the rest.

"Carry on, carry on." Meir Kovner sank into a spare chair at the desk to Zarnitsyn's right and motioned David to the chair next to him, which had appeared from nowhere. At the bottom of the table, Meir's former agent Andronikos avoided the Kovners' eyes.

Zarnitsyn, clad in a tailored three-piece suit of coffee-colored cashmere one size too small, flashed a saccharine smile.

"On behalf of the Institute's Academic Council" (Zarnitsyn made a wide round gesture embracing one and all) "let me tell you, Comrade Kovner, how immensely happy we are to see Major Kovner at your side. He is the pride and glory of our Institute."

"I said to go on," said Meir Kovner impatiently.

"We are winding up Departmental reports. The recent research stimulated by the latest Party directives on the Yiddish roots of the Parusian language."

Meir furtively poked David, who groaned.

"Let me review what we have done," Zarnitsyn said.

"We'll catch up as you go."

"Very well, then. Have your seats, Comrades. Associate Professor Vityushkin, please continue. Moldavia, to prepare."

The man nearest to Zarnitsyn's desk got to his feet again. Meir Kovner winked to David. That was the former Young Communist League Secretary, the student who had brought the

Pravda over to Zarnitsyn at that ill-starred colloquium. Vityushkin's wiry red tufts had been tamed, he had put on weight, his neat double-breasted coat was of passable wool, and the breast welt pocket was where it should be on the man who recycled his suits no more.

"The latest words of the Party wisdom," Vityushkin said, looking devotedly at the space between Zarnitsyn and Meir, "as laid out in the *Thesis on the Origins of the German Language*, gave a powerful impetus to our research. Department of Marxist Philology read the texts by Josephus the Historian with a new insight. And here's what we've found. Walking down the valley of Kedron, Josephus spotted an emaciated man prostrate under a pine tree. Are you a Paruse or a Sadducee? Josephus asked. *Es'n*, answered the man. Josephus thought he discovered a third sect, a monastic one, the community of living solitary and mortifying their flesh. He recorded their name as the Essenes. He was wrong. The poor devil begged him in Yiddish for some food."

Vityushkin sat down. Zarnitsyn looked at him with undisguised love. His smile went off as he switched his gaze to a middle-aged dark-haired woman on the other side of the table, her lips pursed like a nun. She had pulled a pad from the bulky briefcase of black leather in front of her and leafed frantically through it. "Moldavia takes the floor. Go ahead, Comrade Enesca."

Enesca clutched her notes and stood up. Stubby and red-faced, she wore a navy-blue suit over a white batiste blouse.

"The latest Party directives opened our eyes to previously unexplained facts of Moldavian history. We know now that when the Paruses landed on our shores, they brought Yiddishist culture to Bessarabia. It is supported by the finds on the sites recently liberated from Rumanian occupiers, which brought a wealth of paleozoological evidence. Then—"

"Hold on," Meir said. "What kind of paleo-something?"

"Well, for one thing, stockpiles of oxen guts, the spare strings for Paruses' fiddles."

Enesca fumbled in her briefcase and came up with a handful of colorless filaments.

"And for another," Meir asked, "if there is another?"

"For another, immense deposits of pike bone, the waste product of gefilte fish. It was consumed during Parusian klezmer festivals, where the hungry public demanded, *Gimme a fish!*"

Zarnitsyn regarded her with disgust. Meir felt sorry for the unimaginative woman ungainly in her suit.

"Then the music," Enesca said. "So similar, their klezmer and our doinas."

Zarnitsyn said dryly, "That will be all, Comrade Enesca."

Enesca sat down, her cheeks pink.

Zarnitsyn turned to Meir Kovner. "Allow me to pass to a special item on the agenda, Comrade Kovner. We're seeking the Party's protection of a diligent, loyal, and highly gifted collective from a gang of adventurers. Yes, adventurers!" His voice rang with cracked bronze. "A copy of the letter from the Marxist-Leninist Joint School to the Central Committee has fallen into our hands. A brazen attempt to smear our research with destructive, malicious calumny!"

He tugged open his desk drawer, produced a single page, and rose to his feet.

"Our response to the slanderous—"

"No," said Meir Kovner. "First read *their* letter. Aloud."

"What for? My summary is extensive and written from an unimpeachable position. More than enough for passing judgment on an illiterate lampoon."

"I don't think you can skip reading their letter."

"I don't have it on me."

Meir Kovner took a stack of paper from his briefcase and pushed it to Zarnitsyn. After a considerable pause, with a mien of disgust on his face, Zarnitsyn passed it to Vityushkin. The latter stood and cleared his throat for a long while before reading.

"Grateful for the support of the Party and Comrade Stalin in person—"

"Ha," gasped the audience. "What nerve!"

"—we have examined the glorious passage of the Jewish revolutionaries from the bondage in Judea to freedom in Prusa, as highlighted in the directives of the Central Committee. Our findings differ somewhat from our distinguished colleagues at the Institute of Marxism—"

The audience made indignant noises. Vityushkin stopped.

"What's the matter with your associate, Professor Zarnitsyn?" said Meir Kovner.

Zarnitsyn shook his head. "With all due respect, Comrade Kovner, doesn't it smack of bourgeois objectivism? Allowing a public recital of a potentially hostile text? The Academic Council doesn't want to be poisoned. It demands termination of the reading."

The members exchanged worried glances.

Meir Kovner radiated cheer. "Just read the School's letter."

"As you wish." Zarnitsyn sank to his chair, red-faced. "I only hope that it doesn't set a dangerous precedent. Do as requested," he hurled to Vityushkin.

The reading resumed.

"—striving to usurp and monopolize a hefty slice of historical science."

Zarnitsyn's left hand jerked forward, as if to stop Vityushkin, and froze midair.

"Why don't you go on?" said Meir Kovner, affably.

He enjoyed it. The fat bastard who had humiliated his nephew—Meir was giving him a tit for tat with impunity. With his "special item," Zarnitsyn had brought it upon himself. Meir squinted his eyes at David, who gazed straight ahead at the opposite wall, jugular muscles playing under his skin.

Vityushkin turned the page. The rustle was clearly heard in the hush of the room.

"The sorry experts from the Institute of Marxism have grossly misread the sources. Playing with, fussing about, and all but licking certain words, they never realized that the Hebrew letter *peh* might represent not only the occlusive consonant sound *p* but also the fricative *f*, as in Marxist-Leninist *Philosophy*. The Jewish revolutionaries' self-name was not Paruse, but Pharuse."

The audience exploded in angry protests.

Vityushkin's voice trembled with indignation as he read on. "Therefore, an informed scientist would not beat the bushes at the barren boulder of Paros but rather search near the Egyptian coast, on the island of Pharos. Yes, in the harbor of Alexandria! The Institute of Marxism missed their mark by seven hundred kilometers!"

Vityushkin suffered visibly. His forehead was covered with sweat, and he pushed the words from his mouth with an effort.

"Mark-led Pharusian galleys landed at the eastern tip of the narrow island. A four-hundred-feet-high candle loomed against the starry sky. 'Who goes there?' a Roman sentry yelled and fell, his throat cut. The glorious assault began. By the morning, all was over. The Pharuses took control of the island and the tallest building on earth, the Seventh Wonder of the World, the incomparable Lighthouse of Pharos. Atop, Mark would write his Manifesto!"

Zarnitsyn threw glances at the audience, checking whether disapproval and disgust rose to the high standard. The targeted individual made an instant response in the form of a grimace, hemming, and snorting, although not too loudly, out of respect to the lofty office. That reaction ran in ripples along the table, as if Zarnitsyn's gaze was the prow of a man of war cleaving waters.

"Our version of events," Vityushkin read, "besides being factually true—"

"Ha ha ha!" an overly indignant champion of truth burst out laughing, and stopped short.

"—allows for a fuller role of the Pharuses in the class warfare in Roman Empire, the prison of the nations. From liberated Pharos, Mark beamed signals of freedom to passing ships across the Mediterranean. They inspired enslaved Europeans as Radio Moscow does nowadays!"

Inadvertently, Vityushkin became infected with the pathos of the text. That didn't pass unnoticed by Zarnitsyn, who cleared his throat. Vityushkin turned crimson.

"And when Romans returned in force, the Pharuses fought back all their attacks. They were hardly those hapless victims of pogroms and harassment depicted by the—"

Vityushkin stumbled.

"—by the Institute of Marxism."

Meir Kovner snorted but said nothing, magnanimously.

"Beams of light from the great mirror of the lighthouse blinded the attackers; burning lamp oil incinerated them. And the defeated Romans rolled back, as the Germans would from the walls of Stalingrad!"

Enesca started clapping hands, but stopped short under Zarnitsyn's glare.

"Those perished in the battle enjoyed the privilege of resting on the mainland, under stony mounds extending from fence to fence—a great distinction because they shared the burial ground with Comrade Mark. Yes, with Mark's tomb! Because even Comrade Mark was somewhat less than immortal."

"What do they want to say?" Zarnitsyn demanded ominously.

"Clement of Alexandria pinpoints Mark's burial place. The great leader was laid to rest in the mountain-like mausoleum of black Nubian granite, a stark silhouette against the azure skies and yellow sand.

The protests in the room grew loud. Vityushkin stopped and looked at Zarnitsyn in a silent plea. Zarnitsyn let the tumult continue awhile before he tapped at the desktop.

Vityushkin sighed and resumed.

"When the time arrived to carry out Comrade Mark's last will and the Pharuses sailed off in quest of the Promised Land, they left a wake of toponymy and valor from the Isle of Pharos through the Boss-Phorus to the promontory of Phoros in the Crimea. Their Iron Legion under wolf's head insignia crashed all in their way. The Roman Historian Tacitus knew them as the Marcomanni, Mark's men. 'Amongst their neighbors,' he reported, 'they are most signal in force and renown; nay, their habitation itself they acquired through their gallantry.' The bravest of the brave gained Prussia. Theirs was a society of fearless warriors and northern amazons. And when the sorry time came, it was not their 'timidity' but their reckless courage that aborted the Prussian

Millennium. As another poet put it, mourning the Catastrophe: 'Then Prussia hurried to the field, and snatch'd the spear, but left the shield.' "

Vityushkin looked up. Meir Kovner smiled at him, amiably. Vityushkin dropped his eyes.

"On this poetic note," he read, "we close our analysis of mistakes, grave errors and omissions made by the distinguished scholars at the Institute. The centerpiece of our plan is the proposal for Old Prusa Foundation. Please read the script of our film, *Voices from the Yesteryear.*

"A village street. A house of yellow stucco. Flower boxes underscore two rows of windows. Another window looks down from the steep gable. In the court, a tourist group with a guide is going through barns, pigsties, stables . . ."

Vityushkin droned on . . . Meir eyed Zarnitsyn's desk topped with thick beveled glass, just like his. Since Meir saw it last week, Zarnitsyn's photographs on the green baize had been rearranged. Now they formed a circle, the center concealed under a copy of Zarnitsyn's *Basic Memorandum.* Meir went through a number of suppositions, not entirely friendly, of what might lie there . . .

Vityushkin, finished, sank to his seat.

Zarnitsyn, white with suppressed rage, rose. "I will put an end, once and for all, to any doubt that the Paruses—yes, the *Paruses* with a *p!*—did touch at the island of Paros."

At Zarnitsyn's sign, Andronikos took a position at the anteroom door, facing the end of the conference table.

"You will see," Zarnitsyn said solemnly, "an amazing artifact that was discovered, through hard work and serendipity, during the ongoing struggle for the liberation of Greece. The Balkan Department has the floor!"

Andronikos said, "Our men, ugh, cleared the island of Paros of those fascists. The Roman, Teutonic, and Hellenic fascists. Over miles of mountainous terrain we did. The partisan army of General Markos. And came up to this grotto. And there he was, in a stone box."

He pushed open the double door.

A wheeled platform rolled in, draped in white. Two men under fez hats—truncated cones of burgundy felt and black tassels—pushed it. Their bare legs were hairy black between sandals and short blue tunics somewhat matching their knees blue from cold.

The trolley skirted the conference table. Heads swiveled, and eyes followed its course.

It stopped across the desk of Meir.

"The remains of Comrade Mark the Founder!" announced Zarnitsyn.

Andronikos pulled off the white cover.

A set of bones arranged into a human skeleton rested on the red velour: a skull too small for the mighty chest, two sets of arms, a pelvis, two thighbones, two shinbones, and assorted toes. At the feet lay a rusty deteriorated iron chain.

CHAPTER EIGHTEEN

Andronikos broke the stunned silence.

"One of us partisans, he pursued a goat. Saw this stinker of a bee flying in and out of a rock. Grown with shrubbery rock. He looked closer and spied a crevice, then another. Used to be a passageway, now stoned-up. Our boys, they broke through the masonry. Only they had to run for it because of the swarm. Vicious little buggers, them wild bees. Made themselves comfortable right under the sarcophagus. You see, the Paruses had soaked the stiff in honey, but the yum-yum had leaked down. We blew smoke into the cave and destroyed the hive. When the partisans looked above, they saw a stone box. The name of our *archistratigos* was right on the lid. See?" Andronikos scanned the room, triumphantly. "Like, if General Markos falls in battle, the place is his! After we found it, whoever been unhappy with General Markos's authority—they had to clam up."

Meir Kovner twisted his mouth. "What are you going to do with the—with the stuff?"

"Brick it up into the Kremlin Wall."

Zarnitsyn beamed. "Roman imperialists looted Mark's supposed tomb in Alexandria. They could as well have frisked Alexandria Mark Center, ha ha. We'll petition the Government for a ceremonial enshrinement. Comrade Mark belongs to Red Square, not to Mussolini's Venice!"

Enesca got out of her seat. Short-legged and fat, she waddled the short walk to the platform and paused for a closer look.

She returned to her seat. "The hands. They both are left."

"Comrade Mark was left-handed," said Andronikos.

COMRADE STALIN CHANGED HIS HAIRCUT

"Bilaterally left-handed. Fought the right-wing revisionism of the M-L-J gang with both hands."

Enesca scoffed. "The fingers are too short. Only three phalanxes for each."

"And how many should there be?" Andronikos asked, caustically.

"Should be four, in a skeleton."

"No!" The Greek gloated. "Not in Mark's. He was *kolobodaktylos*!"

"And what's that?"

"The Stumpfinger!"

"Ancient authors call Mark The Stumpfinger, Enesca," Zarnitsyn said.

She didn't give up. "And the chain?"

"One that Paruses had left behind. As a token of their liberation."

Zarnitsyn said, "Nowadays the Communist partisans are forging the whole of the Archipelago, link by link, into a new proletarian chain around Greece."

"Pass me the clinker," commanded Meir Kovner.

Andronikos did so. Meir took off his glasses and brought the chain so close to his eyes that it nearly touched his nose. "Met— metalwork, eh, Prokhor Pirogov & Son," he read. "In Russian. Why?"

"Greek looks so much like Cyrillic," said Andronikos making to snatch the chain.

Zarnitsyn bent quickly over the desk and pushed him away.

"You hit it on the mark, Comrade Kovner. An immensely important observation of yours. We see it as a message that came through the ages. Mark's followers foresaw Russia's leading role in the revolutionary movement. Thank you ever so much, Comrade Kovner. Your contributions to Markism, which your *Origins of the German Language* had opened, merit a scientific degree, Doctor of Arts in History. I'm assigning a young assistant to give you a hand in arranging your ideas into a dissertation."

He raised the audience with an orchestra conductor's wave of his arms.

"No need," said Meir Kovner. "I don't feel worthy." He hoped a tinge of regret was not detectable in his voice.

"I truly hope you reconsider," Zarnitsyn said.

David started to go, but Meir held his knee down.

Zarnitsyn gestured the Council down. "We're passing to the last item in the agenda, approval of doctorate topics for Comrade Vityushkin's students."

"Item one," read Vityushkin. *The Uninterrupted Presence of Pruses in the Baltic.* Here we'll develop the story of crypto-Pruses who survived the Order's onslaught and once a week gathered at secret candlelight to recite the Manifesto. We'll trace their Pruse origins through the analysis of their names: Krupp from Krupnitsky, Brahms from Abramson, Kant from—"

"The next item, Vityushkin." Zarnitsyn skewed his eyes at Meir Kovner.

"Item two," Vityushkin read. "*The Echo of the Parusian Revolt in the Peasants' War in Germany.* It wasn't by chance that the peasants' leaders picked blue and white for their flag colors. The reason—"

"Why should it go to Vityushkin?" asked Comrade Enesca sternly. "Item two—it has nothing to do with whatever philology!"

Zarnitsyn huffed in anger. "Are you saying, Enesca, that narrow specialization is more important than a perfect command of Marxist methodology? Let me break it to you that I'm consolidating these two Departments—Marxist Philology and Middle Ages. Associate Professor Vityushkin is taking over the new unit."

Enesca's voice rose with alarm. "And what's the reason for that odd marriage? I don't quite understand."

"There is nothing here to understand. Comrade Vityushkin heads the Jubilee Committee to celebrate the printing of Lenin's first work, *What the 'Friends of the People' Are and How They Are Fighting Us,* fifty years ago this spring. He's up for an early promotion."

"To full professor?" gasped Comrade Enesca. Her face was patched with red and white. No longer did she resemble a nun— she was a Dolores Ibarruri hurling *¡No pasarán!* to the roaring crowds.

"We need new blood in the leadership," said Zarnitsyn.

"Why not in the trenches?" Enesca scoffed. "But surely full professorship would go a long way in extending his deferment."

"I have a flatfoot!" Vityushkin shouted out.

"Such an affliction, and very catching."

"The work of Associate Professor Vityushkin," Zarnitsyn pronounced testily, "is as war-related as they come. Marxist ideology provides a spiritual shield for the Army. Surely Major Kovner will attest to that." Zarnitsyn squinted his eyes at David Kovner, who stared dead-on at the wall. "Marxism vitalizes the world. There is no more honorable occupation than studying Marxism. And you, Enesca, you're a poor team player. Your clapping—what was it supposed to mean? Where does your loyalty belong?"

"I applauded our glorious victory at Stalingrad," Enesca said haughtily.

"The Moldavian Department should determine where it stands. It's high time for the Moldavian Department to specify their intended contribution to Lenin's Jubilee."

"Lenin had never been to Moldavia!"

"Nor to China. But the Chinese comrades have sent us a grain of rice upon which a devotee had engraved the complete text of Lenin's article. In Chinese!"

Vityushkin grinned. "She should try corn. Corn grows well in Moldavia."

David Kovner rose to his feet and walked out.

Zarnitsyn followed him with his eyes.

Then he squinted at Meir Kovner and casually scooped away the copy of the *Basic Memorandum* in front of him.

Meir saw that the mementos and snapshots under the glass top had made a reverential circle about a glossy photo: with a spoon in his hand, Minister Molotov drove a slice of lemon about his tea glass, and Zarnitsyn looked at him with fawning admiration.

Zarnitsyn exacted his revenge . . .

Meir Kovner caught up with his nephew at the trolley bus stop. Light snow melted on Meir's bald pate before he realized that his *papakha* was still in his hand. He thrust it in place, took David by the elbow, and guided him away from the stop. At the spot marked "Positively No Standing," Meir's chauffeur was hastily installing the windshield wipers he'd removed before leaving for the comforts of the Institute's lobby: even the vehicle with an MOC license plate was not immune from petty theft. The auto started and crept along beside Meir and his nephew.

David trembled with suppressed anger. "Why did you take me over there?"

They stopped at the curb. "I just wanted," Meir said innocently, "to show you your idea at work."

"I'm renouncing any relation to it. I regret my ever mentioning it, even in jest."

The chauffeur brought the auto to a stop in front of them. The windshield wipers wigwagged at a measured pace. Meir Kovner beckoned. The chauffeur exited to open the back seat door for them.

Meir installed himself beside his nephew. "You don't have to work directly with Zarnitsyn. How about Enesca? And the Institute isn't the only show in town. Moscow's large enough. Go to the Marxist-Leninist Joint School!"

"To those culture vultures?"

"Don't exaggerate! Would you like me to take you down there?"

"Just give me a lift to the Kremlin, will you please?"

They were silent for the remainder of the ride. Letting David out at the Borovitsky Gate, Meir Kovner said, "Zarnitsyn *is* an asshole. But what can I do if better people turn up their noses at my work? Make up your mind. I cannot wait much longer."

CHAPTER NINETEEN

M eir Kovner rode on. He felt stung to the quick. Such priggishness on the part of his nephew! Then he remembered the complete ease with which the men and women at the Institute of Marxism moved about in the fictitious world of Prusa, and his thoughts became calmer and happier.

The people over there did their best. They didn't indulge in an infantile obsession with "the truth." They didn't check their work against so-called facts. They knew what mattered. It wasn't the "facts." It was the skill in operating within the dogmas that the Party had laid before them. The frame of reference had its own postulates, and they measured their work against them alone.

The model of a world. A virtual world. Created by Meir's fiat. No pathetic Johannine prattle about the truth that made you free could shake its foundations.

Meir Kovner felt proud of himself.

Except for the fact that he'd needled Zarnitsyn. But he couldn't help it! He did it for David's benefit. Meir remembered Zarnitsyn's photo with Molotov. Why had Zarnitsyn kept it from view in the first place? One would expect that he would advertise it right and left, mount it prominently on the wall. There could be only one reason for his not doing so—he'd been told to hold it back. Still, the pompous swine couldn't help bragging to Meir, even if in a flash.

And see what kind of gratitude David showed!

Offence boiled anew in Meir's breast.

If only he had Arnold Hramoy working with him! Meir had made inquiries: Arnold was coming back tonight.

·171·

He had debated leaving Arnold a message and opted against it.

Something was telling Meir that Arnold would come on his own, and soon.

★   ★   ★

Meanwhile, David showed his pass and service book to the sentries at the gatehouse (a glance at his face, at the photo, again at the face), was frisked for arms, and was allowed within the Kremlin walls. The crenels silhouetted against the sky, forked like Grandpa Osher's beard upside down. David passed patrols and sentries wearing the sky-blue insignia of the Kremlin Regiment. Behind the closed main gate in the shorter wall of the Arsenal he heard neighing. Marshal Budyonny kept stables in the Kremlin barracks.

David skirted the Senate Square, away from the elegant main entrance with its four columns. At a corner door he showed his pass, went through a body search, and was admitted to one of the Senate's triangular courts. He presented his pass once more to gain admission to the central, pentagonal court. At its bottom, two teams of guards carried out the relief routine in front of a green door adorned with a huge padlock. "Halt who goes there?"— "The Corporal of the Guard . . ."

David turned to another door, producing his credentials and himself for the final examination: face-photo-face and body frisk. Behind his back, the two teams completed the relief:

"The post's passed over!"

"The post's taken over!"

Entering the annex, David glanced back. Two soldiers drew in their stomachs, pivoted their toes a rifle-butt apart, and froze . . .

David had the reading room nearly all to himself. He presented his powerful authorization at a counter, ordered a book, and settled to wait in a long, narrow hall stuffed with desks of polished oak across its width. The only other reader, a young woman in the first row, lit the emerald disk of a lamp. Radiant points reflected from the dull green glass-shades on the other desks.

A matron brought David his order on a wooden tray and went back behind the counter to her three bored companions.

David opened *Prince Vorontsov's Having a Good Time,* published by Vorontsov's former butler in Munich, 1929. The disgruntled retainer gave away the juicy detail of his former master's life. The pages were untrimmed, the folds still closed except for two dozen pages in the beginning. When David came to a Crimean summer, he had to walk to the counter and ask for a paper knife. The ladies on duty ceased babbling and scaled him. Inspection completed, a heavyset woman in a sober navy-blue two-piece suit, a twin of Enesca's, pushed him a blade—wooden, dented, round-pointed. He couldn't assault Comrade Stalin with it if the same walked into the room; no, he couldn't.

David signed the release form and backtracked, past the young female reader. As he sat down, she threw the ends of her throat-wrap over her padded shoulders. The clawed paws and the head of a silver fox brushed a knitted turban cap and settled down on to the back of her red dress. The beaded glass eyes seamed to spy on him.

David slid the knife between the pages and slit them apart. The fold opened into two pages. He read: "While the Emperor's family stayed at Livadia, the Prince had to call off the fun-making at the manor. The Czarina wouldn't tolerate—"

The double door swung open. In stepped Marshal Semyon Budyonny, parading all ten inches of his cockroach mustachio.

David blinked. The Civil War hero had long been reduced to a museum exponent. His antics were tolerated and shrugged off. A widely believed story made rounds about his beating off an arrest and a certain death. Budyonny and his orderly lay flat behind ancient machine guns at his country house and kept Beria's men at bay until Stalin's order came countermanding the arrest.

It was generally assumed in the army that Budyonny had never read a single book. To judge from their dazed faces, a similar thought had occurred the librarians. But the fox-wrapped girl rose to her feet and crossed to the door, swinging the red panne velvet of her skirt. She passed David unnecessarily, leaving in her wake a whiff of "Red Moscow" perfume mixed with body odor. When her glance brushed his face, David recognized the blue-eyed shepherdess from the fateful Institute colloquium six years ago. Budyonny pulled his mustache and put his other arm round her waist. The door shot behind them.

The four librarians buzzed excitedly.

David returned to his reading. He slit the folds as he read on:

Therefore the Prince resorted to an elaborate scheme. The mountains edging the Yalta coastal strip are rich in karst formations, the voids—caverns and tunnels—formed in limestone by acid waters. At places, they honeycomb, and some are as long as several kilometers. Pagans had their shrines in there; Greek settlers took refuge from Khazar invaders. Later they served as Christian clandestine temples, outlaws' lairs, livestock corrals—they have been in use over millennia. The Prince had a cavern transformed into an Oriental sheik's parlor complete with hard flooring, thick carpets, a wine cellar, stalagmites turned to candelabras, servants dressed as seraglio keepers: The Lair of Ali Baba. For the principal entrance, in the south, the Prince had a secret gallery hewn through, which started within the palace. A trusted man, a young German clock master, took charge of the entrance. A Tatar bodyguard, Ahmed, later fallen in a cavalry charge in the Civil War, was overseeing the northern entrance. Hooded girls rode donkeys in a ravine. At a certain point they had to dismount. Blindfolded, they clambered, clutching a rope, stumbling and falling, with Ahmed at the head. They didn't mind bruises—each scratch was paid for princely.

Once a local beauty sprained her ankle before reaching the northern entrance. She lay on the rocks, unable to move any further. Prince Vorontsov sent over the young German, Max Ebert—

The name leapt out at David like a tiger from Grandpa Osher's silk folding screen. Max Ebert! Clara's uncle had intimately known the secrets of an underground passage to the Vorontsov villa!

> Together with Ahmed, they carried her in their arms. After the belle got delivered to the floor, the Prince found out that the excitement of the trip affected her performance very favorably indeed . . .

When David was returning the book, he heard the librarians' whisper. "And he wraps machine-gun belts around the girls!" "And makes them call his—his you know what—a bazooka!" The matron reluctantly tore herself from picking to pieces the hero of the Civil War and engraved the checkout time in David's pass.

David walked down the stairs. His mind was like his gun's scope. And at the crossbars was his wife's uncle, Max Ebert.

Thank you, Clara.

Tomorrow he'd revisit Lubyanka. He'd have a close look at Max Ebert's files. He'd memorize as much as possible.

Behind him the guards started another relief . . .

Outside the palace, a cart with two grays in harness waited in Ivan Street, the whole back of the cart taken by a crate. The driver in a Circassian coat threw down a running board for Budyonny and his red-velvety date, even as a limousine swept past them into Senate Square. The auto pulled up at the pillared main entrance. A gorilla of a bodyguard jumped out and swung open the back door. A somewhat shortish man alighted, dressed in a light-grey cover coat with a beaver shawl collar. Before another bodyguard pushed David rudely off the square, he took in the clean-shaven cheeks and the cold, dull eyes behind the pince-nez of the Party curator of State Security, Lavrenty P. Beria.

Budyonny spat on the ground.

CHAPTER TWENTY

"Zena wouldn't draw me another pass to the Lubyanka." Meir Kovner raised his eyes from his scribbling. "Oh, it's you. What would you suggest for town names in new Prussia?" Meir gazed serenely at his nephew, as his fingers idly drummed on the tabletop. "Should Königsberg revert to Tel Hamelekh or celebrate a contemporary hero?"

David said, "I wonder whether you've heard me, Uncle."

"Heard what?"

"About the pass."

"What about the pass?"

David repeated.

Meir Kovner said, "I told Zena not to."

David gasped. "Uncle!"

"Yes. It's time for you to contribute to the Project Prusa."

"Didn't I say I wanted nothing to do with it?"

"Let out some steam. You want a pass, don't you?"

"You're resorting to blackmail?"

"No. To the market forces."

"To the contemptible market forces."

"Yes. Goods against payment."

David paused. "What exactly do you want?"

Uncle wanted a Five-Year Plan for Scholarly Research at Philosophy Division of Academy of Sciences, People's Democratic Republic of Prussia.

David proposed writing the music for the anthem of People's Democratic Republic of Prussia.

They shook hands on an essay on Civil Acts and Immigration / Naturalization in medieval Prusa.

·176·

David did his bit then and there, sitting at the bottom of Uncle's long conference table. He felt sparked, almost flippant, his morale boosted by his discovery in the Kremlin library.

He wrote:

The boundaries of Prusa were made by treacherous bogs and vast lakes. The Pruses left one access road and dug moats across all the other. The only remaining access they named Checkpoint Charlie in a mocking reference to the Emperor Charlemagne who coveted their land. Along the water barriers they grew the Hedge—two impassable rows to the height of twelve feet: prickly brambles, brier, and wild rose, a watchtower at each turn. Between the rows walked border police. Large yellowish-grey beasts sniffed, halted, strained their leashes—vicious German shepherd dogs, the only German inhabitants of the land. The police ought to be watchful—offenders were resourceful and inventive. They dug tunnels or swam lakes, flied kites, hid in barrels of sauerkraut in merchants' wagons, or squatted in milk churns, a length of reed in the mouth.

Meir Kovner raised his eyes from his reading. "Don't you think it opens to—to misinterpretation?"

David looked up innocently. "Why?"

Meir persisted, unhappily. "I mean, whom were the border police to stop?"

David returned an angelic look. "Trespassers, of course."

"I know, I know." Meir said impatiently. "But it rather looks as if . . . as if they . . ."

David eagerly nodded, three times in a row. "Oh, I know what you mean. Yes, when the dead bodies were found stuck in the swamps, border police were originally confused by their position. They thought that the wretches attempted to *flee* Prusa."

"Aha!" Meir was relieved: he got there without saying the *f*-word. "And what was it indeed?"

"Then they understood. The appearance was wrong. In fact, the trespassers were desperately trying to get *into* the country."

"So why don't you say that in so many words? You should show that Prusa was a magnet for people all over the world!" Meir pushed the pages across the table.

When he received the text back, it showed some corrections. Meir read on.

Every now and then, border police found dead bodies stuck in the quagmire. True, they faced away from Prusa, but it was only because human smugglers, those infamous traffickers in human beings, didn't shrink from any dirty trick to besmirch Prusa. The coyotes turned the corpses around to kick mud back at Prusa!

Yet the desperate Slavs from the eastern forests and bogs beyond the Lithuanian lands wormed their way into Prussia. The illegal immigrants from Rus took any job. Never mind compulsory tattooing and a shameful red star on their clothes—they ran to the swamps and threatened to take their lives as soon as there was talk of deportation back to Rus.

Meir reread the last sentence and stroke out the "red star" with all modifiers.

Many of their females were smashing beauties, what with their blue eyes and high cheekbones, but they had no chance of marrying a local because their children couldn't be Pruses: Comrade Mark the Founder decreed in his Manifesto that the mother line was the sole bearer of national belonging. So if some love-stricken couple persisted, they bred bastards.

Their quandary oddly paralleled that of *marquises*, to which patrician category belonged any man with his family name on the following list (schoolchildren memorized it along with verbs' conjugation paradigms):

Marcus, Marcos, Marca, Markman, Markey, Markson, Markham, Marks,
Markoff, Markin, Markish, Marquet, Markensohn and Markisyan,

Marquand, Marquette and Marconi, Marcaurelius, Marcabru,
then Markelov, and Markovic, and Markover, and Marqué,
plus Markovnikov, Marcuse, and Marcantoni: amen.

Those men of mark could only marry a virgin with a birthmark on
a buttock, new brides being certified annually during the holiday
festivities. Tante Brokha's underground business, *A-1 Strawberry
Marks and Hymens Installed,* flourished.

Uncle Meir pursed his lips, but said nothing.

To Provide for Better Protection of the Marquisate Prerogatives, a
group of elders brought a motion before the Supreme Council of
Prusa, the Sanhedrin. They proposed putting a fence around
virginity. A fence? A fence around *what?* No, no; we mean a
secondary virginity check, mouth cavity examination. How're you
going to go about it? Well, leave it to professionals who look into
the mouth day in, day out. Which exposed the draft legislation as
the intrigue of toothdrawers jealous of the privileges that the *Law of
Marquises* had afforded to midwives and skin men. Instead, in the
spirit of Markism, a law was promulgated to allow immigration from
Marquesas Islands. The primitive savages tattooed all over their olive-
slick bodies weren't recognized as Pruses, but they fought in the
Prussian army. They were in the first line to meet the approaching
hordes of mounted invaders, those hideous creatures wrapped in
black white-crossed cloaks, standing on all fours on the backs of
their horses. And when a Marquesan javelin found its target, a huge
black dog plopped down to the ground, howling! Those battles
cemented the brotherhood of the Pruses and their Marquesan
auxiliaries. It came to test when five years after a war a transgression
came to light. Inadvertently, a Marquesan warrior had been buried
in the Tel-Hamelekh cemetery. Never mind! This hero had earned
with his blood his place in the Land of Prussia! His remains were
ceremoniously transferred outside the ivy-grown outer walls. As the
body was downed into a pit, a military orchestra played and poets

intoned, "Elsewhere, graveyards guard their bounds against apostates and suicides, but at the Prussian burial grounds it's Marquesan heroes who rest outside!"

Such interments became known as "joining the angels." Few people remembered the original phrase, "joining Angelus." Fewer still could trace it back to the Pruses' Judean past.

It all started when a wealthy Roman patrician sat at the window booth at his Jerusalem branch of *Banca Vespasiana*. Mark walked by. He scooped sesterces and held them to his nose. The coins didn't smell. 'Follow me,' he said to Angelus, and the banker got up and followed him. From then on, Mark's daily bread had always been buttered. Yes, it wasn't buzzards on a mountaintop but waiters from Alexandria restaurants who carried wicker baskets along the Heptastadium causeway. Pulleys hoisted pork chops, oysters and Falernum wine atop the lighthouse, forty-stories high, where Mark wrote.

When Angelus died, his non-Prussian corpse caused controversy bordering on riots. The compromise solution was a sepulcher built just outside the cemetery's walls. Predictably, it fell easy prey to grave looters. They ransacked the vault but found no riches. Angelus's fortune had gone, eaten up by his life-long support of Mark. The sole object found in the hands of the deceased in the bare stone sarcophagus was a scroll with two signatures on it.

Mark had rewarded Angelus's loyalty with co-authorship of the *Manifesto*.

"Disgusting." Meir Kovner crossed out the whole Angelus story. "You have no sense of propriety." The same fate befell Tante Brocha's shop. "There is no place in our society for your sexual fantasies," he muttered while expunging the unsuccessful draft legislature. "And the whole Rus episode won't fly." Meir struck out that part as well. "The contacts between Prussia and Rus were of a friendly, cooperative nature. They ought to be highlighted rather than sneered upon."

He scanned the paragraphs that had escaped his blue pencil, then resolutely x-ed every page.

David's next attempt was as follows.

The tale of Dodo the Archer made its way to all school textbooks in Prusa.

At the World Marpessaic Games on the Isle of Paros, the Pruse teams went places heavily guarded by duennas in grey robes. The objective was to prevent defections—to wit, defections of the locals or other nationals, who were on the lookout for an opportunity to snick into Pruses' rank and shout "Eyzl!" which meant jackass in Yiddish, to the duped chaperone. (Here, of course, we find the origin of the common European root *azil*, asylum.)

Those protective measures were introduced in the wake of the Sixty-fourth Marpessaics, when the entire papal archery team rushed into the Pruses' ranks and demanded asylum in Prussia.

The International Marpessaic Committee reacted quickly. It isolated the troublemakers in the Markos Grotto.

Candles crackled in heavy candelabras placed on the sarcophagus. Their light barely penetrated the gloom at the back wall, where the archers' white berets with red pompons punctuated the blackness. The head of the Pruse delegation explained that the archers were ill informed—that circumcision would change nothing, and besides, it had been discontinued as far back as Comrade Mark the Founder.

An archer named Dodo came forward. He was broad-shouldered, redheaded, and long-nosed.

He turned his satchel upside down over the sarcophagus lid. Scraps of parchment, frail papyrus scrolls, and alabaster writing tablets fell on the engraving "Mark" in red quartzite.

"Here you are," he said. "All forty-three of them."

The Pruse official's fat face contorted into a grimace of disgust. His two fingers hooked the scrap of the parchment that had landed next to him and took it to the candlelight.

He read aloud:

"Five dinars for eating the cardinal's marrow-pudding, two dinars for praying knees up—"

"No," the archer told him. "Wrong side."

The official turned over the soiled scrap. "This is evidence provided by the management of *Da Salome* that the girl Elana is the fruit of Nurgit's womb."

"Elana. My mom," said Dodo shyly.

"And Nurgit?"

"My granny. My beloved granny. *Fructus ventris Rosae*. Here you are. The compendium."

"The—what?"

"I've summarized it. Tsipora bore Rivka, Rivka bore Nekhama, Nekhama—"

"What are you trying to say?"

"You see, *Da Salome* has never taken a girl from without."

The officials went to see the papal nuncio. They found him in the baths. He talked, if reluctantly, keeping his eye on the naked competitors horse-playing. Yes, that's right. Centuries back in time, after that infamous rebellion in Judea, the Roman legionaries brought young women back home. They were the wives and daughters of defeated Paruses, a legitimate booty of the conqueror. After a term in their captors' beds, the girls were put up in an establishment of their own. The merry house in the Trastevere, *Da Salome*, thrived on through centuries. The girls catered to Roman potters, mariners of Ostia, Appian beggars, and patresfamilias from adjacent apartment blocks. But gradually they developed a more sophisticated patronage.

The most memorable of all was chestnut-haired, green-eyed Tsylia. A poet had commented on her wide international clientele. The nuncio quoted the Latin verses:

> You take a Vandal to bed and a Brit and a Dacian
> You are a Spaniard's delight and a Gaul's ruination
> From Alexandria come your Egyptian admirers
> And from the Red Sea an Indian brings you sapphires
> Nor do you flee the embrace of a circumcised Jew

Nor is a Hun's proposition rejected by you.

The last line alluded to Attila's personal envoy who, delirious over the ministrations received, interceded prostrate before his lord on behalf of the defenseless town. Attila tore off the envoy's testicles but spared Rome.

The girls' trademark was their top professionalism. Take the legendary Rachel, Tsylia's buxomly great-great-granddaughter. Even as the waters of the Tiber, once again flooding, reached her bed, she kept uttering breathlessly to the Emperor Justinian's general, eunuch Narses: "More, more, you brute! By Priapus, what a push!"

And yes, all the employees of *Da Salome* had been born and raised in-house, mother teaching daughter the craft of making men happy.

Back in his inn, the Pruse official arranged the forty-three birth certificates in a sequence. Let's see, he muttered. The mother-progenitrix, the originator of the line, had endowed her daughter with one half of Parusian blood. The latter's daughter had retained a quarter, the next in line an eighth . . . The official sat sweating, multiplying two by two and the result by two again, forty-two times so, marking each successive certificate with the result. He was grateful for having learned the new fad, the Arabic numbers; still, he quickly ran out of space. Nor did he know how to pronounce the numbers. Here you are, he said at last. The monster of fifteen digits. Over a thousand of thousands of thousands of thousands of thousands. Against that much of non-Parusian blood, Dodo's mother had but one part of Parusian. Nothing at all. A totally negligible quantity. A drop in the ocean, literally. Even assuming that a couple of the fathers in the line happened to be Paruses—*nec recutitorum fugis inguina Iudaeorum*—it would hardly affect the outcome.

Not so, said Dodo. No fancy arithmetic of murky Islamic provenance was invited. At each reproduction, it was the mother alone who counted. Both the *Manifesto* and the Roman principle of *mater certa* ruled so. Both spoke in his behalf. As his ancestor Tsylia would have said, her ass was international, but her womb, Parusian.

The Marpessaic Committee had to face it. In the small cells at the Tiber, unquestionably Parusian girls had been born and procreated other girls of immaculate Parusian pedigree.

Dodo won his case. The remaining week on the island he spent partying with Prussian athletes and learning about his historic motherland. He left for his new country sailing solo around Europe, escorted by three boats of guards of honor, Prussian slingers. He was shot and killed in the Messina Straight. The incident was pronounced a tragic mistake. The guards, unfamiliar with advanced seagoing techniques, only knew that a step to the right or a step to the left was considered an attempt to escape, and Dodo did his sailing by tacking. In this connection, the hypothesis that Dodo had begun having second thoughts about Prussia should be soundly rejected . . .

The other papal archers had to return to the brutal non-Prussian world, which robbed people of morality, happiness, and sexual potency and reduced them to stinking running dogs.

Meir Kovner finished reading and set David's text aside.

"I can use but a fraction of this. Sexual exploitation of proletarian Parusian women in slave-owning Rome and the feudal Papal State. The ardent desire of the working masses to live in the just and happy Prussian society. That's all. Too bad your Rus part—"

"I can fix it," David told him. "Want a story of the Rus pagan Prince Vladimir picking a religion for himself and his people? He had to choose one of the three great monotheistic creeds. Judaism was an option."

Meir Kovner shook his head. "No. I don't trust you with so delicate a matter. You're irreverent and irresponsible. Besides, the Pruses had nothing to do with religion. Theirs was a secular, progressive enterprise purposed to liberate the Jewish working masses from all sort of oppression. Rabbis figured prominently on their enemy list."

"Sure. And I know why. It was the rabbis who caused the reduction of the daily wages to one *pros*, a half a loaf."

"Now did they?"

"You bet. In days gone by, at the end of the working day the Sadducee landowner dispensed the whole pita bread to each laborer. But the rabbis insisted on saying grace. So they said a *brakhah* and broke the bread into two *proses,* and the landowner took the two *proses* from their hands and gave a *pros* to the Paruse on the rabbi's right and another *pros* to the Paruse on his left."

"Those clericals in the exploiters' service." Uncle Meir scribbled fast. "The Pruses never forgot the offense. They embraced atheism."

"But they had to be careful about the word. It sounded too close to Mattheism."

Uncle Meir put the pen down. "Although in my ordeals, I found some merit in religion."

"Did you?"

"When you're at the bottom, it pays to know your Job."

"Am I hearing that you'd never had any doubts about the Cause?"

"God gave you a pair of good ears." Meir Kovner scratched his pate and sighed. "All right, I'll pick this or that from your notes. Zena will write the pass. Just for tomorrow. After which we talk."

Just for tomorrow was fine with David.

PART FOUR

CHAPTER TWENTY-ONE

B ack in October, on Arnold Hramoy's last day in Moscow, Joseph Ognev phoned to tell him the news. Meir Kovner was back in Moscow. How about the two of them calling on him, tonight?

Arnold thought quickly. In a voice trembling with—with joy, he said he would do all he could, tied up as he was on this last day before the departure.

He put down the receiver, his thoughts in turmoil.

Using the phone—how irresponsible—did Ognev blight Arnold's trip? Meir in Moscow—wonderful, of course, but in which capacity?

His agony ended in twenty minutes when another call, this time from the delegation's head, suggested that Arnold go to see his old friend on the happy occasion of his return to an important party position.

Arnold stormed into Meir's apartment, held him in a bear hug, and uncorked the French champagne he'd saved from his last Paris trip. Right afterwards arrived a photographer sent by the Central Committee.

Even Ognev's resentment didn't spoil the reunion.

Arnold Hramoy received the oversized envelope with the photograph on the platform of the Yaroslav railway terminal. Meir's face had undergone retouching to dispose with the ashen tint.

Arnold had been carrying the picture through his American tour, ready for an occasion. The moment arrived in a hotel lobby in New York. Arnold laughed amiably at the haggard man with a scar and a thick German accent who had asked him about Meir

Kovner and a slave camp. In a loud voice intended to reach the rest of the delegation and above all the KGB chaperone, Arnold said, "At the spot in question, there is no slave camp but a thriving new town with the Semyon Budyonny Regional Library and the Bremen Town Musicians School of Music for miners' children. And a fine restaurant, where they treated me to delicious Siberian meat dumplings. As for my dear friend Meir Kovner, on the eve of my departure I saw him in his Moscow apartment."

He produced the photo from his briefcase. On the glossy paper, Arnold was hugging Meir's shoulders, both faces radiant with smiles. The scar-faced man gazed long at them, at the Lenin on the wall, and whispered, "Dat ist right. Dat ist his place." "It's recent, you see," Arnold said unnecessarily. "Yeah," whispered the haggard man. His eyes traveled between the picture and Arnold's face and back to the picture. Then at last he noticed: in the background, Ognev puffed away at his pipe. The scar-faced man's jaw dropped. He looked up with a silent question. Arnold, also silently, gave a nod.

I didn't lie, he thought as he rode in the Embassy limousine to the final rally.

Twenty minutes later, he scanned the tiers of Carnegie Hall packed to capacity. He shared the stage with the rest of the Soviet delegation and a very senior diplomat from the Soviet Embassy. Seven years ago next week, he had sat up there, at an unseemly distance from the stage. An immigrant named Dora Goodman, whose family he had known back in Russia, had given him a balcony ticket for her son's gala performance; it proved very handy indeed, what with the steep price of eighty-five cents, and one wouldn't even dream about a box seat at $2.75. A memorable evening it was. That's when Arnold fell in love with the King of Swing. At that time, the German-American Bund and Jewish Veterans of War fought in the streets. Now the Bund was history and Arnold a guest of honor and a hot item. *Fine and dandy*, isn't it, Benny? He squinted to the right. The editor-in-chief of a leading Jewish establishment newspaper, dressed in a three-piece business suit and a polka-dot bowtie, shared the stage with the delegation.

Arnold smiled at him. The pundit's gold-rimmed glasses flashed back a greeting.

The blow came forty minutes into the meeting, when Arnold completed his answer to a question—they should rest assured, he said, that Judaism, like any other religion, was safe from harm in the Soviet Union; his own name, Hramoy, came from *khram*, the Russian for *temple* (*yes, yes*, rustle ran through the Russian language experts, that is, nearly everyone in the room), and Arnold was carrying that name proudly. Then a man rose to his feet in the middle of the orchestra seats. He wore round spectacles and a brown wool jacket with yellow leather elbow patches, and he clutched a small tin case. A petty salesman with his samples, perhaps. Or rather a jeweler, reluctant to leave his precious cargo unattended for a moment. Straining his voice, he asked the distinguished members of the Soviet delegation to expand on the postwar plans that the Soviet government might have in store for their country's Jewish population.

A buzz of short exchanges ran around, whereupon a hush descended on the house.

The Soviet delegates squinted their eyes at the very senior diplomat. Failing to read from his impenetrable face, the jovial writer, the delegation's head, set his eyebrows bobbing, jointly and separately, and started speaking. Together with all Soviet peoples . . . healing the wounds . . . the assistance of the American Jewish community . . . grateful in advance—

But the jeweler remained standing by his seat. He shook his head.

"No. I mean administrative plans for the Jews. A statehood."

From the upper tiers, murmurs spattered down. The very senior Soviet diplomat from Washington sat stony-faced. The members of the delegation went into a whispering conference. None of them had the faintest inkling of the cause of the excitement. It seemed that something new had happened while they were away from home. Could New York Jews have learned about the Crimean project? It had been in cold storage since the twenties.

"All right, all right," the delegation's head said at last. They had petitioned the Soviet Government. Now that the Crimea, the home of the pre-war Jewish agricultural colonies, had been rid of the traitorous Tatars and Germans, wasn't it only natural to establish a Jewish autonomy there? A Republic basking in the sun, a California at the Black Sea. Realization of that project will take huge investments, therefore the help of the American Jewry—

"Cut the bull!" A heckler's call came from the peanut gallery. Many swiveled to see, but the gallery vanished in the darkness. Instead, the bowtie pundit rose up in his seat on the stage. He opined it was counterproductive to talk on so sensitive a topic before hearing from the office of the President. The editor won scant applause, but three men rose at once in the orchestra and asked sarcastically why the Jewish worker should take his cue from the president-capitalist; and didn't they have a better source for inspiration over there in heroic Russia; and wouldn't it be wiser to listen to what the envoys of Marshal Stalin had to say on the matter?

Stalin? An acne-cheeked youth with a barely started mustache and fiery eyes jumped up as if kicked in the coccyx. The butcher of Leon Trotsky would end up in the ash heap of history, cheek by jowl with his chum of the recent past, Adolf Hitler. The young man called for no support to Stalin's crafty designs for Jews—no more so than to the Zionist chimera in Palestine, a colonial outlet for Jewish American bourgeoisie. While the youth's neighbors pulled him down by his cuffs, someone of unmistakably professorial comportment and a thick Central-European accent rose up to speak about the mortal danger to the Jewish spirit which lay in the very idea of Jewish statehood. Jeers erupted. Exile and wandering had formed the Jew, the professor raised his voice, whereas statehood would trivialize him, turn him into yet another Salvadoran. So violent did the booing become at that point that only disjoined scraps of the professor's speech struggled through. Arnold strained to hear: ". . . the fomenter of the creative impulses of humanity . . . evaded the chauvinistic traps of blood and soil . . . great not in spite of his rootlessness, but because of it . . ."

Amidst the general hubbub of shouts, insults, and arm waving, someone black-hatted, white-breasted, and long-skirted walked down the aisle. In his right hand the man clutched something oblong and cylindrical. "Comrades, Comrades," whispered the very senior diplomat. Arnold felt small and vulnerable on the huge stage. On reaching its edge, the black-hatted man swung his arm and loped the Thing. The delegation's head squeaked softly. The bundle didn't quite reach their seats as it fell on the proscenium and unfolded flat. The huge letters, *Mazel Tov!* stared in Arnold's eyes in a mocking reference to a song which he'd heard in this hall, but this print was in Yiddish, which Benny's concert brochure couldn't be, and then Arnold took in the rest of the line, the six-column banner in the thick newspaper which lay there, the first page up, "*Mazel Tov!*—Congratulations: Deathblow to G-dless Enterprise," and the paper's title above, *Der Williamsburger.* The diplomat's glance nailed the newspaper to the floor and forbade its recovery. In a high-pitched, shrill voice, the man in the black gaberdine denounced the insolent project of the Zionist apostates, impertinence in the face of the Lord, a Jewish state in Eretz Isroel without the Messiah's okay. "What are they trying to do, manipulate the Almighty? To claim His power and the might of His hand for themselves?" But a Jewish state in Europe was a different story. The man voiced no objections. In fact, he supported it, provided the capital city was Lubavitchi and the Grand Rebbe appointed the czar. Something else that President Roosevelt should negotiate was a permanent seat at the soon-to-be United Nations Security Council. And yes, duty-free status for Antwerp and Trieste!

Now a dozen men sprang to their feet and shouted at once. A voice stood out: "Give God a break!" and another one: "A Jewish foot won't touch the land soaked in Jewish blood!" At this point, a shaggy-haired man, who reminded Arnold of brawny Jewish draymen back in the Ukraine of his youth, cut them short with his mighty bass. Of all the trash he'd just heard, he said into the instant silence, one thing alone did make sense. Take it! Accept what had been offered; accept it on behalf of the Jewish people.

Receive that land as a legitimate booty—and transfer the Palestine Arabs up there. Let the Russians have that dirty, cheating, quarrelsome flock on their front lawn, whereas the Jews would have the whole of the Land of Israel, on the both sides of the Jordan River!

The very senior diplomat, red-faced, tugged Arnold by the cuff. The Soviet delegation, smiling and bowing into the bedlam below and above, retired to the wings. "Crazy people," said the diplomat, wiping his brow. "Talking sheer nonsense. I wonder who leaked it to them." Leaked what, asked the members. But the Embassy man was already gone.

On his arrival to Moscow, Arnold Hramoy went to the Presidium of the Academy. There he tried to sound out his chances in the upcoming election to full membership in Academia, an all-important step for a Soviet scholar—what with its prestige and privilege. The ballot, even if secret, had never, ever gone against the Party recommendation. Arnold believed he had cinched the nomination. Wasn't his American assignment further evidence of the Party's trust in him? But his contacts evaded answer, which worried Arnold.

In the corridors of the Academy he stumbled on Meir's former cadre, Andronikos. The professional revolutionary turned scholar—give me a break! The Greek bragged. He was working on an arch-important, hyper-secret project redressing historical wrongs. "Soon, very soon an ancient *dimokratia* would shine anew with socialist luster!" Arnold smiled and nodded on cue. But it clicked together—Andronikos and the scene in Carnegie Hall. Right from that corridor Arnold went to see Meir Kovner in the Party's Central Committee.

He completed his account of the American trip to Meir, speaking across the latter's ministerial-size desk. The Moscow winter day was wearing out. Car honks were barely audible through the double windowpanes, muffled by awe for the high office.

"I arranged for the leak," Meir said. His skin had lost that ashen hue that had struck Arnold back in October. "As a trial balloon."

Arnold's eyebrows shot up in a sham surprise. Inwardly, he congratulated himself. Once more his antennae hadn't failed him.

Meir pushed a sheaf of pamphlets and assorted sheets across the desk. Arnold read them, turning pages almost continuously— he'd mobilized his extraordinary skill of instant reading.

He tried hard to hide his anxiety under a mask of benign interest.

The Party hacks had concocted an absurd story. Well, not worse than some others. Crazier claims had been made. "Masterpieces" were "discovered" and "lost," but not before "a copy was made." Forgery went on even in empirical fields, such as biological science given as a fief to a charlatan agronomist. Often—alas, too often— instead of crystal-clear currents of gospel truth, stinking sewage coursed through the gutters of the Academy, whirling filthy garbage . . . Now this parody of Arnold's theory of the European languages' migration from Middle East.

He smiled, his eyes alert. "Come to think of it, the Führer will be thrilled to find that he speaks a corruption of Yiddish. You can bet your life against his foreskin."

"So what do you think?" Meir Kovner asked cautiously.

"It should be put in perspective." Arnold played for time. "In view of the new discoveries—and there are some proofs, you're saying," he ruffled the papers—"paleozoological or others, aren't they?"

Meir blinked and said nothing.

"Keeping our full trust in the Party and—" Arnold shuffled the papers again—"and the progressive scholars of the world. Still, some ungenerous people may request hard evidence."

He walked to the window and pressed his thumb to the cold glass. He'd hurt it with a paperweight: he'd brought along a Varga calendar from his trip and hammered a nail in the wall behind Meir's chair, all by himself.

Arnold heard Meir say, "You know, Zarnitsyn doesn't ask tough questions. He's going to turn this theory into an indestructible vehicle for his election to the Academy."

The thrust hit home. Arnold managed not to turn, but he started. Now he knew why the functionary in the Academy's Presidium had hidden his eyes from him. The coveted prize was about to fly away and land at the Institute of Marxism. It was obscene: for years, Zarnitsyn had been known for denying his Jewish origins, and now he was to be elected for the project of a Jewish state! Zarnitsyn's intrigue had to be countered with something distinctive, something bearing a signal of Professor Hramoy's intellect and erudition . . .

Meir's voice went on. "I'm concerned with the Yiddish-to-German part. Some may say it's a weak point."

You bet it is.

Now, nobody like Arnold to give it academic respectability. Here he had something unique to sell. Something Hramoy–esque.

He slowly turned to face Meir.

"The weak point? Not necessarily." Arnold came around Meir's desk and perched his butt casually on the edge. Meir hastily turned over a page. Arnold registered verses: *From Alexandria come your Egyptian admirers / and from the Red Sea . . .* It rang a bell. Later, later . . .

Now that the hands had been thrown up, Arnold felt exited. The winds of inspiration lifted and carried him.

"Let me tell you," he said, "about a little known episode of the German Reformation. At that time, Martin Luther lent his endorsement to a pamphlet, author unknown. The book went through many reprints. It warned good citizens against despicable charlatans. It denounced their tricks, swindles, and con games."

"The Pope's legates," Meir nodded. "The vendors of indulgencies."

"Not this time. Luther aimed at beggars who roamed the

roads of Germany. The falsely sick, quack-doctors, pilgrims to no shrine. Now, why would Luther, in the middle of political, social and religious turmoil, bother to write his *Vorrede*, Introduction, and attack the community of rogues?"

"Did he? He may've had a good reason."

"Such as? I wonder what it could be?" Smiling Arnold invited Meir to give him a good advice.

Meir Kovner grimaced. "The beggars were the reserve of the peasant revolution, weren't they? The revolution that Martin Luther inspired but then feared and betrayed. He went to the other side. That's why."

"Ugh. There could be other motives, too."

"Luther abhorred idleness. And he had an acute sense of truthfulness, hadn't he?"

Arnold nodded. "Granted, all that may have played a role. But there was yet another factor, Meir. The outcasts spoke their own private language. They called it *Rotwelsch*. The linguists know it as Beggar's Welsh. A good deal of its vocabulary was rooted in Hebrew and Aramaic."

Meir shrugged. "*Rotwelsch?* No big deal. I heard it spoken in the port of Hamburg. An argot of the underworld, isn't it? Their thing for privacy? Like—like—"

"—like the Cockney cant or the Russian *blatnaya fenya*? On the face of it, yes. But Luther saw *Rotwelsch* for what it was—the work of the Jews, and he said so in so many words. Now look. There are plenty of Yiddishisms in Beggar's Welsh. As for the Hebraisms—they were also adopted by Yiddish. They weren't independent borrowings. They came by way of Yiddish."

Meir Kovner blinked. "You're saying—" He broke in midsentence. "What are you driving at?"

"You will see it presently. Now what do you think—when did the records of Beggar's Welsh appear first?"

Meir shrugged again. "How could I know? With the first steps of capitalism? When the intensification of exploitation led to pauperization of the proletariat?"

Arnold shook his head. "Much, much earlier. The truly striking thing is that the first recorded evidence of Beggar's Welsh falls in 1250. And this is contemporary with the campaign of the Teutonic Order in Prussia! The language was born even as their invasion of Prussia brought about the most immediate contacts between the Knights and the Pruses."

Meir started. "Did you ever!"

Arnold smiled encouragingly. "At that time, as you have suggested with remarkable insight, the Knights from the Grand Master down set to internalizing Yiddish. Look at the records of that transitional period, at the occasional snippets of Latin-cum-Beggar-Welsh that have come to us. Like this macaronic pearl: *Quare ne guarin du tzi metina?* Why weren't you at matins? wrote a prior to a truant knight. How did the knight reply to the inquiry? Lost in ages."

Arnold made a pause, letting Meir absorb it all before the masterstroke. "Beggar's Welsh wasn't an artificially created argot, after all. It was an archaic stage of German, a station on the route, as the German language developed from the Yiddish of the Pruses onwards. It lends a healthy substantiation to your extraordinary hypothesis, Meir. This is the missing link, which should fill your *Origins* with substance and weight!"

Stretching it, of course. Well, *Paris vault bien une messe.*

Meir Kovner couldn't believe his luck. Such a bonanza. And Arnold Hramoy's reputation to back it!

"The original idea wasn't mine," he said, proud of his honesty.

Arnold beamed back. "But I feel your style, Meir."

"My style. If I could write like Martin Luther. So he—"

"He set to the task of forging the German literary language from the raw material. It took a good deal of smoothing, fitting, and conforming. Luther's anti-beggar *Vorrede* was an important step. He cleansed the contemporary German thoroughly. No trace of that 'damned, rejected race' remained in the language save for the biblical vocabulary, such as hallelujah, amen, etc. But the peculiar tongue of the Knights didn't perish."

Arnold pointed his finger upwards, calling for attention. The gesture was unnecessary. Meir Kovner listened, enthralled.

"When the Reformation swirled into East Prussia and the Order dissolved into chaos, their language went underground! The underworld adopted it and made it their own."

Meir chuckled. "Are you saying the robber knights bequeathed their language to the highway robbers?"

Arnold was building on his success. "You may put it that way. So Luther learned the limits of his power. He may have purged the German books and formal language, but he proved powerless vis-à-vis the jargon of the vagabonds. Beggar's Welsh is still spoken in Germany, alongside other dialects. The underworld keeps using its Yiddishist patterns and Hebrew borrowings. To the researcher's delight—to your luck, Meir— the ancient stage of the German language has survived in oral tradition. As if the dinosaurs descended from Arthur Conan Doyle's *Lost World* and walked in here, into the Central Committee, begging for vivisection."

Silence fell, in which Meir listened to the measured steps of the primordial giants in the corridors. He often felt sorry that revolutionary activity had left little room for his education. How masterly did Hramoy make his improvisation! How naturally it came to him! He just sank his long hairy arm to the bottom of a beggar's sack and retrieved a live dinosaur! The walking proof of the Yiddish-to-German hypothesis, and Martin Luther astride, his star witness! So odd, wasn't it, that Arnold should totally lack in the sphere of music. That fact somewhat reconciled Meir with the overbearing superiority of his friend's personality.

"Arnold," he said. "You've heard—read—from both sides. The Institute of Marxism and the Marxist-Leninist Joint School. How do you feel? Which team should assume the leadership role in the Project Prusa? Lend your enlightened judgment."

Hramoy shot a quick glance at him.

"What can I tell you about the amateur philologists? They've made a sorry mess of the letters *samekh, sin,* and *shin.* The correct self-appellation of the Pharisee was *Perush*. With the *sh*-sound, as in *Prussian* uttered by the English and Americans."

"These we'll do without," Meir Kovner said quickly. "Just tell me who you think should lead. The Institute and the School are at each other's throats. Two harlots before the king. They'd rather have the baby ripped apart than handed over to the rival. Perhaps you prefer a Solomonic ruling? Such as, the Project Prusa should find its home at your Division of Linguistics. How about that?"

He smiled broadly. He'd warmed to Arnold. He was offering the king's gift to his dear old friend.

Inwardly, Arnold exulted. His presentation had carried the day. But he kept his feelings inside.

He looked into Meir's eyes.

"Tell me, old boy, am I reading correctly your intentions? Are you going to proclaim a Jewish state in East Prussia?"

For a moment or two, Meir Kovner said nothing. Then he nodded.

Were he religious, he would have felt himself the Messiah.

CHAPTER TWENTY-TWO

Snow crunched under the feet of Meir Kovner and his nephew as they walked a footpath in a park. Yesterday's fluffy snow lay on the barren branches and crow nests. In the distance, an ice-bound river glittered with black unfrozen patches. The day was bright, sunny, and frosty. They were alone except for a couple of cross-country skiers emerging now and then from the woods.

"The door in the Senate's central court," asked David, "What's so special about it?"

"Which one?"

"The green one. Under the cupola."

"Oh, that one. The basement connects to quite a few passages. Ancient poterns. New tunnels."

"Leading where?"

"To a subway circuit. To bomb shelters. To command posts. To the Mausoleum in Red Square."

"What for? Does Stalin secretly come over to enjoy the view of dead Lenin?"

Meir stopped short and swung about to face his nephew. "Go on, keep kidding. Now, what have you decided?"

David took him by the elbow.

"Listen to me, Uncle Meir. The Project Prusa reeks of a dangerous provocation. A Jewish nation held by the short hairs in Stalin's grasp. At this moment, he needs the Jewish Antifascist Committee to impress the American ally. But after the war? He's sending off entire nations to Siberia and Kazakhstan. Where will he stop? The Jews are to help him legitimize the new acquisition; afterwards we'll become one people too many."

·201·

"How can he? What will he bring up against the Jews?" Meir's voice sounded unsure. "You cannot pin cooperation with Hitler on Jews. We aren't Tatars or Chechens."

"Stalin can do without—you know his ways."

Meir shuddered under the critical eye of a Stalin at the crossroads of two alleys. The Father of All Soviet Peoples except for his Tatar, Chechen, ethnic German, Karachai, Balkar, Ingush, Kalmuk children. He'd chased them away from home, disowned them with his chastising, cast-iron hand, and then put it in the breast of his trench coat, closer to his cast-iron heart, and frozen in cast-iron rigidity, larger-than-life, epaulets of snow on his shoulders . . .

Was it the Jews' turn to join the community of ostracized?

Rubbish. Meir's nephew was grossly exaggerating.

David went on. "Sorry, Uncle, but I'm afraid you live in a fool's paradise. Don't you see that the romance of the Soviet power with the Jews is over? That your project is an anachronism? While you were—away, the very essentials of the Soviet policy changed. Yes, the Jews have been enjoying front-row seats for a while, but the front row also makes a better target. I cannot pinpoint it, but there is a specific trap in Stalin's design. Anyway, in the long run a Jewish state sandwiched between Russia and Germany is but a leaf of lettuce atop the Polish ham. Just think of all the trials and tribulations that have fallen upon the Poles."

During that monologue Meir Kovner jerked his eyebrows and twitched his nose, having difficulty staying calm. "And yet the Poles have their own state."

"Because they have roots there. History. Myths. Traditions."

Now Meir's feelings broke through with long pent-up indignation.

"And what am I doing? Why am I urging you to join me? You only criticize, but people around you are busy with positive activity. They're working hard so that the Jews in Prussia have their chronicles and annals, their poetic legends. The immortal Manifesto. The Great March to the North. The evergreen Prussian epos, the Gilgele."

"All phony."

Meir gasped at the unfairness of the accusation. "Ha! You shouldn't use that word too loosely, David. Do you think that other nations' myths are any better? That Galileo whispered his aside '*and yet it moves*'? Marie-Antoinette's pretty lips uttered '*let them eat cake*'? George Washington's cherry tree—how much truth you think was in that story?"

"That tree has sunk its roots into the American consciousness because it grew up in American soil. Similarly, the Germans have been living in East Prussia for seven hundred years. German kings traveled to Königsberg for coronation. Hoffmann with his fantastic world comes from East Prussia—"

"Tell me more about Hoffmann, Dovidke. And about Kant, and Käthe Kollwitz, won't you? Who else of the great and the good were born there?"

David exhaled puff after white puff. "The land's as German as sauerkraut!"

"So what? You rename sauerkraut liberty cabbage, and it's no longer German! I'm happy for Hoffmann and Frau Kollwitz. But do me a favor and suggest a home for the Jews, too. A desert island. Is it in Palestine? I hate to break this to you, but empty it ain't. There are some living creatures down there, and I'm not talking about camels."

"The Jews had their kingdoms there. No need to make their history out of thin air!"

"Kingdoms-shmingdoms! Herzl was panhandling for any slice of land on the earth for his Jewish state. Africa, South America. Can you imagine his happiness if a piece of prime real estate in Europe had fallen in his lap?"

Meir took off his astrakhan *papakha*. He wiped sweat from his brow and thrust the cap back on.

"Mark it well, David: nobody around here—nobody!—feels for Germany as strongly as I do. But the Germans are to lose East Prussia anyway. It's up for grabs. Don't we deserve it more than anybody else?"

"Acquisition of a lost property is still thievery. I want no added cause for the enmity between the Jews and the Germans. This one will block an eventual reconciliation for generations!"

Meir ran out of patience. "You're pipe-dreaming about reconciliation—at *this* moment? You a castle-builder! A knight-errant! Rescuing German ladies in distress—why did you go poking your nose into that mess in the first place?"

"Because it was the right thing to do!"

"But there are right things we do and others that we don't. You must be sick! And what did you achieve anyway? New gangs of troops may've come. Raped them all over again. Ten times a day, some women've been."

They stood in the alley, glaring each other down. Somewhere below the escarpment chugged a train. Two youngsters slid on the trail between them, the tips of their felt top boots in the leather loops of their skis.

Meir Kovner broke the pause.

"Now you listen here, David. It's a grand objective, a Jewish socialist state in Europe. Not in a Birobidjan on the Chinese border, where good Communists walk around through the clouds of gnats, hatted and buttoned up like Hassidim. Not in mandated Palestine. Ha! Herzl, the little heart! Turning the Jews into a Near Eastern, Asian nation—just think of the sheer stupidity of that! We are Europeans! The Jews—the Ashkenazim— have lived in Europe for at least two thousand years. Longer than— than the Hungarians! The Jewish creativity thrived on European soil! Look at the turn-of-the-century Jewish Vienna—it was the quintessence of Europeism! Think what'll happen when the Jews gain a permanent place in Europe, in full right and equality! Hitler came pretty close to clearing Europe of Jews. If the rest give up on Europe and withdraw to Palestine—I don't want him to celebrate victory down there, in the hell where he belongs! No! The Jews will fulfill their historic mission to get Nationalism and Communism married, and they'll do it in the heart of Europe!"

David shook his head.

"Uncle, it beats me. How can you fail to see that the Project Prusa is nonsense? Explosive nonsense! Our Fifth Point will soon mean something like Article Five of the Nuremberg Laws—remember the one that had stripped the German Jews of their citizenship?"

Meir grabbed his nephew by his lapels. He spoke in a whistling whisper.

"Did you say nonsense? What do you know about nonsense? Care to hear about the nonsense my jailers pressed on me to sign? I was more mad than sane from countless sleepless days and nights while three interrogators took turns—I'll spare you the detail, but one day I'll show you where they put out their cigarettes on my breast. They gave me a choice between being an agent of Franco's Guardia Civil, Hitler's Gestapo, or Mussolini's Black Shirts. But best of all they wanted to style me as a Japanese spy. You see, some years before that my people carried out Lubyanka's request and—well, got hold of some vital data on the Panama Canal. The KGB sold our booty to the Japanese. With the proceeds, they bought cars in America for middle-level Party functionaries. Not from dealers, not from factories—stolen cars, dirt-cheap. Remember the Pierce-Arrow back in Yalta? One of those. Now they wanted extra mileage from that deal."

The outpouring had worn Meir out. He pulled a flask topped with Hathaway's Johnny Walker's out of his bosom pocket and helped himself to a generous gulp.

"So I confessed. I even went an extra mile. They wanted a piece of nonsense? They'd get nonsense squared. I had betrayed the Commune of Paris to the advancing Japanese troops. I had sold my Communist virginity for a controlling package of shares in Mitsubishi Zaibatsu. I proposed a deal. The Party would send me to Tokyo; I'd come into ownership rights and transfer them to the Communist International. As simple as this."

He swigged another one.

"I signed my statement and began waiting. Did I think that they'd let me go? Of course I didn't! But I gambled that my outlandish lie would strike any observant eye and bring about a revision of my case."

Meir Kovner chuckled with his new, cackling laughter.

"Apparently, there was no observant eye. Or they couldn't care less once I'd signed. Two weeks later they called me out of the prison cell. As usual, they yelled from the corridor. Anyone whose name starts with a *k*? And you're supposed to shout back your yes. If more than one answered, then: The next letter an *o*? And so on, until they said to the sole remaining voice: out here! That's their way to put you on the carpet without letting the neighboring cells hear your name. Why? The jailors are crazy about secrecy. In his cabinet, the interrogator read me my sentence. Ten years' hard labor."

"But they finally got it, didn't they?" David's voice lacked conviction. "Four years of your term still to go, and—"

Meir shook his head. "I doubt there was some belated flash on the road to Damascus. They just needed me. My skills. My cadre. My network. They brought me to Moscow in time for Arnold to see me before his American trip."

He felt hot, in spite of the bracing cold in the air. A snowball fell from a twig and flattened to a cake. Only now did Meir realize that the snow around them had become tinged with blue.

He had no energy left to press David.

After all, with Arnold Hramoy at his side he'd do without.

He sighed. "Well, if that's how you feel about it. Stay with your virtue intact, you fastidious old maid. But before going back to the Army—why don't you make a trip to the Crimea?"

David gave out a burst of relieved laughter. But he hid his eyes. The ingrate felt some guilt, after all, Meir thought bitterly.

"To the Crimea. Sure, Uncle. I'll apply to my local and request a voucher to the Sacco-Vanzetti Sanatorium and buy a ticket to Sevastopol at the Kursk Terminal. That simple."

"I'll fix you up with travel documents. And I'll second you to the KGB—that'll open a few doors for you. Drop me picture postcards. Write about the beauties you'll sleep with. In small handwriting to cut the expense."

Fat chance, Meir thought to himself. Still in love with his German wife.

The following day, David Kovner received a telephone call from Arnold Hramoy.

CHAPTER TWENTY-THREE

I *t's got to be somewhere, after all!*
Arnold pulled books from the shelves, peered into the gaps, thrust his hand behind the front rows.

So much for the photographical memory. Arnold Hramoy couldn't locate the book he'd placed out of sight.

Aha! Here you are. A thin, carton-binding volume. The thick, dark brown cover with black, irregular texture and tousled, whitish corners.

Arnold went to his desk and copied a line.

> *The conquered Jews have given laws to the conquerors.*
> —Seneca

Sitting in his Division of Linguistics office, Arnold Hramoy admired the epigraph to the book that he would be writing.

Any Party hack could quote Lenin, but Hramoy invoked the Roman stoic philosopher, which surely was more chic. The allusion was neat. If the Jews could so profoundly have affected the Greco-Roman world of top culture, should it come as a surprise that the primitive knights of the German Order succumbed to their influence?

Arnold placed a bookmark in the book and returned it.

Meir's folly was a godsend. Many in the Academy frowned on Arnold's theory. They wanted the homeland of the great Indo-European family of languages to lie in the Russian steppe. The natural cultural chauvinism. The British, on behalf of the Indians, championed the Indus valley, the Germans favored the southern shores of the Baltic, the Swedes backed Scandinavia, and the

Chinese stood behind Eastern Turkestan. Something irresistible lay in the idea of bringing a tourist to this or that rock and saying: here, in the shadow of the Hill of Dnghu, the proto-Indo-Europeans breakfasted before embarking on their earth-shaking journey. And all along they cherished the memory of their Russian (read: Indian, German, Scandinavian, Chinese) Dnghu wolf yogurt!

Compared to the above contenders, Arnold was under a heavy handicap. He championed a homeland of the Indo-Europeans located outside his country. He had no constituency to fall back upon except for Kurdish shepherds, and Kurdish shepherds didn't vote in the Soviet Academy of Sciences.

But what with Meir's offer, Arnold at the head of Project Prusa could enlist the support of the State! Arnold's hypothesis amended with the Pruses clause—Arnold's mind was ready supplying images: the rod to link his horseshoe's ends! the string for his longbow!—would become orthodoxy, the linchpin of an enterprise of enormous political importance. Arnold would wrap himself in the purple mantle of the Party ideology. He'd smash the Indo-Germanists to smithereens. They had already been wounded by the fact that their home base was also Hitler's—they would breath their last under Hramoy's *coup de grace*. Arnold smiled to think of them reporting to work at Indo-Yiddish departments!

He sat back in his chair and drew on his cigar. Come to think about it, his own name, Hramoy, had come straight from *aramei*. Aramaean savants, his ancestors. The initial *aleph* had survived only as an aspiration, an *h*-sound.

He warmed to Meir Kovner. The dear old friend. Still, the original idea wasn't his, Meir had told him. Then whose?

He slapped his forehead. But of course! The verses Arnold that got a glimpse of in Meir's office! *From Alexandria come . . .* An epigram by the Roman poet, Martial. Eons ago, young David Kovner had shown his translations to Arnold, seeking his commendation. Arnold walked to the shelves, but he knew it before checking. *To Caelia.* It was Martial indeed.

Arnold pressed a button. The door opened at once, and the secretary came in. This young woman with a large wet mouth deeply suffered whenever Arnold had female company. She sported the new pink nylon blouse with brown diagonal stripes that Arnold had bought at Macy's. Its effect was somewhat marred by her bra's black shoulder straps, which showed. Mercifully, her slip screened off the cups. After five minutes of deft questioning Arnold learned that Meir Kovner's nephew was in town, a wounded artillery major, bemedaled for Smolensk and Minsk.

Arnold called Meir's home and was in luck: the younger voice answering the phone belonged unmistakably to David Kovner. Arnold affected surprise and immediate recognition, dumped tons of charm on David, and invited him to visit anytime and browse through his books, together.

He again took out the book with Seneca's quotation and placed it in a strategic position.

David Kovner came later in the afternoon. Arnold hung out a *Don't Disturb* tag on his door, borrowed from his New York hotel room. Arnold's office was a far cry from that of other Academy moguls, who fashioned their environment after the Party functionaries. Arnold's was a labyrinth of book stacks, reception bays, and cozy nooks smelling of old print and fresh coffee— ideally suited for entertaining in style a foreign luminary or a female visitor with intellectual pretenses.

Arnold gave a guided tour of the stacks to "the colleague." Now and then Arnold climbed a stepladder, a cigar stuck between his teeth. He pulled a book, let his guest feel its covers, enjoy its smell, leaf through its yellowish pages, savor a quotation; then he offered another book, and yet another. The secretary brought in a copper coffeepot and lingered for a bit more than necessary before leaving. Arnold served rich, dark coffee on a Louis XV little dressing table edged between two stacks, where the room was just right for two poufs. Eastern Mediterranean coffee, he said; that's the only region they know how to make coffee. "You have a sister in Palestine, don't you?"

David Kovner nodded. "Her husband—name Legume—came down there from Germany, back in the thirties."

Arnold screwed up his eyes. "One of those starched-shirt, silk-cravat, Goethe-worshipping yekkes?"

"Precisely. Although he's been progressively shedding off his yekke-ism. Accepted the prevailing dress code and general outward sloppiness. Learned to shout instead of speaking. But making only slow progress in Hebrew. Three weeks before the wedding he ran back to my sister yelling: *Katabt la maktub! Katabt la maktub!* What's a big deal, Malka says; so you wrote him a letter. Who did you write the letter to? And why this terrible accent? Didn't I teach you to speak the right way? Say it again, *katabti lo miktab*. No, the former yekke shouts. *Katabt la maktub!*"

"This is Arabic, of course," Arnold laughed.

"Yes, that's what he told to his bride, this is Arabic! Look how closely Hebrew and Arabic are in the basics! And he pulls a red lump out of his pocket, spreads it on his knee, and puts the fez on his head. If you want to look like an Arab, Malka says, why don't you wear a *kaffiyeh*, rather than this vestige of Turkish imperialism? But watch your step, because our guys may give you a whack on your *kaffiyeh* in the darkness of night. No, the former yekke shouts again, you miss the point! I don't want to wear an Arab *kaffiyeh*, no better than a *yarmulke*, or a Hasidic *shtreimel*, or my former homburg. I'm opting for the East-Mediterranean fez! The Arabs and we are cousins, members of the same extended family. We are Semites! And our languages are no more distant than some German dialects. But nobody says Bavarian and Berliner are separate languages, right? Even if I bust my guts, quite rightly, at the Viennese sissy-britches turning every second word of theirs into an endearment, and they, full of spite, call my beautiful *Mundart* a *pifke* grunt. So I want the same here. I want Hebrew and local Arabic merge into one language. The Palestinian Semitic language. With two dialects."

"An instinctive linguist," laughed Arnold. "Even if oversimplistic."

All went well. Arnold watched his charisma envelope his guest. David Kovner seemed truly relaxed as he continued with the tale of his sister's fiancé.

"And so we'll smooth our differences, he says, reduce our misunderstandings, and live side by side in our common patrimony, Palestine. Fine, Malka says. Two dialects. But can you read any of their terrible dialectic scrawls? I can't, admits the former yekke and presently the Palestinian Semite. And they have problems with ours, Malka says. So they'd better learn our letters and our superior ways. They won't, says her Semite sadly. But I have a better suggestion. What if we both, he and I, the Palestinian Arab and the Palestinian Jew—if the two of us throw away our medieval letters? As the Turks did with theirs? He and I, we switch to the Roman alphabet, the script of modernity and progress. Not only will we speak mutually intelligibly, we'll understand each other's writings! *Katabti lo miktav,* I wrote him a letter, and he understood my letter instantly! We'll feel closer to one another than we've ever been since Abraham chased Ishmael off to the desert. We, in our common country. So you rather fancy the Roman alphabet, my sister says icily, the letters of the Spanish Inquisition, Nazis' dirty papers, and the medieval pamphlets soaking with blood as in "blood libel." Not so, her Semite says; the medieval pamphleteers and *Der Stürmer*—they used Gothic script. Not Roman letters. My reform will help thousands of new immigrants to come quicker over the culture shock. I'm thinking also, he says, about our sons and grandsons—it will help them in the wider world, will make it easier for them to communicate. Here we come to the source of the problem, my sister says. You're just too lazy to study. Besides, I don't want my grandson to ever speak to a grandson of an SS-man. So perhaps we should have different sets of grandsons, she says. That's when she broke their engagement for the first time."

"Quite a lady, your sister." Arnold sincerely enjoyed the conversation. "And what happened next?"

"Of course he came back and said that he didn't mean it, that he was just an indolent ingrate, that for a youngster of forty-five as he, it was a helpful mental gymnastic, switching to a new language in a peculiar alphabet. There were more crises, but now they're married after all. Although she's considering divorce—trouble is, he's speaking German in his sleep."

Arnold turned grave. "I see some merit in her attitude. After all that happened—"

Arnold's telephone rang. He cursed internally—the secretary had been issued clear instructions to leave them alone. The call—it better be important! He walked to his desk and picked up the receiver. "Yes?"

The secretary. She'd found it out: Major Kovner had gotten wounded saving German civilians from marauding troops.

Clever girl. Arnold laid down the receiver. He walked back to the little table and sank to the chair. "After all that happened—it would be tragic to sow the seeds of bloodshed, of another catastrophe. Certainly, we'll never forget, and we'll never forgive. But there is something that is neither short memory nor forgiveness. And not revenge, either." He took a sip of his coffee. "Reconciliation. That's when you sit with your offender at the same table and talk. And we'll have to! In our world we're bound to live together, Jews and Germans. It's a small planet, after all. I keep saying it: we have to overcome our passions and start out on a new road, beyond vengeance."

David's eyes flashed, which showed Arnold that his words weren't taken at face value. Major Kovner must have read some of Arnold's incendiary articles in the Army newspaper, *The Red Star*. The drawbacks of being a popular writer.

He would appreciate some help, he said. A newspaper wanted an article from him. The humanism of the Soviet Army in Germany. Could Major Kovner advise him? Some examples from his battlefront life, perhaps? Saving civilians from—eh, the darker side of the war? David told him about his surgeon, Doctor Petrov, treating abused German women. His pad on the coffee table, Arnold took notes, asked questions, made sympathetic noises. "Only don't tell me, major, about just revenge. Our troops don't discriminate between a German woman and an *ostarbeiter*, the Russian or Ukrainian girl the Germans had dragged along—

our glorious liberators rape all in the end, age eight through eighty."

To make room for his pad, he incidentally pushed a book towards David. When David took it in his hands, the book opened at a thick bookmark.

Arnold looked up over his notes. "Oh, St. Augustine," he said casually. "Have you ever seen his *City of God*, Major?"

David Kovner shrugged. "It wasn't in our Marxist Philosophy recommended list."

Arnold raised his eyes to the ceiling in mock horror. "A philosophy curriculum without St. Augustine! But you went far beyond the curriculum, didn't you? I do recall—you were well grounded in Latin. I remember your translations. *Quod Romana tibi mentula nulla placet.*"

David Kovner smiled. His glance glided over the yellowed page and stopped, as Arnold had intended, at an underscored passage. The major read, translating from Latin: " 'The conquered Jews have given laws to the conquerors.' " He looked up in a silent question.

"Augustine is quoting Seneca," Arnold explained. "Augustine was more fortunate than we are—he read Seneca's book, but we can't. No copy has survived to our days. I'm saving the item for my new book." He smiled. "Quoting prominently Seneca—that much unorthodoxy I can afford, I think. But I won't highlight my source. Augustine, the Christian saint? The *City of God*? That would be too much for *them* to swallow."

Once again, as ten years before, they were two like-minded thinkers closing ranks against *them*, the Party troglodytes.

David Kovner asked what book Arnold was writing.

Arnold made his move.

"It's titled *The Perushes*, David. A mythical tribe, a.k.a. Paruses or Pharuses or Pruses, that your uncle and his collaborators have discovered."

Arnold could read nothing on Kovner's face.

"Their creation is thoroughly consistent," Arnold went on saying. "The key figure is one Mark, the lawgiver, propagandist, revolutionary. Synthesis of Moses, Marx, and Bar Kokhba."

David Kovner grimaced. "A mythological chimera. The cross between a lion, a goat, and a snake."

"If you want, David. But look at the chronology. The Parushes arrived at their Promised Land in AD 255. Their capital, Tel Hamelekh, fell to Teutonic Knights in 1255. Medieval Prussia lasted a thousand years. You will recognize the Millennium, the Paradise on Earth. I take it that the Prussian mosquitoes bore no malaria, the Prussian paralysis was the world's most progressive, and the Prussian lullabies, the loudest—they meant to keep the baby awake. The utopian Ashkenazi state in Prussia, David, is another Third Kingdom, *hamalkut hashlishit*, the fusion of Old Testament prophesies with apocalyptic Revelations of John, plus Marx's promise of Communism."

"Is that going to be in your book?"

Was Arnold mistaken in detecting irony? He smiled and shook his head. "No. I'm leaving it to the philosophers."

"To Marxist-Leninist philosophers?"

Arnold shrugged. "My interest is restricted to a linguistic aspect. The Yiddish-to-German hypothesis."

David dropped his gaze. "An exceptional absurdity."

Oh-oh. "Don't be too harsh, David. I admire the daring. Sort of a perverse elegance. After all, Jews did migrate north from Judea after the Great Revolts, didn't they? A change of the language did occur, and as a result, the Germans and the European Jews, the Ashkenazim, speak close languages. The rest is the Marxist method, which Engels defined as turning Hegelian dialectics upside down."

Arnold's smiling eyes sought David's, who wouldn't look up from the *City of God* in his hands.

"Whoever turned the language story topsy-turvy had a healthy sense of humor," Arnold went on. "It would be a privilege to work with him," he added after a pause.

Major Kovner blushed, almost imperceptibly. He returned the book to Arnold, rose to his feet, and thanked Professor Hramoy for the perusal of rare books; he had to go—he was leaving Moscow in a couple of days.

The common bond was no longer.

"I wish I knew you were in town," said Arnold. Indeed, why hadn't Meir told him about David? Then Arnold remembered the admiration in the eyes of the student David, his uncle's frown, and he understood.

Meir Kovner was jealous.

Well, he had no grounds anymore, had he?

Arnold said, "I wanted to tell you something. One day before the war, a doctoral thesis came from the Institute of Marxism to my desk for a reference."

Davis stared at him, silently.

"Authored by that former student of Zarnitsyn. The name was Vityushkin. I recognized your synopsis on early Marx. He made it, putting it elegantly, the material base for his doctorate. He elaborated Zarnitsyn's 'discovery' of Mounted Hounds, of course."

"And what kind of a reference did you give, Professor Hramoy?"

Arnold smiled. "Rapturous, of course. What harm could another lousy dissertation do? I didn't care for Marx anyway, even in your lucid and succinct rendering. His was pathetic. I praised it anyway. I hope you don't mind."

"I couldn't care less," David said.

"So I thought. Thank you for the interview, major."

"Hardly an interview, professor."

Arnold walked David Kovner to the door and returned to his shelves. He placed the book by St. Augustine back where it lived, hidden behind the Sanskrit-Lithuanian comparative grammar. Now he knew all that he wanted to.

He sat at his desk. The idea of the *Origins of the German Language* had come from David Kovner indeed, but the major wanted none of it anymore. The good news was that Arnold didn't have to tread on the toes of a young, take-charge, sharp-elbowed fellow who also happened to be the nephew of the project's curator. The bad news was that the sharp young fellow wasn't about to develop his success but rather was slipping away. Why? What had scared him off? Arnold, who had eagerly seized the opportunity to work for Abay Kunayev's nation, couldn't comprehend David's lack of enthusiasm for the Project Prusa . . .

Arnold hadn't arrived this far without developing a nose for danger. He had witnessed many a research project end up on the face of the investigator in a way much nastier than the proverbial egg . . .

The phone rang. The secretary asked if Arnold had forgotten that the *Don't Disturb* sign still hung on his door. She giggled. Arnold paused before saying no, he had not. She could take the afternoon off and do some shopping for her little Hasmik— Arnold had brought her a Mickey Mouse watch from his trip to America.

His trip. Christmas dinner and Professor Gibbs. The Scottish-American had talked of the Millennium and Prussia in the same breath. Arnold suspected now that the professor had been privy to the Project Prusa and wanted to determine if Arnold was in the know—which he wasn't. He was trusted less than an American Professor! Now Arnold sorely regretted his own imprudence: he wished he'd never stayed behind in that midwestern town, unchaperoned . . .

He remembered and sprang to his feet. What a piece of childishness! Why should he parade notes *in English?* People went under for much less than that!

He ran to the door, opened it, tore away the *Do Not Disturb* sign, and crumpled it in his fist.

He returned to his desk, threw the sign into a wastebasket, and wiped his brow. He'd gotten carried away. It would be reckless stupidity, his embarking on the Project Prusa. After all, he was responsible for his children (Arnold supported three families). And for his students, wasn't he?

But if he had invented things? He would be a fool to overreact and let the golden opportunity disappear, now that election to the Academy was a month away!

He sat undecided, absentmindedly clicking his lighter. On and off. The flashes of genius. The Hramoy genius . . . He started another cigar and sent smoke billowing towards the peeling molding.

Tread water, that's what he would do. He would publish an article on Red Welsh. It would bring the matter to the fore and establish his credentials without an outright commitment.

Then it hit him. How could he be so blind? A capital threat was emerging from different quarters. The whole matter of the Project Prusa concerned him more deeply than he preferred. What if somebody said, the Prussian Academy of Sciences could use people like Arnold Hramoy?

But I'm not even a Party member! Let Meir Kovner go there!

Comrade Kovner is already there. Now it's Professor Hramoy's turn. The internationally renowned scholar made an important contribution to Prussian history and linguistics. Our primary expert. Our pride.

The pitiless hand would grab him and toss him away from his Moscow office, his Bolshoy ballet, his Russian women.

Even if he'd managed to dodge the transfer, his life would never be the same. The very emergence of Jewish Prussia would change it forever. His cosmopolitan identity would be torn asunder. A narrow tribal characterization would stick to him. Wherever he went, they would identify him with—with Prussia! What an irony! Are you from Prussia, Monsieur Rahmwah? No, decidedly not. *Pas grave*; just tell me: why do your people mistreat the natives so harshly? . . . And back at home, they would yell from doorways, hiss at his back in streetcars: "Beat it to your Prussia!" Or: "What have we shed our blood for? To conquer Prussia for the Jews while they sat the war out in safety?" No use in showing them a Major Kovner and his medals.

He groaned. If Meir had resented transforming the Jews into a Middle Eastern nation, Arnold saw the fault in cooping the Jews up in a state, period. Some believed the Jews were the salt of the earth. But if you gathered all the salt together, you would have a brine pan. No fish, no birds, no plants. A Dead Sea.

The man of the world felt pushed and dragged into the shell of a mini-nation, ethnocentric and provincial, burdened with the arrogance of two ideologies.

It was unfair!

He sat there deep into the dark hours. Then he remembered: the newspaper's deadline was tonight.

Arnold traced out the title of his article with his Parker pen. *The Hour of Just Revenge Has Struck.*

At this hour of our imminent triumph, he wrote, there should be no slackening of the merciless sacred rage that has carried us into the Mounted Hounds' den.

CHAPTER TWENTY-FOUR

"Marshal Budyonny having a date at the Kremlin library?" Ognev said. "No big deal."

They'd veered off their regular path. Above their heads the trams came from the boulevard and rumbled onto the bridge. Across the empty embankment, wind whirled snow curls.

A flock of crows, attracted by steaming horse's droppings, landed at the piers. Ognev picked up a chunk of ice and tossed it into the congregation. The birds lifted off with indignant croaking.

"Minister Beria abducts girls in the streets," said Ognev. "A sadistic rapist. And a serial murderer. In Stalin's place—"

He broke off in midsentence.

"What do you feel when playing Stalin?" asked David.

The actor's eyes shone. "Confidence. Elation. When I'm playing Stalin I'm playing myself. Stalin's mission is mine."

"Which is—"

"Beating the living daylights out of the Germans. Making them pay for what they've done to us. Breaking Germany's spine. Humbling her into the dust so that she can never again raise her ugly head."

"And if the Allies don't go along?"

Stalin's notes in Ognev's voice grew in strength with each phrase. "Then I'll divide Germany. There won't be a Germany anymore. Just an East Germany and a West Germany. I'll put a stake down Germany's map. To this aspen stake I'll nail a horizontal bar, the crosspiece that Martin Luther set in place when he cut the Protestant North from the Catholic South. And on that cross, I'll crucify Germany. She'll hang all right, but not as a Christ—no such distinction, no sir. I'll crucify the thief and outlaw. I, Joseph Stalin."

His jaw set forward, he glared across the river.

David felt awed, against his will. "And Berlin?"

"Berlin the capital. The head. Yes. I'll place a ring around Berlin, a crown of barbed wire. A ghetto for a ghetto, a barb for a barb."

Ognev checked himself and smiled. "It's but an actor's monologue. The bad habit, turning everything into theater. Because acting isn't a trade; it's a disease; an incurable disease."

The crows came back and worked hard on the dung.

"Did you ever think of playing Stalin for real?"

Ognev paused. "Meaning what?"

"Being Stalin under the eyes and cameras of dozens of those who believe they're watching Stalin."

Ognev said nothing.

They took the route back through the maze of alleyways, between the rows of decrepit two—and three-story dwellings. At a colonnaded mansion to their right, they had to make their way through a gathering. Dark eyes examined them, then relaxed on recognizing one of their own.

Ognev made a wry face. "Friday night. The synagogue. I forgot. Should've taken another route."

David asked casually, "How would you feel if a Jewish state was carved out of East Prussia?"

Ognev stopped short, causing David to do so. "What are you talking about?"

"Germany's going to lose East Prussia."

Ognev resumed walking. "Of course she will. We'll screw every German who remains there. Dispossess and expel every damn one of them. But Jews are weak-hearted softies. Twisted minds. On the one hand and on the other hand. We'd rather do it by ourselves."

"We who?"

"We the Russians," said Ognev with Stalin's Georgian accent. He grinned. "We'll rename each and every damned place. Like Hoffmann's Clara in *The Nutcracker*—isn't she better off as an all-Russian Masha? Now more of that will come. We'll Ivangelize them. We'll bring them a gospel according to Joseph."

They were at their house but halted before entering, as if by an unspoken understanding. Ognev said, "About your question. In my pipe dreams, yes, I have."

David didn't ask what the hell of a question the actor was responding to.

He said, "You'll play Stalin before an international audience—live. Sit for historic photos—as Stalin. Put your signature on agreements deciding the fate of millions—as Stalin. You'll be remembered as the Stalin of the most momentous conference that's ever been. The role of your life."

Ognev opened the door and entered the lobby, first. In the elevator, they spoke not a word.

★　★　★

"So it looks like the old aesthete Hramoy is going to come aboard. The idol of your youth, wasn't he?"

In his dining room, Meir Kovner didn't hide his triumph.

"No longer," said David.

"Why?"

Meir received no answer and walked to the safe, glancing over his shoulder at the alarm clock. Using his body to screen what he was doing, he fiddled with the safe and flung open the door.

He beckoned his nephew. "Come along."

On the upper shelf of the strongbox lay neat piles of booklets. Meir took some, felt them in his hand, and tossed them back. Red, black, dark blue, olive green. Passports. Military service cards. Letterhead stationary. A bronze, cash-register-like contraption in the left corner of the lower shelf. And a heap of rubber-stamps complete with an inkpad.

David whistled. "An impressive collection." He stared at the heaps. "Could I have my pick?"

"No. I don't trust you. You're unreliable." Meir Kovner handed David two booklets. "Your KGB papers." He reached behind the door, fumbled there. When he clanged it shut, the front of the safe looked as it was previously; that is, with all the levers down. "And hurry up. The Crimea will soon become closed to all. Even with my passes."

"A lot of action there, eh?"

"Refurbishing the Greater Yalta after the German occupation. Setting in place an awesome security system. Building roads and a new airfield in the steppe."

"Is Stalin going to fly down there?"

"He doesn't like flying, even if he does keep an emergency seaplane at his South Coast residence."

"Where will he put his guests up?"

"Livadia and Alupka palaces. The villa at Koreïz he's reserved for himself, modestly. The smallest of the three. Now, I'm replacing the old comrade who ran the safe house in Djankoi. I'm sending another old comrade there. You'll find an acquaintance. He's Heinrich. He'll provide you with a motorcycle for the trip to Palai. When are you leaving?"

David paused. "Have something else for me to do down there?"

Uncle Meir opened his eyes wide. "Now, what brought that one on?"

"Searching for traces of our family shouldn't take such elaborate preparation."

Uncle drew close and laid his hands on David's shoulders.

"You won't survive here, Dovidke. I realized it when you bolted from the Institute. And then again, you wrote that joke of an essay. Get moving! The SMERSH is again pressing its case against you, the one I'd hushed up. Unlawful disarmament of an Army patrol. They seem to be particularly mad at you. The same mortar round that hit you—you see, it also killed one of them, who came to arrest you. Go to Palai, and then right back to Heinrich. He'll pass you to the right people. They'll get you safely out of the country."

David stared at him. "And where to?"

"Perhaps, joining Malka in your land of—how did you put it—the ancient kingdoms?"

David hugged Uncle Meir.

"If I follow your advice, I'll let you know. I'll write a postcard."

He remembered Hramoy's bony face behind horn-rim spectacles, when Arnold thanked him for the interview.

"I'll tell you that I departed for an interview."

★　★　★

David and Ognev were near the former monastery when Ognev said, "Playing Stalin. For how long?"

"For a couple of hours."

"And then?"

"You'll be a hero of the Yishuv."

"What's that?"

"The Jewish community in British Palestine. The emerging Jewish nation."

"You saying Jews will send a submarine from Palestine to pick me up?"

"Not really," admitted David. "But you'll get there all right."

"Doesn't sound sexy, feeding Levantine fleas."

"How about playing Stalin in Hollywood?"

They walked a good ten minutes in silence before Ognev asked, "And what is on your wish list?"

David explained. Ognev stopped and turned his head away. They stood at the boulevard crossing, before a six-story apartment building with a sign *Polyclinics* at a cut-off obtuse corner.

David's heart thumped. He didn't know how much time passed before he looked up at the actor.

Ognev gazed into the distance, his eyes narrowed.

"Whenever I lay with women, they demanded my Stalin's accent. They wanted me to call them whores in Stalin's voice. Not my wife. She loved me, not his awesome power. In fact, she abhorred him. Not only for what he was, but also because I'd been transforming myself into him. She said my role took me over. She was afraid to see in me—" He checked himself. "I was Stalin, with all his present and past. Do you know that his second wife couldn't bear it? She took her life. My wife was glad that I didn't have Stalin's pockmarks. Now that my wife is dead—"

He set his jaw.

"You'll get your Stalin, pockmarks and all. For once, Comrade Stalin will go through a great personal sacrifice. Comrade Stalin will make pockmarks chemically. With his own hand."

CHAPTER TWENTY-FIVE

The next morning, in high spirits because of Ognev's assent to his plan, David went to see Heinrich. He found his uncle's friend packing for the Crimea and had a long talk with him. From Heinrich's place near the Riga Railway Terminal, there was a short walk to an open market. An officer of the Soviet Army wasn't supposed to set foot in the semi-legal zone of abject poverty and war profiteering. David wore a sheepskin overcoat and an old black flap-ear cap, rabbit dyed to imitate sealskin, which he'd found in Uncle Meir's back closets—and wondered why Uncle would have kept the unseemly attire.

David walked among the buyers and sellers standing in a just-passing-through crowd. The vendors paraded their motley wares. A second-hand coat . . . knitted mittens . . . kitchen utensils . . . a gold watch . . . a loaf of bread . . . Soon David stumbled on what he'd been looking for. As if advertising the wares, a red cross called in from the mat glass of a wall cabinet placed on the ground. On a low self-made cart—a piece of plywood mounted on ball bearings, barely above the ground—a rump of a man presided over a pile of hospital supplies displayed on a length of canvas spread on the ground. Nearby, two brawny men in British-made leather flying jackets threw glances over their raised fur collars.

David squatted. He regarded the legless man's wares. Bandages . . . hypodermic syringes . . . plum-purple crystals of permanganate . . . chocolate-brown little bottles of iodine . . . rubber enemas . . . valerian root . . .

"Want some Salvarsan?" somebody uttered. "Makes you like new."

David looked up flying pants and met the appraising eyes of one of the two biggies, who had come over and loomed over him. The thickset man crack-opened the door of a wall cabinet, then made the opening wider.

David peered in. The two shelves were crammed with bottles, paper bags, and packages . . . red tablets of streptocide . . . ointments in tubes . . .

A yellow bottle labeled *Ether,* large and sealed with wax. David hesitated. Not exactly the right stuff.

Here you are. An ampoule marked in Indian ink, CH_3CH_2Cl. Ethyl chloride, an instant, short-term anesthetic—that much he'd learned back in the Minsk hospital.

David resolved to trust the inscription. He paid the man in the flight suit, made some other purchases, and returned home.

In Uncle Meir's dining room, David walked straight to the safe. He'd seen it hundreds of times in his pre-war life and fiddled with it without giving it much thought. It wasn't an assault-proof fortress that you would want for your bank. With its bronze face and four bronze legs in the shape of lion's paws, it rather resembled an elegant plaything. Uncle had said once, it had belonged to "an aristocrat" and was requisitioned at the aristocrat's arrest. The rotten representative of the defeated class of exploiters had hidden his amorous correspondence there. The Party obliged Meir Kovner to install the safe in his apartment, but he used it frivolously as a dish collector. Now it again served its primary purpose. Plaything or not, it must've given headaches to the aristocrat's jealous wife. On the face of the strongbox, five horizontal lines—black, ingrained—intersected seven vertical slits at right angles. From the slits protruded bronze levers crowned with white ivory knobs. David dragged a knob and pitched the lever. It clicked on a line. He slid it up to the next line, then tried in between—it snapped there, too. If you pitched all the knobs to a sequence, the safe's face looked like sheet music. He set the first seven notes of a song from Uncle Meir and Heinrich's program on that New Year night and pulled the handle. The door didn't budge. Why should it indeed? He couldn't even check a minute fraction of Uncle's repertory: Russian folk ballads, Yiddish lullabies, German carols, Italian opera arias, or revolutionary songs of the Comintern. It was impossible to try them all. Moreover, for each tune he needed to know something else; namely, the key in which the tune was entered into the lock, like C major or E-sharp major. Without that knowledge he had to try the tune repeatedly, up to twelve times. Twelve times a thousand of tunes—impossible to handle.

He sighed, walked to Uncle's bedroom, and carried Uncle's typewriter from there to the dining room. After an unsuccessful attempt at safecracking David would try his hand at counterfeiting. The Remington churned out manifold paper and coarse grey sheets with brown glossy grains of pulp. The stack to David's left grew steadily. But the safe teased him, taunted him by its very presence each time when he raised his eyes of his work. David moved the typewriter so that the safe was behind his back.

When he was done, David sorted up the loose leaves, punched them through, and skewered them on two pliable tin strips fixed inside a grey cardboard binder. He crowned the impaled stack with a shiny narrow two-hole plate, bent one strip up and another down, and locked them with sliders.

He held a make-believe KGB dossier of Max Ebert.

A farmer's son, a boy of sixteen, Max started at the Greek watchmaker Stavraki's and stayed there through all the storms of the Revolution and Civil War until it finally became the Twenty-Six-Baku-Commissars First Alupka Cooperative of Watchmakers, named after the Baku Communist leaders who perished in 1919 during the Civil War and British intervention in the Caucasus. In his small town one had to diversify, so he was also a master locksmith. How had he gained the acquaintance of Prince Vorontsov? How did he become privy to the secrets of one of the most powerful men in the pre-Revolutionary Crimea?

Not a word about that in his KGB file. Max Ebert had hidden his past; faded into the mass of nameless laborers. Who'd blame him? After the Revolution, the new masters of the land sent the likes of him to dig canals in northern swamps.

Actually, that was too good for Ebert. The aristocrats had fled the Crimea and left their lackey behind. With his knowledge of the secret passage he was to assassinate the villa's new residents, their pants down or skirts up, right? A monk Clement stabbing King Henry the Third on the royal *chaise percée*. A Charlotte Corday turning Marat's bath very bloody indeed.

Ebert's very knowledge had made him a terrorist. Terror through intention, articles 58-8 and 58-11 of the Criminal Code. No labor camp for Max Ebert. A slug to the back of his head, kneeling in a cellar.

No wonder that he'd kept his secrets behind his tight teeth. Only once did he break the silence to impress his pretty niece, and even then he dropped no better than a hint.

David needed that secret.

Ever since his unfortunate quip about Yiddish, David had felt nagging guilt. He had given a boost to the cock-and-bull story concocted by the Party bosses and ambitious academics—the one that would only bring more trouble to both Jews and Germans. He felt personally responsible. He had to destroy the shady undertaking.

But how?

David's discovery in the Kremlin library was the first breakthrough. He had learned about the secret gallery that led to a meeting site—the meeting that would decide the fate of East Prussia. And his wife's uncle was privy to the gallery's secrets!

Max Ebert's movements during his war odyssey in the Crimea were consistent with the suggestion that Max had twice used the cave and gallery. The gallery was operational!

Uncle Meir's offer to arrange David's travel to the Crimea could not have come at a better moment. From that point in time his ideas, still hazy, began taking shape.

When Ognev agreed to play Stalin, David had his plan.

Disguised as a KGB officer, he'd show up at Ebert's Kazakhstan exile, where Max lived on borrowed time. Ebert's fake file would give David extra credibility as a KGB officer. He'd take Max Ebert from the street and interrogate him. If he found the man trustworthy, he'd disclose himself before his wife's uncle. He'd secure his cooperation. He'd debrief Max in minute detail. He'd learn the secrets of the Lair of Ali Baba.

"Well, Cousin Max," David said aloud. "I hope we'll get along quite well."

Still, it was touch and go. He was supposed to find the secret entrance to a cave, at night, with Ognev in tow.

If he could bring Max along to the Crimea, things would be different.

But that looked equally impossible. The runaway exile didn't stand a chance of traveling over four thousand miles across the half-length of the Soviet Union, through innumerable cordons of the Railroad Ministry, the SMERSH, and the KGB.

Impossible . . .

And so David was painfully aware of the inadequacy of his plan when the next day he took a bus to the railway station, destination Kazakhstan.

Sharing David's seat, an old man in rags belched vodka. At David's left cheek, a cold draft came from a window frosted with icy flowers. Tiny ice crystals had nearly skinned over the wound of graffito scratched across the white fluffy surface.

David allowed his thoughts to drift. In his ear hummed a tune, the flea that had been there for the last two days. The song about the drunken tramp Augustin. *Ach du lieber Augustin, alles ist hin . . .*

With his fingernail, David scratched out five horizontal lines across the frosted window, turning it to music paper. Using his fingers, he thawed through seven round spots—some on the lines, some between. The light of the day appeared through.

Why the intrusive tune, the *ohrwurm*, earworm, as Clara would say? Oh yes; it had started in Hramoy's office. David had perused the book by St. Augustine, and the name had recalled Augustin the tramp. It took David back to Palai, under an apricot tree, where Uncle, having finished his dessert of bread and honey, told the parable of musical farmers with perfect pitch inhabiting his romantic daydream. The clock on the village tower chimed the *Augustin* every hour on the hour, didn't it, each time in a different key. The farmers listened to the tune and knew the hour from the key: the hour was equal to the number of the sharps. The key D major, for example, required two sharps, so at two o'clock the chimes played the tune in D major. The farmers—or rather Uncle Meir—had cleverly used the fact that there were exactly twelve steps in the musical scale, the same number as the hour marks on the clock face . . .

Back in the dining room, before entering his combination into the safe, Uncle had thrown a myopic glance at the alarm clock.

What if he'd taken the key from the hour?

And inverted the farmers' routine . . .

A shadow of a tall vehicle appeared on the mat glass. Perhaps a truck with soldiers under tarpaulin, its diesel rumbling. His speed slightly higher than that of the bus, it advanced, blocking light in the marks one by one as if striking on the notes of the tune, *Ach-Du-lie-ber-Au-gus-tin*.

The geezer sat hunching, a dejected lump. His forehead leaned against the back of the seat before him. David tilted him backward by the shoulders and squeezed himself and his suitcase past the man. At the door David looked back: the wretch had tumbled into the former position.

David got off, crossed the street, and took a bus back home. When he walked down the lane, the clock on a Kremlin tower struck four. At this moment, the hidden switch in the strongbox had adjusted the mechanism to the key with four sharps in the signature, E-major.

David made up a story of a train ticket left behind on the table and coaxed a spare key from the janitor—his own key he had dropped through a mail slot. Having gained the entry to the apartment, he walked straight to the strongbox.

Seven knobs, left to right, to be coordinated with the five staffs of the treble clef. He was to enter the first seven notes of the little catchy tune in E-major.

David hummed the first note. That would be a B, on the middle staff. He pitched the first lever to the middle horizontal line and kept humming. The second knob went one notch up, between the middle staff and the one above it. With a sharp in the signature key, it made it a C-sharp. The next note slipped down, back to the B-staff. Another notch down, an A. Once more, a down-step to a G-sharp. The sixth and the seventh knobs rested at the bottom line, the E-staff.

Ach-Du-lie-ber-Au-gus-tin . . .

He pulled the handle, and the door opened smoothly. It went like clockwork. The treasure throve of his uncle's was his to pick from. Now he had the means to pull Ebert out of his exile and imminent death. He'd take Max along, all the way to the Crimea.

Into a blank passport David glued the mug shot of Max Ebert that he'd palmed at the Lubyanka.

And what name should he give to the born-again one?

He caught a glimpse of Clara Zetkin's magazine, the *Women's Communist International*, sticking out from behind the shelves where Uncle Meir had relegated it. Clara Zetkin, née Eissner . . . David smiled and filled the line out, *Aisner*.

Sorry for the burglary, Uncle. We the bad lot are expected to say: when I grow up, I'll do restitution. Well, I won't. Your tough luck: back in Palai, you felt so superior that you thought it safe to drop a clue to your little nephew. Your little nephew has grown up—grown out of your books and banners, papers and portraits, meetings and marches. Of your Prusa.

CHAPTER TWENTY-SIX

M eir Kovner examined his strongbox. Several forms were missing. How had David put it? "Acquisition of stolen property is still thievery." Now what about a box work on your uncle's safe before leaving his home?

In a sense, Meir was pettishly glad. He felt he'd one-upped the prude. That's like him, he thought. How did that joke go, the one about Marxist-Leninist philosophers' brains? . . . Feeling guilty, Meir raised his eyes to the portrait on the wall. I didn't mean it, Comrade Lenin. It's just a silly jest.

Meir sniffed at the rubberstamps for evidence of a recent use. Who was the partner his nephew wanted to take along on the dangerous road to Palestine? Good for him if it was a female companion. But David had also lifted a military service card. On the other hand, there were servicewomen in the army, right? Like in the good old times during the Civil War, when he was a regimental commissar. The regiment's best machine gunner was a girl. His one and forever love. Long dead . . .

He went out onto the landing. A neighbor, pug-nosed, freckled, dressed in a grey pullover and shapeless slacks, was disposing of garbage. It flew down with a scraping sound that ended with a thud. Meir nodded hello. The fancier of flamboyant dressing gowns was no longer a lodger when Meir returned from Siberia. Meir had made inquiries. Rem Adler was arrested as a British spy. Pity not a Japanese spy, Meir thought. Neighbors on the landing, neighbors on death row. Always nice to see a familiar face.

Meir wouldn't wait for the elevator. As he walked down the staircase, Ognev's face flashed behind the glass door in a brightly

·233·

lit cabin. Their eyes met, and Ognev turned away. Still sulking about the silly fight on New Year' Eve? Meir felt sorry. He should have gone over and reached out for his old friend. He would—as soon as the present feverish work for Yalta was complete.

Dusk was falling as Meir crossed back to his Central Committee office.

An Army colonel had been waiting on a sofa in Zena's anteroom. The little mirror in the sofa's back reflected his stout neck. Meir let him in. Now the colonel faced Meir across his desk.

"We're complying with your request, Comrade Kovner. Locating the men named Ashkenazi in all branches."

"Fine. Step it up." The Ashkenazi Guards Regiment was to take a prominent part in liberating the ancient land of Ashkenazi Jews.

"But they hole up. They turn to any dirty trick to conceal their name. Their favorite ruse is misspelling. Some do it Askanci. Others Eskenasi. The most creative spell it Ashkenudze and claim the Georgian Fifth Point. Why should they, I beg your pardon, be concealing their Jewish name?"

Indeed, why? Meir thought sadly. David's words about the end of the romance of the Soviet power and Jews rang in his ears.

The colonel grumbled. "'Fraid they'll have to do latrines. Yes, before joining the new unit. Fifteen days of brig for the tricksters!"

Meir suggested suspending the punishment, fair as it was, by invoking emergency reasons. The colonel left, puffing in disgust. Meir draped his coat over the back of his chair and remained in a shirt and tie, his thin upper arms ringed with coiled metal garters.

He unfurled columns of paper smelling of fresh ink. Arnold had done him the courtesy of sending his article's galley, soon to appear in the *Proceedings of the Academy*. Meir put it off for tomorrow.

The red telephone in the multicolored desk array rang imperiously—Zena put through the call from the Ministry of Foreign Affairs. The Middle Eastern Bureau wondered if the Project Prusa could extend its operations into Iran, where the

Soviet forces held the country's northern part in a war-time arrangement. The Foreign Affairs was exploring ways to make that stay permanent. "Remember those Paruses who didn't go with Mark? Your—what's the title? Your *Manifesto* mentions those schismatics. What if they went east and ended up in Persia? Our experts say the Hebrew for Persia is *Paras*. How come you people aren't exploring that goldmine?" The young aide's voice was impudent. Meir Kovner choked back a sarcastic reply, which he could ill afford: the smart aleck's boss, Foreign Minister Molotov, was Stalin's second in command. Meir pledged to give his full attention to the valuable suggestion of the Foreign Affairs, and waited for the other man to hang up.

Meir's heart pounded. Those bastards! Before long they would claim that the Paruses had founded Paris! No, Paris he wouldn't let them have. Although he personally had felt better at home in Vienna—

He started. Wait a moment, Meir, a taunting voice said in his ear. You're calling them *them?*—And what else should I call them? Should I call them *us?* "Them" ain't "us"; that much of grammar doesn't take an Arnold Hramoy.—No, Meir; don't you ditch. The matter is clear for the record. You're calling them *them*.

But I've always said *them* about my principals!

Exactly; about the bosses. But you have just said *them* about— about—about the Party! About the Cause!

The realization struck him. Even in Siberian labor camps he didn't think of himself as separate from the Revolution. He belonged to the Revolution since Arnold, Ognev, and he—yes, they shooed three cats into the synagogue during a Friday-night service. It was their parting salvo onto the old world!

Arnold's Paris. The decaying West. Yes, it did rot. But the smell was so delicious. When Meir was released, Hramoy and Ognev came to see him. "The last bottle of *Pommery!*" Arnold had fussed. "The best quality-to-price ratio, as the French put it. I've kept it for the Victory Day, but now—isn't your liberation as sweet? On the Victory Day we'll drink vodka." Whereupon Ognev said, his eyes glinting maliciously, he could wage a small bread,

Arnold, that you've stowed away yet another bottle. Meir Kovner kept quiet. He understood. He, Meir, had crisscrossed Europe. So had Arnold, and he was leaving for America on that very night. Of the three, Ognev had no chance of ever being allowed abroad. Too risky. Too damn risky. Just think of what the yellow press could make of snapshots captioned *Incognito—Stalin on Place Pigale!*

Meir sighed and went back to sketching the outlines of the Paruses' life in Paras. The reactionary shahs and fascist mullahs; the original accumulation of an economic surplus. The Anti-Vilification Alliance, the brainchild of one Esther Bat Mordecai. The Black-Hundreder Haman plotting against Paruses. The wise leader of the country, Artaxerxes, seeing through the plot. Haman executed by the firing squad of archers.

Meir laid down his pen. The work didn't go well. He pushed the pad off. Let Zarnitsyn's pack gnaw at this bone! Meir ruffled the pages of his desk calendar until they opened at March 18, the page red-bannered "The Parisian Commune Day." He took pleasure in correcting "Parisian" to "Parusian" and printed "by the fiat of V. M. Molotov." He tore out the page and pinned it to the tits of Mae West on his Varga wall calendar, Arnold's gift.

Meir looked around, jerked down his note, and burned it in an ashtray.

Just in time. Zena came in with a cup of tea. "Lemon, Mark Semyonovich?" She set the cup and a bowl with sugar chips on the desk. She sucked in the air, cast a disapproving glance at Miss West's nipple with the triangular paper scrap under the thumbtack, and opened the window's little ventilation hatch.

"You can go, Zena, and good night." Meir Kovner put his coat back on. He absentmindedly stirred his tea. Ever more often he allowed his associates to use that gentrified version of his name.

Meir opened his wall safe, a standard affair, the title product of a Urals tank plant. He removed a bottle and served himself a generous measure of vodka. Next, he pulled out a dented aluminum kettle, on whose surface rudely engraved dots grouped to form the letters M and K. He filled it with the water from a carafe and set the kettle on the floor rug. Next, a heating element emerged from the safe and dragged along a cord. Meir sank the loop into the kettle and ran the cord to an outlet, for which purpose he had to unplug the desk lamp. The room plunged in gloom. Meir leaned back and closed his eyes, nursing his headache. As the murmur of the heating water reached its peak and changed pitch, signaling boiling, Meir pulled out the heating element and restored the desk light. From inside the safe he fished two three-inch tea cubes adorned with a bright green-and-red landscape picture and the inscription *Ceylon Tea*, grown in the USSR. Meir emptied the packs into the kettle. He carried the cup with Zena's tea to the rubber plant beside the glassed bookshelves and drained the cup into the pot soil. Back in his chair, he poured the tar-black liquid into the cup, inhaled the steam, and slackened in his chair, warming his hands on the cup. He closed his eyes and let his body relax against the cushioned back of his chair, as he sipped the hot *chefir'*, the Siberian camp substitute for narcotics. The leaden weight in the back of his head was dissolving, giving way to the high.

He sat thus until he drifted off to slumber—

His body sprawled in the air. He flew above a mournful expanse, flat and bleak, low marshy banks under plumb-grey skies—an early northern autumn. A dirt road snaked among shallow ponds, and upon it a jeep led a column of men in grey trench coats, rifles slung over the shoulders.

An officer craned his neck from the jeep.

"Anyone starting with an A?"

"Yes, sir!" shouted out every single one.

"Second letter a Sh?"

"Yes, sir!" responded as many.

"The third a K?"

"Yes, sir!"

The officer spit and swore. "Guards Sergeant Ashkenazi-219, the song!"

A tenor started, and hundreds of male voices joined in unison.

Raise high the flag!
Shut up, vituperators!
The Pruses march
With firm and steady stride.
Souls of the friends
Shot by the Romans and the traitors
Are in our ranks
And marching side by side!

The first rows did the last bits of singing, marking time in front of a fence that barred the road, while the rest pulled up, shrinking the column like a concertino.

Meir heard himself singing the last line: *"Marschier'n im Geist in unsern Reihen mit!"*

The officer threw his head back. "Krauts up!"

His eyes met Meir Kovner's. He started. "Forgive my stupid joke, sir. Guards Colonel Ashkenazi-1469 is reporting to you, sir."

"Attaboy," said Meir and fingered his pate. But no, he had no general's *papakha* on him. "Keep doing good work."

The colonel's face brightened. He hurled back to the column, "104 Battalion—over the hurdle!"

The troops hopped the fence and scrambled down into a short ditch behind it. Hoisting one another by hand, they emerged on the far side and regrouped. The jeep rode around the barrier. Meir heard the command: "To Bridge One!" and the column marched away.

A short man, his face round and sweaty under a floppy mushroom of a fishing hat, was kneeling at the edge of the trench. He put his sieve aside and watched the soldiers disappear.

"The eighth century," he said to Meir Kovner hovering above him. "They are trampling artifacts of the eighth century." He resumed his sifting.

"Any luck?" asked Meir.

The archeologist measured him longitudinally. "I beg your pardon?"

"Well, I don't know. Papyruses or clay tablets or something. They communicated with one another, didn't they?"

"Papyruses, parchments, paper, bamboo tablets, and other inferior means of communications are conspicuous by their absence," said the archeologist firmly. "The same holds for typewriters, printed presses and telephone gadgetry. Moreover, the very nonpresence of ancient wires in eighth-century Prusa is the best material evidence of the fact that as early as the epoch of nascent feudalism the Pruses had mastered the art of the wireless. So I'm in luck indeed. Yes, in luck, because I've found nothing. The most promising find in my job is a non-find. Absence is presence."

He squinted at Meir. "But please fly somewhat away, because I'm farsighted."

Which Meir did.

The man sprang to his feet. "Forgive me, sir. I . . . I—" He dropped the sieve into the trench and looked helplessly down.

What's happened to them? thought Meir Kovner flying away. Below lay monotonous grey fields and tussocky bogs, then posts and palings and again posts and palings, and farmsteads, few and far between, pressed down against the level ground. It smelled of burning leaves. Then huts grew thicker. Here and there, two- or three-story houses were scattered like the teeth of a sick horse. Meir overtook a woman wearing a top-to-toe Moslem dress. She dodged along the streets from shadow to shadow in rapid, man-like bounds, a baby bundle dangling from her neck. Somewhere a gong sounded, or rather a hammer hit a suspended length of rail, and people clad in greased grey coveralls poured out onto the streets. Meir landed amid the cries, "All to the Mountain!" Men and women ran, pushing Meir about. He held tight his glasses in his hand lest he lose them, his arms pinned to his chest, and floated in the thickening torrent swirling about him, pressed hard to others, shoved and shaped like Arnold's pebble, until he found himself in a vast open square packed with people. They pressed at a long, breast-high timber barrier. Behind it, at a distance, stood two structures of roughly equal size at an angle to each other and the barrier, making a sort of a triangular plaza, unpaved, at whose apex loomed a huge tree stump. The last workers hastily filled potholes and carted away wheelbarrows.

The construction on the left looked to Meir's myopic eyes like an oversized bookcase stuffed with huge books. Here and there red book spines showed like odd volumes of Lenin's *Complete Works.* From the upper edge of the volumes protruded bookmarks, which swayed. Meir got some breathing space. He restored his glasses onto the bridge of his nose and clarity to his vision. The book spines turned people crammed together, men dressed in somber brown business suits and women mostly in red dresses, waving their hands above their heads. They stood behind guardrails, three tiers stacked up.

A reviewing stand of sorts, Meir guessed. He spied a familiar face. Of course! Doctor Markman, the Kremlin hospital's surgeon who lived in Doorway Two of Meir's house in Solyanka Street.

On a parapeted platform crowning the stand appeared a man, sporting a heavy raven-black mustache and a uniform cap. He had the platform all to himself. Wide-shouldered, tall and brawny, he firmly grasped the guardrail.

His deep baritone filled the square from front to back.

"Comrades, six minutes ago, that is, two minutes and eleven seconds before the deadline, demonstrating the Prussian efficiency and attendance to detail, we completed the last section of this memorial ensemble!"

His left hand made a wide circular gesture towards the other structure. It was draped in canvas, upon which images of red flames rushed about like red roosters on Rem Adler's gowns, or perhaps like stormy manes of fire and red manes of horses pulling *tachanka* chariots.

The man under the military cap shouted. "We've built our masterpiece at the place of enormous importance. Here the girl of the Pirgul's fame once stood tied up to the tree trunk. Here she took the punishment that ushered the birth of our nation.

The German invaders cut off the sacred oak, the focus of our collective memory over centuries. Never mind—new suckers keep growing from the stump!"

He leaned over the railing. "Say a couple of words, Rudolph."

One tier below him, a man with a mane of white hair, a fluffy mustache, and sad brown eyes started and straightened a necktie under his starched collar.

"Yes, Chairman Mark, Mark Two Hundred and Eighty-Seven. I am opening the Jubilee celebration marking the passage of nineteen centuries since the public appearance of the first work by Comrade Mark the Founder. The work of a genius—"

"—wherein he took a rap at the false Friends of the People," Chairman Mark CCLXXXVII took over. "The Gang of Three, despicable Mattheas, Lucas and Johannes."

He waved his hands, and the crowd shouted:

"Hey, hey, M-L-J! How many lies did you tell today?"

Chairman Mark's hand sliced the air downward. "The blatant lies! Take this Mattheas-Lucas's mantra. 'Man does not live by *pros* alone.' The turncoats are dead wrong. Pruses do! Your temporary meat shortages are perfectly explainable by our defense needs. Can you imagine how much beef one single Yiddish shepherd dog consumes per annum? At a rate of four pounds per day, eh? Those uncounted canine heroes! Tirelessly and self-denyingly, they guard our borders. But if a Roman worms himself into Prusa—how do we tell a Roman?"

"By his Roman nose!" barked somebody at Meir's left ear.

"And a Mattheist-Lucaist-Johannist?"

"By his beard!" answered a dozen voices at once. "By his wedge-shaped goatee!"

Meir fingered his chin only to realize that his Vandyke, long ago shaved off, was now back in place. Soaked in cold sweat, he cringed. He pulled up his collar and tucked in his criminal chin.

Chairman Mark shouted, "You have exercised your democratic right to the Q & A, which session I'm declaring closed. Now, Rudolph!"

Rudolph started. "I'm inviting our distinguished foreign guest to the parade ground."

A puny middle-aged man appeared from the distant left and strutted on the far side of the barrier, shaking the hands that reached out to him from behind the barrier. He had narrow, sloping shoulders, wide hips, and a red-pomponed white beret cocked to cover one of his big ears.

Chairman Mark Two Hundred and Eighty-Seven smiled friendly. "Over here, Comrade André!"

The little man under the beret entered the triangular plaza. He walked to the apex, placed a kiss on the stump, spit out a bark snippet, and moved to the left, facing the stand. Silent figures in black leather jackets appeared from behind the stump. Swift hands stuffed Comrade André in a pair of boots with sharp steel teeth; others buckled a harness around his waist; still others installed a sleeping bag, a tent, and a camping stove, all humping on his back. They stuffed his waist straps with an ice ax, water bottles, bays of rope, a canteen, and flashlights. Directed by Chairman Mark from above, Comrade André tossed up a grapnel, a rope ladder dangling. Surgeon Markman caught and passed it to Rudolph, who secured it to the guardrail. The little man began to climb rung-by-rung, swaying and twirling with the ladder.

Hands reached down and helped André over the guardrail. The little man stood alongside Rudolph, both men beaming. And the crowd cheered.

Rudolph handed him a red booklet.

"Comrade André, here you are. Be it remembered that you have accomplished the *Ascension* to the Moral Top of the World. Presently you will see that it has entirely transformed your psyche and cured your asthma and sexual frustrations. You're being invested with a First Class Mountaineer card, its Fifth Point entry stating *Pruse*. Show it around and shout as loudly as the poet did: 'Read it and envy—I happened to be a Pruse, a Pruse, a Pruse!'"

"Look at the painted parchment," sighed the man at Meir's side. Only then did Meir notice that the man was missing his entire left arm. "Like a marquis they treat him. And we—we have it on birch bark." He drew a white square from his bosom and let Meir finger the unpainted soiled pine edging and read the inscription *Manuel Kantorovich* scratched out on the white bark. "Framed," he added proudly, "because I'm a veteran."

Then Comrade André spoke, and his machine-gun French sent the marquises on the stand into a frenzy. Rudolph's translation began with greetings from the whole of progressive mankind. "Prusa is the world that the spirit of Mark the Founder created for himself, the Hegelian idea materialized on Earth, the perfect paragon, the apotheosis!" When Comrade André announced that he had brought a gift from French comrades, twenty barrels of *marc*, grape brandy, the crowd became hysterical. Some yelled, "Veev Camarad Andray." On the stand, an improvised choir attempted singing, *Tout va très bien, Madame la Marquise*. A shadow crossed Chairman Mark's face.

The little man beamed. He straightened his beret. "Let me tell you about our French version of Markism." Rudolph dutifully translated, even as his face grew longer with every word. "Our Social La Marckism—"

"No way," Chairman Mark cut him short. "There is no such thing as another version of Markism. Who do you think you are? Such a pygmy, and as cheeky as those yellow fish with their Malakisam. "He pulled back the skin on his temples, turning his eyes into narrow slits. "Now that Prusa is locked in mortal combat with the forces of imperialism, from irredentist neighbors to Reform rabbis to perfidious trolls—the Pruse system is the only true model. Toe the mark!"

"Long live Chairman Mark!" rolled over the plaza.

Chairman Mark stood on his captain's bridge against the low lead-grey sky like a monument to himself, his hands firmly grasping the handrail. A blood-dropping prepuce, blown up many times over, soared above him like a nimbus.

CHAPTER TWENTY-SEVEN

They pushed André behind their backs. Rudolph said quickly, "I am herewith opening the anniversary parade."

The structure to the right of the stump came to life. The cover cloth dropped, opening the entrails to view. Meir saw a huge metal P-frame and within it, two large plywood boxes, open in front. They hung side by side, suspended on a common chain, which passed somewhere under the lintel.

The throngs hummed, excited.

Chairman Mark rumbled, "We have built this object of an enormous symbolic value, embodying the spirit of *Ascension*. Once a year, every citizen of Prusa will enjoy the wonderful, elevating experience of going to the pinnacle!"

He called. "Masha!"

"Over here!" A tall woman in coveralls in front of Meir began making her way through the crowd to the left end of the barrier. Four other figures joined her. Marshals in black leather jackets frisked them, pinned on papers flowers, provided them with a furled banner, its two long handles brought together, and admitted them to the parade ground. Once in the triangular plaza, the five placed a kiss on the face of the stump. Other black-leather marshals arranged them in a rank with their backs to the frame, three women flanked by two men. Masha was at the center, pressing the banner between her good-size breasts. Now that Meir could see her face, he knew whom she resembled. Clara Zetkin, the Communist International's firebrand.

Chairman Mark shouted, "The Sewing Shop of Top Mark is to become our first riding squad. Forward, the lot of you!"

"Excelsior," Rudolph said.

Behind the structure something clanged, gnashed, ground, winched. The two cabins set out on a slow, hesitant motion, the left one upward and the right, sinking into a pit. A chain appeared, pulled by the upbound cabin.

Now Meir knew it. The cabins and the two lengths of connecting chain formed the loop of a rudimentary *paternoster* lift.

As if having read his thoughts, Chairman Mark said, "Of course, the construction isn't a so-called *Paternoster*, Our Father, for Mark the Founder commanded this: 'You have no other Father but Me.' No; it is Your Mother. Your mother of the saying, 'Go ride your mother!' "

"We named our construction *Parousia Mark One*," Rudolph said. He added shyly, "Nickname: Tsylia."

A cabin began to emerge from the pit. A marshal shouted, "Three, two, one—mark!"

Without looking back, the quintuplet in coveralls stepped backwards into the cabin, which continued to drag upward— slowly, squeaking.

"Funiculì Funiculà!" thundered Chairman Mark.

The square roared. By fits and starts, the cabin lumbered to the top, shifted to the middle, and halted there. Masha Zetkin opened her arms, unfurling the banner, and passed the two flagstaffs to the women at her sides. They kept unrolling it into the hands of the two men on the row's flanks, who lifted the banner, so all could see the white lettering on red bunting:

NO MAN SEWETH A PIECE OF NEW CLOTH
TO AN OLD GARMENT

Chairman Mark-287 shouted, his eyes filled with blood. "Behold Comrade Mark's immortal behest, which the M-L-J pack of mad dogs tried hard to conceal! Read their scribbles (I say *read* as a figure of speech, of course), and you'll find not a single piece of instruction for the personnel of the apparel industry, the traditional Ashkenazi activity. By suppressing this wise dictum, the bloody M-L-J gang sabotaged our efforts to provide every Pruse with a boilersuit lasting his lifetime."

The proletarians of the needle trades chanted, *"Hey, hey, M-L-J! How many robes did you ruin today?"*

The cabin, now on the right, began its descent. Once on the ground level, the riders, their faces flushed with excitement, stepped out, made a left, and proceeded to the end of the parade ground where they surrendered the prop, curled around the barrier's end, and melted back to the cheering crowd.

The cabin they had abandoned emerged from the pit and accepted another rank. Those five carried plywood placards mounted on poles: three clusters of Roman ciphers, an equals sign, and a peculiar symbol looking like an inverted T. Before stepping into the Tsylia, they arranged them into the line, III $\perp$ V = VIII. The cabin dragged upward, while Rudolph read from a book in his hands:

"The pupil starts drawing the Prussian plus sign with the horizontal bar, and the teacher sees to it that the vertical stroke reach not below the bar."

A tall, scraggy, bespectacled schoolmarm in the cabin shouted, "The Teachers Union stands guard!"

The crowd hoorayed, as Chairman Mark assured: "Your innocent, unprotected children will never be exposed to the hateful symbol of Mattheism-Lucaism-Johannism!"

Another rank took the teachers' place. Banners swam by. Men and women marched into the plaza, placed a kiss on the stump, lined up, retreated into the Tsylia, and rode up past the reviewing stand, chanting slogans. And the marquises on the stand waved and shouted back. The banners screamed: "Forward to the past!" "To the great paragon, medieval Prusa!" "A people not oppressing another cannot be free!" "Who's afraid of wicked trolls?"

"I am, for one," the one-armed man murmured.

"Why?" Meir whispered, falling in line.

"Them trolls, they live underground."

"How'd you know?"

"Every now and then, they poke at the ceilings of their caverns."

"Oh. I wonder why," Meir said, still under his breath.

"They can't stand our patriotic singing."

While they exchanged their whispers, five well-nourished men riding up the Tsylia unfurled their banner, sheet music of four notes and the inscription "The Union of Composers." Rudolph, a happy smile on his face, produced a violin and played, his eyes on the banner,

do do do
doo!

over and over again.

"When Comrade Mark the Founder," shouted the Chairman, "perfected his lighthouse to broadcast *marconigrams*—right, Rudolph?"

"Of course, Chairman Mark," said Rudolph, his voice choked with emotion. He kept fiddling. "Do-do-do-doo!"

"—the Pharos signature tune became the hope of enslaved humanity. It passed down through the generations like a cherished secret until a father whistled it to his son within the hearing range of Ludwig van Beethoven. The latter, inspired by the Pruses' epic past, expanded the tune into his best creation, the Fifth Point Symphony."

"Do-do-do-doo!" Rudolph's eyes followed the banner's downward movement.

"*As you were*, Rudolph! Now, we in the People's Democratic Republic of Prusa adopted the line as our anthem. The text is presently unavailable, going through the third revision. Salute to the anthem!"

Chairman Mark threw his left arm forward in a clenched-fist salute, and so did everyone on the stand and in the square, except for the one-armed Kantorovich. After an instant of hesitation he used his right arm. Before he had a chance to lower it, the crowd knocked him down.

"See this Wagnerite?" they shouted, trampling him down. "The right-hand salute—what nerve!"

Meir Kovner started to protest but was quick to remember his handicap and only sank his chin deeper.

Kantorovich propped himself up on his good elbow and pronounced, with a happy smile, "It's good to die for one's music," whereupon he breathed his last.

"Where are you, Rudolph?" The Chairman bent over the parapet.

"Over here. I'd rather be in Princeton, though."

"Nothing doing, Rudolph. No nostalgic self-indulgence. Just do the scientists."

"Yes, of course. The Institute of Very Specific Physics is invited to the tribune."

The woman in the Muslim *burka* materialized next to Rudolph.

Rudolph said, "I cannot, eh, properly identify the presenter, who goes under the assumed name, Imelda."

The woman laid her baby bundle on the guardrail. Through the thick gauze covering her face came a croaking, rasping bass. "Following the wise directives of Chairman Mark, we in the Institute have marked the Great Anniversary by reproducing the ancient Parusian radio. Our starting point was the capacitor that you found in a sixth-century Baltic amber block."

"I beg your pardon," shouted the archeologist from the square. Under his slouch hat, he cupped his hands in a megaphone. "We haven't dug yet below the eighth century."

"Correction. The capacitor that you *will* find in a sixth-century Baltic amber block."

"Are you a man or a woman?" asked Rudolph.

The black gauze swung about to him. "Keep your wandering paws to yourself, mutant. I'm a man all right."

The man Imelda unwrapped the bundle. Out came a chunk of yellow rock, upon which rested a spiral of barbed wire. Guarding the rock with his left hand from falling, Imelda pinched the wire's tip and began slowly, carefully to scrape about the surface of the crystal. Something crackled. A burring voice said, "I we'ally see thwu you, the MLJ basta'ds."

"A historic statement," said the Chairman.

Imelda's disembodied voice explained. "Our script recognition system has just vocalized the previously unknown note by Comrade Mark the Founder on the margins of his *Good Tidings* manuscript. *I really see through you, bastards*—followed by seven exclamation marks."

"Comrade Mark was a passionate man," said Rudolph.

"We recognized the seven seemingly innocuous bars and dots as the barcode of what is wrongly called Roentgen rays, or equally wrongly, X-rays. What with the above phrase—*see through you*—clearly Comrade Mark had made an epochal discovery in physics and medicine!"

On his perch, Chairman Mark Two Hundred and Eighty-Seven thrust his left fist forward.

"Long live the Mark rays!"

"Long live—live—live—live," the call rolled down the square. *"Hey, hey, M-L-J, get a scrotumful of Mark's ray!"*

"Are you in charge of the project?" asked Rudolph.

"Negative," Imelda said. "The people in charge never leave the underground."

"But why do you have a bunch of frogs in your throat? Couldn't you say it like all men?"

"I can't. My voice—it's being electronically scrambled to prevent identification."

"Now, Rudolph! No idle yekkish chat! Just give the man—eh, Imelda—his medal."

"Yes, of course. Here you are, Comrade. The insignia of the Order, title classified. An arm and hammer on a chain forged of uranium-235. I'm pinning it at your heart."

As Rudolph spoke, the lid of a manhole in the left end of the parade grounds broke from its bed. It shifted sidewise to open a crescent of a gape. Two hands pushed the lid by the edge all the way off. A head popped out and swiveled about; a human figure climbed out, looked around, and made an all-clear sign. One after another, three more shapes emerged. The file of four moved silently towards the Tsylia, the faceless shadows wearing identical black robes that fell to the ground. On the breast of the figure in front dangled a placard:

$$E=mC^3$$

"The Division of Physics," said Rudolph and whined softly. *"Of Peeziks!"* Zarnitsyn's voice squealed somewhere. *"Peeziks! Peeziks!* Say *no* to the MLJ accent!"

"Of progressive physics-pizziks," said the man Imelda. "Watch the people's power."

He descended André's ladder with agility unimpaired by his long *burka.* Rudolph made to follow, prompting a tut-tut from Chairman Mark and "you've got no security clearance, Rudolph," upon which Rudolph calmed down. Imelda joined the row in front of the Tsylia, making it a full five. The cabin with the physicists went up. The marquises whispered greetings, and the riders mouthed it back. On returning to the ground, they marched to the hole.

Chairman Mark watched them disappear. "Now, Rudolph, a couple of words for the Division of Mathematics."

"The Division of Mathematics, yes. They have succeeded where generations of mathematicians failed. Even the Swiss genius, Leonard Euler—"

"Prussian genius!"

"Even the Prussian genius, Leonard Euler, stopped short of solving the problem which consisted of crossing over all seven bridges of Königsberg—"

"Kovnergrad, Rudolph!"

Meir Kovner started. Did he hear it? His mind reeled back to the archeologist and colonel on the road, and their strange behavior began making sense. He felt utterly happy. He threw back his collar and tried to shout, "I'm here, brothers! Proletarian salute!" and was angry that his voice failed him, as happens in dreams.

"Forgive my slips of tongue," Rudolph said. "The problem of passing through the seven bridges of Kovnergrad in one continuous route and none of them twice. Leonard Euler declared it impossible. But—"

Chairman Mark raised his hand. Men in grey trench coats began rolling from a side street onto the square. The formation plunged through the parting crowd towards the parade grounds. Meir recognized the outfit that he'd seen on the road. Colonel Ashkenazi-1469 marched in front. Three soldiers brought up the rear, rolling a piano. It rumbled, rattled, screamed.

The Chairman's triumphant voice rose over the din. "But our glorious Academy of Sciences, armed with the solely true, Markist mathematics, have licked the Seven Bridges Problem. They blew up a bridge!"

"We have a very, very strong Division of Mathematics," said Rudolph proudly. "Second only to the Kantemirov Tank Division."

The entire column was now in the parade grounds. The piano came to rest in the plaza. Somebody brought a chair.

Chairman Mark shouted, "Guards Captain Ashkenazi-864!"

"Yessir!"

"Action!"

Captain Vladimir Ashkenazi left the ranks and goose-stepped towards the instrument. He shed his fatigues, revealing tails and a white tie, sunk into the chair, and threw up the lid of the Piano Arithmometer. The opening sounds of the *Pas de Deux* from *Swan Lake* served as a signal. Shouting, people climbed over the barrier, formed couples, and danced in the plaza.

Doctor Markman on the stand at last recognized Meir and pointed at him, laughing. Marquises fed André under the guardrail and passed him down from level to level, until the men on the ground received him into the ready hands. To the music's beat, they began tossing the little man. His painted parchment locked with both hands, he took off and fell back and sailed up again, guffawing happily.

"Up-n-down, up-n-down, ten more times and he's mine," said a man at Meir's side. Flat-nosed and wide-eyed, dressed in a long black mackintosh and a grey felt fedora, he watched the tossing nonchalantly. "Do you think we can allow the man who walked our streets—allow him to go back and slander us under the neon lights of Montmartre?"

"You're mistaken," said Meir Kovner, still savoring his triumph. "Ain't no neon in Montmartre. You mean Broadway. Broadway is in America."

"America," the man beneath the fedora said gravely. "Why should your thoughts turn to America? I'll tell you why, Kovner. Your dalliance with America goes back to the 1920s, when an American spy ring, the Agro-Joint, purportedly sponsored the Jewish agricultural settlements in the Crimea."

"The Joint was a humanitarian organization."

The tossers set the little man down, bound his hands behind his back, and frog-marched him away.

"It was the Zionist-capitalist enemy outfit all right." The erect, unsmiling figure loomed over Meir. "They took cover behind a charity front, but their long-term objective was chopping the Crimea off the Soviet Union. You made frequent trips to the area, where you conspired with their emissaries. You, Meir Kovner, code name *Early Mark*, exposed long ago as an American spy—"

"You're mistaken again," said Meir Kovner. "I was exposed as a Japanese spy." A familiar twinge hit his stomach.

"So you were a Japano-American spy. A go-between for Roosevelt and the Mikado. A vital link in the global anti-Soviet ring, emerging from under Marco Polo Bridge in Japanese-occupied China, arcing at the 40th parallel to Market Street, Philadelphia, and continuing across the Pacific all the way back to your Japanese masters. You enciphered your cabal's records into impenetrable German Gothic handwriting. You concealed them in shoeboxes at the Institute of Marxism's library, and you inscribed the boxes *Early Marx*, cynically exploiting the sacred name."

Now Captain Ashkenazi jammed the *Tannenbaum* tune. Above the piano soared a placard, G L G L, and the crowd sang *O Gilgele, O Gilgele, your gentle sounds will teach me.* "Another vocalization," demanded the voice of Chairman Mark, and the song morphed to *Gulagele, Gulagele, from bogs to shiny sea.* The voice, soft and grey as the felt fedora, kept purling at Meir's ear.

"Let's pass to your last name, Kovner. It's no accident that the town of Kovno should sit in close proximity to the Prussian border. You, Meir 'Mark' Kovner, have long fashioned yourself in the role of Mark-288 of Prusa. You and your traitorous friends, the gang of Jewish bourgeois nationalists and foreign spies, have infiltrated the Sanhedrin of the People's Democratic Republic of Prusa. You have secretly petitioned the United States Senate to admit Prusa to the Union as a borough of New York City. Upon which admission, you'll open the Baltic harbors for the American Navy. Confess now!"

"I do," Meir Kovner said quickly. Sickness rose into his throat.

He heard rumbling that seemed to come from underground. Somebody behind Meir screamed, "Stop singing, now!" The crowd burst into shouts. Meir made out, "The wicked troll struck again!" The ground under Meir's feet shook. Suddenly, a large chunk of the parade grounds caved in. The piano jolted, banked, and sank down into an open void, together with Captain Ashkenazi-864 and his chair.

In a wild uproar, pandemonium broke loose. The yawning sinkhole spread, eating into the ground around it. Dancers and tossers alike got caught in the sinkhole and vanished, swallowed by the void. It closed in on the pit under the Tsylia. The structure staggered. The boxes swung forward pulling the frame along. It fell face down, the right side caught on the exposed stump roots. For a moment, the structure held horizontally, bringing to light its tin back, gear and handles. Then the left shoulder pivoted down. The Mother of the Nation cleared the roots and collapsed into the abyss.

Marquises jumped from the stand, which quivered but held its ground. In front of Meir, the barrier crumbled and disintegrated.

Timber split apart and fell into the crater. People on the rim tried to flee but the crowd held them back. The jagged edge of the precipice crawled Meir's way, unavoidably, irrevocably. Meir stood put, unable to run away, head on fire, feet riveted, heart about to burst.

Chairman Mark, dark against the crimson sky, screamed from his vantage point atop the stand:

"No panic! A great opportunity! We'll turn the pit into the world's largest swimming pool!"

The chasm stopped at Meir's feet. Meir wouldn't look down, from where dust and moans wafted. In what remained of the parade grounds, Colonel Ashkenazi gathered his troops. "In order of size! Ash-502, where're you barging? Here you aren't in your math class—it takes brains over here!"

Captain Vladimir Ashkenazi, disheveled and pale, climbed out of the pit, pulled up by a blond Valkyrie, the false prophet Johannes' daughter.

"Forward—harch!" The 104 Battalion pulled away, the public falling in step behind them in a long, meandering band.

The song of the Guards went on *a cappella*:

> The trumpet blows
> The final call to onslaught
> We're on the march
> To battle and prevail.
> Blood-colored flags
> Lead us to better common folk's lot
> Hurray, Paruse! There looms your Holy Grail!

"Move your ass, Prusifalchik," the man beneath the fedora said to Meir, derisively.

Snow started falling, first slowly, reluctantly, every flake by itself, then thickened up into one whirling mess. The wind picked up. Meir felt grains of biting snow against his cheeks. The snowstorm, blowing and drifting, rushed along the streets and out to the country. The head of the column with Colonel Ashkenazi was gone from sight. Then the rest became invisible to Meir, except for the hunched shoulders of people trudging in front of him.

"Move on! Move on!"

The temperature rose. The snow on the ground was no more. Hot wind burned the skin of Meir's face and hampered his breathing. It carried particles of sand, as sharp and biting as the snow.

Meir Kovner brought up the rear, his warden following in a jeep.

PART
FIVE

CHAPTER TWENTY-EIGHT

This afternoon, a Russian lorry drew up to the villa's northern doorway. Four burly men in mufti craned a tub into the ballroom. They eased it into a window bay and pulled off the burlap.

A lemon tree, complete with golden fruits. Flown in—from where?

Winston Churchill wished his staff had been more careful with their tongues within Russians' earshot. The other day at a cocktail party some British aides had heaved a sigh or two for lemon peel. The Russians must have overheard.

"See to it," Churchill said to the aide reporting the lemon episode, "that no one among the staff utters the words *Swan Lake* to the Russians."

"Why, sir? The Whitehall recommended Tchaikovsky as a safe conversation piece."

"Isn't it the name of a pond on the estate? For all I know, the Russians may fill it in and fly in a couple of cygnets overnight."

The balding aide with washed-out eyelashes giggled. Lagging behind at Churchill's flank, he minced his steps across the villa's lawn.

"Like the gold fish in Livadia," he contributed. "The other day an American said a couple of the fishies'd look swell behind the glass. The next day the Russians stuffed the grand aquarium to the rim."

Obscene largesse in the midst of the starving country . . .

Dusk was falling. Churchill's chauffeur had just brought him back to the villa from Livadia, the former Palace of the Czar's,

·259·

where plenary meetings were held. Livadia was an Italianate palace with large bright bedrooms. In there, Stalin had put up the American president, whereas Churchill had to be content with a daily commute. The winding road passed Stalin's residence. Twenty-four miles, circular tour. Daily. No grievances, of course— only natural considering Roosevelt's sad state of health. Half a world away from home and showing every inch of it. But it added to the feeling that three's a crowd. Roosevelt cuddling up to Stalin. Roosevelt's little jokes at Churchill's expense. Roosevelt's indifference, bordering on hostility, to the interests of the Empire. Roosevelt's refusal to stay with Churchill in Malta for more than one day. He wouldn't give Stalin the impression that the Western allies were conspiring against him. Conspiring against *him!*

The aide said, "I wonder, sir, how the State Department might have instructed our American colleagues about Tchaikovsky. The one with 'the fishes' said Tchaikovsky was a swell guy. He'd written the *Overture 1812* to celebrate the Americans' gallant resistance when we the perfidious Brits burned the White House in Washington. I wonder whether he ever heard about Napoleon."

Winston Churchill couldn't stand cheap America-baiting. The son of an American mother and himself a great admirer of the spirit of the New World, he would have no part of it. What was even worse, with his slur the aide may've been trying to ingratiate himself with Churchill. Had the staff noticed Roosevelt's unfortunate slights? Had it gone *that* far?

He barked, "Watch your tongue, Gates!"

The aide pinked. "Yes, sir."

Ah, well. For better or for worse, the conference was practically over. Reduced to a dinner party tonight for Churchill to host. Some finishing touches before the late-night signing of the communiqué. And the East Prussia issue still in limbo.

That morning, Stalin said, "I like those *Gilgele* songs. They remind me of the *Suliko*." The latter, a gooey Georgian ballad, was on the homework list of anyone dealing with Stalin, but *Gilgele*? Churchill's aides found out that it was an equally schmaltzy cycle of Yiddish songs. The Soviets promoted it within the framework of a pseudo-scholarly project, Stalin's substantiation for his designs on East Prussia. A very good sign, his mentioning it. The Prussia thing must have turned the corner.

Past marble lions watching the sea, Churchill descended wide stone steps. The aide tagged along, two steps behind. Churchill breathed in the salt-tinged air. The sea was at his feet, grey and heavy. The *Franconia*, his floating headquarters, was invisible behind the promontory of Phoros. And then not a patch of land all the way to the Strait of Bosphorus. A strange sea. An ominous expanse, without a single island.

He glanced back up the stairs. The building was no more—it had receded into the greenery. Two minaret towers alone remained visible, flanking the pointed arch of the mosque-like terracotta façade and Byzantine cupolas. Byzantine? Nonsense. They were Mogul cupolas. And above the villa a primordial chaos of slabs bordered an oppressive crag of a mountain.

He glanced over at the aide. A young man, baby-faced, not over forty. His face was still slightly pink with embarrassment.

"Do you care for this place, Gates?"

The aide shot him a quick glance. "This palace, sir?"

"Yes, this villa."

"Very impressive."

"Drop the lingo. Say it straight."

"I find it somewhat eclectic."

"Eclectic?"

"Yes, sir. A blend of Yorkshire and Punjab."

Churchill hemmed. "Back to our muttons, Gates."

"Yes, sir. After the lemon lorry, a swarm of grimy Russians descended upon this place. The KGB men, uniformed or plain-clothed. Security men."

Churchill cut him short. "You don't have to explain to me who the hell the KGB are."

"No, sir." The aide pinked again, heavily. His skin took to pink easily, Churchill noticed. "They checked the reception rooms, got under the tables and behind the curtains, then into the kitchens. They have placed their men all over the place. And they've designated the first-floor bathroom for Stalin alone. I fear, sir, you have to use one of the staff facilities."

The facilities in question were dingy closets.

The aide was a sorry sight.

"They took over the reception area completely. Turning back any staff who'd wish to pass through the halls. From one doorway to another we have to cross outside."

Back in his parlor, Winston Churchill helped himself to a generous scotch and soda.

His nostrils flared.

Let them dare. Let some blasted Russki try to step in his path.

He walked the halls, his jaw thrust forward. Aides and servants dashed aside merging with the walls or retreating to the kitchen.

Hot inside his collar, he flung the door open and halted in the middle of the bathroom, scanning two stalls, a red-leather-upholstered bench, and a white marble tub.

Why did he come here?

Nuts. A man of his age can always make use of a trip to a loo.

He stood at a urinal when a Russian colonel pulled up to his right. "How do you do, sir Primal Minister?"

Winston Churchill carried what he held in his right hand to his left hand. His idled right hand he shoved to the KGB colonel.

He washed his hands after the handshaking and took pleasure in wiping them on Stalin's starched towel . . .

He checked the ballroom. The lemon tree was there all right, the greenery and golden drops. Churchill jerked off one fruit.

In the court, the sun was bright not in a winter fashion. Not in the English winter fashion, at any rate. He felt a sudden bout of homesickness.

He kicked at the green stone of the façade. His shoe's toe left a dent in the damp blanket of moss. A pseudo-Gothic English abbey, except for the gaudy entry.

A blend of Yorkshire and Punjab.

He snorted. The mousy young man had his choice of words.

Churchill went along the wing of the building, bobbing the lemon in his palm. Good that Sarah was here tonight. His daughter had first met Stalin in Tehran and got on well with him since. Besides—why, she's always been her Papa's favorite, in spite of her stunts. Or maybe because of her stunts.

Back in London, Churchill had shown Sarah a Soviet film that he'd obtained through the Embassy in Moscow. Sort of a documentary with limited distribution.

On the screen, Stalin had pushed tobacco into his pipe with a short, stained thumb as his generals gazed at him lovingly and hung on his every word. He passed the pipe's stem over the gigantic map on a table, laying out the plan of the Battle of Stalingrad. It was Stalin all right. The Stalin whom he knew in Moscow and Tehran. Except his Stalin had multiple marks of smallpox, and the Stalin on the screen had none. The editors had re-touched them. Churchill nodded an approval. The gods should show no blemish before the mortals.

Documentaries, for what they were worth. Just the other day he'd watched a French newsreel. Troops taking over a German town. Charles de Gaulle against the backdrop of burning houses. Impressive footage. The trouble was, the French had captured the town a week before filming. When de Gaulle caught up with the troops, they staged the battle scenes for the movie. What if they had to burn down a couple of houses for that beanpole in a kepi! Churchill had the stupid film pulled out of the machine and relaxed with *The Iron Mask*, the last silent moving picture of great Douglas Fairbanks. The kidnapping of Louis XIV; his twin brother subbing for him. Churchill had a favorite in the Dumas story. It was noble Fouquet, who wouldn't tolerate the act of high treason committed against his guest, even if the host had everything to gain from the royal swap and everything to lose in case of failure.

Churchill entered the living quarters and knocked at Sarah's door.

"Yes?" Her voice was muffled as if she held a toothbrush in

her mouth. She had that habit, walking about with a toothbrush in her mouth. Like a horse with a mouthpiece. Or a mule. Her pet name was Mule, for her stubbornness. My blood. Churchill felt a warm wave of empathy.

"You have fifty minutes, darling."

"Aye, aye, Prime Minister."

He still held that lemon. He smelled it and placed it on the carpet runner at Sarah's door.

An hour later he stood at the center of the brightly illuminated grand ballroom, his guests clutching their cocktail glasses. The swarms grew thicker towards the glowing fireplaces. Through the blur of moving coats, suits, and uniforms with medals making a brave show, Churchill spotted Stalin's white jacket.

Winston Churchill inched towards Stalin, smiling to his guests, exchanging a couple of words with others . . . past two experts, a Scottish-American in tortoise-shell spectacles and a Russian. The Soviet man, stout and imposing in white tie, was in charge of Stalin's East Prussia project. Churchill was glad it wasn't Meir Kovner, who reportedly had something to do with the project. Churchill didn't trust the old troublemaker.

He slowed down near Sarah who was entertaining a Royal Navy officer smartly accoutered in white and gold.

"What a treat," the seaman was saying, "seeing you in civvies for a change, even though you shine in any attire."

So did she, with her bright reddish, almost orange-colored hair and large green eyes. And her deeply décolleté chartreuse worked wonders on the perfect figure of Churchill's daughter.

The lieutenant commander went on. "Any chance you desert to the Navy?"

"Nothing doing, Jim Hathaway. My choice among the Services was decided by the uniform. Carrying black about my neck in mourning for Horatio Nelson? It doesn't jazz me up. Besides, the RAF colors agree with my hair and eyes."

"I knew that the uniform makes the man, but I didn't ponder its effect on women."

"I say, it affected Eve same as Adam."

The man had a clear-cut profile, Wellington-type . . . Winston Churchill sighed inwardly on the subject of Sarah's unsettled life. Simultaneously, he was smiling to Stalin's top minister engaged with a British career diplomat. Molotov's snub-nosed face with prominent cheekbones revealed no emotion.

The brass and tailcoat crowd stopped dead at an invisible semicircle drawn before the central fireplace. A fireside scene formed the focal point of tonight's invisible tensions. Next to President Roosevelt's chair sat Marshal Stalin, pipe in hand, gold-braided high collar buttoned-up, legs in white trousers with blue-and-red seam stripes stretched in front of him.

Two fellow emperors dividing the world at a chat. Look at the president who reclined in his chair and laughed at Stalin's every utterance! Completely under the Georgian's spell. Roosevelt's eyes met Churchill's. The smile went off. Churchill felt pangs of resentment—not for himself, of course: for the Tight Little Island.

Back where he'd left her, Sarah tried out her five Russian phrases on the Soviet State Security czar.

"And the last one. *Can I have a hot water bottle, please?*"

Lavrenty Beria's eyebrows flew up in a mock surprise.

"But surely you don't need one. There is enough fire in you!"

His enthusiasm went as far as squeezing Sarah's arm.

Sarah pulled back. "You're one of the few Russians here who speak English. Did you learn it in India?"

"Why?" Beria dropped his hand.

"It's tinted with a charming Indian accent."

"I must've acquired the accent in Baku back in 1919, when Indian troops of the Royal Army invaded that sovereign Russian territory."

Churchill passed by, his mouth twisted.

His mood didn't improve as he took his place at the banquet table set with white cones of napkins. Tonight again he felt Stalin's unfortunate dominance. If in Moscow and Teheran it was bad enough, here it became even worse. Today at Livadia, when Stalin, habitually late, entered the conference room, Churchill had had to suppress an urge to stand up like a schoolboy. He couldn't help raising his rump a few inches before sinking back.

He turned to Stalin on his right. "That's a jewel of a place you've put us up in, Marshal Stalin."

Some jewel. Lacking in bathrooms. Churchill thought longingly about his customized bathtub on board the *Franconia*.

The interpreter rustled a running translation behind their backs.

Stalin nodded. "Prince Vorontsov was an Anglophile. Commissioned an architect from England." He wrinkled his eyes. "Vorontsov even wished that you the British had stayed in the Crimea after that unfortunate war—some ninety years ago? A bit of British occupation wouldn't have hurt, he said. Just long enough to open the English markets for his port."

The diners respectfully cocked an ear to the conversation among the principals.

Churchill laughed. "As we did for the claret of Bordeaux. Cultivated, if not the wine, then the thirst for it. But Vorontsov's *Ai-Petri* port had a reputation with the connoisseurs."

Stalin made a helpless gesture. "Unfortunately, nothing has survived the trials of wars and revolutions." He smiled at Sarah. "As for jewels, you have a jewel of a daughter, Prime Minister. A daughter that I would've been proud to call mine."

"Too bad that she can have but one father," Churchill smiled.

Roosevelt leaned on the table in his intimate, charming manner of bonhomie. "That makes Sarah Churchill your grandniece, Marshal Stalin." He flashed his winning smile.

The murmur hushed. In the ensuing silence, Roosevelt's voice sounded loud and clear. "That comes from the informal way that we, the Prime Minister and I, refer to you in our communications."

Stalin stared at him without blinking. Churchill cast a warning glance. But Roosevelt wouldn't be stopped.

"We call you Uncle Joe."

He glanced triumphantly from one to another around the table, waiting for a burst of good-natured laughter.

Churchill shrank inwardly. What a blunder! Nay, a *lèse majesté!* You cannot joke in such a manner at the expense of an Asiatic despot and demigod. In private, perhaps. But not in front of his humble subjects and worshipers!

Stalin's cheeks grew pale. He crumpled his napkin and threw it off.

"When could I leave this table?"

An ominous silence hung. Molotov's impenetrable eyes changed hue from dove-grey to steel grey.

Sarah Churchill sent down a charming smile. "But, Marshal Stalin, don't you people refer to the U.S. as Uncle Sam? Why can't the president and my father talk about Russia in a similar vein? With the same friendly intimacy?"

How very clever. Bravo, my darling Mule.

Stalin got up, but his feisty mood clearly was no longer there. He curtly apologized to the hostess and walked out, an elderly man on his way to the gents.

CHAPTER TWENTY-NINE

The brooms and rags lay in the tunnel. The wooden panel leaned against the wall. David Kovner stood behind the door of the broom cupboard. He could feel Ebert's breath on his neck. Further back on the staircase landing, Ognev sported Vorontsov's Turkish gown over his long underwear.

Two gorillas with colonel's shoulder stripes came into the room.

David poised, horrified.

They opened the stalls, poked under the bathtub—

Stalin came in and motioned the security men out. They closed the door noiselessly behind them. He walked to a spigot, took his pipe shining with brown varnish from his lips, and placed it on the sink's edge. Placed his face under the stream; massaged his cheeks. Reached out to a handle bar, jerked off a towel, wiped his face dry, and dropped the towel on the floor. The pipe back in his mouth, he stepped to his left, to a urinal; unbuttoned his fly. Stood long, puffing smoke, until first urine started to drip in the trickle of an old man.

Stalin tightened his grip and cut off the flow. In a while, he let it go again. The streamlet made a little burst and reduced to close to nothing. Stalin sighed and repeated the cycle. Shook it off. Smelled his fingers. Stroke his mustache.

The large mirror in front of the spigot didn't reflect the cupboard door. He couldn't see the wall open up and a man step into the room. He felt it only when a powerful arm clamped hard around his neck and something damp and stinking pressed against his mouth and nose, and he fainted.

·268·

They stripped him on the red-leather couch. He remained in soldier's drawers, the dull aluminum of the covered buttons showing through the worn fabric, his socks clipped to garters around his calves. Ognev shuffled on the white trousers with blue-and-red seam stripes and a marshal's vest. "The watch!" hissed David.

They carried the unconscious body through the secret door—Ebert, under the armpits, and David, by the feet. Farther on in the tunnel, Ebert had to make do by himself.

Ognev remained at the urinal, puffing on Stalin's pipe. His fly unbuttoned, he watched the old man's weak dribble. He sighed and smelled his fingers.

★   ★   ★

In the dining room reigned the banquet din, voices blurred by alcohol, unrestrained laughter, and silverware clatter.

Molotov gobbled another tumbler of vodka. He tucked his chin into his chest, tilted his cannonball head for a charge, and stuttered, "Your t-t-turn!" The British diplomat sighed and drew a trembling snifter to his lips. "Bottoms up," said Molotov. "It would be wiser," said the British diplomat putting down the snifter, "for the news about East Prussia to appear first in the free press."

"I see no p-p-problem," said Molotov. "In the Soviet Union, all p-p-press is free. All the other is p-p-prohibited. Don't shirk it. Drink to dregs! It isn't the Molotov cocktail after all, just v-v-vodka."

Further down, the two professors were getting cozier with every new glass. The Russian pressed for drinking brotherhood with a due kiss on the mouth; the American demurred, but slapped Zarnitsyn on the back and wanted to hear more about his outstanding project. "We've raised our eyes to a larger goal," Zarnitsyn said and served himself another shot. His cheeks had turned florid.

All hushed momentarily: Stalin was returning to his seat.

His eyes traveling with Stalin, Zarnitsyn went on. "Language is the key. The German language bears the lion's share of responsibility for Prussian militarism, Bavarian boorishness, and ultimately for the Nazi page in German history. Martin Luther blundered. As the raw material for the German language, he picked the wrong dialect. He opted for the one in use in the Saxon princes' chancellery. We're going to correct his error of judgment. The corrupted German language, the language of universal hatred, will be reshaped by proletarian Beggar's Welsh."

The American slapped his forehead. "Beggar's Welsh! I've just read an article by Professor Hramoy. I've requested an appointment with him in Moscow" (he looked at his wristwatch, unnecessarily) "in four days."

"Hramoy doesn't own the language," Zarnitsyn said testily. "And he never fathomed the potential of Beggar's Welsh. Never made a connection with the medieval Prussia—how could he? He's out of the loop. It's we at the Institute of Marxism, the world-renowned discoverers of Marx's crushing characterization of Teutonic Mounted Hounds—we started working on Beggar's Welsh revival even before Hramoy's paper. We'll carry the precious legacy of the Great Peasants' War into the twentieth century! We'll infuse the German language with the politically correct idiom!"

Zarnitsyn picked a peach from the tray of an approaching waiter. "Stalin attaches the first-rate priority to the project. He's kept the name Project Prusa for official use, but he himself always refers to it as Operation Haman."

"Do you discuss your work with Marshal Stalin?" the American asked, awestruck. He absentmindedly took a peach from the tray of the lingering waiter.

Zarnitsyn fought off the dangerous temptation to lie. He sighed. "No, but I'm getting his ideas through Minister Molotov."

He stood up. Vodka splashed from the glass in his raised hand.

"At the moment of truth, the German language will come back to its roots for rejuvenation. Push Germany back to her glorious past when Königsberg was still Tel Hamelekh!"

He gobbled his shot and sank back. Couldn't agree more, Professor Gibbs said. They drank their glasses and kissed.

Mopping peach juice from his lips, Zarnitsyn sprung to his feet—his stomach weakened by decades of boozing demanded relief. His thought continued to flow in a pleasant spirits-induced stream. Come March, he thought while walking across the courtyard, he'd be voted into the Academy as a full member. His project would develop into a grandiose scheme. In People's Republic of Prussia, children would be taken at birth from their parents and raised in state institutions. Their tutors and teachers would have taken a crash course in Beggar's Welsh from Rostock pimps and Berlin hookers. They would swear to be faithful to Beggar's Welsh at all times. Their diplomas in hand, they'd descend on nurseries, kindergartens, and schools. They would compensate for the inadequacies of their vocabulary by humming and gesturing, but most of all, by their enthusiasm. They would make up new words on the spot, the great innovators, each one of them a Samuel Johnson of Beggar's Welsh, a Ben Yehuda, and l'Académie Française! The pupils would be exposed to nothing but the ancient tongue. Nothing foreign should affect the wonderful sensibility of their ears. No horse neighing, no bird chirping, because those were also languages of sort. The first all-Rotwelsch-speaking children in modern history . . . He reached the distant shack— lath and tarpaper, three holes in the floor—assigned to his ilk. There, under the relentless light of a bulb in the ceiling, choking on the murderous smell, he squatted, assuaged his intestines, and reached for the nail in the wall. He pulled off the impaled paperclip, the last one from the nail, and threw a glance at it while bringing it to the destination. His arm froze halfway: Stalin's face, minus one cheek and ear, looked at him from the newspaper cut. In Zarnitsyn's ears, voices thundered, "Death to the blasphemer!" and his eyes, bugged in horror, seemed to watch men with assault rifles popping out from the other two holes and filling up the shack. He closed his eyes and remained thus until the tumult in his head died down. With his trembling hand, Zarnitsyn returned the paperclip to the nail, the portrait facing the wall. His trousers down, he stole out on half-bent legs and scooped wet leaves from the ground . . .

The two professors were too far from Churchill for him to follow their chat, but he heard Zarnitsyn's indiscreet toast. The Prussia thing had been secured. An important victory. Opposite him, at the far wall, the victory goddess, Nika, balanced her brass body on the tip of her sandal, supporting massive candelabra in her raised hands. Churchill counted five candles, which tended sometimes to double to ten.

Goddam Russians. Hard to catch up with. But they wouldn't beat *him.*

Churchill caught sight of Lavrenty Beria. Stalin's henchman was demolishing a chicken. Having wrenched a leg from the chicken's body, he tore off pieces of flesh with his fingers and threw them into his mouth. His eyes behind the glistening pince-nez openly devoured Sarah.

Fury rose up Churchill's throat. The last straw! He'd tell Stalin what he'd found in the Whitehall archives: back in 1919, in the city of Baku in the Caucasus, Beria was the British occupiers' informant.

The fit of anger cleared Churchill's head of alcohol fumes better that sal ammoniac. He stood up, drank to the Grand Alliance. The words came easily to his trained lips. The Soviet people could rest assured that they had two faithful and reliable allies.

Stalin narrowed his eyes. "In Livadia, where we hold our plenary sessions, Czar Alexander stayed and died. He had said Russia had two allies. Who was Russia's first ally? Russia's first ally was her army. Who was Russia's second ally? Russia's second ally was her fleet."

Behind Churchill's back, a dark-eyed waiter stopped with a heavy gilded tray of wine glasses. The waiter offered a bottle for the host's examination. Churchill's eyebrows went up at the golden circles and the mountain on the label. "*Ai-Petri* port! So they found some of Vorontsov's stock, Marshal Stalin!"

Churchill took a sip. Superb. Exquisite color, rich in bouquet, what with extra years of aging. He nodded his approval.

The waiter placed a glass in front of Churchill, then two more for Stalin and Roosevelt.

Stalin narrowed his eyes to a smile. "As you can see, I do carry some clout in the kitchen and cellars."

He rose to his feet. "Ladies and gentlemen, comrades! Allow me to use this occasion for a communication. The Presidium of the Supreme Soviet insists on the inclusion of East Prussia into the Russian Federation. Can we go against the will of our parliament? No, we cannot go against the will of our parliament. It's incumbent on me to announce it at this dinner, which has fully met our expectations. And now I drink to the host, a man who is born once in a hundred years."

He took a sip from his class of port and sat down. His eyes shifted from Roosevelt to Churchill and back. "A Jewish state in the Baltic? No one but provocateurs could come with so weird an idea. The Soviet Union has never had any intention whatsoever to participate in that chimerical enterprise."

Churchill reached to the waiter's tray and washed down his defeat with the second helping of Vorontsov's port.

The waiter with Hindu eyes moved on and offered the port to the British diplomat vis-à-vis Molotov.

Sarah Churchill took a glass, too. She was certain those eyes of black velvet had not been in the room before. Another Russian spook? Or did we slip in one of ours, above the agreed-upon number?

She squinted and smiled at him.

The waiter winked in return.

Across the table, Beria watched the silent exchange of signs between the hostess and the British spy. The bastard had appeared out of thin air, past Beria's men, carrying two bottles of Vorontsov's port! Beria called page after page of British agents' files to his formidable memory but couldn't match that face. Was the Sarah in the spy business, too? She had done a stint as a scantily clad chorus girl, then as a dramatic actress. Married an Austrian-born comedian. The marriage had gone sour. Now at thirty, Section Officer of the Royal Air Force, she interpreted aerial photos— why, quite a spy's job. His glance ripped through her gown from the cleavage down and disposed of it in one jerk.

Zarnitsyn had been out of the banquet room long enough to miss the last exchange of toasts. He paused behind Molotov's back. Stalin's number two sat upright in his chair, staring at the cut-off head, dead eyes closed, of the defeated British diplomat in his plate. Molotov's pate retained its yellowish tint despite the alcohol he had drunk. Zarnitsyn bent to Molotov with an easy intimacy of a favorite retainer. "The great new idea of yours, Comrade Minister. Paruses and Persia, ha ha. Being done." Molotov's glance didn't swerve. "P-p-paruses? Never heard." He weighed in his hand a peach offered by a passing waiter, flattened its bottom against the table with a whack, and placed it on the head of the British diplomat. The eyes opened for a moment and closed again.

Alarmed, Zarnitsyn went down and squeezed into his seat. The cup on his saucer tinkled, as if worried. He raised a smile for the American's benefit. "Let me tell you the one about Paruses on Place Pigale. You'll die laughing."

The American expert gave him an angry look. "Hell if I know what you're talking about." He turned his back on the Russian. In a moment he glanced over his shoulder. "Why don't you go and take some Prussic acid, my Socratic friend? In place of hemlock."

Zarnitsyn suppressed another urge to the toilet; at least, he hoped he did. Nothing would force him back to the shack with the paperclip on the wall.

Across the table, Jim Hathaway struggled with a nagging thought. Where else had he seen those dark eyes?

He sat through the dessert, his uneasiness growing . . .

He found the British duty officer in the library. The officer oversaw preparations for the signing ceremony. Along the wall, the photographers violently moved their tripods and flashguns about. Barred from the banquet rooms, they seemed set for revenge.

The officer kept his eyes on the aides arranging chairs. "The telephones in the main building are out of reach, Hathy. The Russians have taken over for the night—no, no!" he yelled to the aides. "Leave more room for the President!"

He glanced back at Hathaway.

"Excuse me, old chap."

Outside, gusts of wind brought in the odors of a salty, tepid sea hinting at distant outhouses. The marble lions kept watch for enemy submarines. In that spy-congested place, Hathaway half-expected the big cats to turn their heads at the crunch of the twigs under his feet.

He shared a room with three signals officers in the garden hands' hut. The telephone line wasn't safe.

"Would you give me Moscow—now?"

The operator in Simferopol called back almost right away.

"I'm sorry for the late-night call. It pertains to your nephew."

Meir Kovner's voice was stifled. "What about my nephew"?

"He promised me an interview. Could I speak to him now? . . . Oh, he isn't. What's the best time to call him tomorrow? . . . I see. I understand."

He strode back. The Mogul cupolas stood black against the dark sky. Behind them, rows of chimneystacks reared up like flak batteries. Hathaway felt the spooky presence of invisible Russians behind every shrub. In the gardens, at Swan Lake, a crafty sorcerer was readying Odile to sub for Odette.

Hathaway plunged back into the atmosphere of warmed-up bodies, alcohol vapors, and quick deception. The dark-eyed waiter in the white linen jacket collected half-eaten fruit. Hathaway crossed to him.

"How about our interview, Major?"

The waiter gazed emptily past him and moved on to the door.

Beria registered the contact of two British spies. He went to the corridor. Two uniformed guards stood to attention.

"The waiter who just left—where'd he go?"

The guard pointed to the kitchens and the VIP men's room. "Over there, sir."

"How did he get to the banquet room in the first place?"

The lieutenant turned red in face. "I dunno, sir. Comrade Stalin was returning from—from the bathroom, and the waiter minced at his side. Comrade Stalin was kind of giving him instructions, pointing at two bottles in his hands. I—I didn't challenge him, walking as he was with Comrade Stalin."

Beria's furious gaze incinerated the guard. He spoke to the cinders in a violent whisper.

"You will this time, idiot. Find out, and unless he is Jesus Christ, you'll detain him."

He returned to the banquet room, into the armor clank of cutlery and the all-inspecting glances of his well-positioned scouts. How much better he was qualified to issue battle orders, he thought, than that old fart who couldn't hold his piss for the duration of the dinner.

The British Navy officer who'd spoken to the waiter made his way to Sarah Churchill, who was sipping tea from a white-and-red china cup. They were too far from Beria to hear. To add insult to injury, the crafty Englisher maneuvered Sarah away from the lemon tree with its mike.

"You seem to know that waiter," Hathaway said.

"Which one?" Sarah professed innocence.

"You know who I mean. The bloke who left the room a minute ago. If one enterprising Russian major weren't back in his hospital, as his uncle is protesting rather unconvincingly, I could've sworn that he was here passing about wine and dessert."

"Oh well, one more rug merchant on the Northwestern Frontier."

"Why change the rules of the engagement? They keep their men in the open. Even on the balcony above us."

Under the yellow Gothic ribs on the red ceiling, two brawny men in grey business suits stared down at the partying.

Sarah Churchill shot her eyes up and shrugged. "Well, no secrets to keep. I wear falsies only on stage."

"There'll be no signing tonight," Hathaway heard behind his back. The mousy aide, Gates, spoke to Sarah alone.

"And why so?" Hathaway said and paid for that.

"That's not to be disclosed to lower-level personnel."

"Now, Gates, don't be a pompous arse," Sarah told him. "Disclose to humble us the great secret of the great men."

"What with the last-minute snag about East Prussia. Stalin doesn't want to rush it. They'll do the signatures tomorrow, at Livadia."

Sarah brought her gaze onto Stalin at the door. His face stern, he listened to Winston Churchill speaking to his ear. The rest of the party had fallen back, respecting the leaders' privacy.

"Excuse me, Jim. Will you hold this for me?"

She pushed the cup adorned with a golden monogram, N & A, into Hathaway's hands and went to her father's help. Gates, the senior-level aide, threw an openly hostile glance at Hathaway.

Jim Hathaway watched Sarah talking to Stalin, who stared at her. Then a smile ran under his mustache. He curtly bowed and was gone.

Beria followed him. Passing by Sarah Churchill, he stopped short. "But one thing in the English language I could never fathom. Why do you people write your father's initials on the doors of your toilets?" He snorted and was gone.

Streams of Russian guests flowed towards the door. They kept a distance from Professor Zarnitsyn.

I'm dead meat, Zarnitsyn thought. The empty place around him grew. He physically felt silver threads multiply in his full head of hair. Making use of both hands, he snatched two tumblers from the tray of a passing waiter and knocked them down, back-to-back.

Without any apparent reason, David Kovner came to his mind. What could it mean, this recollection so out of place?

He made hasty steps to intercept Molotov. "How could I have known?"

"You should've," the minister said, icily. His gaze bore through Zarnitsyn and moved away.

Zarnitsyn crossed on his shaky legs to the waiters' sideboard. He stole a look around, snatched hold of a barely started bottle of Gordon's, and slipped it underneath his tailcoat, under the armpit. The long corridors of the Lubyanka with their blood-red carpet runners came into his internal vision. Zarnitsyn knew that nothing would save him when they started looking for a scapegoat. Little comfort that Meir Kovner would perish too.

He grabbed another bottle, openly.

★   ★   ★

Later in the night, Sarah Churchill knocked at the door of her father's suite.

"Enter!"

Winston Churchill, clad in a tasseled crimson silk robe, was chasing the alcohol of the banquet with cognac. He cast an admiring glance at his daughter.

"You've saved the day, darling. Made a marvelous hostess and a new admirer."

Sarah shook her head. "He's a property of Francis B—."

Her father choked over his reply. "Why, Stalin wants you for a daughter."

"Nothing new. He'd said as much back in Tehran. But another Russian monster opened a very promising conversation indeed, and his glances were far from fatherly." She shuddered. "As for a father, I have one and he's the best of the kind."

She came along and patted his shoulder.

Churchill stroked the back of her hand. She'd always had her way with him, whether it was about her childhood follies or her theatrical career.

She said, "Did you notice anything strange about Stalin tonight?"

"Strange? What do you mean?"

"I don't know. Just a feeling."

Winston Churchill smiled. "Tonight was the first occasion when there was nothing strange in him. His omnipresent, overbearing personality—I didn't feel it towards the end. I've overcome it!"

She served him another *Hine* and kissed him goodnight. Churchill sat back nursing the snifter.

Hard cheese. Too bad Stalin had put paid to the East Prussia project. Too bad for the British Empire. The most magnificent formation in the history of mankind, she might prove so short-lived. Bled white and bankrupt as she was, faint, spent and weary, she'd won a war and was losing a peace. The last thing she needed was yet another punch at her solar plexus. Churchill dreaded hordes of death camps' survivors wading from clandestine boats, oozing through the borders into Palestine; and then—the Arab world radicalized, the Suez Canal blocked, the jugular vein of the Empire squeezed down.

Had he made a mistake in the old days, during his tenure at the Colonial Office? Back then, Jews sought to establish a world Bolshevik empire under their domination, didn't they? True zealots, Meir Kovner type. Churchill encouraged them to work instead towards a simple, true, and attainable goal, a Hebrew state in Palestine. Now that communism had resumed its westward march, the Jews no longer played any leading role in it, but no credit belonged to Churchill. It was Stalin who had curbed the Jewish Commissars' power. Meanwhile, Zionism had grown into a real menace for the British Empire. It rocked the Middle East. Churchill had counted on the East Prussia project to defuse that threat. Now that hope had evaporated.

Was it Roosevelt's unfortunate joke that made Stalin retaliate? Then Sarah had saved the conference from a still greater disaster. The war was virtually over, and yet anything unforeseen might ruin the whole effort. There was a very relevant historical precedent, the sudden death of a Russian empress, which had saved the King of Prussia, Frederic the Great, from a crashing defeat in the Seven-Year

War. This episode reportedly fortified Hitler's resolution to fight to the very end. Waiting for a miracle, he.

Winston Churchill sipped from his glass. Something strange in Stalin, Sarah had asked . . .

During the entire dinner he had seen Stalin's right side alone. But as his guest was leaving and Churchill was telling Stalin about Beria's doings in Baku back in 1919, he spoke to Stalin's left ear. He could solemnly swear that Stalin of yesterday, and of the last week, and in Tehran last year, and in Moscow in 1942—that all those Stalins had had a small pockmark behind the left earlobe, right beyond the hairline. With his eye of a painter, Churchill had noticed it well. Now he wasn't sure if Stalin had that mark tonight.

Stalin, the wily rascal. He'd manipulated them into coming here, to his turf. Churchill and Roosevelt suggested Cairo, sort of halfway. He said no; after Tehran his doctors forbade him flying. A mighty flimsy excuse, but even faulty logic can get the better of you if backed by so many artillery barrels.

Churchill grunted in contempt. Guns or no guns, Stalin would never have had it his way were it not for Churchill childhood's passion. Back at Harrow, the boy Winston recited the ringing verses: *Into the jaws of Death, into the mouth of Hell rode the six hundred,* and felt creepy all over. A cadet at Sandhurst, he pledged to hike one day the hills above Sevastopol, where the horsemen of the Thirteenth Dragoons Light Brigade had charged Russian canons— off they rode in the ecstasy of blind obedience and gave their lives to the finest nation in the world. What grandeur of the spirit!

He got up. He deserved a treat. As soon as he could, he would head to the killing fields of Balaklava.

★   ★   ★

Meir Kovner laid the telephone receiver down.

He'd heard something that Jim Hathaway hadn't. After the shrill persistent tones of a long-distance call awakened him, an impatient female voice came on the line. "Here's Simferopol. Go ahead!" and another click, before Hathaway's voice reached him.

So Hathaway had called from the Crimea.

And he talked about David.

Why on earth should an interview with David Kovner be so important to him that he placed a late-night call from the Crimea?

And David was in the Crimea too.

David had arrived at the safe house all right, although with a week's delay. "Sasha" reported the other man with him—Meir had no qualms about keeping an eye on the old comrade, and see? Seemed that Heinrich was disloyal to him, after all.

What's David up to?

The interview. The code word indicating that David was on his way out of the country. Did he ask Hathaway to place a call? Back at the party they had hit it off, David and Jim, soldier to soldier.

The code word was there, but the phrase was wrong.

Meir Kovner jackknifed in his bed. *Was David in harm's way?*

He missed David terribly . . .

Since that nightmarish trance in his office, half-dream, half-hallucination, Meir had experienced sleeping problems. And he could no longer feel about the Project Prusa, his cherished baby, as he did before. The words from his dream came again and again to his mind, the reading of Gilgele as Gulagele, the little Gulag.

He had seen clouds gathering. Was it because he had left Zarnitsyn's office so abruptly? Who cared that you had a crazy nephew in need of smoothing his feathers? And yet Meir had hoped against all hope that they would take him to Yalta! That would have meant full forgiveness, acceptance, and security . . . Something else, he'd love to meet Winston Churchill—be introduced to him and see the face of the old adversary. He knew his chances of joining the team were slim, and yet he hoped.

They left him high and dry; they took Zarnitsyn in his stead.

Now Hramoy. Arnold was game for cooperation, oh yes he was when he pulled out his dinosaur! But his new article was a disappointment. A vintage Arnold. Expressive, eloquent, graphic . . . established his expertise in the area. But no mention of Prusa. Just about Beggar's Welsh.

Arnold's dodging. Arnold Hramoy, the most sensitive barometer of all . . .

And he, Meir, wasn't he an anachronistic dinosaur clinging to the high ideals of yesterday?

Meir Kovner, who had once been condemned to hell and then furloughed from hell, was bound to return to hell.

"Rock ist weg, Stock ist weg, Augustin liegt im Dreck . . ."

In Zena's old files, Meir had come across a photo of a pre-war Party conference. Most of the faces scraped off. Erased from existence, from people's memory—the faces of "traitors," denounced and wiped out by the system. Meir's face, too, was a white spot.

No exalted position of today could restore the photo paper to its former wholeness.

Did David have a reason to hurry his message to his uncle? Make it arrive more quickly than a postcard?

Was it a *warning*?

He lay fully awake while hours passed by, and when at last he fell asleep there was the patchwork of leaden and crimson stripes in the sky and fiery horses galloped and the earth shook again and a black piano vanished into a void and a crater spread, encroaching to Meir's feet, to drag him into the abyss.

CHAPTER THIRTY

G reen suspenders smudged with Stalin's vomit crossed his undershirt under a Turkish robe. His back felt a soft touch of a chair. Silent rage burned in his yellow eyes. The taller gangster sat across on an ottoman, his eyes in the slits of a mask dead on Stalin.

At least they hadn't restrained or blindfolded him. Restrain or blindfold! That would've been the limit! No, all the limits had already been transgressed. He, the absolute lord of every soul in Russia—

Stalin choked on the implausibility of what had happened to him.

His aching head added to the bitterness of humiliation and helpless rage . . . The thug stretched out his hand with another aspirin. Stalin ignored it.

Behind a Chinese silk screen, the other gangster changed out of his waiter's jacket.

Stalin said, "That stooge of yours thinks he can pass for Stalin. That he can duplicate my unique personality."

The ringleader came out from the screen, his dark eyes showing in his mask's openings. "He'll do all right for a couple of hours. He'll play it safe."

Why on earth, Stalin thought, did these men conspire against his East Prussia project?

"That arrangement, that statement on Prussia—what do you hope for? I'll disown it the very next day."

The insolent thug said, though respectfully enough, "No, Comrade Stalin, I don't think you will. Not after Marshall Stalin's table announcement. Not after Marshall Stalin signed the protocols.

You wouldn't show disrespect of signed agreements. Much as you're angry now, you don't want to look erratic. One more change of mind is one too many. Besides, it doesn't turn out that bad, does it? Jewish emigration to Palestine picking new strength. The British Empire greatly inconvenienced. The capitalist world supply of oil endangered. A wedge driven between Great Britain and the US."

Stalin scornfully said, "A bandit talking about state interests!"

The ringleader's eyes flashed. "Over there at the banquet, your fat minion blabbed out your plans. You wanted to provoke another clash between the Germans and the Jews, didn't you? Completing Hitler's work with different means. His crimes have burdened the Germans' guilty conscience—"

Stalin broke in, impatiently. "Guilty conscience? Bookish nonsense, you schoolboy! One *hates* those who one wronged. Cain's children will always hate Abel's!"

"And your design was, wasn't it, to help it. It would be the Jews—not you, not the Russians, but the Jews—who would have deprived the Germans of the quintessential German land, East Prussia. With this single stroke the German guilt would evaporate. Wiped clean. The Germans' hatred for the Jew would surge up anew. For the Jew the robber. The Jew the aggressor. The Jew the invader and usurper, enslaver and land grabber—why, even Goebbels couldn't have pulled off such a perfect one."

The gangster has figured it out.

And he wouldn't stop! He babbled on! "To crown everything, you've ordered tinkering with the German language."

Stalin sniffed scornfully. "Those scholars of mine came up with the idea that German came from Yiddish. A singular folly."

The gangster's ears, protruding from his mask, flushed crimson. "You jumped on it, didn't you? You know that people may put up with hunger and deprivation, but they never reconcile themselves to the loss of their identity. And language is the ultimate identity mark. Even the rumors leaked at the right moment would suffice to whip up the Germans' rage sky-high. A wagonload of hay into the fire of your gigantic provocation."

Stalin shrugged his shoulders. "I would never authorize such an absurdity."

"Precisely. This little embellishment to the project would never be given a wide circulation, other than by rumor. You would use it for the purpose and discard it. And soon afterward you'd repudiate the whole Operation Haman! You would disown the offender. Denounce the terrible Jewish chutzpah. What with your seminarian's background—you know your Book of Esther. The evil courtier Haman, a.k.a. Meir Kovner, plotted against the helpless, captive people—by the irony of fate, this time the German people. You aren't without a sense of humor: your lunatic Haman is a Jew. Your just, omnipotent hand, the hand of King Artaxerxes, would bring deliverance to the Germans. And punishment to the Jews! Thousands of pickup trucks with troops and dogs would converge on Prussia. Long trains of cattle cars packed with Jews would chug off to the East, farther and father from the ill-conceived People's Republic of Prussia."

Stalin kept his rage under control. "There is a great deal our Jewish citizens can make themselves helpful with in Siberia. Our Jewish violinists can play to our Jewish doctors, and our Jewish doctors can treat our Jewish violinists."

The gangster ignored the interruption. "You would promise the Germans to give them back East Prussia—later on, you'd easily find an excuse to renege on your pledge. Meanwhile, the grateful German nation would turn her devotion to you. What with their propensity to idolize—the Germans would only have to reroute their adoration. From the man with a short brown mustache, to the man with a bushy reddish mustache. From the red flag with a swastika, to the red flag with a hammer and sickle."

Stalin sprang to his feet. His eyes flashed with rage. "You imbecile! Don't you see? Yes, I'll squash the Jewish Republic. And what will happen the next day? Jews all over the world will scream bloody murder. And screaming the loudest will be the American Jews. They will raise hell! Protests, rallies, Congressional acts. Excellent. Scream louder! Gather multitudes in front of my embassies and consulates! With luck, some helpful idiot throws a bomb into the window!"

Stalin grabbed a low stalactite and broke the brittle limestone off. He held it in his hand as a dagger and jabbed the air, his face contorted.

The gangster said, "You won't leave it to chance, will you? Your people will be among the protesters, your people armed with Molotov cocktails."

Stalin calmed down. His breast was bursting with pride for the perfect intrigue. "The entire progressive mankind will denounce the neo-fascist provocateurs. The blame will be his, the blame for the breakdown of the wartime alliance. I will lay the new war guilt squarely on the Jews! In order to prevent the Fascist-Zionist takeover of Western Europe, my tanks will move in. With the German nation raining flowers onto my tanks, it will be a cakewalk, all the way to the Atlantic. I'll crash capitalist Europe! I'll carry out mankind's dearest dream!"

He stood panting heavily, fist clenched, one foot set aggressively forward.

Such beauty of the plan—destroyed by these shit-heads!

"And you—" Stalin showed his teeth, stained yellow with nicotine. "You know what I'll do to you? What Lavrenty will do?"

"Ah, well, we'll be far from your reach."

"I'll find on you any place on the face of the Earth. Like I did to Trotsky. Lavrenty's long arm will snatch you and bring you to Moscow."

"I hope not."

Stalin spoke slowly, as if in a trance. "He'll deal you the most painful death at his disposal." Stalin's eyes rolled up, showing the whites. "But before, I'll string you up by your prick with my own hands. It's a promise!"

The gangster smiled and beckoned the other one to follow.

The taller outlaw hesitated.

"That's all right, partner," said the ringleader. "Comrade Stalin has nowhere to run. And Comrade Stalin knows, doesn't he, it will all be much easier if he makes no wrong move. He'll be returned where we took him. Very soon and discreetly."

Stalin was barking abuse into their receding backs. David and Ebert stopped out of Stalin's earshot.

David gritted his teeth.

"A charming personality." He unbuttoned his breast pocket, but he found that he needed his hand to talk. "The would-be Artaxerxes. The last peg in the great Prusa charade. It was Stalin himself who shaped the *Basic Memorandum*. When I first read it, the Marxist clichés came as no surprise, but the biblical allusions? Now we know why. You see, Stalin attended a religious seminary in his youth. That made a lasting imprint on his style. He couldn't help throwing in a biblical format for the *Basic Memorandum*. A New Testament Judean setting. The rebellious prophet, Mark, who blends with Moses the Lawgiver. The Devil's scheming. The Israelites in quest of the Promised Land. Stalin channeled his instructions to Zarnitsyn through Molotov. Uncle Meir bragged, 'The guidelines come from here!' But he was only a front—a dummy who thought he directed the project, and a sucker to bear the responsibility!"

Ebert motioned. "Look at the great mastermind going mad."

They silently watched Stalin tear down pendant after emerald pendant from the lamp's hem and throw them about. David pulled from his breast pocket a stack of booklets tied with an elastic band. He handed them to Ebert. "Your task is over, Max. Well done. Feel free to leave. The Crimea's large enough." He slapped Ebert's shoulder. "Isn't it your country, eh? We'll skip the wrap party. As for the Fifth Point in your ID, chalk it up to my sense of humor."

"And you?"

"Stalin doesn't know about the northern exit. He'll think we're trapped. He won't start wrecking the place right while Churchill is still here—that would mean losing face terribly. He'll post guards but make no move before the last Brit leaves the palace. Then his men will come to the steel door, blow up the locks. By that time, Ognev and I will be speeding the bike in the steppe. What are you going to do for the rest of your life, Aisner?"

Ebert leafed through the papers. The military status of Master Sergeant Aisner was now entered as *demobilized*. "I heard you two speak. You and Heinrich, back in Djankoi. Is Ognev coming back to Heinrich's?"

"Why?"

"Heinrich's running an underground road to Palestine, isn't he?"

Stalin drew closer. Ebert switched into German.

"I would come along, if I may."

In place of an answer, David said, "There will soon be rough going down there. They're looking for men with war experience."

"They—who?"

"The Jews."

"Are you saying that Stalin's men are smuggling out Jews to Palestine?"

"Why not? Sticking a communist thorn or two in the backside of our British chums of convenience. Besides who says this operation isn't a private affair of one repentant anti-Zionist? Haifa may remind you of Alupka. Feel ready for that?"

"Fine by me." Ebert smirked. "I guess, David, you meant it from the very beginning. So much for your sense of humor."

David grinned back. "I'm glad you share in mine."

"And you? If you get out of this mess. Going overseas too?"

David's thoughts drifted momentarily to the junipers that he planted in the steppe. Then to his uncle, Clara's parents . . . He kept silence.

Ebert touched him at the shoulder. "You cannot stay now that the Englishman has recognized you."

David smiled. "Why should he be telling? I'll play a U-boat."

He lifted Ognev's pipe above his head like a periscope, bowl-up.

"Lying at the bottom."

But there was no certainty in his voice. The truth was, he didn't know himself.

At half-past eleven, they gathered down the tunnel. Stalin panted heavily.

The agreed-upon time for Cinderella to return from the Palace was midnight.

They waited. Tension rose.

Midnight came and went.

Forty past twelve.

The tension became unbearable.

At half-past one, British officers, three by the sound of them, used the bathroom.

"One hustle less, the signing. Let the Americans handle it. You leaving with the P.M.?"

"No, staying one more day to wind things up. The whole blooming palace will be mine. I've exchanged a couple of winks with a Russian waitress."

"They all are KGB."

"Screw the KGB!"

By 0215 hours, all sounds had gone dead. David and Stalin returned to the hall. Ebert stayed to restore the panels.

Stalin's eyes burned. "I'll get that bandit!"

David shrugged. "He has certainly taken his precautions."

"What precautions? What orders in this country can stand against Stalin's declaring them null and void?"

"Your staff and guards have just seen Stalin off. And then we show up and someone declares—"

"Someone? Stalin himself!"

"For them you'll be just a madman. They'll get in touch with Beria. Do you want everything to ride on his will and pleasure? So that he chooses the Stalin who suits him best? And eliminates the other one?"

Stalin's eyes were ready to pop out.

Ebert came back. He pulled David aside. "We might as well leave it as is."

"A loose canon on the imperial throne?"

"Can't be worse than this one."

Somewhere from the depth of David's memory a voice came, rich in lordly overtones.

Tell me whether you liked the town of P—

Ebert waited.

"Stalin is the Supreme Commander," David said at last, "and the war ain't over yet."

"Do the generals really need his meddling?"

David shook his head. "It's damn risky. I'd rather stick with the devil we know."

Wish I knew if I'm right.

Ebert said, "When Ognev pestered me about the murder-bus that the SS used on Jews—what did you tell him?"

David averted his eyes.

Ebert went on. "He'd kept playing his record. Then you spoke to him, and he shut up."

"I told him to give you a break. You were at the end of your tether, weren't you? Back in Moscow, I was afraid he'd attack Heinrich in the safe house. Well, he didn't. But he unloaded his frustration onto you, right?"

Ebert persisted. "He was a shaken man afterwards. What did you tell him, David?"

David spoke, still reluctantly. "Something that I'd found at the Lubyanka archives. The first ever murder-bus was a product of the KGB, back in 1937. By that time the Great Terror came to culmination, and the volume of the work overwhelmed the butchers. Then a KGB man rose to the challenge. He converted a van into Death on Wheels. Alleviated the logistical burden on the agency. A certain Adler. Rem Adler. They gave him a medal."

After a pause, Ebert said, "It must've whacked Ognev."

David grimaced. "We have more pressing concerns now. What to do with this character." He motioned towards Stalin, who demolished screen after folding screen.

"You think he'll play the team?"

David shrugged. "He's got no choice. His best bet is to stick with us. We'd better steal away before they trap us here. Now we have Ognev up against us—it's a whole new ballgame. He'll seal it all, the mountain exit too. Even if we make it to the mountains, they'll take us with bare hands."

"That's why we'll split now. Out of the palace, to the town."

COMRADE STALIN CHANGED HIS HAIRCUT   ·291·

"We still will be in the security zone, sealed-off."

"We'll hide there. It's my town; I'll find a nook for us."

"Masks off?" David took his off and tossed it into the pool.

"Masks off." Ebert's went the same way.

David explained the plan to Stalin. The prisoner said not a word. His nostrils flared. Than he nodded curtly.

★   ★   ★

The lounge area of the railway car is separated from the larger dining and çonference room by a sliding wall. A mahogany wine cabinet stands at the opposite bulkhead. The lights are dimmed, the windows shut blind.

"Stalin" lies on a fore-to-aft sofa, toes up, calves fit into soft yellow-leather top boots. He wears a brown flannel shirt with frayed cuffs, tucked into shapeless satin trousers gathered with elastics on the ankles. His head rests on a blue velvet cushion. On a low stool at his feet sits Lavrenty Beria, dressed in a grey three-piece business suit, a glass in his hand, a bottle at his feet.

"Stalin" is nursing a glass of golden wine. His gaze is glued to Beria's face. But instead of the thin-lipped, sadistic face of his minister he sees David Kovner.

"Stalin" is engaged in a mental dialog with Major Kovner.

How come you didn't keep your word? the major asks angrily.

I only kept to the letter and spirit of our agreement, "Stalin" says. Didn't you pledge that I'd sign treaties? That my signature would stand alongside those of the President and Prime Minister? That my face would be immortalized in photographs? Now, with the signing pushed to the next day—could I come back to you at midnight? Besides, your after-the-action plans—they were laughable. Yes, that's the word. Laughable. Palestine, Hollywood. And what has the leader of the Soviet People and whole progressive mankind lost in Palestine or Hollywood?

The major has no reply. The gravity of his mistakes and the absurdity of his arguments cannot escape him. He changes his tactic. He says, they'll find you out. You can never imitate the real Stalin, not for long.

He is *my* Stalin who is real, answers the Stalin on the coach. My art creates the real Stalin. The other one is but an imitation of what I've devised. The great artist, I dictate laws to reality.

Beautiful words, says the major. They'll win a storm of applause from the gallery. But what are you going to do about the records? There are piles of documentation that wouldn't tally up. Like dental records. Quite a problem, eh?

Stalin smiles. A problem? What problem? There is a dentist— there is a problem. No dentist—no problem. Lavrenty knows how to deal with things like that.

And Stalin's daughter, the major asks in desperation. The other man's daughter—what are you going to do about her?

Stalin frowns. She's a Jew-lover. I'm going to see her as little as possible.

And if somebody speaks Georgian to you?

I have forbidden speaking Georgian to me. I'm Russian, period. You keep forgetting my natural rights. My privilege to initiate a talk. Answer anything with no more than a cold, impenetrable gaze . . . The next day the man is gone. Forever.

The major loses his face. You will need, he shouts, special knowledge! Thousands of minute clues!

A man will be at hand, "Stalin" says. A madman. Carried away by his remote likeness to Stalin. Called himself Stalin, until Lavrenty's men beat his brain out of him. Now the madman doesn't look like Stalin anymore, what with his shaven head and broken nose and toothless mouth.

You are mad!

Major Kovner is saying to Comrade Stalin that Comrade Stalin is mad. Who is mad after all?

"Stalin" sips his wine. His face hardens. There is one hell of a system in your madness, he says. The Germans orphaned you by murdering your Jewish parents. They widowed you by dropping a bomb on your wife—why, that must've been a punishment for her crime of race defiling. For her sleeping with a Jew, eh? They killed your little son, the product of the criminal liaison. Then they nearly did you in when you dared to sit on the bench *For Aryans Only*. The Germans push you off, and you cling to them. Weird, isn't it? Rushing to the rescue of those two miserable whores, a legitimate trophy of my Army. So who is lunatic, *moghitkhun sheni deda*?

"Lavrenty, did you instruct them well?"

"Of course I did."

"What did you tell them?"

"Highest alarm on northern slopes of Ai Petri. Search for three criminals. The first, the youngest one—overpower and manacle. The oldest—gag and shave, then and there. The third one, the tallest—shoot down on the spot."

See you soon, David Kovner. I'm sparing your life once again but not your freedom. As for East Prussia, I'll go along with your design. I'll place the land directly under the Russian boot. The iron-shod hobnailed boot of Mother Russia.

"Lavrenty?"

"Yes?"

"After he's done, have the barber shot."

CHAPTER THIRTY-ONE

The following morning five sentries chattered happily at the roadblock near Koreïz, where the spike to Stalin's villa hooked into the corniche road. The long ordeal of securing Stalin's stay was over. The dreadful responsibility. The bulldog jaw of General Vlasik. The cold fishy eyes of Beria. The KGB colonels playing gardeners and electricians. All were gone. Night emergency orders had lifted them and hurled them to a mission on the far side of the mountain chain, to strengthen the outer ring of guards. The outer ring—now that the game was over! Some idiocy. Still, the coastal area remained tightly secured at the exits and patrolled inside.

Captain Savelov, left behind in charge of a squad, was small fry. He had rarely, if ever, spoken to General Vlasik, let aside Beria. He'd caught fleeting glimpses of Stalin and once heard Stalin utter a word or two. Only once; but that encounter had filled him with immense pride.

That night Stalin had stopped in front of a laurel bush. On his beat, Savelov had squatted behind the plant. He heard Stalin puffing at his pipe, which apparently didn't want to draw. Savelov hunkered down clutching at his knees, paralyzed with fear. Soon he heard gentle rustling. A drop fell on the back of his left hand, then another. The dripping turned into a streamlet. In a while Stalin puffed once more at his pipe, said *"moghitkhunshenideda,"* and left.

Captain Savelov drew his hand to his nose. The urine of the Great Leader scented of white wine.

Savelov bandaged his left hand with two layers of gauze. That way he could protect the precious substance and still smell it.

Now and then he inhaled the ravishing odor. He went around with the bandaging while he could still catch the minutest whiff. When asked about his wound, he only smiled enigmatically. His chest was about to burst open with pride mixed with regrets that he could share the secret with no one.

After he removed the gauze, he kept it as a memento.

Savelov tried to look up the arcane phrase that was engraved in his memory. Every uttering of the Father of the Peoples should find its proper place! Recorded and commented on. As the *Propagandist's Notebook* on his nightstand offered no explanation, he turned to the *Concise Soviet Encyclopedia* in the Lenin Room of the caserne. M. Mo. Moghitkhun? Nothing of the sort. Many pages of the *Encyclopedia* were missing, razored out. They contained the articles mentioning the denounced enemies of the people or authored by them. Perhaps the clue was in those missing pages.

Then he considered. Perhaps the phrase was in the Georgian language. Their political officer had lectured them on the humble origins of Comrade Stalin, the son of a cobbler in the empire's Georgian borderland.

Savelov went to the caserne's canteen. A gaunt, tall girl named Tamar did the floors there. She'd been transferred from the Georgian capital, Tbilisi, where she scraped the KGB cellar floors clean of blood.

The charwoman was at the canteen all right. She looked up at him from the floor where she was nudging a puddle of grey water around. She had raven-black hair, an oversized, aquiline nose, and an uninterrupted line of thick, black eyebrows.

He offered her a piece of candy in a wrap that featured three bear cubs frolicking in a forest.

The charwoman Tamar took the "Bears in the North", ripped open the wrapper at one end, and carefully bit at the chocolate.

She savored the bit and smiled up at him.

Savelov said "moghitkhunshenideda" and flashed a smile.

The charwoman Tamar sprung to her feet. She swung the dripping mop into Captain Savelov's face. She hurled the rag and the candy on the floor and ran to the door. On reaching it she stopped short and wheeled. She came back in two strides and retrieved the candy. Then she was gone.

Savelov had to wash his face in the men's room and wipe the celluloid collar of his shirt with his handkerchief, but otherwise the episode brought no trouble.

His luck had held. Nothing wrong happened during this stay of Stalin's.

Captain Savelov made a sigh of relief.

A miracle that nobody had been thrown down to penal battalions . . .

He saw a patrol jeep stop at a distance and let out three men. A uniformed officer waved a thank-you to the driver. The jeep belched out a puff and was gone. The threesome drew closer to the checkpoint. That's when the captain's jaw sank, and so did his heart. Dressed in some theatrical garb of a coat, blue with a red breast, which wouldn't button on his waist, straight towards Savelov, walked Stalin. Of course, it couldn't be Stalin—Savelov had caught a glimpse of Stalin in the convoy of long black autos yesterday as it drove towards the exit of the security zone. And what in the name of hell could Stalin, head uncovered, be doing in the company of a KGB major and a character in boots with tarpaulin tops?

The captain pinched himself on the wrist but Stalin didn't fade away. The Great Leader kept his gaze frozen straight ahead and his jaws tightly closed. Knots of muscle played below his cheekbones.

Captain Savelov stirred back from his stupor and threw up a salute, as did the four sergeants in his charge.

"Good morning, boys." The major saluted back. He winked. "Tell me. Does this man resemble somebody you know?"

"It depends, sir," said Savelov cautiously. He was thinking fast.

"Well?" the major said.

The other guards looked aside. The grave responsibility was Savelov's to shoulder.

Captain Savelov made up his mind.

"He may look like his father, but I've never met his father."

"Good. Forgive my silly joke. Meet the People's Actor of the USSR, Ognev."

Savelov laughed happily. He had heard whispers about the actor Ognev, Stalin's look-alike, appearing only so rarely before the public.

The dreadful nightmare was clearing up pleasantly.

"Ognev? Joseph Ognev?"

"In person. What, really looks alike, right? Like—eh?" He motioned up the spike road.

"Why," the captain said. "Now that you mentioned it, sir, some resemblance is there. No denying it. But I'd never confuse the two. Never!"

The other guards shook their heads. "No." "Never." "Never in my world."

The man Ognev fixed his glare on the captain, and Savelov turned cold inside.

He said, "I didn't know that Comrade Ognev was around here."

"You weren't supposed to," sighed the major. "I'm sorry about that, Captain. Lavrenty Pavlovich Beria's orders. No one was to get a whiff of it. Understand?" The major lowered his voice. "The Boss's schedule was a killer. You know it better than others. He could benefit from—understand? Like, some occasions weren't that important. He had a break while his stupid guests stuffed themselves with more liquor than they could possibly handle, all in the company of the People's Actor."

Savelov guffawed. "That's neat! High class!"

Still, he knew that he had to go through the motions. "I've got to log in your identities, sir."

The major held out his ready hand.

In his guardhouse, Captain Savelov browsed through the identity booklets. The Union of Cinematographers, certificate of the People's Actor, Josef Ognev. All right.

The KGB Major, David Plesetsky. Fine.

The third man, a tall, quiet one with pale blue eyes. Master Sergeant Max Aisner. A glance at his face—at the photo . . .

Savelov logged in the three names and the time and came back to the road.

"What can I do for you, sir?"

"We're going back to Moscow. Straight to filming where all the klieg lights are blazing, and the cameras are on standby, and Napoleon is drinking flat lemonade with Count Bezukhov, and the director is looking nervously at his watch, all ready to resume the shooting as soon as the star is back. Comrade Ognev interrupted his work in a patriotic history movie for this assignment. Now, how did the Boss travel? By plane?"

"They drove up to the train, of course. Comrade Stalin doesn't like no flying. Back from Tehran, the plane didn't go well with him."

"He pretended," said the man Ognev. "He is tougher than any of you."

These were his first words, and Captain Savelov started. *Moghitkhunshenideda*, what a voice!

"So his seaplane's here and available, isn't it?" said Major Plesetsky quickly.

"Yes," said the captain. "In the sea-side hangar, on thirty-minute standby. Not to be moved by any circumstances without personal permission of General Vlasik."

"This beats Vlasik, doesn't it?" The major took an envelope from his shoulder briefcase and offered it to Savelov.

Captain Savelov pulled the KGB stationary from the unsealed envelope and read, moving his lips: "We are hereby requesting the use of Comrade Stalin's personal transportation means on February 12, 1945, for People's Actor Ognev and two accompanying persons on a special mission." Across the upper left corner ran lettering in red pencil, *granted—J Stalin.*

"But . . ." Savelov looked from the actor to the major.

"This captain is thinking too slowly," said actor Ognev. "This captain is a slow thinker."

Captain Savelov didn't hesitate anymore. He simply couldn't help obeying the yellow eyes of a wildcat. He turned his head and hurled to a sergeant:

"Go and get it going!"

The sergeant started but remained in place.

"What now?" roared Savelov.

"Before I go—could he draw me an autograph?"

Holding it with the other hand on a concrete road block, actor Ognev was signing on an ace of diamonds, the stub of a movie ticket, the court summons in a child-support case, a certificate "to an outstanding swimmer," and a lewd snapshot penciled "your kitty" in an interesting spot. In a sure and accustomed hand, he inscribed *J Stalin.*

The sentries burst into jackass laughter. "You certainly know how to joke!"

They slapped the actor on the back, while the major was giving away bottles of wine with golden disks and a mountain on the label.

Actor Ognev's face was frozen. His eyes alone ran from one man to another, as if memorizing.

★   ★   ★

Through the half-open window, a draft had deposited a handful of wet snow onto the windowsill. In Meir Kovner's dining room, Lenin's open mouth seemed to inhale the shags of grey smoke as they dragged under the ceiling towards the crack.

The smoke rose from the bronze tray on top of the chest of drawers. There burned notes, photographs, letters . . .

Meir smiled. He hadn't accumulated much stuff since his release from the camp. He felt good, as he'd felt in his youth, when he lived from his suitcase.

He opened the safe. Foreign passports—long time since he had last used the likes of them. Meir selected several and shoved them into his briefcase. He added for good measure a long envelope carrying the return address on the flap and King George's stamps cancelled at a Tel Aviv post office.

Meir dragged the bronze gadget out of the low left corner of the safe. He picked a brown rectangle of a card from a neat stack, fed it into a slot, did his settings, and cranked a handle. The punch machine spat out a ticket to Djankoi. Meir raised it to look through it at the light above him. The tiny holes had grouped into contours of digits, like constellations in the night sky. He pocketed it and filled in a reserved seat form by hand.

Two tickets for one place—so what, conductor? What with a rush on every available place, mistakes are made, right? Even in our socialist railways, the best in the world. People are to remedy the mistakes, aren't they, my friend? Here's something for your little children. Don't mention it.

In the hall he put on a sheepskin overcoat and a black flap-ear cap that he'd brought up from a back closet. He inspected himself in the mirror. A low-level functionary looked at him, an accountant perhaps. He chuckled. The dimple in his chin jerked. He walked to the door, humming *Der Prus marschiert mit ruhig festern Schritt*. He put his hand on the doorknob, but had a second thought and returned to the dining room. He pulled out a book, which barely cleared the span between the shelves. He used the hem of the tablecloth to dust it. He leafed through the pages. The paper was of a somewhat better quality, photography passable. A white hen ruffled its feathers in the lap of a smiling peasant woman, bedecked with a babushka headscarf. *Poultry Raising in Model Farms of Moscow Region*.

Oversized, he sighed.

But it made a perfect gift.

Captain Savelov wasn't sure that he did it right. A British military officer, therefore an ally and a guest of honor, was generously dispensing packs of Pall Mall to his men. Mind if I take your name, said Savelov. The Englishman came over and stood at the entrance to the guardhouse. A violation. Captain Savelov suffered silently. He leafed through the logbook, playing for time and throwing glances at the telephone, which he'd love to use.

A seaplane took off from behind the ridge and turned inland.

"Comrade Stalin's double," said one of the soldiers outside and chuckled.

"Where will they touch the drink?" asked another. "Did you hear what the major said to the pilot?"

"Straight on that stinking puddle near chemical plant-36. Never gets frozen."

"Bumpin' good of him to leave us his wine."

"I wish I had a corkscrew."

"I can open any bottle with my bare hands and teeth. Wanna see?"

"Petrov!" Captain Savelov barked from the guardhouse. "I'll twist *you* into a corkscrew!" He logged the entry "James Hathaway" under the names of actor Ognev and his escorts.

"Is it a good booze, Mister Englisher?" The sergeant turned the bottle so that the label with its two golden discs faced Hathaway.

The next moment Hathaway was in the guardhouse, peering over Savelov's shoulder.

"Not allowed!" yelled Savelov.

Of course, Hathaway said sheepishly. He regretted causing any trouble.

Captain Savelov watched the back clothed in a tight tunic jacket getting smaller. Making gigantic strides, the Britisher walked to his jeep.

Should Savelov detain the brazen intruder?

That could bring on a lot of trouble. He'd rather pretend that nothing had happened.

Jim Hathaway thought fast. He had just witnessed another appearance of the port. Vorontsov's port, *Ai-Petri*, believed out of existence outside museums of vine. This cache had been well stashed away. Nobody had discovered it—neither the revolutionary bands nor the pre-war communist masters, nor von Manstein's orderlies, nor the liberators' troops, nor the Conference's own security. The dark-eyed waiter, a.k.a. Artillery Major Kovner, a.k.a.

K.G.B. Major Plesetsky—he alone had a seemingly limitless supply of the wine.

He had just flown off to Moscow in the company of—of People's actor Ognev . . .

Hathaway reached the palace and the signals room with a secure telephone. The duty officer was happy to let him field the calls.

"I'll be packing, Hathy, old sport. If anything comes up, holler me, there's a good man." Female laughter and squeals were heard down the corridor. "The PM's party has left for Sevastopol and the *Franconia*. They took all available vehicles. They'll come and pick me up in the morning. I'll give you a lift to Sevastopol. And then what, beautiful Moscow again for you?" His voice betrayed his condescension.

Hathaway took the receiver off the cradle and hesitantly placed his fingers on the black disk. He started dialing, halted, and let the disk go. The white numbers in the round holes winked at him, mockingly. He knew he hadn't placated his principal back in Moscow with the extravagant present to his son.

And what was Jim actually going to report to Colonel Davenport? What weird tale?

Frank Davenport would sneer into the receiver.

Make it short, Hathaway.

Back in Moscow, sir, I accepted the invitation of a Soviet *apparatchik* for the New Year gathering at the latter's flat. There I met two individuals. One, Artillery Major David Kovner, the host's nephew. Another, a perfect double of Stalin, actor Joseph Ognev. A couple of days later I saw the two, chummy in Pokrovsky Boulevard.

Then in Alupka, at the dinner at the PM's residence—

The dinner party at Prime Minister's residence, eh?

Yes, sir. There was a small talk about a local port. A connoisseur's item, long gone. Stalin said he had none around. Then he left for a short break. When he was back, a new waiter appeared in the banquet room. He brought in two bottles of that long extinct port.

The salesman's hackneyed trick. Referring to an item as gone, and then producing it, for an effect. Did Stalin impress the PM?

The thing is, the waiter who went around the room with the port was Major Kovner.

Or so you imagined.

Now, under the watchful eye of Major Kovner, Stalin changed his mind about an important political matter. Vital for the Empire.

Are you crazy? An artillery major—a waiter—controls the dictator of Russia?

If it was Stalin.

And who was it? I told you, Hathaway, make it short.

I'm afraid it was that actor, Major Kovner's buddy. You see, back in Moscow, before the guests came, Kovner read *The Iron Mask*. It must've given him an idea, an inspiration—

It gave an inspiration to your fairy tales.

Now at the banquet I recognized Kovner and made it known to him that I did. He split. Away from his watchful eye, the actor stayed till the end of the party and left with Stalin's coterie. The next day, he went to Moscow.

You've got fifteen seconds to go.

The following day, Kovner reappeared near Stalin's villa, this time as a KGB major.

Are you saying that you sat through a New Year party with a KGBist and didn't identify him as such? Where was your professional vigilance, Hathaway? Five seconds to go.

He rushed to Moscow in Stalin's flying boat to get ahead of the train. And he was escorting—

Stalin, no doubt.

Yes, Stalin. Posing as actor Ognev.

That will be all, Hathaway. Are you entirely out of your wits? Or your head's just gone dizzy from sniffing the big wigs' fart?

The sonuvabitch's long equine face would twitch. *You busted your gut to worm yourself in there, what? Who the hell were the major-league names who pulled ropes for you, Hathaway? Was it Lord B—? Or rather Lady B—?*

Forget it. The signals officer on board the *Franconia* gave Jim a hard time over the phone. Lieutenant Commander James Hathaway? Colonel Davenport was supposed to represent the Moscow mission, wasn't he? Too bad he hadn't come to Yalta on account of some, ugh, intrigues. No, the officer couldn't put Lieutenant Commander through to Miss Sarah Churchill.

Jim placed a call to the Russian security. No, they couldn't spare a vehicle, to their regret.

It took all of Jim's Russian money plus a windproof, chrome Zippo lighter to buy a used bicycle from a block in town.

On leaving the restricted zone, he noticed an extraordinary level of security, no lesser than at the time of the Conference.

At the dead of night he climbed up the ladder of the *Franconia* and had his tea in the first class salon, waiting for Sarah. Last time he was on board the *Franconia*, the venerable Cunarder was on trooping service, poor old thing. They had smartly refurbished her for this occasion, he thought . . .

Sarah came out to him dressed in her blue uniform. She let him talk almost without interruption, her large green eyes on him, which made him feel somewhat at variance with the subject of his talk.

Her questions were to the point. When he finished, she only said:

"I'll try to see what I can do. I promise."

As she walked away, he wondered if his fidelity to Francis cost him too much.

In Stalin's armored train, Ognev sips wine.

There is something else, David Kovner. You lied through your teeth about the Death on Wheels, made in the KGB. I knew instantly I couldn't trust you anymore. That's when my decision to break with you became final.

Why? Kovner enquires with an air of innocence.

I have no love lost for the KGB. And yet, and yet, and yet— what you're saying is too much to stomach. Once again you're absolving the Germans—

No such thing. They're guilty as charged. Just making a point for you to leave Max in peace—the Germans were neither the only ones nor the first. Lenin, Trotsky, and Stalin—

"Stalin" explodes. Don't you dare touch Stalin! Stalin, that's me!

David Kovner narrows his eyes. *I thought I've been talking to Joseph Ognev, who'd popped his cork because of my tall tale—*

Ognev waves his hand. Don't carp. Because you *are* a liar. You know what exposed your pack of lies? You pinned the murder-bus on Rem Adler. The point is, I knew Rem Adler. You've laid eyes on him too, even if you didn't know his name. He lived across the fifth-floor landing from your Uncle Meir—how about that? He couldn't have done what you're saying. He was no monster.

Yes, Ognev remembered him well. Rem Adler was a jovial mixer. He loved flashy garb. Dressing gowns of silk or satin were his passion. Chinese dragons or Persian peacocks or Ukrainian roosters. Each time Ognev saw him in the staircase, there was a new dressing gown. And a new joke at call, usually bawdy, never political. Once he rang Ognev's door with a bottle of the "Soviet Champagne." He wanted the Ognevs to share in his joy. A brand-new insignia, the Red Flag Order, shone on his breast. A charming man, Ognev's wife said when he left. Ognev didn't know what he was, what he did when away from their house in Solyanka Street.

One day Rem Adler disappeared like so many others. Ognev didn't ask where and why. It wasn't done, asking.

"Lavrenty."

"Yes, Joseph Vissarionovich?"

"Arrest Rem Adler."

Beria cleared his throat. "I can't."

"You—*cannot*?"

"We executed him. Back in 1939."

"Why? Did he sabotage anything? Squandered exhaust fumes?"

"No, Josef Vissarionovich. The murder-bus was all right. Worked well for us. We abandoned one of ours in Vilnius in 1941, and the Germans laid their hands on it. Three months later an SS–Obersturmbannführer, Walter Rauff, came forward with his own *sonderwagen.* But Rem Adler—let me remember—he came through the paperwork as a British spy."

In the silence of the car, the wheels clattered softly.

Then "Stalin" spoke. Very deliberately. "How very interesting, Lavrenty. Rem Adler, a British spy. By the way, what did you do back in Baku in 1919? People tell stories about it, you know."

Beria walked to the bottom of the salon and bent over the map of Germany.

He breathed, "Mustachioed swine."

"Who, Lavrenty?"

"What did you say, Josef Vissarionovich?"

"Whose mustache are you critical of?"

"Hitler's of course. Who else's? I'm so glad your hearing has improved."

"Stalin" paused, glaring.

"Don't you dare to speak about my hearing, Lavrenty."

★ ★ ★

Meir Kovner walked down the passageway in a railway sleeper, first class. Compartment seven, the conductor had told him.

Five, six. In the corridor's window the moonlit station building began to crawl back. Seven. Through the half-open door tobacco smell wafted out. A stooped passenger, his back turned to the door, laid out his articles onto a window table. He straightened up. His felt homburg touched the ceiling lamp. He took the hat off and laid it on the berth. The lamp reflected from the bald, knobby surface of his head glossy with sweat.

Meir Kovner recoiled. He tiptoed backwards, turned around, and quickened his steps.

Arnold Hramoy, in person. The clever ass of a dodger had smelled the imminent brushfire and made off. He would sit it out in a remote hole.

Meir Kovner sat in conductors' compartment, complaining of his allergy to cigar smoke.

The locomotive steamed around a curve. The conductor's relief snored on the upper berth. He came down, lured by Meir's offer of vodka. Meir drank with the two from thin tea glasses jingling in zinc-plated holders and related how he, a Marxism-Leninism professor ("just call me Mark") had, in Lenin's Zurich archives, found an unknown work of Lenin's on physics put on the margins of his manuscript *What the "Friends of the People" Are and How They Fight Us*, and how Wilhelm Roentgen, that German plagiarizer, stole the idea from under Lenin's nose. That said, we should be grateful to Roentgen. Back in 1895, Lenin looked forward to a promising academic career. Had he gotten credit for his work, he would have stayed in physics and enjoyed the fame and all. What a loss for the world communist movement! Fortunately, fate ruled differently. His Nobel Prize stolen, Lenin redirected his energy elsewhere.

The relief conductor stared at the bottle of vodka. He brooded over his father's execution by the Reds of the Lenin Regiment in the Civil War, and he wished Roentgen had never been born.

Meir kept the conductors company until the morning, when he relocated to the restaurant. He kept his cash payment on the table and his eyes on the entrance door. He jumped to his feet and escaped, leaving the omelet partly uneaten, as soon as a lanky figure with a shaven head peeped in the door, ducking under the lintel.

Meir didn't know that Arnold Hramoy also didn't sleep that night. His life story spread before him. Endless politicking, lies and compromises. Locked in the Soviet Union, he, with his agile and powerful brain, was a prisoner of his Indo-European studies. The stint with the Sorbonne, the gift of the gods, the thing that distinguished him from his colleagues and made them burst with envy—what did it amount to? A bone picked clean. He was allowed to rummage in the waste dirt of linguistics, a subject that in France had been left to epigones, politicians, and sophomore students. New goldmines opened elsewhere. His friend who had arranged Arnold's stay had wasted no time letting him feel it. Behind the smokescreen of intimate collegiality, having "forgotten" about special circumstances of this *russe sympa*, he preached to Arnold. "Keep your eye on the South Seas, *mon vieux*, and on sub-Saharan Africa! There languages are born and grow, free of the straightjacket of written conventions! There the linguist can watch mumbling and gestures becoming a pidgin, the pidgin morphing into a creole, and the creole graduating to a *koine*. There he has a chance to smell the highest mystery of all, the Holy Grail of linguistics—the First Language! Go where the action is, my friend!" To the South Seas, thought Arnold bitterly. Exactly the best proposal to put forward in the Soviet Academy of Sciences.

Nothing could be set right. The life was screwed up. Arnold said that phrase in thirty languages. That kept him alive till the grey morning dawned in the window.

He walked to the restaurant. Somebody sitting at the opposite door hid his face behind his forearm, jumped to his feet, and disappeared. Did *they* follow him?

Arnold spent most of the day in the restaurant, poking his fork at the dishes brought in and taken away uneaten, one after another, until he paid for the whole short menu.

In Kursk he stepped out into the arms of doting locals.

Meir Kovner, hungry and unshaved, tried to catch up on some sleep on the soft plush berth in the compartment stunk up by the imperialist cigar.

The car stood in sidetracks, hopelessly behind the timetable, until a short train zoomed by, rushing to Moscow.

"Where are we now, Lavrenty?"

"Just passed Kursk."

"Send a word to Moscow. Nobody and I mean *nobody*—let *no* vehicle into downtown within the Sadovoye Ring. From now on and till we're in the Kremlin. One-way traffic. Outward yes. Inward no . . . What? To the Kremlin maternity ward? It's packed with Jewish obstetricians. Who's having babies in the Kremlin maternity ward? Jews. They'll make new babies."

Beria left at once. He walked past the guards' compartment, over the armored connecting bridge, to the grand salon car, and further on to the security car.

He felt alarmed.

Why should Stalin have teased him about Baku? Stalin must have known Beria's dark secret from day one. They all had some skeletons in the closet, the revolutionaries of the days of yore. Stalin himself, Beria fumed—hadn't he robbed banks? The knowledge of his cohorts' shameful past served Stalin as a weapon against them, a proverbial leash to hold them in. When Stalin wanted to eliminate a man, the little smudge on the man's pajamas fly came in handy.

Did it mean that Beria's turn to perish had come?

In the radio compartment, heavy boxes hummed and blinked with green and red. A lieutenant with earphones completed his feverish scribbling, jumped to his feet, and saluted. Beria grabbed the pad. The commanding officer of the Yalta security zone radioed that Stalin's seaplane with actor Ognev and two escorts on board had taken off, destination Moscow.

Beria frowned. How come Ognev had been in Yalta? Looked like Stalin had wished to have his double at hand. But why without Beria's knowledge?

Yet another sign of his falling out of the dictator's favor?

Those three who'd flown from Koreïz, what if they were the same men whom Stalin ordered to capture and brutalize? Then why should Stalin turn against his double with vengeance?

"Radio to the seaplane," Beria hurled. "Order route change. Landing in Kupavna. Another radio, to the Kupavna KGB base. Prepare the lake for an urgent seaplane landing. Upon landing, apprehend and isolate the passengers. Yet another radio, to Yalta: request description of Ognev's escorts."

He'd get his hand on the little kike and his friends before anybody else could.

And he had no intention to follow Stalin's instructions about the three.

You gonna love it, Pocky.

He almost forgot. Stalin's command to Moscow traffic cops. He sent it all right.

CHAPTER THIRTY-TWO

The four engines of the flying boat droned on. In the aircraft's salon, red electric lights were dimmed. Behind porthole windows lay blackness. Stalin, still in the pre-Revolutionary Uhlan cavalry coat, reposed buckled down to a couch. David and Ebert had taken seats in the aft. They spoke softly.

"You sure that the lake isn't frozen solid?"

"It never does. A chemical plant drains in there."

"How'd you know?"

"Clara and I worked on a construction site on the shore."

"The Englishman saw us to take off."

"Yes, what about the Englishman?"

"Will he stir up trouble?"

"Meaning what?"

"You know what I mean. I wonder if we land into the open arms of a welcoming committee."

David shrugged. "Better the Brits than Beria's men. *I* wonder if we land where we want to. If the pilot's going to get some new instructions on the radio."

"He won't."

"Why?"

"I've sabotaged his radio."

David laughed. "When did you pull this one?"

"While we waited for the crew to come to the plane."

The seats shook. The plane dropped down in an air pocket. Holding at the seatbacks, David walked up the aisle.

"Does the plane bother you, Comrade Stalin?"

Stalin stared to his face. Then he shook his head, barely perceptibly.

David took the seat across the aisle from Stalin. "Down there, on your home field, you were a true master. No big deal if the travel shortens the days of President Roosevelt. Only why did you hold the conference in Yalta—had Siberia been booked up, or what?"

Stalin shrugged. "I put him up in Livadia, didn't I?"

"You bet you did. You've deserved your Certificate of the People's Actor, Ognev."

It seemed to David that he saw a little glitter of laughter on the bottom of the yellow eyes.

Then the spark in Stalin's eyes changed hue. With a silent menace he glared at David.

David held his stare . . .

Stalin shifted his gaze . . .

He rested lying on his couch, buckled up for the remainder of the flight.

The bandits. He had to share a crouching room with them in a half-destroyed cinematograph in Alupka. Hiding with his kidnappers from his troops!

Back in the cavern, as soon as the ringleader took off his mask Stalin had seen he was a Jew. All checked. The "major" had as much as spelled it out when he shouted his stupid arguments. The Jews had destroyed Stalin's Project Haman, a.k.a. Project Prusa, because it meant a death sentence for their state in Palestine.

Zionists. David Ben-Gurion's agents.

The ringleader had carried the KGB major shoulder boards. A fake, of course. Stalin frowned at a passing thought: the Germany's shining SS hero, Otto Skorczeny who had rescued Mussolini in a glider assault, had the *sturmbannführer's* rank. Equivalent to major. Looked like it was customary among his adversaries. Dispatching daredevil majors to kidnap heads of state.

Why had the "major" and his sidekick spoken German back in the cavern? The other goon, the blond one whom the "major" called Max, could easily be a German. Then what? A joint Zionist-Nazi enterprise? The Jews who would ally with Germany to fight the British colonialists. There were like those in Palestine, he'd been told. Stalin mentally tried the black-and-silver SS uniform on the "major." But of course he was a local. One of those Jews who had the nerve to speak Russian better than the Russians. Better than he, the Lord of Russia.

Hatred for Jews choked Stalin . . .

By the time the plane made a wide turn and swooped down, Stalin sat erect, staring in the window. Darker shadows grew instantly and moved out of eyeshot. The water surface sprang into view, overwhelming the visual field.

Stalin felt a thud. The flying boat touched the water. Max unbolted the air-stair clamshell door and threw it open. "Not yet!" shouted the pilot from his cockpit. Stalin stepped out before the two spies did and descended the metal ladder welded on the door. Gloom reigned, slightly thinned above the water surface by the reflected light. The seaplane rocked gently amidst flotsam. His hand on the handrail, Stalin stood on a rung, taking in the predawn cold, the chemical stench, and a dark shadow that bounced on a path along the lakeshore.

The pilot pulled the plane towards the shore when it jolted and stopped. The pontoons ran aground. Stalin lost his balance, momentarily. Max caught him from falling. Stalin freed himself from the dirty fascist's arm.

The shadow on the shore drew up and took the outlines of an auto. The doors flung open. Two smaller shadows split. For a quick instant, a beam of light caught out a pennant. Then gloved fingers entered the beam and drew the end of the fabric off, spreading the pennant to be seen.

Stalin blinked. The local accomplices—why should they pick something like the British flag, the Union Jack, for a countersign?

The flashlight went out. The local team busied itself with something on the ground. Foot-pumping—Stalin made it out, at last. They pushed the inflatable boat into the pond. The men clambered in and set to paddle.

Max's feet walked past Stalin on the ladder, his body hanging outside, like a passenger on a running board of overcrowded bus. Stalin gave no way to help the goon. He didn't feel the impact of the boat touching the pontoon. Inside were a uniformed man and a civilian in a grey covert coat, both men in high rubber boots. The uniformed man threw a line; the "major" caught it. Max hopped into the dinghy and offered Stalin a hand. Stalin disregarded the offer and stepped in by himself. He searched for a helm and found none. Still, he sat where the helm would have been.

The "major" jumped in. His local accomplices paddled, throwing glances at Stalin. Stalin turned away his head. The seaplane's pilot with his mate in the door opening slowly dissolved in the gloom . . . Stalin's self-confidence rose with every invisible drop splashing from the paddles into the stinking water.

The boat slid onto the soggy marsh touched by frost. The kidnappers and the locals stepped out. Stalin reluctantly let Max and the uniformed one carry him to the dry shore in their arms.

He stood up. He instantly identified the grey Rolls Royce with a little pennant on the hood. The British Embassy auto indeed. The perfidious Albion. Where were they taking him?

But the "major" asked him, deferentially, "Where to, sir?"

A victory! Now that he was in his capital, his personality had overwhelmed the plotters.

"The Kremlin."

The two Brits took off their top boots. Stalin rode in the back, between the sturmbannführer and his goon of an orderly, gaze set straight ahead, a storm in his heart. Shoot them down, everyone who could bear witness to this outrage!

Not exactly everyone, though.

Without turning his head, Stalin circled the air above the ringleader's lap and jerked his hand up.

The six-lane avenue was void of traffic. The Rolls Royce ripped southeast at a neck-breaking speed when a shadow rushed from the median to the curb. Police. The man frantically cranked a winch. The tracery swing arm of a semaphore came down level. The red reflecting disc hung poised in midair. The sergeant put a whistle to his lips and began walking towards the auto.

Without slowing down, the auto whooshed by under the arm.

The sergeant furiously blew the whistle. He ran back to the median, jumped into the saddle of his motorcycle, gunned the engine, and raced forward.

He caught up with the offender four blocks down. Riding alongside the driver and continuing to whistle, the sergeant flagged the auto down and flashed the beam of a spot lamp into the cabin.

The front-seat passenger pointed forward with his gloved hand.

The police sergeant barked orders into a bullhorn, but he swiveled the light beam to the left. Red and white broken lines on a blue background. He let the squawk box drop to his chest and swore. He whistled once more, but more softly, and kept flagging down. His face expressed purpose: he wouldn't let the smart-alecky diplomat off the hook.

The left backseat window rolled down. A KGB major made a sign: suck it and get lost.

That must have broken the sergeant's resolve. He made a sharp U-turn and disappeared.

Stalin set back and attempted once more to button his coat. No way. The trousers were even worse off the mark, so the kidnappers had to cut through the waist at the back, where the tunic concealed the gaping wedge. This circus uniform, the choice of the fake major back in the cavern when he'd fumbled through Prince Vorontsov's operatic garb! But Stalin had steadfastly refused to touch any of the little actor's rags. *That* humiliation he couldn't allow to happen!

The avenue was coming to a large square. Must be the Byelorusskaya. Some thirty meters before it, the auto drew to a halt in front of blinding lights and police sawhorses. Behind the barrier, pickup trucks, parked head to nose, blocked the avenue. From a taxi car that had also pulled up before the barrier, wild, animal howls were heard—a woman in labor.

A police captain made for the car and saluted the flag of the allies.

The front-seat passenger window rolled down. The grey-clad gentleman spoke. The captain shook his head. "No one's allowed, sir. No matter who."

The gentleman in the front seat persisted. His head emanated indignation and the smell of a good aftershave.

The captain kept shaking his head.

The "major" opened his door, stepped out, closed the door behind him, and walked around to the other side. The captain saluted and listened, but seemed unmoved by either words or rank.

Now.

Stalin scooted over to the left door and reached for the handle. He flung open the door and climbed out, dressed in the blue and red Imperial Uhlan's coat over white buckskins.

Max got out at the other side.

Stalin skirted the auto and marched towards the KGBist. Adrenalin rushed in his blood.

The captain's head jerked up. He saluted and stretched up to attention.

"You idiot," Stalin yelled, eyes red for blood, frosted breath bellowing from his mouth.

The sergeant stood, trembling.

A uniformed man alighted from a white ZIS auto on the far side of the truck's line. He was short and stout and wore the large stars of a general's rank on his blue shoulder boards. He swaggered to Stalin, his chin up, shoulders squared.

"You clown, you son of a bitch!" he yelled.

The grey gentleman motioned his chauffeur. The Rolls Royce backed up, turned around, and sped off, up the avenue. The two Ben-Gurion's agents watched it disappear, their faces tense.

Good. You're trapped.

The imbecile of a general squeezed his body through the gap between the parked trucks. He stopped short, his eyes goggled with terror. Stalin crossed to him. He shouted into the general's fat, flabby face, level with his. "You'll rot in a swamp, *sheni deda'tz—* " With a jerk of both hands, he tried to tear off the general's shoulder boards, but they didn't budge. Stalin turned to the captain. "Quick!" The captain ran to the general's back, produced a Russian imitation of the Swiss Army knife, and ripped the shoulder boards off with a vengeance.

The general stripped of rank stood bolt upright. Stalin slapped him hard, forehand and backhand. He watched the dummy's head rock. He slapped twice more and tugged at the lapels of the general's greatcoat. "Take it off!"

The ex-general unbuttoned. The captain took the coat from his shoulders.

Stalin hurled, "The shoes! And the pants!" He snatched off the general's cap.

The erstwhile general did as told, with an amazing speed, and froze.

"Bring this over!" Stalin walked to the white ZIS-101, cap on head.

The corpse, formerly a general, kept standing at attention, oblivious to the cold. A wet spot grew in his underwear groin and moved down his legs.

The police chauffeur jumped out and flung open a door. Stalin put his foot in when he remembered.

The Jews.

He swung about to see.

The two agents of the Elders of Zion walked towards the Byelorusskaya railway station.

"Get those two!" Stalin yelled, pointing out.

Four policemen ran to the spies. They grabbed them by the shoulders, clicked handcuffs on their wrists behind them, and dragged them back to Stalin. The two didn't resist.

Stalin walked over to the front seat and climbed in, angrily warding off the chauffeur's helpful hand.

The captain stood by with the general's clothes in his hands.

Stalin motioned to his seat. "Put it here."

He couldn't leave the two behind, their tongues loose. "And shove those rascals to the back."

Which was done, unceremoniously.

The chauffeur raised the bulletproof glass divider behind him and drew the curtain.

The white ZIS rushed down Gorky Street.

Stalin began tearing the pathetic garb off his body. His heart beat fast. He'd lost none of his facilities. He was still the young revolutionary of steel will and quick decisions.

To his left, the driver closed his right eye and half-turned off, his jaw quivering uncontrollably.

Dead man, this chauffeur; and he knows that.

Behind, a new sound came from the taxicab.

The cry of a newborn . . .

CHAPTER THIRTY-THREE

Tom Davenport pushed off the attic's hatch. Tom was thin, freckled, and twelve. Maneuvering his load through the opening was somewhat of a problem but Tom managed it. First he climbed out without it and placed a few bricks in strategic positions on the roof. They would serve as stoppers against sliding. The roof sloped only gently, but Tom didn't take chances. He jumped back into the attic and lifted the bird. First the tail and the fuselage went through. Then Tom slid her sidewise until she came against the right doorframe, swiveled her to the right with his left hand so that the wing passed through, and gently pushed the whole thing out.

Once again on the roof, Tom lay down. He was atop the living quarters of the British Embassy compound, above his father's flat. Tom watched the embankment and the Kremlin. The walled town was barely seen in the darkness on the far side of the Moskva River. Tom knew the scene well. When he was—well, small, he would steal with the grown-ups to guard against the German firebombs even if Mother blew her top over it.

It was a perfect night for his enterprise. The Embassy officer on duty had come to Father in the middle of the night. Father had gone over there, as he did when he needed a secure telephone line, and then returned and begun packing. Tom lay in his room pretending to be asleep. When Father tiptoed into Tom's room, Tom lifted his eyelids only once, just to see that Father took along his Wellies from the utility cupboard. That's what he usually wore when angling. But what kind of angling could he do in the middle of a Russian winter night? Then the door lock clicked once more.

And Tom's mother—a week ago she'd flown to London and

Father had begun hinting about storks and cabbage. Tom couldn't get it: why did adults speak so silly about the simple facts of human reproduction?

Flat on his belly, Tom watched the streets below. Meager as the night traffic was, it never ceased completely across Great Stone Bridge, a major Moscow link. On clearing the bridge, the outbound motors, military trucks, or vans made a right to the quay and a quick left into Yakimanka Street.

The outbound vehicles, yes.

But there was no traffic in the other direction, towards the Kremlin. Not a single vehicle.

Odd. Why?

Didn't matter why. The Russkies had clapped on yet another idiotic regulation.

It sat well with his project. Father, with his angling boots, must have left town. What with the inbound traffic interdicted, he wouldn't be back before Tom was done.

The armored train glided to a stop at the Kursk Terminal in Moscow, pushing first a platform with naval artillery and heavy-caliber machine guns. The railcars disgorged a pack of men. Whether uniformed, as Beria was, or in civvies, like Molotov in his grey coat and fedora, they emanated awesome power. It was hard to tell whether their eyes had acquired the look of authority and cruelty because the men were at the summit of power, or they had climbed to the summit of power because they had had that look of authority and cruelty in their eyes in the first place.

Perhaps, real Stalin wouldn't have pondered on what came first—power or its outward attributes—but Ognev did. The steps of his salon car pulled up precisely against a carpet runner lined with security men. He descended the steps, dressed in a greatcoat with no shoulder boards. "Stalin" gave the assemblage a once-over. His hand tore nervously at the second top button. It parted with the coat. He threw the button off, under the car, and walked into the VIP salon of the terminal thoroughly cleansed of all regular passengers.

Beria's eyes followed the button . . .

Back in the train, on Beria's return to Stalin's car, the old tyrant hadn't let him leave the salon for a single moment, not even to bathroom—Beria was given a privilege of using Stalin's. He forced Beria to drink wine, glass after glass, himself only sipping. It wasn't until their arrival that a signals officer in the passageway whispered to Beria that the seaplane hadn't acknowledged receipt of the message.

Beria swore. Something very wrong was in the air. His instincts signaled both danger and opportunity.

Five black Packards with mighty steel flanks, surrounded by motorcycle escorts in glittering headgear, roared past police in white gloves, southward onto Chkalov Street.

Beria sat in the third Packard, with Molotov. Using his flashlight, he read the dispatches from his Kupavna base that the signals officer had slipped him. The lake surface had been cleared for landing. Then a boat appeared on the lake. The crew pretended to be drunken anglers happily exploring the surface freed of ice. They were arrested and confessed of espionage.

"Idiots!" Beria cried.

Molotov squinted his eyes. Beria crumpled the messages and shoved them in his greatcoat's pocket.

This one was from Yalta. The security zone commanding officer sent in detail on Ognev and his two escorts. Counter-Revolutionary uniform of the actor . . . Tarpaulin-top boots of the orderly . . . The female guard at the seaplane's mooring reported the major's eyes of black velour.

Black velour, indeed! Those brainless broads . . . *Wait a moment.* Beria thought back to Sarah Churchill's smiling at the British spy in a waiter's disguise. The knave had never returned from his trip to the kitchens. Could those eyes be his? . . . Beria read it to the end: "—of Major David Plesetsky of the KGB."

The British spy penetrated his KGB?

The colonel in charge of the radio car, using his judgment,

had sent a request to the KGB Personnel Office. The reply: there was no Major Plesetsky in the KGB rosters . . .

The motorcade made a right to a narrow quay. Beria made an effort to hide his emotions from Molotov.

One more message. A telephonic one, taken in the Kursk terminal. The name PLESETSKY stared him in the face. ". . . arrested two spies . . . a KGB ID issued to David PLESETSKY . . ."

Beria broke into laughter. He guffawed long and happily, with squealing and screeching. He paid no attention to Molotov's astonished looks.

Having laughed to his heart's content, Beria savored the message.

"February 13, 03:12." He looked at his watch. 03:31. "At the roadblock at Byelorusskaya Square, the post of the KGB and police arrested two spies attempting to penetrate into the capital. One carried a KGB ID issued to David PLESETSKY, another to Infantry Master Sergeant Max AISNER.

"The arrests were commanded by Comrade STALIN. The spies were handed over to the personal custody of Comrade STALIN."

Stalin? Twenty minutes ago, in Byelorusskaya Square?

Beria sat, stunned.

★   ★   ★

Behind the bulletproof glass and curtain, Ebert rubbed his bound wrists against the back of the seat. He persisted until a little screwdriver slid down from under the leather bracelet that had once held his watch. His fingers got hold of the handle. He nudged David, mouthed, "Your nippers," and turned his back to David, who offered his wrists. Now they sat back-to-back. Slowly, intently, his fingers contorted, Ebert was picking the lock on David's steel cuffs.

Outside, searchlights flashed momentarily and went out, as the patrols in Gorky Street identified the Moscow police general's car. The lights effected moving images on the drawn curtain, the shadows of the driver and Stalin wriggling in contortions while changing into the general's trousers.

David's hands free, he massaged his wrists. Now he picked up the screwdriver. Ebert all focused on the barely felt pulses of his wrists. He whispered instructions to David working on his cuffs.

The auto crossed Manege Square. It was about to enter Red Square through History Museum Drive when on the far side motorcycle outriders arced around St. Basil's and fanned off. Following them, autos darted from the embankment.

Stalin swore and gave a command.

The ZIS-101 hung a sharp U-turn.

★   ★   ★

Beria's car rolled up into Red Square. He saw the head auto with security men loop away and Stalin's car steer towards a tall, slender wall tower, whose spire topped with a five-pointed star vanished in the darkness.

"Follow him," Beria hurled to the driver.

The KGB lieutenant colonel in charge of the Savior Gate shouted command and depressed a button. A motor hummed; the door crawled to open.

The auto slowed down. A back-seat window rolled down. A bodyguard barked, "Admit no one! And pass the word to all gates—now!"

The black Packard drove through the sixteen-foot deep archway as the sentries stood at attention.

Behind, Beria shouted to his driver:

"Step on it!"

★   ★   ★

The sharp turn of the white ZIS-101 threw David off his work on Ebert's manacles. He resumed as the auto raced along the fifty-foot Kremlin wall towards the stocky Kutafya Tower, the barbican set at a distance before the wall.

There was another jolt when the driver brought the car to a stop in front of the closed gate.

In Red Square, the guards began closing the Savior Gate after "Stalin" rode by, when the head of another black limousine rammed into the folds, obstructing the closure. The lieutenant colonel in charge, his hand on a phone, saw Minister Beria jump out of the car. On hurling furiously, "You're as good as dead," Beria ran through the opening, following "Stalin's" auto, which was making a right in the Cathedral Square. The lieutenant colonel debated belatedly whether the order of letting nobody in had covered Stalin's State Security Chief entering on foot, when Molotov, too, made his way out of the car, his hand on his nose bleeding from the crash.

Enough is enough. The lieutenant colonel shouted the car back. The gap closed and left Molotov outside demanding the name of the insolent officer.

The lieutenant colonel's hand trembling, he resumed dialing. He was to pass Stalin's command to the other gates.

Six hundred yards from the Savior Gate, the white ZIS pulled up at Kutafya Tower. Stalin craned to see. His glance met the wide-eyed guard at the gatehouse door.

"Make way!"

The guard had known that Stalin was arriving tonight. But why through this gate? His hesitation lasted no more than a second. The gate started opening. The limo lurched into the gap. It rolled across the ancient overpass to Trinity Gate, which also let the white auto in, as telephones in both gatehouses started ringing.

Stalin pulled his head back into the auto. He'd made it! His ZIS-101 turned along the shorter Arsenal wall when he spotted an oncoming black Packard speeding past the Senate's flank. Right before they should have smashed into one another, the black Packard swerved to the right, tires screaming, even as the white ZIS carved a left. They skidded in the Senate Square, Stalin's white ZIS-101 caroming off the heavy black Packard to its right.

The autos stopped. Stalin squinted against the bright lights above the Senate's entry that flooded the square and the longer Arsenal wall. The shoulder boards of two sentries at the principal entrance to the Senate shone with cyanine blue, but their cap bands and lapel tabs and the whole front of them seemed dark against the lights.

The back doors of the Packard—his Packard! hijacked!—flew open. The muzzle of a submachine gun trained at the ZIS. A bodyguard jumped out of the left door holding his aim, whereas another one held open the other door for a man to climb out. Stalin saw the man, familiar to him as his own mirror reflection, stride to the front of the auto. Pointing to the ZIS, he shouted, "Get them!"

The driver of the white ZIS didn't see him. He had run around, behind his auto, and was busy opening the front passenger door. Kicking out the Uhlan jacket that tangled in his feet, Stalin came out to face the brazen impostor, the spearhead of the Ashke-Nazi conspiracy, who stood there, hiding cowardly behind the two security men.

The Packard's driver stepped out, too. The two drivers gasped at the two Stalins, as their car engines kept running. Stalin felt their confusion as another personal humiliation of his. The idiots should have gotten it right away which of the two was real Stalin! Instead, panic-stricken, they ran away, towards the Arsenal and further on—away, away from the sacrilegious, devastating spectacle of two Gods, two suns on the sky!

Stalin advanced silently, shaking his fists, his glare impaling the impostor.

"Stalin's" bodyguards stood agape, their submachine guns aimed at Stalin. He flung them off with his left hand. The burly men, as if impelled by an air gust, recoiled in front of the black Packard.

The monstrous boosted engine revved up. The enormous hulk of a car surged forward and knocked the security men down, as one of them let out a burst of fire from his Schmeisser up in the air.

★   ★   ★

The two blue-lapelled sentries at the Senate door had waited for Stalin's arrival nervously, alerted through the security circuit. As the two cars came to a screeching stop, the sentries showed arms and froze.

Now that the extraordinary scene evolved before their eyes, they shifted their eyes from one Stalin to another as if watching a fast table-tennis ball. Then the back door of the white ZIS flung open, a KGB major darted out and jumped in behind the wheel of the black Packard. The engine roared. The auto jumped forward. The two bodyguards who'd arrived in the Packard fell, knocked down to the sentries' feet. The enormous auto rolled over them and pulled up short of the entrance. Who was the friend and who the foe? The sentries frantically searched their minds for a suitable protocol, their guns at the port. It was an empty gesture. Their bolt-action Mosin 1891 / 1930 served ceremonial purpose only. There was no ammo in them. The soldiers, however thoroughly vetted, wouldn't be trusted with live weapons in front of Comrade Stalin. He had his own bodyguards to protect him, armed with the best gun around, the German assault rifle, Schmeisser MP-44. And now those bodyguards lay knocked down.

One of the sentries, his hands trembling, opened the Senate's door and pulled the other one by the half-belt of his trench coat into the lobby. They ran all the way across it and further on, through the back door, to the inner court.

★   ★   ★

Ten seconds before, when the ZIS skidded to a stop, David was still attempting to unlock Ebert's handcuffs. He registered two bodyguards jumping from inside the black Packard, Ognev and Stalin entering the scene, and the fleeing drivers. Now that the car steadied, he finally pulled it off. The manacles fell on the seat. Then the motion of Stalin's hand threw the bodyguards in front of the Packard. The next move of David's came instinctively. He pushed the door out, in a split second gained the Packard driver's seat, and gunned the auto. The next moment, the front wheels rolled on the limbs of the guards.

David slammed his foot on the brake. *Now, quick.* He jumped out. The bodyguards lay knocked down, and nobody remained at the post at the door. David and Ebert were alone with the two Stalins.

David stooped and picked up a Schmeisser *Sturmgewehr.* He grabbed "Stalin" by the hand and dragged him through the door into the Senate's vestibule.

"Enough, Ognev. Your hand's beaten."

Ognev's heavy glare drilled through David. "Your murderbus story. You didn't lie, after all. Rem Adler. He's kissed the dust. I'll see to it that Hitler and Beria—"

"Save your skin. Get the hell out of here. Now!"

Outside, Ebert denied entry to the lobby to Stalin, who yelled, "You fascist! Let me get the blackguard kike!"

Ognev's eyes grew glassy as he spoke with a thick Stalin's accent.

"Comrade Stalin has faith in his destiny. Comrade Stalin trusts in his mission. Comrade Stalin remains at his post. What would happen to Russia without Comrade Stalin?"

"You stand no chance against real Stalin!"

The glassy eyes flashed again with vigor and hatred.

"The real Stalin—that's me! Hands off Comrade Stalin!"

Ognev pivoted and strode off, running into Ebert's back.

Ebert swung about. He caught "Stalin" by the shoulder and glanced at David, who shrugged and waved his hand in resignation.

Ebert held the two Stalins at arm's distance. Like two drops of water they were, and their attire similar, except for the button missing from Ognev's greatcoat. The men, breathing noisily, glowered at each other past Ebert, their eyes burning with hatred. Ebert pushed "Stalin" off and reached for Stalin's breast. He wrenched loose the second top button. Unrestrained, "Stalin" charged. Ebert tackled him with one hand and shoved the two Stalins apart, towards the autos, like an umpire after a clinch.

"Farewell, kindred spirits!"

He strode between them and attempted to get hold of the other Schmeisser, but it had the awful weight of the Packard upon it. Ebert ran back to the Senate's lobby, bolted the door, and walked across to join David at the back door. From their cover, they watched the pentagonal court where four armed, blue-lapelled men shouted at one another. Two sentinels at the green door poorly lit with a shielded bulb trained their arms at the two fellow guards who had dropped their post at the main entrance. The newcomers were yelling, one over another, their voices filled with horror. The two at the door shook their heads. "No talking to the sentry!"

"Where does the door lead?" Ebert asked.

To the Mausoleum. To Prusa. To hell. Keeping his eyes on the guards, David whispered furiously, "Why did you? The button—why?"

Ebert smirked. "For the sake of fair play. Even break for either one. Besides, I'm Jewish."

"Now are you?"

"Wanna see my papers? I have a vested interest in seeing a Jew Czar of all Russias. If the dice fall Ognev's way—it's good for the Jews."

David cooled down. "On that point you may prove grossly mistaken, Aisner."

In the pentagonal court, the screaming went on. A sentry held up his hand. "You two! One does the talking, the other one shuts up."

A front door sentry spoke, choking on his words. The soldiers at the door looked at each other, speechless. Then one of them drew a key chain from his pocket. The padlock fell down. He fumbled with the lock in the door and opened it. All four ducked into the door opening. David heard the sound of the key turning inside.

David and Ebert gave them a minute before crossing to the door. David tried the door. Locked. With a short burst from the bodyguard's Schmeisser he broke the lock open.

David halted in the door opening and looked back. Something held him back. He took in the dark angularity of the court, small snowdrifts in the corners, and the edge of the roof against the blackness of the sky.

Ebert, already in, hurried him. "*Poshlee!*"

David stepped in. "You don't care to prolong your exclusive tour of Kremlin?" He drew the door closed behind him.

★ ★ ★

Along the length of Ivan Street in the Kremlin, the night patrols in twos and threes spotted a man in a greatcoat and a pince-nez, running towards the Senate. They challenged him but stopped dumbstruck, recognizing the Minister of Internal Affairs, Lavrenty Pavlovich Beria. A few started to follow him but he angrily waved them away.

He didn't need a witness. Stalin had tried to prevent his entry to the Kremlin—why? And this on the heels of the other developments: Stalin's threatening posture back in the train; Stalin's putting him virtually under arrest in his salon; Stalin—simultaneously—in the train approaching the Kursky Terminal and in Byelorusskaya Square.

He knew it. His men had failed to direct Stalin's personal plane to the KGB base in Kupavna and apprehend the passengers. Stalin—or his look-alike—had made it to Moscow. Perhaps to the Kremlin. Both of them might've made it to the Kremlin.

Beria had to take action. He'd play it by ear.

A round of automatic gunfire sounded ahead, from the Senate Square.

Beria turned briefly and hurled, without stopping, "You all—
form a guard line!" He turned again. "Your backs to the square!"
And again. "Let nobody pass!"

He turned round the Senate's corner to another burst of fire.

He saw two autos parked crookedly in the square and two
men in greatcoats, their peak caps fallen on the ground, hair
disheveled, trying to wrench an assault gun from under the front
wheel of the white car and from one another. The men in the
greatcoats turned their faces at the report and straightened up.

"Lavrenty, at last!"

"Arrest the impostor! Now!"

Beria was far from being awed by those two pathetic figures.
One of the Stalins in Senate Square was an impostor. Which one?
Beria didn't give a damn. The other Stalin was reduced to the
level of the actor. Beria knew who should go, the real McCoy or
not. He had to liquidate the bastard who'd ridden with him in
the train and threatened him.

On arrival to Kursk Station, that very Stalin had lost a button
from his greatcoat . . .

Beria's hand crept towards his holster.

The Stalins yelled, one over another, walking towards him.

"Arrest the bandit!"

"Lavrenty, now!"

Beria drew the handgun. "Hands up!"

The two Stalins froze.

Beria's narrowed eyes kept shifting between them, trying to
catch a clue from their appearances. He couldn't; not against the
dazzling floodlights above the main entrance. Similar greatcoats
over similar-looking blue trousers and shoes—

The Stalin on the left swiveled momentarily. Shining dots
flashed on his breast as the brass buttons reflected the floodlights.

All but the second top button.

Keeping his gaze fixed, Beria took a bead. *Straight through the
hated mustache!*

Joseph Ognev looked into the business end of the barrel. He
wished he'd never taken Beria by the tooth, back in the train.

Beria remembered: at the shot, the muzzle would jump up, and the bullet would pass above the head. He lowered his aim and drew the hammer back to full cock, even as a door banged on his left. The two Stalins wheeled to see. Now the light fell on the breast of the Stalin on the right. It shone with brass, whereas the left greatcoat faded in the shade.

Beria shaded his eyes. Holy shit! It was the other coat, after all, that lacked the second top button. Somehow, he'd goofed. The wine the sneak had forced on him back in the salon car . . .

Beria changed his mark.

His mouth contorted in a grimace, he pulled the hammer all the way back.

CHAPTER THIRTY-FOUR

The Political Affairs Officer at the U.S. Embassy would guess it right, later in the morning. There was indeed a party in the Kremlin Arsenal barracks that night, a clandestine one. The occasion was five four-gallon canisters of moonshine smuggled into the Kremlin under disguise of motorcycle fuel. An added incentive was the parcel of salted pork fat a mother had shipped from the Urals to her Petya. One canister bought the loyalty of the noncom on night duty. The soldiers crowded into one of the bedrooms. They were all village boys of Slavic blood, selected for their health and appearance. They'd started quite a while back, right after the tattoo, and by the small hours they felt spent, sitting four on a bed in long johns, red-faced, nursing enameled cups, no snacks anymore on their nightstands.

The fusillade in the square roused them instantly. Plunging their arms into their sleeves and tightening their trouser belts, the soldiers rolled down the stairway to the gun stalls and then to the emergency exit.

There they came to a halt. The door, the only one that wasn't sealed for the night, was locked. The duty sergeant held the keys, and he was nowhere to be seen.

Another burst of gunfire, somewhat farther away, perhaps shielded by a building. The soldiers, horrified, herded at the exit while volunteers searched for their man. They found him by his snoring. He rested on the floor in the Lenin Room, wrapped in the red wool cloth that he had dragged off the table, bringing down magazines and newspapers. The canister lay nearby. The soldier who came across the noncom heaved it. The canister jumped up, empty.

They found the key in the noncom's pocket.

When the door finally flung open, the human flood gushed out into the Senate Square, smashing Beria's makeshift cordon. The front men attempted to halt, awestruck by the spectacle of Beria taking aim at the twin Gods, but those in the back pushed on.

The crowd bumped into the minister with all the momentum of charging bulls. They propelled him sidewise, into the Senate's wall. His pince-nez fell down, under their feet.

Beria's revolver slipped out of his hand. The bullet ricocheted off a column and got buried in an Arsenal's window frame.

He heard a screech and a bang. The great gates at the Arsenal's shorter wall flung wide open. Through the deep archway, Marshal Budyonny burst out astride a white stallion. He made a quick left and barged into the square knocking down all in his way. His immense mustachio pointed to the long earflaps of the peaked felt helmet emblazoned with a red star. A felt cloak with broad, ridged shoulders, clasped under his chin, billowed behind him and fell back.

Trailing his élan, a horse cart rushed in, with two grey stallions and a man in a Circassian coat in the driver's seat. The wooden cover was gone, revealing a machine gun trained back, the mount's leading edge curved up like a sled.

Behind it slouched a woman, head turbaned, red panne skirt hiked up, high galoshes pushing onto the back of the driver's seat. A cotton belt with bronze cartridges crisscrossed her jacketed back and shoulders and looped out of view under her breast. She clutched at the receiver's handles with both hands, thumbs ready near the trigger.

The driver brought the *tachanka* around. Now the gun commanded the square.

A Stalin yelled, pointing at the other, "Cut him down!"

The other Stalin shouted, "Wipe him out, Semyon!" and ran behind the black Packard.

Beria ran to the Senate's main entry. How very fortunate! He had an opportunity to get rid of both Stalins! Then he'd announce his ascendancy on the spot, from the seat of power—who could challenge him?

He shouted, "For the Motherland—for Stalin—" and tore at the handle. The door didn't budge.

Budyonny flashed up the saber above his head, ready to give a signal. The remaining Stalin ducked behind another car. Several soldiers hit the ground. The rest, more confused than hindered, remained standing in front of the gun.

Beria took cover behind a Senate column.

"At the impostor—fire!"

Budyonny thrust the thumb of his left hand between two fingers into an obscene combination and flung his fist towards Beria. "Suck it, you bandit!"

"Fire!" Beria repeated in a desperate falsetto.

No one in the brightly illuminated Senate Square was aware of an airborne object traveling up along Ivan Street. The contraption was fast losing altitude as it flew into the plaza.

It hit Budyonny in the neck and fell down.

With lightning speed, Budyonny's saber sliced the air. It sheared off a wing and ripped apart the fuselage inscribed in block Roman letters, *DAVENPO—*

Responding to the signal, the machine gun exploded in a rattle.

The barrel swiveled about on the tripod. The flashes at the business end merged in one continuous flare. The deadly slugs spit out from the muzzle. They cut a swath through the crowd and landed in the Senate's façade and columns. Stucco and brick chips splashed off. The slugs ricocheted from the reinforced steel body of the Packard, pierced through the white ZIS, and shattered its windows.

Budyonny, agape, looked at the carnage.

"As you were!"

He poked the gunner in her red-panne buttocks. The barrel jerked down. The lying bodies of the guards jigged under the last burst of fire. The awesome power of the Maxim's bullets lifted them, shoved them back, and turned them about. Shreds of gory flesh, uniform, and bone splinters flew about in the pink spray of blood.

The shooting stopped. Steam rose from the holes of the cooling jacket. A thin stream of whitish smoke drifted from the Maxim's muzzle. The torn-up bodies lay on the ground. Cries of the wounded and dying began to be heard. Red streamlets inched across the dented blacktop into the snow.

Beria tiptoed from behind the column. He slunk behind the white vehicle and sank on his heels.

He steadied his knees and rolled over the body in a grey greatcoat.

The glassy eyes stared at Beria. From a single hole in the breast oozed a little blood. The red stain spread slowly to a cluster of torn treads where once was a button.

His face beaming, Beria yelled, "The impostor is dead!"

From behind the black bulletproof Packard the other Stalin stepped out, his greatcoat bereft of a button.

CHAPTER THIRTY-FIVE

Mr. Hathaway's gift to Tom Davenport on his twelfth birthday was princely indeed. The model fighter plane boasted a forty-eight-inch wingspan and reproduced the exterior to the smallest detail. But that wasn't all. It could fly as far as eight hundred yards, or possibly more, Mr. Hathaway had said. Tom was the lucky owner of a spic and span flying model of the Seafire fighter, the pride of the Royal Navy!

Father had said, why don't you fly it in the Embassy courtyard? A pathetic hypocrisy! The white bird would smash into the walls. Tom had begged Father to take him and the plane to the countryside, but Father flatly refused. War time; Russian paranoia; the ambassador would never permit it—but Tom suspected the real reason was Father's dislike of the giver, the dashing subordinate of his. Father's antipathy only added to Tom's admiration for the lieutenant commander.

Biding his time, Tom did what he could. He neatly printed *DAVENPORT Mark One* in black ink along the white fuselage, next to the small Union Jack. And then he did something more substantial.

He cleverly modernized the fighter. His installation utilized lengths of rubber band, two empty spools, a clock's spring, and the lever of a toaster. The bird would make a full circle above the river and land back at the feet of its master. With his brilliant creation, Tom was going to impress Mr. Hathaway on his return . . .

Now he had taken his plane onto the roof for a test flight.

The silhouette of the Kremlin across the river loomed against the sky. His heart pumping, Tom let go of the propeller and pushed the plane. It rolled off the edge and faded into the dark, downriver.

What Tom didn't know was that one of the spools jammed shortly after the plane took off, so the arc of turn was much gentler than planned. Then the spool came off the axis. A rubber band went limp, dooming the plane to a straight route for the remainder of the flight.

★   ★   ★

At the Mausoleum outside the Kremlin, two guards of honor faced each other across the wide door niche. Other than the two sentinels, no one was in evidence in Red Square. But it wasn't deserted. Ensconced in doorways of the offices edging the square, in niches and nooks, patrolmen watched out, shivering with the cold of the Russian winter morning.

A hundred yards away from the Mausoleum, Afanasy Glebov, the rookie on his first watch on Red Square, shared his post in a nook of St. Basil's exterior with a fellow guard of the Kremlin regiment. They had just seen a cavalcade of black Packards rolling into the square, one car admitted through the Savior Gate and the second one attempting to enter but turned away. It joined the remaining two and moved away, past History Museum and towards Gorky Street . . . Afanasy looked wistfully towards the Arsenal behind the Kremlin wall, where his luckier roommates enjoyed a party in the barracks.

Sounds of automatic gunfire didn't disturb the sentinels at the Mausoleum. The men remained standing still, their eyes open unnaturally wide, a feat which only those well trained in the skill of sleeping upright could master.

But the commander of Afanasy's outfit ran from his hiding place towards the Kremlin wall and stopped short, peering towards the Senate, from where the sound seemed to have come. Another fusillade. The moon peered out of the clouds and lit the crenels. The blackness above the river became smoky. Against that background a whitish speck appeared. The moonlight glinted briefly off it, as it moved towards the Kremlin.

Afanasy yelled, "Up above, Comrade Colonel!" The colonel

raised his eyes to the apparition. It advanced and grew in size, losing altitude over the embankment. For an instant it was lost against the façades of the Kremlin cathedrals to reappear briefly above the darker roofs. The colonel ran a few steps from the wall, took a shooting position, and discharged his handgun at the airborne intruder.

Afanasy joined the shooting without waiting for a command. He didn't see two halves of the Mausoleum door fling open at once and two arms spring out. The edge of a hand hit each sentinel under the chin. Two bodies fell and were dragged into the Mausoleum.

At this point Afanasy turned his head towards the Mausoleum. He rubbed his eyes. Was he dreaming?

He nudged his mate. "Look, Nikita! Quick!"

"What's that?" Nikita had riveted his eyes to the left bank, where the flying object came from.

Afanasy shouted angrily to his companion's face.

"Ain't no sentinels! You said it's never like that at the Tomb!"

Nikita swiveled his eyes towards the Mausoleum. He rested them a moment, spit on the snow, and returned to his watching the air above the river, as Afanasy gasped at the two sentinels standing in their usual place, in the Mausoleum niche.

The flying object must have landed at Senate Square, and the Kremlin burst at once with a staccato of gunfire, long and deafening as a jackhammer, magnified by Red Square's expanse. The colonel turned back and swept the air with his arm. "All out!" The soldiers poured out to the square. The colonel ran to the Savior Gate and got engaged in a heated exchange with the guards. The searchlights opposite the Kremlin threw powerful beams up in the sky and fell to shallow angles, even as the tower's clock struck the hour.

Impervious to the hustle, two soldiers goose-stepped towards the Mausoleum. They threw forth their straight, stiff-kneed legs. The gleaming toes rose precisely forty centimeters from the ground, to a hair. The iron shoes smashed thin ice into smithereens.

Afanasy Glebov, fascinated, watched the free show at the Post Number One of the Soviet Union.

The squad walked into the door niche and stopped. They swiveled away from each other—left turn! right turn!—and froze back to back, facing those whom they'd come to replace. The latter moved aside. The relief shift stepped into the vacated places. They did an about-face, took right-shoulder-arm, and froze dead, facing each other.

The relieved guards stepped forward, turned away from the door, and marched off.

Now a searchlight fell on St. Basil's. The cupolas caught the beam. They blazed with Las Vegas blue, green and brown, as if wrapped in striped Asiatic robes. Light danced on the cones and dots, making them sparkle. A long shadow cast across the square and broke on the Kremlin wall. A blade of light fell on Red Square's cobbles, along the guards' marching path.

The guards made a right and crossed the line.

The two men walked towards the bridge, their backs getting small, their goosestep gradually giving way to a carefree stroll.

EPILOG

Five months later, in defeated Germany, Winston Churchill's Rolls Royce pulled up in the inner courtyard of a mock Tudor estate. All the way from Babelsberg to Potsdam, near Berlin, Soviet troops had lined the route and tanks stood in crossroads.

Winston Churchill alighted. The large flowerbed in the center was in the shape of a Soviet red star in a green circle. It said, loud and clear, make no mistake about who's calling the shots here.

The president's motorcar was already parked. Like Churchill's, his was a short ride. The last meeting of the Big Three, this one with Harry Truman in the deceased Roosevelt's place. And again in a Stalin-controlled territory. The wily master of intrigue knew how to take advantage of the situation.

In the wood-paneled room on the ground floor Churchill shook hands with Harry Truman and took his seat at a gigantic round oak table that occupied almost the whole floor. Made expressly for the occasion and flown in from Moscow—another symbol of the Soviet might. Three desk flags at the center tilted towards three equidistant points on the rim. Fourteen out of fifteen red-backed chairs filled. In the background, aides had taken position, Royal Navy Commander Jim Hathaway among them.

Stalin entered. Late as usual, as befit the great leader. His white tunic in the sea of khaki, navy blue, and grey once again emphasized his uniqueness. Some changes since Yalta, understandably. Heavy bags under his eyes, face sagging and red with hypertonia. New insignia; he'd promoted himself to Generalissimo. Churchill's bottom felt no impulse to rise. A good sign.

Or a bad one?

Stalin took a seat under the cluster of large framed photographs taken at the previous meetings of the Grand Alliance leaders. Stalin with Churchill in Moscow. Stalin shaking hands with Sarah Churchill at Teheran, her father and President Roosevelt admiring the scene.

There was one from the Crimea.

On the closing morning they had sat outside the Livadia Palace, three men on a hard wooden bench. Partitioned in three sections by elbow-rests, the bench was no loveseat.

In the center, Roosevelt was wrapped in a navy woolen cape with a fur collar, locked at his breast with a single buckle. An ashen, lined face. The absent, faraway look in his eyes was the putout gaze of a man about to meet his Maker. One hand, half-covered with the cape, lay limp on his knee. In the other hand, a cigarette had choked.

To Roosevelt's right, Churchill had clasped a black fur cap that rested on his lap. His head had sunk deeply into the collar of his loose overcoat. He'd raised a smile, the brave façade of a man who'd suffered defeat in the guise of victory.

And Stalin.

A greatcoat buttoned up to the collar. Hands locked in his lap. A peak-cap above his face set in iron. The face of a winner. The only clear winner, the emerging master of half-universe.

But was it Stalin? Churchill thought, regarding the photo. On that February day in Livadia—was it Stalin who signed the agreements, sat with them for the picture, and saw them off?

Churchill had an early night on the *Franconia*, after the extended pleasures of his bathtub. The next morning he left early for the hills of Balaclava, disregarding Sarah's written note that she'd liked to join him and have an *important* talk with him. Battlefields were for boys. It's profanation, ladies in the Vale of Death. And Sarah's matter could certainly wait until the flight if not until Athens—hadn't he made it clear that this was his well-deserved holiday? On the way to the hills he asked the aides what Miss Sarah had done in the evening, and they said she had a long late-night talk with the Royal Navy lieutenant commander. Ladies' *important* news! he snorted indignantly to mask his impatience and guilt while his party discussed the movement of troops: "the 17th Lancers . . . the 11th Hussars . . ." and somebody recited *sotto voce* the stanzas of the Poet Laureate. Nearby, the British military cemetery had been damaged heavily by the war. He'd ask Stalin to restore it. And he thought of mothers whose boys perished at that old war and ladies' matters of proposals, weddings, and births that might indeed be the most important subjects of all.

Sarah joined him at the airport, in time for the band and military honor guard, and he lent her his fatherly ear on the flight, and was stunned to hear her hot whisper. There was more of it in Athens, and something about female intuition, and he remembered that missing pockmark behind Stalin's ear; and it all fell together in a wild story which he couldn't afford to disregard, however incredible.

Half-convinced half-incredulous, he placed a call to Moscow around midnight and had that strained conversation on a secure line with a fellow Harrovian—Frank Davenport wanted to hear directly from the Prime Minister. Churchill couldn't blame him. The mission did look bizarre. Speed to the lake in northwest outskirts of Moscow to meet a landing seaplane, take those on board into the Embassy limo, and assist the elderly passenger whom Davenport should find resembling somewhat a certain person. Churchill himself was very tense, even if the signals men had assured him that the communications were impenetrable.

Why did Churchill make the call, probably saving the unspeakable despot and formidable foe? Churchill could justify his actions on an entirely pragmatic basis. By no means should the outcome of the war be put in jeopardy: you don't change horses midstream.

But in his heart Winston Churchill knew something else. Something might have contributed to his decision. The brazen substitution had happened in Churchill's residence, even if a temporary residence. It was *his* guest who was kidnapped. It was *his* hospitality that was abused. He couldn't act less nobly than Dumas' Fouquet . . .

But could he be sure that he'd succeeded? Who was the short man in pompous garb, sitting against the little red flag, his left half-profile exposed? By now Churchill had learned by heart the layout of the man's left ear: the dots edging the stark-drawn bends inside the large auricle, the cartilage guarding the orifice, and a brush of shaved-off white hair on the yellowish lobe . . .

Well, quite a few dreadful things had happened since Yalta, yet none of them seemed out of character with Stalin as Churchill knew him. Churchill had cautiously assumed that in front of him sat real Stalin. But if that were true, why would the Russians kick Davenport out of the country? Frank Davenport, who'd fished Stalin out of the seaplane in the middle of an icy pond and saved the day for him? Wasn't that rather a sign that the impostor Stalin had won the doubles' contest and retaliated against the British meddler? And why did the Soviets cast Davenport's expulsion into that ridiculous form, their protest against "aerial espionage over the Kremlin"? An absurd allegation, any substance to which Frank Davenport, on his debriefing back in London, flatly denied. But two Embassy typists, overheard gossiping, were summoned to the ambassador. A yarn about a glider landing in the middle of the Kremlin on that night. And what was so special about that aircraft? the ambassador asked icily. Well, the girls said; Davenport's name was all over it, on the fuselage and tail, and the crew's handkerchiefs had also borne the monogram FD. The ambassador sent the dumb Doras packing . . . Right afterwards Stalin ordered the bulldozing of the British cemeteries of the Crimean War.

The Special Service Bureau had gleaned some information from those three Jews—two Kovners and one Aisner—who turned up in British Palestine. An MI6 agent, with whom the elder Kovner had had some not entirely pleasant encounters back in Berlin, 1931, spotted him in the streets of Rishon le-Zion. The trail led to the flat of Malka and Eli Kov'Ner-Lagoyim. All three houseguests of her and her husband's were arrested, in spite of her violent resistance. Hathaway flew to Lidda to assist at their interrogation. It appeared that the vainglorious actor Josef Ognev had concocted the whole abduction plan in his crazy head. He'd long daydreamed of taking Stalin's place. Then a man whom he could trust showed up in Moscow, Major David Kovner, whose life Ognev had saved by enlisting him in a war college after his uncle's arrest. Ognev demanded a payback, and David Kovner went along—reluctantly, as he maintained. An opportunity arrived when Stalin came to Greater Yalta. David Kovner, who had grown up in the Crimea, knew about a stalactite cavern hooked to the Vorontsov's Alupka palace, one of the conference sites. Together with Kovner's orderly, Max Aisner, they made it to the cavern, jumped Stalin in the VIP gents', and launched Ognev to rule Russia. David Kovner, too, slipped into the banquet premises. To his astonishment, he heard "Stalin" nixing the Jewish state in East Prussia! By doing so, Ognev, an ardent if secret Zionist, destroyed the competition to the emerging State of Israel or whatever name Ben-Gurion was going to give to his creation. That's where Kovner first heard about the Project Prusa. On his return to the cavern he demanded Stalin's explanations, which the kidnapped dictator provided. David Kovner was excited by the prospect of a Jewish national home in Prussia, but he rather favored a binational Jewish–German state there, a realization of his dream for which he had paid with expulsion from the Institute of Marxism back in 1938. Stung by Ognev's duplicity, Kovner changed sides, what with Stalin's pledge that the dream of Kovner's youth would come true. The trio rushed to Moscow in Stalin's seaplane. (Here the MI6 report recorded Royal Navy Commander James Hathaway's suggestion that the prisoners might as well not divulge the means by which they had gotten from the suburbs to downtown Moscow lest they jeopardize the brave Russians who helped them, a point well taken.) Kovner and Aisner escorted Stalin to the Kremlin's gate and left him before he entered the compound. Soon afterward they heard the shooting. Uncertain as to who had prevailed, they fled the country, taking Kovner's uncle along. So far, Stalin's promise of the binational state in Prussia had not materialized, which made them fear that it was Ognev who had arrived first at the Kremlin and ambushed their Stalin.

That's what they reported, and the background check on David Kovner confirmed his Crimean roots. The story of his disastrous talk at the colloquium in the Institute of Marxism was found in old Embassy reports, and David Kovner's name in the rosters of the P— artillery school was quietly verified. Furthermore, it was confirmed that actor Ognev had disappeared from his Moscow residence. All checked on the surface, but Churchill smelled fish. David Kovner's story might have been the truth all right and yet not the whole truth. Churchill strongly suspected that Ognev's boyhood friend, the elder Kovner, played a crucial part in Stalin's abduction and the reversal of his East Prussia policy. It must have been Meir Kovner, the mastermind of the intrigue, who stood behind Ognev. Just like him, wasn't it, working mischief with the British Empire, flooding British Palestine with Jewish refuges. It was his *emploi*, his shtick, the work of an old Comintern hand, instigator and spy.

Churchill was furious with the Kovners for their meddling in his great project. But the milk had been spilled; no use in crying. The last thing Churchill wanted at the moment was publicity. Besides, there was nothing to incriminate the Kovners with in the British judicial system above and beyond their illegal entering the British mandated territory under false identity. Max Aisner seemed to have had proper papers and just obeyed orders and was therefore released. The remaining two were about to be expelled back to the Soviet Union, strictly to the letter of the law and the spirit of Yalta agreements and quite humanely indeed, when they disappeared from the top-security Acre jail. An investigation revealed that Max Aisner had organized their bold escape. Later reports confirmed that Aisner joined a radical branch of Jewish military underground. As for the Kovners, no news since . . .

The head of Stalin's security, youthful General Vlasik, came into the room and bent over his master's right shoulder. Churchill was told that Stalin had fallen to taking General Vlasik along to the men's room . . .

Stalin turned his head to listen.

Churchill glued his eyes to the spot behind Stalin's left ear, but the shadow of the lobe hindered his vision.

Hathaway inched to his right behind the chairs, gaining a better view. He had to stop, having come against Russian aides and the heavy gaze of General Vlasik. But he could now see.

Hathaway swung about to Churchill and shrugged his shoulders.

Behind Generalissimo's ear, a thick grey thatch had grown.

Stalin had changed his haircut.

Author's *Postscripts*

History has written some ironic footnotes. It lent notoriety to a place-name Phoros, and it enriched Russian political lexicon with a special metaphor, the *Swan Lake*.

In 1991, die-hard Communist putschists locked up President Gorbachev in his summer retreat, Phoros in the Crimea. For days in a row all channels of State television broadcast little other than the *Swan Lake*, back-to-back, one performance after another. In the few intervals, the conspirators' flustered faces flashed momentarily on the screens, as if to announce yet another rerun. As though the coup were arranged by passionate lovers of Tchaikovsky with the sole purpose to ram their beloved score down the throats of the captive audience. The putsch failed, and the Soviet Union imploded under its own weight. For a while, people of Russia tried to play their own music, starting nervously whenever they heard the sounds of the *Swan Lake* drifting over from a television set . . . And so it went until the exercise in polyphony ended, and a KGB colonel with a deliberately soft voice and heavy stare brought back the sounds of Stalin's *State Anthem*.

And what happened to East Prussia? After World War II, Stalin appropriated the coastal areas. The German population either fled or was exiled; consequently, Slavic settlers moved in and around Königsberg renamed Kaliningrad. German East Prussia of spired churches and groomed lawns was fast becoming yet another Russian province, with poor roads, drunks in the streets, and crumbling, inferior housing.

After the demise of the Soviet Union, Russia retained its outpost in the Baltic. Kaliningrad Region boasted more armament and military personnel per square mile than any place in Europe: in there retreated the Soviet Army from occupied Germany and the Soviet Fleet from their lost bases in the Baltic republics, now independent. The Kaliningrad *oblast'* excelled in smuggling, money laundering, and narcotic dealings. Here thieves first brought Mercedeses and Audis stolen in Germany, on their way to garages of provincial governments and "new Russians." Once more in its recent history East Prussia was an exclave, separated from the hinterland by foreign territory with an apprehensive, uneasy population. The picture had an uncanny similarity with the situation between the World Wars, when the contiguity of Germany was broken by the "Polish corridor."

The Kaliningrad Region became an eyesore to the expanding European Union. Will it ever become a bridge of cooperation?

No design for a Jewish Soviet republic came to fruition. Stalin's after-war policy towards his Jews was brutal. The repressions culminated in the notorious "doctors' plot." Reportedly, the entire Jewish population of the Soviet Union was to be exiled to Siberia and Kazakhstan. Stalin's death on the eve of the show trials of "the murderers in white coats," "agents of the Zionist-American 'Joint'" aborted the plans.

Many Jewish communities celebrate the deliverance as *Stalin-Purim,* paralleling the biblical story.

Printed in the United States
25012LVS00002B/380